"ARE YOU TELLING ME YOU ARE GOING TO RUN AWAY?"

Windrider waited for her answer.

She tossed back her hair and tilted her chin. Always full of spirit, this small one. Then her lushly curved lips lifted at the corners in a ghost of a smile. He grinned back at her.

"No," he said, speaking in a slow rhythm that betrayed exactly what he was feeling. "I knew that you would want to stay." The pulse at the base of her smooth, pale throat fluttered hard, calling to his hands like the song of the wind. Her high, rounded breasts rose and fell with her deepening breath.

He pulled her into his embrace. His lids drifted closed, and he heard and saw no more. He could only feel, as raw and fresh as if he had never kissed before, the tingling thrill from the heat, the silkiness of her mouth . . .

D0451598

If You've Enjoyed This Book,
Be Sure to Read These Other
AVON ROMANTIC TREASURES

FORTUNE'S MISTRESS *by Judith E. French*
HIS MAGIC TOUCH *by Stella Cameron*
THE MASTER'S BRIDE *by Suzannah Davis*
MIDNIGHT AND MAGNOLIAS *by Rebecca Paisley*
MY WILD ROSE *by Deborah Camp*
A ROSE AT MIDNIGHT *by Anne Stuart*

Coming Soon

THEN CAME YOU *by Lisa Kleypas*

Avon Books are available at special quantity discounts for bulk purchases for sales promotions, premiums, fund raising or educational use. Special books, or book excerpts, can also be created to fit specific needs.

For details write or telephone the office of the Director of Special Markets, Avon Books, Dept. FP, 1350 Avenue of the Americas, New York, New York 10019, 1-800-238-0658.

COMANCHE WIND

GENELL DELLIN

An Avon Romantic Treasure

AVON BOOKS NEW YORK

If you purchased this book without a cover, you should be aware that this book is stolen property. It was reported as "unsold and destroyed" to the publisher, and neither the author nor the publisher has received any payment for this "stripped book."

COMANCHE WIND is an original publication of Avon Books. This work has never before appeared in book form. This work is a novel. Any similarity to actual persons or events is purely coincidental.

AVON BOOKS
A division of
The Hearst Corporation
1350 Avenue of the Americas
New York, New York 10019

Copyright © 1993 by Genell Smith Dellin
Published by arrangement with the author
Library of Congress Catalog Card Number: 92-97293
ISBN: 0-380-76717-1

All rights reserved, which includes the right to reproduce this book or portions thereof in any form whatsoever except as provided by the U.S. Copyright Law. For information address Alice Harron Orr, 305 Madison Avenue, Suite 1166, New York, New York 10017.

First Avon Books Printing: May 1993

AVON TRADEMARK REG. U.S. PAT OFF. AND IN OTHER COUNTRIES, MARCA REGISTRADA, HECHO EN U.S.A.

Printed in the U.S.A.

RA 10 9 8 7 6 5 4 3 2 1

For my readers,
who make my heart sing
with the letters you send

Thank you all.

We shall ride again
We shall ride again
The wind's voices are singing—He'e'yo'!
The wind's wing-feathered voices are singing—
Ahi'ni'yo'!

—Inspired by
traditional Comanche song

Chapter 1

Republic of Texas, 1838

The darkness beyond the open double doors of the chapel yawned like a chasm. Through the misty cloth of her long wedding veil, Jennie O'Bannion clutched at her mother's hand and stopped walking, blinking hard against the bright sunlight, struggling to hold back her tears.

"I can't do this, Mama," she whispered. "I thought I could, but I can't."

Her father, two steps ahead, turned and came back, his boot heels striking hard on the boards of the porch. The men of Rowan's Fort, standing around outside until the last minute to go into the church for the ceremony, cut their eyes at them and listened.

"You *will* do it, daughter," Papa muttered, trying to keep his voice low, trying to hide his chagrin.

Jennie met his angry stare. Her mouth flew open to contradict the direct command.

Mama precluded her. "Now, now, darlin'," she said, "you'll seal our secure place in this shelterin' community, won't you, love?"

"For sure and for certain she will," Papa

1

growled. The breeze lifted his long white hair and
blew it away from his face; his icy blue eyes never
left Jennie's.

"Papa's not able to farm us a livin'," Mama
coaxed. "And all his sons are in Heaven now.
You're our only child left, our only hope, dear
Jennie."

She lifted her free hand and arranged Jennie's
veil for the dozenth time. "There," she said,
"your pretty face and your hair can show. I didn't
make this lace with me own hands for to cover
up them splendid red curls."

Papa snorted, glancing over his shoulders at the
curious onlookers. "Women!" he sighed. "Take
an hour gettin' dressed, and still they ain't
ready."

Sympathetic chuckles answered him. The men
made a few quiet remarks among themselves.

"I've got to have some freedom, Mama," Jennie choked as her mother made frantic shushing
sounds. "I'm eighteen years old and I've never
made one single choice to direct my own life!"

She jerked her hand free and whirled on her
heel, away from the dim chapel that was waiting
to swallow her. Her white skirts swished merrily.
She pulled at them with both hands, wishing she
could rip them off her body and burn them.

From far away, so far to the south that it must
be in Mexico, thunder rumbled. Even God was
angry that she had to go through with this.

Then why didn't He save her?

"I wish it'd rain fire and brimstone," she
blurted. "I wish there'd come a wind to blow me
back to Ireland. I wish it was the end of the
world!"

Mama grabbed her arms and held them,
squeezing hard. "Jennie! What a thing to say!"

Jennie's eyes searched her mother's worn face for a sign, just one glimmer, of understanding.

"I didn't have the choice to leave Ireland and come to the Irish Colony," Jennie said hoarsely. "Nor to leave there for San Antonio de Béxar, nor to leave *there* for this . . . this godforsaken *religious* cult in this horrible fort out here on the edge of nowhere!"

"Quiet, girl!" Mama threw her arms around Jennie and hugged her tight. But she spoke into her ear in the extra-stern tone that had always forbidden the luxury of tears to her brood of six children. "A woman don't have much choice," she said, firmly. "A dreamer and a rebel you are, but you'll do what you must, just like every other woman that went before you has done."

Jennie bit her lip, but the tears didn't even threaten to come. This hurt went too deep for tears. She would never be able to cry again.

Kathleen pulled away and picked at the lace-trimmed veil once more. "Your papa's not able to farm," she whispered. "He can work in the store for Mr. Nordstrom and keep us the rest of our lives without us having to depend on charity."

The plea in her mother's trembling voice took the strength from Jennie's body.

"It'll be all right," her mother whispered.

So she let them turn her around, lead her across the porch, between the knots of curious men, and through the fateful opening between the rough slab doors of the church.

The Reverend Rowan stood waiting for her at the altar like a handsome, smiling spider looking for a fly. Behind her, the men of Rowan's Fort shuffled in to take seats beside their women. Mama and Papa, each holding one of Jennie's hands, drew her on into the room toward the preacher.

And toward the big, solemn man standing beside him, Trammel Nordstrom. His gaze swung to Jennie. Unsmiling, indeed, frowning a bit, he watched her slow progress.

The awful silence in the room cried out for some sort of music. A processional. Didn't all weddings have that?

Well, hers didn't. It didn't have a groom whom she knew, either. Much less one she loved.

As they neared the front of the room, Papa muttered into Jennie's ear, "We'll be safe here in this fort. Your papa knows what's best, daughter."

She couldn't answer. In her heart she was screaming, *That's what you said when we left Ireland, and all my brothers and sisters died on the way!*

Mama stopped at the end of the front pew and hugged her one more time. "It's only that you're becoming a woman today, my Jennie," she whispered. "And there's one big satisfaction for a woman—running her own house. Remember that."

Mama sat down then. Jennie took a deep breath and let Papa take her on to a spot directly in front of the reverend and Mr. Nordstrom. Reverend Rowan broadened his captivating smile and cleared his throat.

"Brothers and sisters," he said, "we are gathered here in our communal home of Rowan's Fort to witness the wedding vows of Elder Trammel Monroe Nordstrom and one of our newest sisters, Miss Jeneen Mary Sigourney O'Bannion."

Then, his every word imbued with resonant sincerity as always, he began a long prayer, thanking God for giving him the wisdom and the authority to bring these two people together.

To a sizzling hell with your authority, Jennie thought.

Then she opened her eyes and stared down at the toes of her shoes: new, white shoes that the reverend's own wife had lent her. The very dress she stood in was made from cloth that was a gift from her bridegroom's store. By the time she and Mama and Papa had finally ended up here on the edge of the world, on the western frontier of the Texas Republic, all they'd had left was the few yards of lace and a broken-down ox and cart.

Well, they would have clothes here in Rowan's Fort, and food. They would be safe here after so many long months of danger from the sea and sickness aboard the *Caroline* and the cruel rejection of their own people at the Irish Colony. They were accepted here. She was doing what she had to do, and she mustn't rebel.

Every woman in the world, every woman for centuries back in time, had done this. She could do it, too.

But was it worth giving up her whole life to somebody else? To another man who would make all the big decisions for her, just as Papa always had done? Would she become an old woman and die without ever having had any freedom?

The reverend didn't say anything about freedom. It was duty that he mentioned over and over again when he began his homily. Duty. *And* he used the word "obey" a great deal. Every time he said it, a chill passed over Jennie.

It was a scriptural duty, he said, for a woman to obey her husband. Her husband's duty was to take over from her father in providing for her and protecting her in every aspect of her life. He felt certain that Jennie and Trammel would faithfully uphold these responsibilities.

Trammel cleared his throat; Jennie glanced up at him. He looked back at her with hard, relentless eyes. They were exactly the color of mud. Her stomach tightened into a hard knot.

Finally the sermon stopped and the vows began.

From a far distance, much farther than where he stood right beside her, she heard Papa say that he was the one who gave Jeneen Mary Sigourney to Trammel Monroe Nordstom, and then the reverend began pronouncing phrases and telling Trammel Nordstrom and her to repeat them. Mr. Nordstrom did so in his loud, harsh voice.

Jennie listened, not to the reverend's words, but to the rise and fall of his fine tenor tones, and when they stopped, she stood as silent as one of the posts that held up the roof.

The reverend stared at her, then said, "Repeat your vows, my dear."

Jennie couldn't even part her lips.

From outside, through the open door, floated the sweet springtime fragrances of the grasses and the wildflowers that covered the low, rolling hills. For one insane instant, Jennie pictured herself running out of the church, throwing herself onto a horse, and galloping off, never to be seen at Rowan's Fort again.

Reverend Rowan looked at her with his intense, piercing gaze.

"Trepidation at going into such a solemn state as marriage is becoming to a modest young bride," he intoned. "However, you, Jeneen Mary Sigourney, must have no fear. My judgment comes from God; He has decreed this wedding."

Papa squeezed her arm, hard.

Trammel Nordstrom threw a commanding glance at her. His broad face had begun to redden.

"Speak up, Jeneen," he ordered in a hoarse whisper.

But it was poor, tired Mama who finally forced her to speak. Poor Mama, who had a perpetual, lifelong fear of living on charity. Into the stifling silence of the room, she whispered shakily, "Please, Jennie!"

She could just see Mama, trudging wearily behind the ox and cart, going down the endless miles of road again if they were thrown out of the fort. It was true that Papa couldn't provide for them anymore. The journey, the cholera, and the deaths of his children had weakened him physically and turned his hair white overnight. Being sent away from the Irish Colony because they might still be carrying the disease had ruined his mind and his judgment.

If the three of them were to survive, Jennie would have to marry Trammel Nordstrom.

She straightened her backbone, squared her shoulders, and opened her mouth. She would become a grown-up woman, running her own home.

"I, Jeneen Mary Sigourney O'Bannion . . ."

In an instant, it seemed, the ceremony was done. Papa moved to sit beside Mama. Reverend Rowan lifted his arms high and wide and swept them downward with a flourish, taking Jennie and Trammel each by the shoulder to turn them around to face the audience. He said, "The two of you will now make your home among these brothers and sisters of our sacred community, this one brave bastion of civilization on the western frontier of the Republic of Texas."

Trammel Nordstrom, without taking his eyes from the beaming faces of the congregation, reached over and grabbed up Jennie's hand into his huge, sweaty one.

She fought the instinctive urge to snatch it back. She belonged to him now, that possessive gesture said.

And so said the reverend. "By the authority of God Almighty and the Republic of Texas," he proclaimed, "as founder and leader of the Community of Rowan, I now pronounce you man and wife: Mr. and Mrs. Trammel Nordstrom."

So. She wasn't Jennie O'Bannion anymore.

She was Jennie Nordstrom, a woman grown. A woman free of a child's restrictions to run her own house.

But just before Reverend Rowan began the benediction, Jennie Nordstrom's husband leaned over and whispered, "Put that flaming hair up and cover it before the celebration gathering at the store. If you're so modest you can't say your vows, you've no business having the look of a barroom wench!"

For the rest of her life, the only thing that Jennie could remember about her wedding reception was those few minutes inside Trammel's store's back room with Mama, who went to help her put up her hair as Trammel had ordered.

Jennie's hands shook so with anger and trepidation that Mama had to do all the combing and pinning it took to secure the mass of unruly curls to the top of her head.

"I *hate* him," Jennie said, through teeth chattering from the chill chasing through her blood and her bones. "Mama, I hate Trammel Nordstrom. I thought a wife was supposed to love her husband.''

''You don't even know him,'' Mama replied, calmly. ''You have to live with a man to know him, and that's the way you'll come to love him. That's how it was with me and your papa.''

Jennie clenched her teeth harder and rubbed her hands together to warm them. In the cool dimness of the storeroom, the April afternoon suddenly felt like a night in January.

''Then it's a strange, rotten way for things to be!'' she cried. ''Whatever happened to loving a man the first time you see him and *then* marrying him?''

''That's nothing but a fairy tale.''

''Mama,'' Jennie said, her voice stretching desperately thin. ''Ever since I was a wee girl, I imagined that when I grew up, there'd be a handsome man on a big white horse a-ridin' into the field while we worked. I'd take one look at him and I'd know that I loved him.''

Her mother made a *tsk*ing noise. ''You're a dreamer, Jen, darlin'—''

Jennie interrupted with a sound like a sob, holding up her hand as if that gesture could stop the train of events, could change them to fit her words.

''Wait, Ma! His eyes would flash, he'd trot his horse straight to me, scoop me up, and gallop away with me in front of his saddle to live happily ever after.''

''See what I tell you? That's a fairy tale.''

''Ma, but I don't *love* Trammel Nordstrom!'' Jennie choked. ''If I have to marry, I need to marry a man I love!''

''Every woman dreams of such, but none of 'em gets it. No woman gets to marry for love.''

"But I'm different! I can't bear to be a drudge, letting a man order me around . . ."

"You *can't* be different, you can't be your own self, Jennie," her mother said, with flat conviction. "Not and be married. You'll have a wife's lot in life now, and you'll behave as all wives do."

Kathleen O'Bannion tilted Jennie's chin up then, and looked deep into her eyes in the calming way that had had the power to quiet Jennie's rebellious heart since she was a tiny girl.

"Ah, my sweet colleen," she said. "I look into your wild green eyes and I see my own passionate, rebelling self when I was eighteen. But I learned. You will, too."

She stroked Jennie's brow and hugged her again.

"Just think," she whispered. "You've been wishing to be out from under Papa's thumb. Well, now you are."

But her soft tone had lost its charm, just as her familiar caresses had lost their comfort, and her loving look had lost its power to pacify.

Jennie grabbed the handkerchief her mother offered and buried her face in it, soaking it with scalding tears. There was no hope. She should have run away when she had the chance.

Rides-on-a-Rushing-Wind put his heels to his horse. The big black and white spotted stallion leapt forward.

"Your talk is that of an old man!" he shouted over his shoulder to his brother, Ten Bears. "The same words over and over! You're so old, you can't even race your horse to that mesquite bush over there!"

He heard Ten Bears' roar of anger. After that,

the sounds of the wind filled his ears, and beneath it, the noise of hoofbeats.

Good. Let the old grouch see that he must lose once in a while. Maybe then he'd remember that his brother had power, too.

Windrider reached the top of the knoll and leaned down to touch the mesquite bush, like counting coup, a moment before Ten Bears came pounding up to him.

"You ride like an old man, too," Windrider teased, laughing, willing his humor to rise up and smooth out the resentment churning in his stomach. "Go sit in the smoke lodge and quit telling a warrior what to do."

"I am not in the smoke lodge yet," Ten Bears grunted sourly. "*I'm* a warrior protecting The People."

The jibing insult sent Windrider's anger shooting hot into his veins, but he held it back. He and Ten Bears had come a long way in burying their bad feelings; they hardly had argued during this whole trip. For the sake of the band, they must remain companions, even if they were friends no longer.

So he said, forcing a mild tone, "Learning to speak the language of the Spanish is a way to protect the *Nermernuh*."

"Making friends of the Spanish is *not*," Ten Bears countered harshly. "I don't trust them."

"Then trust *me*," Windrider said, in a voice gone suddenly hard as a rock.

Ten Bears threw him a sharp look, and the brothers held each other's eye as they circled their horses on top of the hill in the warm afternoon sun. He knew it, too. Windrider could see the thought in Ten Bears' eyes: The fate of the band, the lives of the people, depended on them, as brothers, acting together instead of pulling part.

The wind from the south blew sweet as the beans of the mesquite bush beside them. It lifted the feathers bound into their hair and turned their faces to it, toward the river that the Spaniards called the Colorado. The sky hung low, blue-black, rimmed in white, catching the sunlight's dance.

"The Thunderbird is rising," Ten Bears said.

Windrider nodded. "He throws his shadow."

He spoke quietly, hiding the fact that his heart was lifting because his stubborn, ill-tempered brother had actually changed the subject. It was an offer to make peace. They kept watching the sky, not looking at each other.

Far, far in the distance, so far that their ears could barely catch the sound, the Thunderbird had begun to flap his enormous wings.

"He will fly soon," Windrider said.

Taking a deep breath of the rain-smelling air, he lifted his hand high in greeting. Thunder, lightning, wind, the pure power of the storm, always carried his spirits high into the sky.

"The Thunderbird returns from wintering in the warm country with Sun Father," Ten Bears grumbled. "We'll soon be wet as fishes."

"No matter, I welcome him *and* the lake on his back," Windrider said, with the teasing grin that never failed to nettle the humorless Ten Bears. "Already he has changed your talk, which I have been trying to do since Sun Father rose this morning and these ponies took their first steps back toward the camp of The People."

"My talk has not changed!" Ten Bears shouted, hitting his bare thigh with his fist, but this time his anger was not as strong. He simply could never give up an argument as long as he had breath to speak.

Windrider bit his tongue. *Why* had he not resisted making the joke? Now he would have to hear it all again.

"I speak in the language of The People!" Ten Bears said. "You insult The *Nermernuh* when you use another's language. If you must be so friendly with Oñate and those other Spanish, force them to speak Comanche!"

"Ten Bears," Windrider said lightly, starting his mount at a lope down the hill toward their loaded packhorses, "don't you know that using their language got me seven more packets of beads and another copper pot for every buffalo hide we traded?"

He turned in his saddle to look directly at his brother. "And did you ever think that knowing another man's language could do another good thing? We might understand something he didn't want us to hear."

Ten Bears answered with a derisive snort. He turned his face away, but not before Windrider had seen the glint of surprised agreement in his eyes.

Chuckling at having bested his older brother with words as well as with the speed of his horse, Windrider chirruped to the fleet-footed paint, called Echo-of-the-Wolf's-Cry because he could travel far and fast on the wind, and galloped ahead of Ten Bears' favorite dun, named simply *Maana* for its color. Happiness covered over his anger. The sounds of the breezes moving through the tall grasses were too beautiful to mar with more words.

And the warm rays of Sun Father, lighting up the deep blue and orange of the blankets of wild-

flowers, fingering down between them to stroke
Earth Mother's face, were too bright to darken
with more glances at the eternally sullen Ten
Bears. Windrider slowed Echo, walked up to the
packhorses, and gathered their lead ropes into his
hand.

Then he turned, and while he rode slowly,
waiting for his brother to catch up, he let his eyes
go roaming over the rolling plains.

That was when he saw the beaded bag.

It lay crumpled like a wounded yellow bird in
the green of the grass, the red buckbush berries
spilling from its mouth like blood. They repeated
the red in the beads, arranged with white and
yellow ones to make a large blazing sun design.

His flesh chilled. He pulled the paint horse
around into a quick, tight stop.

The carrying strap on the bag had been broken.

He sat, staring, as if he expected the bag to take
on life and move, while all the laughter and anger
at his brother and the pleasure from making peace
and having done such interesting trading flowed
out of his belly and drained away.

This bag belonged to his mother. Her hands had
prepared the elk hide and smoked it to this beautiful yellow color. They had sewn the beads onto
it to make a blazing sun, her favorite design. Because her name was Voice of the Sunrise.

She shouldn't be anywhere near this place. The
People were in camp another day's ride away.

His hand went to the buckskin medicine pouch
tied at his waist and closed around it.

Ten Bears rode up, and kneed his horse to a
stop.

Finally he said, "There." His voice held a sickening dread.

Windrider tore his gaze from the bag of berries

and looked where his brother pointed. To the north, where the vultures circled.

Without another word spoken between them, they lifted the horses into a long lope and rode toward the death on the ground.

Their mother's body lay sprawled in a shallow dry wash, her face turned to Earth Mother. Her long, black hair streamed over her naked back.

Windrider's eyes changed into stones in their sockets; the flesh of his face froze onto its bones.

Mother. His own dear mother.

When he was a very little boy, he had gone berry-hunting with her. His father and Ten Bears had disapproved of his helping with women's work, even though he wasn't yet big enough to ride a pony alone, too small to practice all day at shooting arrows from horseback and picking fallen ''warriors'' off the ground. In spite of the men's teasing scorn, he had loved those days of wandering over the land, lulled and then thrilled by the soft voices of the women. His mother had let him help, had made finding the berries a game.

She'd made a game of all work, his sweet mother. Always, always, she was the laughing one, the one all the camp came to for advice and for cheering.

Her dark eyes had looked at him every day, full of laughter, full of love. Now they stared against the ground.

''No!'' he roared, and half leaped, half fell off Echo, bending over his lurching stomach, running, reaching to touch her. This body must belong to somebody else.

He turned it over, raising a puff of dust in the powdery soil where the blood hadn't pooled.

It was his mother's, shot with a bullet through the heart.

Windrider's whole body began to shake. He sank to his knees, twisted over her, protecting her, peering into her frozen, frightened face, holding his breath, listening for her to speak. Her lips remained stiff, silent. A trickle of blood was drying in one corner of her mouth.

He dropped back onto his heels like a stone in deep water, his hand falling away from her arm, trembling so that he could hardly make a fist. He did it, though, and lifted it high toward the sky.

"Who has done this?" he yelled. "*Who?*"

He called on his anger then, to hold the grief at bay, bringing it ripping and tearing at the pain to drive it back, willing it to burn all over his skin like wounds from the teeth of a wolf.

Ten Bears answered in a voice suddenly gone thin as a child's. "A white man," he said. "There's the mark of his boot."

Windrider touched his mother again, lightly, placing the tips of his fingers against the cooling skin of her arm in good-bye. Then he stood up and left her to look at the tracks. The small crescents of two heels led up out of the wash.

Halfway, two different boots, coming down, met the first pair. Both pairs had gone back up. The brothers moved, Ten Bears going first, to backtrack them.

They led, side by side, off the dry dirt into the waving grasses. In a wide circle, the vegetation had been crushed down and cut into pieces by iron-shod hooves. Windrider ran to that spot and knelt down to touch the marks, to take them into his fingers so he would forever know them again. The sweet smell of the wounded prairie, grass, flowers, and soil, filled his nostrils. The juices of the dying grass wet his fingers.

"Come!" Ten Bears shouted. "Here!"

Windrider pressed his hands flat against the ground. He closed his ears and told his legs not to move. He filled his sight with the blades of green grass bent in every direction.

There would be another body. At least one other woman or girl. Voice of the Sunrise wouldn't have left camp to go hunting for berries alone; someone always wanted to be with her.

The two murdering white men, riding two horses, had snatched up two Comanche women for their pleasure. They had thrown them across their saddles and carried them a day's ride from the camp before . . .

He prayed without words, hoped without strength that it wasn't She Blushes.

But it was.

"My wife," Ten Bears cried. "My mother and my favorite wife."

Windrider forced his arms to raise him to his feet, his legs to carry him to where his brother stood. The wind blowing out of the coming storm held him upright beside Ten Bears. It blew strong, smelling wonderfully of rain and sky and Sun Father and far places, but for the first time in his life, his heart couldn't rise to meet it.

Windrider looked down at the smooth, brown hand, reaching toward him, still clutching her mother-in-law's skinning knife, the soft hand of the only woman he had ever loved.

He had loved her first. Ten Bears had never loved her.

"She *wasn't* your favorite wife," he blurted, his tone low and bitter. "You didn't love her. You took her for Third Wife only because *I* loved her. I've been waiting for her to come to me, and now she never will!"

Chapter 2

T he old sickening-hot fury surged up, searing the skin at the back of Windrider's neck, churning his blood in his veins.

"You bought her before I had enough horses, simply to show that you could," he cried, the pain tearing the words from his mouth as he willed it to tear the heart from his body. "To prove that you were the wiser, the richer, the more powerful brother as well as the older one!"

But for once in his life, Ten Bears didn't take up the old argument. "They went gathering berries," he said, still in that new, shaky voice. "And wandered so far from camp that the white men could take them without The People hearing their cries."

He turned his face away from Windrider, but he kept on standing between him and She Blushes' body.

Windrider stepped aside and walked past him as if he weren't even there. He knelt beside her, barely able to breathe. He couldn't move, couldn't touch her, couldn't shift his gaze from the beauty of her face, frozen forever in fear. Her curving lips would never smile at him again.

He stayed there, perfectly still, while his heart

ripped loose from its place in his chest and lurched downward like a crazed thing to crash from one side of his ribs to the other, pounding hard as the hoofbeats of a herd of buffalo.

While the jealous anger rolled.

It picked him up and threw him to his feet. He swung around on his heel, with the fury flowing through him like a drum's song, wanting to smash his fist into his brother's face, yearning to give out hurt rather than take more of it in.

But if he hit Ten Bears once, he would surely kill him.

"She's gone!" He lashed the words at his brother like the end of a whip. "You took her from me and kept her from me until she was gone!"

The cry took all his breath. He panted, drawing air uselessly into the tops of his closed lungs. Then gradually they opened again, and he sucked it in, long, slow, and deep.

"Why didn't you take her away from me?" Ten Bears said.

"You would've cut off her nose as an unfaithful wife!" Windrider cried. "Just to hurt us!"

"I loved her, too!"

"You did not!"

Windrider hit him then, sending his right fist hard into Ten Bears' face, bracing for the return blow. His anger grew wonderfully stronger, almost as strong as his grief, as strong as a whole running pack of wolves.

But Ten Bears didn't hit him back.

"The white men killed them!" he hissed into Windrider's face. "And behind you, there is their trail. Do we find them and kill them or do we fight each other?"

The truth of the words, like a drenching wave of cold water, put out the fire of Windrider's fury, changed it back to the ice of his grief. He stared into the face of his brother.

"Them," he said, the words grating harsh in his throat. "We kill them."

Without another word between them, the brothers loosed the loads from the spare horses and dug through them for blankets to wrap their mother and She Blushes in. They hurried, leaving the trade goods where they lay, lashing the pitifully lightweight bodies to the pack saddles, then stepped onto their mounts.

Each leading one burdened pony, they loped along the path of the iron-shod hooves of two horses, watching always for the cut stems of the blue and orange flowers, bent stalks of the gray and green grasses, lifting their eyes to the horizon for a glimpse of the murdering riders in the white skins ahead.

The Thunderbird flapped his wings again.

They rode faster, galloping ahead of the rain that would damage the careless trail that showed so clear, heading straight toward the place where the sun rose, stopping finally on a hill overlooking the fort of the Texans.

The tracks they'd been following showed in the grass ahead, shining like silver in the low-slanting rays of the sun. They led off down the hillside straight toward the yawning gates, standing wide open in the sharp-topped fence.

Ten Bears reached to take his bow from its case.

"They are so scornful of us that they don't even close the door opening! We'll be all the way inside before they know we've come to kill them!"

"No!" Windrider spoke with a pulsing force that stopped Ten Bears' hand on the rawhide ties. "We will kill them all," he said, and to make it a sacred vow, he glanced at the Sun Father, sliding toward the horizon beside the blue clouds.

He fought to keep his voice low and calm against the high, keening sounds trying to take hold in his throat. "Their souls live," he said, deliberately not using the names of the dead as was the custom, "for they were not strangled nor scalped, nor did they die in the dark. A good funeral will send them into the afterworld."

He turned to look into Ten Bears' hard eyes, then let his gaze flick away, from one doleful bundle atop its packhorse to the other. His eyes remained stones, but his blood roared high, like a river in flood.

"Then we will make much medicine and bring war parties that will kill every Texan."

Windrider turned away from the fort, into the last of the day, riding hard from the first flying step, heading the horses west toward the place where they had last seen their band of The People. Ten Bears followed. Dark came up from the ground behind them. The Thunderbird flapped closer from the south.

A long ride in front of them, their father, Half Horse, was waiting for Sun Father's light to come again so he could send out searchers for his wife and his daughter-in-law. Half Horse's heart was full of worry and grief tonight, but not as full as it would be tomorrow.

The Thunderbird found the brothers then, and tipped its body to spill the lake it carried on its back. The raindrops hit Windrider in the face and rolled down his cheeks like tears.

Jennie lay in Trammel Nordstrom's bed, *her* bed, too, now, listening to the rain drumming on the roof, wishing for a glass-paned window in the

room so she could hear the drops beat against it.
No, so she could open it, climb through, and run
far, far away.

Too late now. She clutched the covers tighter,
pulled them closer beneath her chin, and willed
the rain to fall harder, to drown out the sounds
coming through the storeroom's wall at the head
of the bed.

Those men were going to sleep in there tonight!

She still couldn't believe that Trammel had invited overnight guests on this, their wedding
night, and with the place so small that every
sound carried into each of the four rooms, but he
had. He might be entertaining angels unaware,
he said.

Now he was telling them good night, calling
them Digger and Nate as if they were old friends
of his. The rain wasn't loud enough. She could
hear every word. That meant that they would be
able to hear whatever sounds she and Trammel
made, too.

A high, thin voice and a low, rumbly one returned Trammel's good-nights. The door creaked
closed and his footsteps trudged heavily out into
the store.

"How come you ain't asked him for no bandages?" the low voice said. "That Comanche
bitch cut my shoulder pretty good; it might get
bad."

The high voice answered. "Let 'im git to sleep,
Digger, and I'll find you somethin' in the store.
No sense tellin' the world."

"You think they'd care what we done to some
Injun squaws? Nate, you done gone outta yore
head."

"Never can tell 'bout these religious fellers,"
said the other.

"But it hurts like hell . . ."

"Wait!" snapped the high voice. "I told you to wait!"

The conversation stopped. Jennie heard only the rustling noises of bedrolls being spread out and the thud of boots being dropped. She stared at the wall, its boards silvery gray in the faint light thrown by the lamp, trying to remember the faces of the two rough strangers who had ridden into the fort.

What had they done to the Indian women? She turned the question over and over in her mind, trying to make it blot out the question of what Trammel was going to do to her.

It couldn't. Her blood rose in desperate rebellion, and she threw back the quilt and sat up, ready to run. She made herself lie back down.

She had no choice. She wanted to keep Papa alive, didn't she?

The strange voices came again, so close to the wall, they made her jump.

"Reckon that was some kinda curse the old woman was spittin' at you?" the low voice said.

"You don't know *what* she was sayin' to me!" the high voice answered. "If you don't wanta stagger around in the dark huntin' your own bandages, you'd best shut your trap and leave me be!"

"Still raining," Trammel said suddenly, from the foot of the bed.

Jennie's eyes flew to see him. He had pushed aside the curtain that closed off the alcove and come in without making a sound.

"Fields oughtta be just right for plantin' if it stops before morning."

"That's . . . good," she said.

He is my husband, she thought over and over as

he made his slow way up the side of the bed. She watched him lean down and blow out the lamp. *He is my husband and I must do my duty. All women do this.*

But how could she? Especially with those strange men bedded down just on the other side of the wall.

Trammel's body loomed large, somehow bigger and darker than all the rest of the room.

"We'll put in the wheat tomorrow," he said, dropping heavily onto his side of the bed, grunting as he bent over to untie his shoes. "Barring drought or plague, this oughtta be the best year yet for the crops."

"How long have you been here?" Jennie asked, the old, sinking realization sweeping through her for the thousandth time that she and her husband knew nothing about each other. Maybe, on their wedding night, they could begin getting acquainted.

"Six years," he said, dismissively, as he shrugged out of his shirt. "Come morning, you'll need to cook extra; we'll have company for breakfast."

"All right," she said. "Did you come here from Ohio with Reverend Rowan?"

"Never mind the questions," Trammel snapped. "What's past is past. All you need to know is that we must both work hard to make the present and the future prosperous."

A feeling of total hopelessness swept over Jennie, dragging her down against the bed like the undertow of a river. She felt as if it could pull her through the cornhusk mattress and the floor into the earth itself.

She was tied for life to a man who would always be a stranger. A stranger and a boor.

With a creak of the ropes holding up the mattress, Trammel stood and unbuckled his belt. "You'll have to watch the store tomorrow. Cook plenty for supper, too. If we feed them good, them guests of ours'll work harder."

Before she could ask if her papa should work in the store, too, he threw back the covers, making a great gust of cool air that blew every sane thought right out of her head.

Gooseflesh popped out all over her.

His weight sank into the bed. His body was beside hers, too close, looming over her. He was lying on his side, looking toward her. Panic took her. Her arms and legs tingled, wanting to push against his big body, roll it right back out of the bed and onto the floor.

Without a word, he closed one of his large hands around her breast.

Instinctively she gasped and tried to pull away.

"I like modesty in a woman," he muttered, as he pressed her down against the mattress and slipped his other hand into her hair, "even if you did nearly carry it too far, hesitatin' so at the weddin'. But you'll have to forget it now. This here's your marriage bed."

Marriage bed. This was her duty, the duty of every woman. Every woman went through this.

He brought his wet mouth down onto hers.

She tried to twist away, but her head was caught in a vise. Her mind scrambled desperately to escape, since her body could not. Soon it would be over; tomorrow he would be gone to the fields.

Tomorrow she could begin to put her new house in order, she thought, shouting the words in her brain for distraction from her husband's rough hands at the hem of her gown. He pulled it up and up, unceremoniously, until it was bunched at her waist. Her mind rushed to her mother's comforting words and held on to them.

There's a big satisfaction in running your own house, she had said, with the ring of truth in her tired voice.

But the words slipped away when Trammel Nordstrom parted her legs. He ran his rough hand up and down inside her thighs while she shivered and bit her lip and tried not to cry. Why, it was the rudest, most embarrassing thing she had ever experienced!

Until he heaved himself up onto his elbows and rolled over on her. That was worse, much worse. She shrank away, as far down into the creaking bed as she could go, her stomach drawing up into a knot that would never untie. She tried to pull her legs together, but he was between them; she pushed at his chest, but he pinned her hands above her head as if she were no stronger than a child.

Then his body invaded hers, and the sharp stab of pain tore a cry from her lips. "No!" she said. "No!"

As she writhed beneath him, helpless, Jennie's thoughts ran like frightened rabbits around and around. If this was what every woman went through, how did any of them stay sane? She would rather always be a girl. She should have stayed in Ireland and become a nun. She should have made Mama tell her the truth, so at least she'd have known what to expect.

She should have run away when she had the chance.

Tomorrow. Tomorrow she would arrange the furniture in the two rooms to please herself and she would straighten up the store. For the first time in her life she had a house and a business to run. There would be lots of satisfaction in that.

She would think only of tomorrow.

But when Trammel had finished and had dropped back onto his side of the bed with a shuddering sigh of relief, when Jennie had pulled the sheet and the quilt up to her chin to lie beneath them, still as a statue of stone, the realities of the present moment came back in a wave that threatened to drown her. She was married to Trammel Nordstrom forever. No matter how many times he silently took her body, he would never know her mind or her heart. Nor would he ever want to.

Her wonderful prince on a white horse could never rescue her now. It was forever too late.

During all the miserable hours that followed, while Trammel whistled and snored beside her, and the low-voiced stranger in the storage room talked out in his sleep, Jennie lay awake. Mama was wise, she had lived a long time. But could it really be true that no one ever married for love?

If that was so, then why did every woman have that dream?

Just after daylight, the brothers rode into the Comanche village, opening the people's eyes with the hoofbeats of the horses, closing them again with the awful sight of the bodies they brought. The dogs barked and the women cried and the features of Half Horse's face broke apart like rocks scattered in a river while the tears ran over his cheeks.

But worst of all was the look on Eagle Tail Feather's face, the face of a child who had lived only ten winters. He ran to Windrider's side and stared at his uncle with eyes gone empty and flat

as those of the oldest man in the camp. His
straight, square body lost its shape, became as
bowed as Half Horse's in the breath it took to tell
him that his beloved grandmother was gone.

The searing, grieving anger hit Windrider again
with the force of a fist to his gut.

"Hear me!" he cried, and rode Echo out into
the open space between lodges to call The People
to listen to him speak.

"The white Texans have decided to come
deeper into Comanchería!" he shouted. "They
have raped and murdered our innocent women!
We must make medicine and many war parties so
that we will see the Texas fort burn in flames that
leap into the sky like red wolves attacking!"

Great shouts and yells of agreement met his
words in the air. The fire in his belly grew hotter.

Its heat never lessened while he sat and smoked
with the men, while the women readied the
bodies for burial. Sun Father had reached the
height of his sky track when they were done, had
dropped down past the horizon when the camp
had finished placing She Blushes and Voice of the
Sunrise with their traveling equipment into sitting positions in the side of a hill, had killed their
ponies on their graves for them to ride into the
spirit land, had slashed their arms and cut chunks
of their hair, had begun to fill the night with the
wailing notes of the grief song. Still Windrider's
anger loomed bigger than his sorrow.

All night it was the same, as he lay in his lodge
listening to Mumshukawa, the medicine man,
singing a death song long past the rising of the
moon. Windrider's arms burned to shoot the arrows and throw the lance, his legs twitched and
ached to ride Echo through the welcoming gates

of the fort. His heart rushed out of his body, crying for justice.

The night after this one, he wouldn't lie down at all. The night after this one, he would ride the warpath.

During the first day of her married life, Jennie learned a lesson that, according to her mother (who came at noontime to visit before she had to hurry back to the kettle of soap boiling in the yard of the fort), every married woman, even, perhaps, the wives of the wealthiest men, had to learn. A woman grown and married had very little time to do as she pleased in a day.

"I'm glad of it," Jennie had answered, before she'd clamped her lips tightly shut so as not to blurt out the fact that pouring all her energy into work was the only way she could stop thinking about Trammel's body violating hers.

Early that morning, long before dawn, he had gone out to milk his two cows, insisting that their guests go with him, and Jennie had drawn her first easy breath since the wedding. The relief of finally being alone gave her such a sense of freedom that she was able to push him out of her mind as she carried in wood, built a fire, and, while it was heating the stove, packed jerked beef, bread, and water for the men to eat at noon in the fields.

Then, dizzy and tense from sleeping so little, she cooked enough breakfast for six men. The first thing upon waking, Trammel had repeated his orders to be generous with the food, along with a lengthy homily on the blessings of charity to strangers. The simple abatement of the sound of his self-righteous, bossy voice had been a happiness to her when he, Nate, and Digger left the house.

They returned to eat smoked ham left over from the winter and all the eggs she had fried, along with a dozen or more of the cornmeal griddle cakes Mrs. Rowan had taught her to make. Then, with copious thanks from Trammel to God for the meal but no compliments from any of them to Jennie as to its contents or quality, they had departed at first light for the fields.

She closed the door behind them with a hand that trembled. Thank the Lord! The whole day was hers before their return. She blanked her tired mind as she washed the dishes and the skillets, then went into the store to greet her first customer.

Helping find everything on cheerful Mrs. Allen's list banished Trammel further from Jennie's mind. She was running an entire business establishment! After the woman left, she dusted the shelves and rearranged everything, stacking all the bolts of cloth according to their colors and patterns, hoping that Papa wouldn't mess them up when he came in to work.

No other customers arrived, and her thoughts turned to the living quarters. She explored and cleaned them, too, running back into the store whenever she was needed. Papa never came to work, and she was glad.

She liked being on her own. She didn't want him bossing her around. She was beginning to understand what Mama had meant about the satisfactions of being in charge.

Late in the afternoon, with business in the store at a standstill, she ran a critical eye over the newly clean, meagerly furnished rooms while she boiled potatoes and apples and put a beef roast on to cook for supper. This was her home now, to manage as she pleased.

When she put the lid on the last pot, she left the stove, ran to angle the two worn armchairs toward each other on either side of the window, and stood back to look at them. Better, definitely better.

But bright covers would be wonderful! She dashed to the small cache of gifts Trammel had stacked in the corner and shook out the two new quilts they had received. As she worked, she avoided even glancing at the bed. Summer was coming. The quilts would be of much more use on the chairs.

They looked beautiful: one a flying geese pattern in greens and blues, the other a drunkard's path done in scraps of every color of the rainbow.

The effect was charming! She dragged a narrow twig table from the corner, set it between the chairs, and placed a candle holder on it for the final touch. Perfect, she thought, standing back to enjoy her handiwork for a moment. Mama was right. There *was* a lot of satisfaction for a woman in running her own home.

But at dusk, when the men came in from the fields, her first glimpse of Trammel destroyed every shred of her pleasure. He stepped into the living quarters, just ahead of Digger and Nate, scowling, his hair damp and his face red from washing up in the watering trough.

His narrow eyes flicked from the burning candle to the quilts, to the eating table, set with four places.

"What've you been doing all day, anyhow?" he roared.

Jennie stopped stock-still halfway between the

stove and the table. The heavy Dutch oven in her hands suddenly weighed seven stone.

"What does it look like?" she retorted, her voice rising with each word. "Cooking dinner, cleaning the house, and tending the store!"

"Wasting all the resources I've slaved for's more like it!"

He stalked straight to the candle glowing between the two now colorful armchairs and blew it out, then he turned and motioned Digger and Nate to take seats at the table.

Jennie stared at him so hard, she thought her eyes would go blind, so angry that her usual tears of rage didn't even threaten to come. She hated him. She really and truly hated this man; she didn't care if it *was* a terrible sin.

"Why'd you do that?" she cried. "I want the place to look pretty!"

He threw a disgusted glance in her direction, not even taking the trouble to meet her eyes as he strode to his seat at the head of the table.

"If you don't know no better than to waste candles," he said, "I reckon I'll be obliged to lock 'em all up."

Jennie's hands gripped the handles of the pot so hard, she could feel the heat of the iron through two thick pot holders. She walked jerkily to the table, all the joints of her body gone stiff as a puppet's.

"I wanted the room to look homey," she said, through tight lips, willing her arms to unlock at the elbow so she could set her burden down. They wouldn't.

"It's been home for several years now, just the way it was," he snapped, and leaned back, motioning for her to put the Dutch oven on the table in front of his place. Her arms trembled; she had a sudden, wild vision of letting go, of dropping the hot kettle into his lap. He took it from her and set it down.

"Pass your plates, boys," he said, and grabbed a pot holder from her hand to use in removing the lid. "You both earned your keep and more this day."

No word of praise for his wife. No comment that *she* had certainly earned *her* keep.

Jennie's thin thread of control snapped in two. She turned and stalked the short distance to the candle he'd blown out, snatched it from its holder, and returned to the table. She walked to its foot, leaned in, lifted the globe from the lamp, and held the candle's wick to the flame.

When it blazed, she cupped her palm around it and returned it to the holder between the quilt-covered chairs. Then she went back to the table and took her seat opposite Trammel.

He was eating so fast and furiously that he barely gave her a glance, but both of their guests eyed her curiously. The one closest to her picked up her plate and passed it. Trammel filled it without a word and passed it back. Jennie took it and set it down.

When the pot was empty, Trammel pushed back his chair.

"We got milking to do," he said, glancing from the black-bearded man to his slight, blond partner. "Then we better hit the hay. Tomorrow's another long day."

Jennie pressed her hands, palms down, flat against the table on each side of her untouched plate.

"Before you go," she said, in a voice so high and clear, she didn't know whose it was, "I want to say that this is my house to run as I see fit."

Trammel stood up heavily and sighed. He swung his head around to give her a look that brought shivers to the flesh on her arms. He looked at the candle. Its disputed light flared high in the breeze from the door, then burned lower again.

"This is *my* house," he said flatly, "and it always will be. Move them chairs back to where they was and save th' quilts for the winter. Waste another candle and you'll be fumblin' around in the dark."

Jennie's disappointment filled her heart to the point of bursting.

He looked past her shoulder at the wall. "Don't be changing things around in here," he added. "Never."

He turned and went out.

Digger and Nate pushed back their chairs and got up, barely glancing at Jennie. The argument was settled, their attitude said. Trammel had won. And they were too tired to care. Every movement they made screamed total exhaustion.

"What'd he mean, tomorrow's another long day?" the blond with the high-pitched voice demanded, as he followed his partner. "We're ridin' outta here before daylight, ain't we?"

The dark-bearded man shot a quick, furtive look back at Jennie. "Look outside," he rumbled. "Iffen ever I seen one, that there's a Comanche moon." He walked through the door, following Trammel. "I ain't riskin' no attack on two lone riders."

"Have you already told that slave driver that we'd stay?" the blond man whined. "Goddammit, Digger, I could kill you for that."

The answer floated faintly to Jennie across the

small room as they stepped outside. ''Look at that moon,'' the big man said.

Jennie's mind clung to their words, trying to remember and fit them with their conversation about Comanches that she'd heard through the wall the night before. She batted the snatches of talk around in her head like a kitten with a ball of yarn. She *had* to think about those mysterious remarks so she wouldn't think about Trammel Nordstrom. Her husband. Who *wouldn't* let her run her own house as she saw fit. She had gained no freedom at all in getting out from under Papa's thumb.

For once in her life, Mama was wrong. There was *nothing* about marriage that held any satisfaction.

Chapter 3

The only thing Jennie had to be thankful for on the morning of her second day of married life, as she worked through the same chores she had done on the first day, was the fact that Trammel had been too tired to bother her during the night just past. That was the only thing that had saved her sanity. She spent the morning praying, as she worked, that Trammel would be too tired *every* night.

By midmorning, though, prayer had lost its comfort. She had to have human arms around her, a warm shoulder to cry on. Because cry she would. All the tears that had been gathering in the deep, deep well of her hopeless heart were about to spill over the top.

Papa still had not come to work, so she closed the front door to the store, dropped the bar into its holder, and ran out through the living quarters to look for her mama, hoping that she would find her alone.

Several women were in the yard of the fort, scattering corn to their chickens, washing clothes, or keeping an eye on the playing children. Jennie didn't glance toward any of them so she wouldn't have to speak; she dashed desperately across the large, open square.

Just the thought of the relief it would be to pour out the bitter unhappiness that filled her almost made her tears start falling.

She blinked and ran on toward her parents' small quarters. The door stood open to the April sunshine.

She rushed inside.

Kathleen O'Bannion was bending over her stove, rattling the stove lids as she adjusted the heat of her fire. She was humming "Oh, My Killarney" in her ethereal soprano voice that Jennie had always loved. The sound of it created Ireland and home and all her precious brothers and sisters. It brought them back to life. It showed Jennie her entire childhood as if Mama had thrown open a window between this new world and the old.

This was the first time she had heard Mama sing a note since Brianna, the first of the children to die, had fallen sick with the cholera aboard the ship.

Jennie stood rooted to the floor, fighting to swallow the words that had been rising to the tip of her tongue all the way across the courtyard.

Kathleen straightened up and turned.

"Jennie!" she cried happily, and dropped the stove lid handle to hold out her arms in welcome to her daughter.

Jennie ran into them, terrified that the embrace would make her cry in spite of her suddenly desperate wish to hide her pain-filled face from her mother. She could never share her unhappiness with her now; she must conceal it forever so as not to ruin the fragile contentment Kathleen had achieved at last.

''Ah! How good it is to have a grown-up, married daughter a-droppin' in to see me in th' mornin'!'' Kathleen said, giving Jennie a mighty squeeze. She squeezed her again, then held her at arm's length to look into her face.

''I'm just boilin' water for tea. Let's sit and have a cup, with some good housewives' gossip for spice!''

Jennie willed the tears to stay inside and forced her lips into a smile.

''I guess that's true, isn't it, Ma? Both of us are housewives now.''

An endless hour later, on her way back to the store, back to the cage that held her, married and miserable, Jennie finally cried. But by that time, the hot tears were no relief.

When she'd crossed the yard, had almost reached Trammel's store, she heard a loud voice shouting, ''Heave, there, O'Bannion! One notch higher, now!''

Jennie whirled at the sound of her name, the name that *used to be* hers. Papa was there, at the edge of a group of four or five men who were working to repair the palisaded wall of the fort.

Her own father who had married her off to Trammel Nordstrom so that he could have easy work in the store, her own father whose back had gone so bad that he couldn't farm a living for her and her mother, her own father who had bartered off Jennie's whole life without looking back, was working alongside all the other men!

Jennie stood there and watched as he bent his knees and lifted the heavy peeled pole into its place in the wall.

* * *

In the late afternoon, when all was in readiness, Windrider sat down outside the door to his lodge and looked into the mirror propped against a pole. The girl, Breaks Something, spoke to him as she walked by.

"I will sing for you, Windrider," she said. "I will call out many warriors to take the warpath with you."

He should have replied politely, "I will reward you with a pony."

But he ignored her. He, his lance, and his bow and arrows were soaking up the *puha*, the power, of the Sun Father's heat and were not to be distracted with words. The stupid girl should know that.

Windrider dipped into the white paint, drew a diagonal line across his face from hairline to chin, down his neck, and onto one shoulder, and wiped his finger clean on a clump of grass.

Then he reached into the black and painted all his skin on one side of the line with the color of death.

The songs and the drums began at dusk. Windrider's blood pounded in his veins like thunder as he rode through the village to signify that his war party was leaving that night. It beat higher and hotter as many warriors joined him, as he lifted Echo into a lope, bent down, and swung a man called Mountain up behind him to ride double, showing that, in past battles, he had performed the most honorable deed of carrying a wounded or dead warrior out of danger.

It roared like a raging river in his head as he rode out to the high, leaping fire Mumshukawa had built, stood up in his stirrups, and called to his men.

"The Crossing Place," he shouted.

They answered with a lifted hand or a nod.

Windrider dropped his reins and leaped to the ground. Now everyone knew where to meet him when they drifted away from the crowd to start on the trail. Now it was dark. The War Dance could begin.

He danced in the closing circle, in the rising, falling rhythms of the rattles and the drums, coming closer and closer to the hot glow of the flames until the full moon rode high. Then he slipped away into the shadows.

Echo grazed just outside the firelight. Windrider mounted him, leaving at a gallop in a wide semicircle from the camp. His shield hung hidden in an old cottonwood tree that grew in the bend of a narrow, nameless creek, about a half mile from camp.

His father's father, Iron Shirt, had given the shield to Windrider when he'd made his first medicine. The old man had imbued the shield with much power. Windrider could feel that power now, pulling him in.

The moon poured light all around him, and Echo flew across the ground. Ten Bears and the other war leaders still had to do their dances, but Windrider would gather his men and be gone. He wanted to be first to attack the fort.

Soon the bend in the creek was to his left, to the west, down a slight slope. He went straight to it, slowing only when he had to duck his head to ride beneath the low, crooked branches of the old whispering tree.

There. The large, round shape of the shield encased in its buckskin cover caught the yellow of the moon as its light moved gently toward him and then away among the big leaves.

He stopped Echo beneath it, reached up, and slid the shield reverently off of the branch that held it, sitting very still until the rustling leaves had given up the responsibility of hiding his most precious possession and had fallen silent except for their slight movements in the wind. Then he held out the shield in both hands and moved it in a complete circle.

That done, he slipped it onto his arm.

"Windrider?"

His hand lifted his lance from the stirrup as he twisted his body to look behind him.

The moonlight caught up with a shadow that stepped out from behind the tree. Breaks Something.

His jaw clenched in anger, at her for being in his sacred place, at himself for not sensing her presence.

"What in the name of the Sun Father are you doing out here?"

"Waiting for you," she replied calmly. "I will go on this raid with you and take care of your equipment and your horses."

"Are you crazy, woman?"

She took a step toward Echo's head.

Windrider turned the horse sideways, dropped the shield into his hand on the off side, and held it down behind Echo.

"Get away from this shield," he growled.

"You have the right to take a woman with you," she said, but she didn't come any closer. "Two women, even, because you are the leader and because you have a sacred shield."

"I am taking *no* women with me," he said, his tone hard as the tip of his lance. "Do you *tsihhabuhkamaru*? Does your blood flow?"

A quick fury flashed through her. "No, I know the taboos," she said.

Then his horse danced a little, out into the moonlight, and Breaks Something's anger died as quickly as it had been born. Because she could see his face.

Windrider. Handsomest, bravest war chief The People had ever known. A man who made the women's juices flow when he strode through the village with his commanding, pantherlike walk. A man who possessed medicine to become one with any horse, no matter how wild, and to snatch a woman's heart from her breast to hold high on his lance as he galloped by.

A man who had no wives.

Bitter longing swelled in her, rising and falling with the notes of the war drums. She would do anything to be First Wife to him. This was her chance.

"I watched you hang the shield here when The People first camped in this place," she said softly. "I watch you always because I love you, Windrider. I want to be your wife."

"I will never have a wife I do not love," he said, bluntly.

She would not let that deter her. "You will love me," she said, in her sweetest tones. "Someday."

"I will never love a woman again."

His flat, sure tones slashed at her heart like a knife's stroke; they brought the anger out of it, welling up like standing drops of blood. Her incorrigible tongue took control; she forgot her careful plan.

"You might love your own wife instead of your brother's!"

The rude, daring mention of She Blushes

brought back his grief. It became huge and fierce
as a mountain lion dropping onto his back, trying
to drag him from the horse and into the ground.
Into the ground where She Blushes' beautiful
body rested while her spirit rode far, far away
from him

He kneed Echo to one side and sent him galloping past the spiteful girl, riding fast and then
faster to shake the grief-panther from his back.
But even with the sorrow twisting in his belly and
hardening the sides of his throat until he couldn't
swallow, he followed the path that the shield's
medicine required.

Its great arc carried him back to the camp in the
opposite direction from the way he had left it,
making the sacred circle complete.

By the time he reached his tipi, gathered his
bow and arrows, a lasso, food, and extra clothing,
and rode through the warm, moon-washed night
out to the herd for his extra horses . . . by the
time he reached the Crossing Place, a broad, shallow ford in the river where his men had begun to
gather, his sorrow had surrendered once more to
his anger. Both She Blushes and Breaks Something were gone from his mind.

Only the Texans existed for him. He could not
wait to see their women-killers' faces.

Jennie lay awake for a long time, clinging to her
side of the bed, praying, again, that Trammel
wouldn't touch her. Finally, while he snored and
moaned beside her, she fell asleep.

At first her dream was the one she had many
times in her childhood: she rode a magnificent
horse through a flower-filled meadow with the
sun shining on her face, sitting the spirited mount
as if she had been born to the saddle. The dream

had come to her again and again over the years, sometimes easing her disappointment over never having a horse of her own, other times filling her with a furious frustration. No matter how many times she dreamed it, her reality never changed— she never got near a horse except for the half dozen or so times that the landlord's hostler lifted her to the back of a slow, shaggy pony.

But tonight the dream was different. She started out in the bright meadow, on a prancing bay horse, but soon they were galloping, running flat out, straight over the edge of the land, and then they were flying, up and up, into a sky of boundless blue.

The wind was whipping her hair into her face, then lifting it up to fly out behind her like a flag, making her skin come to tingling life everywhere it touched her, flattening her thin dress against her breasts and her legs as she thrust her powerful way through the air. She felt as free as if she were wearing nothing at all. There were clouds in this sky, soft, puffy, huge white ones, and horses, dozens and hundreds more horses.

A great buoyancy came floating between her and the bay horse, took her flying from its back to land on a sleek, leggy gray. She slipped onto its bare back, wrapped her legs around its warm sides. It tossed its head in welcome and flew through the heavens even faster.

Jennie threw back her head and laughed, drew in great drafts of the exhilarating air. Never, ever had she felt such an invigorating freedom.

Nothing could slow her, nothing could stop her, ever. No one could catch her.

She floated from the gray to a tall, black jumper who immediately took aim at a cloud. They glided up and over it, leaving it far behind.

But all of a sudden, a weight dragged her off the black horse, ripped her fingers from his mane, and brought her plummeting down, down, straight down through the sparkling sky. All the way to the earth and then through it.

She landed hard; it knocked the breath from her. She couldn't move, she couldn't breathe.

Consciousness came back in a rush. She was lying in bed, Trammel Nordstrom's bed, with his heavy hand on her breast.

She jerked awake, twisting her body like an animal caught in a trap. He tightened his grip until it pinched her painfully.

"Lay still," he hissed, his breath hot against her cheek. "A wife obeys her husband, and you ain't put them chairs and quilts back where they was like I told you. When I let you outta this bed, you'll do it or you'll wish to God that you had."

Her living heart changed into a cold stone.

"Raise up," he muttered, and grabbed the back of the gown to pull it up, too, as he had done to the front while she slept.

Instead of obeying, Jennie pressed her hips harder into the cornhusk mattress, sinking into it until she could feel the rope supports crisscrossed beneath it.

"Quit that!" he said, yanking at the gown so hard that it tore. "You're my wife and you'll damn sure learn to act like it!"

Her one pretty nightgown. The only unpatched one she had.

He rose over her then, like a mountain of flesh, and forced himself between her legs. His hands pushed down on her shoulders, his knees knocked her thighs apart in two powerful kicks.

His swollen manhood tore its way into her.

She turned her head to the side, away from his

baleful breath, and clenched her teeth to hold the screams inside. This was it. The last straw. This would be the last time she ever endured such shame.

She would become Jennie O'Bannion again.

When he was done, he collapsed, with his face turned away from her, snoring once more. Jennie made herself lie there until she knew he was truly asleep. She managed to do it by reciting a litany of promises to the wild, furious, impulsive self screaming inside her.

She would slip out of bed and out of this house—Trammel Nordstrom's house and never her own—into the clean air of the night. She would gather a few supplies from the store, steal one of Trammel's horses from the herd held in the pasture just outside the walls, and she would find her way back to San Antonio de Béxar. She would find a job there.

She didn't need Papa to make her a living, nor Trammel, nor any man. She was a grown woman. She would never depend on a man again, so long as God let her live.

Never mind that she didn't know the way, didn't know how to ride a horse or even how to catch one. She would go anyway. Nothing would stop her.

When Trammel truly slept, she slid out from under the covers, grabbed her dress from the chair, tiptoed through the living quarters and into the store, found a saddlebag and filled it—dried peaches, matches, beef jerky, hardtack. She took a blanket for a bedroll and a bucket with some oats in it, blessing the fact that she had arranged all the shelves and thus knew where to find everything in the dark. Then she ran, the dress still over her arm. She would put it on in the trees by the river before she went for the horse. Pray God, the gentlest one in the herd would come after the oats.

Thousands, millions of stars glittered. Through her dry-eyed despair, they appeared to be fragile and brittle as crystal glass, breaking into pieces as she glanced up while she ran. *She* wouldn't break, though, never again. She was Jennie O'Bannion now.

The huge gates of the fort loomed open as usual, forming a wide, barely lighter rectangle against the predawn blackness of the sky. Beyond them, less than a quarter mile away, ran the river.

She could almost feel its water washing the stickiness from her legs and the smell of Trammel's sweat from her body! She would leave without a trace of him on her anywhere.

The cool, damp grass sloped downward beneath her bare feet. Then she felt the smooth dirt path that the women used for bringing water into the fort and ran faster, plunging down it into the scattered cottonwoods that grew thick along the low eastern bank of the river, all the way to the water.

She dropped her burdens at its edge and dashed in. The coldness of the river made her gasp, but she forged on out into the middle, ignoring the rocks cutting at her feet, until she stood in it waist-deep. She picked up the soaking tail of her gown and scrubbed at her thighs, then bent her knees and held her breath, ducking under, letting the water wash all of her clean.

Especially her mind. She mustn't be afraid; she had to live by her wits from now on.

She stood up, tilting her head against the weight of her wet hair, and turned around in the coming light, knowing instinctively where to find her things. A bird called from downriver, one of the many prairie larks, by the sound of it, and from somewhere in a tree very near to Jennie, another one answered. Shades and shadows of light hovered around her.

A lessening of the blackness began to move over the water.

Day would soon be here; she had to hurry to escape.

A breeze swept down the high western bank of the river, coming off the endless plains to touch her cheek and ruffle her hair. Jennie turned, lifted her face to it, and took a deep, trembling breath.

That wind carried the scent of freedom.

She crossed her arms over her body and grasped the wet gown on each side, ready to pull it over her head. But as she stared into the western sky, the faint line of the horizon began to show against it. The gentle, grassy knoll above the river was lit in one spot, and then in another, by the first, pale touches of the sun.

And all the blackness began to fade to gray.

Except on the highest point of the riverbank. Jennie, looking straight at it while the coming dawn broadened its reach, didn't move. The brightening light crept up behind her and flitted across the river.

Something white there, high on the western bank, caught and held the paleness, glowed bright for a long instant against the last of the dark. More pink light flared out of the east. A shape materialized.

A horse, a spotted horse! Sharp excitement hit her and danced through her veins.

Then, with a chasing chill that froze the soles

of her feet to the bank where she stood, she watched as, piece by piece, the rest of the apparition came clear. The horse carried a person on his back.

One sharp shaft of bright light caught on the vision and glinted at her. Off the tip of his lance.

An Indian!

A Comanche, no doubt. A Comanche who sat that animal as arrogantly as if he ruled the earth.

He stayed as still as Jennie did, and so did the horse.

The light washed over them all, more and more strongly. The Indian sat tall as a cliff there on the rise of the land.

He held the lance upright in one hand; the other rested on the bow slung across his shoulder. The morning breeze came up stronger; it blew his black hair away from his wide, muscular shoulders and stirred the feathers tied in it and in the mane of the horse.

Still, other than that, neither man nor horse moved at all.

A lord of the plains come to look down on the river at dawn.

Jennie felt a soaring lift of admiration at the magnificent sight.

Then, before her heart beat again, the Indian raised his lance high into the air and sent his horse leaping over the crest and down, straight at Jennie, screaming a yell that ripped the morning in two. For one fleeting instant, the piercing shine of his dark gaze stabbed into hers.

Echoes of his shriek came at her from all over the world, and just before she tore her feet from the bank and straightened her legs out to run, Jennie had her last coherent thought. She had heard the Comanche war cry.

She stumbled through the cottonwoods, half
falling forward, instinctively reaching out with her
hands for the safety of the earth, the trees, a bush,
any hiding place. Her toes pushed against rocks,
then dug into the dirt, throwing her forward to
fling her arms around the trunk of a large cottonwood tree.

Thundering hooves made a continuous, omi-
nous roar beneath the high, undulating cries of
the Indians. There must be hundreds of them,
thousands, and she was too late to warn the fort.

Mama and Papa! *Mama!*

Jennie turned loose of the big tree and ran to
the shelter of a smaller one, closer to the fort, and
peered around it toward the gates. A river of
mounted Indians was pouring through them.

She could do nothing. Mama and Papa were
trapped inside the walls, and Jennie could do
nothing to save them.

Tears filled her eyes and the awful sight wavered, then blurred into a slash of mixed colors.
The only thing she saw clearly, as she turned to
run in the opposite direction, was the yellow-red
tongue of the flames. The lookout post atop one
corner of the wall had already burst into a blaze.

She dashed downstream along the river, trying
to stay away from the edge in case another wave
of Indians waited on the opposite bank to attack,
yet desperate to hide herself from the ones at the
fort. She had to get away from them—staying
alive was all she could do for Mama and Papa.

She could do nothing to save them, she could
do nothing to save them. *Nothing. Nothing.* The
word rang in her mind over and over again like
the tolling of a funeral bell.

Jennie ran until she couldn't. Her feet slowed

and then stopped with no commands from her mind to guide them. She wiped the sweat from her eyes with the back of her hand and looked desperately around for a safe place to drop. Somehow, back there somewhere, she must have left the river; here there were no trees at all.

A bush! There, not too far away, was a bush that was bigger than she was.

She staggered to it and let her body drop to the ground, barely able to call up the strength to curl into the smallest ball she could make. Surely they were all gone by now. Surely. Hadn't a long, long time passed since she had been running?

Jennie dragged air into her lungs through her mouth as well as her nose, keeping her eyes tightly closed. In a minute she would look back to see if the fort had all burned down.

But not yet.

Fear and exhaustion pulled the last shreds of strength from her limbs, and she sank into a numbed stupor. In a minute or two, she would look back to see if anyone else had escaped. She would look back to see if the Indians had all gone.

In a minute she would run some more. But not yet.

She came to herself when something tore her body from its warm nest and lifted her into the air, moving fast, already moving like the wind. Her eyes flew open.

Hooves flashed so close to her face that she thought they surely would crush her cheekbones, then they dropped away, and after a fleeting glimpse of white and black horse's spotted legs and neck, she saw that she lay across its withers, staring in shock down at the ground rushing past.

And at the beaded, fringed moccasin enclosing a foot pressed close to the horse's side.

The leg attached to it was muscular beyond belief, copper-skinned, and perfectly bare.

Her blood stopped flowing.

The Comanche had caught her.

Chapter 4

Crazily, beneath the noise of the hooves, Jennie could hear Mama's voice, teasing her, back in the old days in the old country, when Uncle Sean would swoop down on Jennie and throw her onto his shoulder.

"Well, who'd ye think had ye, Jennie?" she'd say. "Saint Patrick himself?"

Saint Patrick had to help her now, because Mama never could. These murdering savages had, most likely, killed her mama.

As this one would kill her. She hadn't run far enough, after all.

She turned loose the screams that had filled her throat since dawn, kicking and hitting at her captor, fighting to free herself from his hand that held her to the horse.

"Let me up!" she yelled, "I won't be hauled around like a sack of potatoes before I die!"

He made no response. The pressure on her back didn't lessen or increase.

She was going to die. She must make him angry enough to kill her now before he had time to ravish her, too.

Jennie took a frantic swipe at his bare leg. Her nails dug in and her fingertips felt wetness. Good!

She'd drawn blood. Surely he would run his lance through her now and put her out of her misery.

She scratched him again.

He chuckled. The low, musical sound poured like warm honey over her skin even while a deeper cold chilled her. She wasn't even hurting him—her best try at striking out had had no effect on him at all!

"What do you plan," he taunted, amusement echoing in his tone, "to drain life from me drop by drop?"

She froze, hanging upside down over the running horse with the ground rushing past below. "You speak English," she gasped, straining to make him hear her over the noise of the hooves, "yet you treat me this way!"

He laughed, really laughed this time. "You and my brother," he said, "worried always about what language I am using."

Every word he spoke vibrated through her bones. His voice was wondrous; it possessed a life of its own, a deep melody that rose and fell on the wind.

Struggling against the strange lassitude it created in her, Jennie kicked out, fighting once more to sit up.

"We can talk!" she cried. "Let me up . . . "

"Say to me, 'please.' "

His teasing, seductive tone made her limbs go weak. But his words filled her mind with fury.

"I will *not*!" she shouted. "Never!"

"Then stay as you are," he growled.

They turned to the right, galloping fast, following a faintly visible path. She caught jolting glimpses of the grass growing thinner and shorter on its harder earth, then, farther down it, something looming in the corner of her eye. She managed to turn her head enough to see a tall cactus, then another, reaching stickery arms out toward the trail.

The Comanche showed no intention of swerving to miss them.

They would rip her to shreds!

"Please!" she screamed. "Let me up!"

In the next breath she sat in front of him, lifted into place as easily and quickly as he had snatched her up from beneath the bush. He laid a huge, hard-muscled arm across her abdomen.

Its implacable weight, its warm skin pressing against hers through the thin fabric of her gown, sent a shivering thrill all through her. She pushed at it, then twisted against it to face him.

"You might as well kill me now! I'm . . ."

All her words died in her throat.

The sight of his commanding face, made even more terrifying by its nearness—not to mention its awful war paint—stopped the last breath in her lungs. That, and the infinitesimal tightening of his arm around her rib cage when her eyes met his.

How could she *ever* have thought, lying in bed this very morning, that she was a prisoner, that her life could not be any worse?

His dark eyes looked down into hers.

They glinted at her, surprisingly human in the menacing mask of diagonal black and white paint that covered his skin. His hair shone in the sun, black as the night had been the moment before she'd first seen him.

"I swear you an oath," he said, in that soul-subduing voice. "Someday you will say 'please' to me, and not because you are afraid of some cactus."

His eyes gleamed, deep and dark, with an arrogant sureness that paralyzed her.

The white feathers tied low in one long, leather-bound lock of his hair lifted in the wind and blew forward to brush her cheek.

She whipped her face away from them, turned her back on him, fighting with all her might to still the trembling that took her the moment she could move at all. *What* was the matter with her? He was repulsive, a heartless barbarian!

She stared straight ahead. But instead of the endless, rolling green prairie, she saw the authoritative eyes of the warrior who held her life, as well as her body, between his hard hands.

Her fists clenched. He was a raiding, murdering savage, someone so far from her own kind that the only thing they had in common was the fact that they were both human beings.

The startling attraction she felt for him was laced with fear. What would he do to make her say "please"?

He held her utterly helpless within his power.

The black and white mount carried them at a smooth, rocking gait, moving faster now, so fast that everything blurred in front of Jennie's eyes. It made a wind that dried the tears on her cheeks. She held her face up to heaven and prayed without words.

The sensuous rhythm of the horse moving beneath her throbbed through the muscles of her legs and warmed them with the heat of its skin in the sun. It possessed a primal power that drew her in and brushed the backs of her thighs against the warrior's legs. For one dizzying instant she wanted, with all her heart, to live.

They rode over a rise in the land and started back down it. She caught a glimpse of trees at the bottom and, in front of them, lots of horses and people.

As they raced closer to them, the fear grew until it became her only emotion; her heart swelled with dread. They were painted savages, every one, with weapons waving in the air. The only people left in the world, except for her, were Indians on horseback. Gathered into one place. Did they make a public sport of killing their captives?

Terror roared in her head like thunder.

"Are you going to kill me now?"

The warrior's rich chuckle rumbled in her ear.

"No. Remember—first I must make you say 'please.' "

Jennie shivered.

The spotted horse carried her closer. War paint, the hideous, garish war paint, flashed in the sun, its white and blue and yellow bright enough to blind her. And each appalling face wore streaks of sinister black.

Several of the warriors looked at her, but she couldn't meet their quick, bright glances. There were too many of them, on horses that were constantly, nervously moving. And she felt too afraid.

She fought to keep her churning stomach quiet, not to disgrace herself by retching over the horse's withers onto the ground. Her siblings, and her parents, had always told her how brave she was, but her bravery was about to fail her now.

One Comanche riding a dun-colored horse and carrying a heavily decorated lance rode through the crowd to meet them. He exchanged words with her captor.

His voice rumbled heavily in her ear, his chest pulsed against her back. She straightened her spine until she sat away from him. He was one of this crowd of barbarians, and she'd better not forget it!

The wide-faced Comanche on the dun-colored horse looked at her, looked again, and spit a brief spate of words at the man at her back.

He dropped his hand onto her hipbone. It was big and hard and utterly unyielding.

It said that she belonged to him.

Panic sent her heart thrusting into her mouth.

Dear God in Heaven, to think that in trying to escape from being Trammel's slave, she had gotten into this!

The two men hurled rapid remarks back and forth in low tones that vibrated with anger. Jennie tried to believe that they weren't talking about her. But they were. By some instinct, she just knew it.

They were deciding her fate this instant, as if she were a sheep or a cow or one of their horses. Were they arguing about which one would ravish her first? Or when to tie her to a post and burn her alive?

The panic rose like a fever in her blood. It didn't matter that this painted savage had said they weren't going to kill her now. Why did she think she could trust him?

"Turn me loose!" she cried, pushing at her captor's hand with both of hers in an entirely futile effort. "Let me go!"

The man on the dun smiled in a derisive way, and her captor's hand grew heavier.

"Quiet!"

The whiplash of an order made her catch her lip in her teeth to stop the next words. She forced her body to go still and her mind to push away every single one of the horrible tales told at the fort about the Comanches.

The narrow, black eyes of the man arguing with her captor darted over her face and then dropped to peruse her body. She watched him warily, every nerve screaming to run from his greedy interest. He was shorter and more stockily built than the warrior who had captured her, and even with the war paint, she could tell that he was not nearly so handsome. His features were broader and coarser; he lacked the high cheekbones and arrogant hawk nose, the sinuous, curving lips burned into her memory from that one, long look he had shared with the man behind her.

Then, at the stocky Comanche's back, the crowd opened up and a line of horses and riders came out of its center. The first was a painted Comanche, but the second . . .

She stared, for a moment not believing her eyes.

Two white women rode the second horse! Women from the fort!

"Mrs. Allen!" Jennie cried, trying to remember the name of the other woman, Mrs. Allen's cousin, as if calling it out would immediately save them all.

But it wouldn't. Nothing would. Mrs. Allen didn't even show a sign of having heard or seen Jennie. Both women, their faces gone slack with terror, were tied to the horse.

Behind them came four children, two to a mount, also.

Mama wasn't there. It was Mrs. Allen and her cousin and some children Jennie didn't know. Mama wasn't there.

The man on the dun began to speak rapidly.

Her captor's hand tightened on Jennie's hipbone, searing its shape into her skin as surely as if there were no cloth between them. It stirred the strange, provocative feeling in her, something more, something much different from the oppression she had felt under the weight of Trammel's hand.

That, and knowing that she *was* completely oppressed, all over again, hopelessly so, brought her temper rising past her fear. Oh, what she'd give to have a gun and be able to use it! To get away from him!

She could get a deep breath. She couldn't get any breath.

The Comanches and the white women and children rode past them. The lead warrior broke his horse into a fast trot and headed away from the gathering.

"Where are they going?" she demanded, turning to look at her captor. "Stop them, right now! Keep them here."

The man leading Mrs. Allen's horse kicked his mount into a lope. They all rode off toward the north.

"Stop them!" Jennie screamed.

"They are not mine," her captor said, in a voice that fell across her heart like a blow from an ax. "But you are, and your noise shames me. Be quiet."

Jennie's body strained after the others from the fort, her eyes glued to the backs of the women as they grew smaller and smaller against the green of the prairie. She was being left behind!

But where were they going? Certainly not to safety!

A leaping, surging terror filled her. What would happen to them? To her? Desperately she looked around.

The Comanche on the dun horse fixed his glittering stare on her again and urged his mount a step closer, shifting the lance he held in his right hand into his left. All its decorations swung back and forth with the movement.

He tried to catch Jennie's eye, but she kept her gaze stubbornly on his weapon. Her glance clung to it, moved over every feather, every braided leather thong, every beaded ornament tied to its handle. Her mind couldn't absorb everything she saw.

Just as her mind couldn't accept that her only destiny was to end up in his bed or in her captor's. Or, perhaps, dead.

The man spoke sharply as he set the end of the lance into his stirrup. The sound drew her eyes to his face, and she saw raw desire, determined desire, gleaming all over it.

Her hands flew to cross her arms over her breasts, as if to protect herself.

"Get away!" she screamed. "You have no right to touch me!"

And then both her hands fell limp to her sides. She fainted dead away.

Jennie came back to consciousness once, in the black dark. She was flying through the night, held fast in arms strong and resilient as rawhide, the same arms that had caught her when she collapsed.

Her own limbs contained no strength at all.

The horror had kept its power, though. It filled her memory. She was a captive. That stocky Comanche lusted for her, and he was determined to have her.

She tried to struggle, but her mind couldn't make her body work; it had enough energy only to draw her back into sleep again. Feebly she collapsed, limp as wet cloth against her warrior's chest.

* * *

The sun on her cheek pulled her toward waking. Something inside her, though, like a voice in a dream, pulled her back. It called, *No! No! There's danger!*

She settled more deeply into the warm nest of her sleeping, lulled by the rocking motion of the horse. Her face rested against something hard and smooth, something with a drum beating inside it. The rhythm would help draw her back from the danger.

The danger was Comanches!

Her eyes flew open, stretched wide with fear from the instant the word hit her brain. Copper-colored skin filled her vision. Beneath it beat the Indian heart she had dreamed was a drum.

She scrambled to get away, to get out of the cradle made by his arms. The chill early morning air swirled in to find every warm place on her that had been against him, to set her to shivering like a sheep just shorn. Her traitorous body tried to lean back for the heat of his body again, but she strained with her numb legs and scrabbled with her hands to sit up.

The warrior took hold of her at the waist and set her up masterfully, as if she were a doll. His long, strong fingers burned their shapes into her skin; his hard palms sent a sweet pressure spiraling down into the core of her.

Oh, dear Lord, she had to wake up, to get away from his touch, away from this awful attraction he held for her.

She plunged her fingers into the horse's mane, tangled them in the coarse hairs to aid her balance, and moved her legs back and forth to get the blood flowing. She shaped them to the sides of the horse. That done, she pushed at the Comanche's hands until he removed them.

Escape. She must figure out a way to escape before she completely lost her sanity.

"Where are we?" she muttered, her tongue still thick with sleep.

"Not far."

"From where?"

"From village," he said, in a tone that told her plainly he would say no more.

She turned to look past him at the sun, yellow now after rising, but still trailing streaks of pink. Between her and the sun, silhouetted against it, rode warrior after warrior after warrior, their horses' hooves pounding, pounding behind her. There could be no hope of escape.

Besides, everywhere that she could see, the prairie looked the same. The green and gray grasses, sparkling with dew, covered a rolling sea of land as trackless as the mighty ocean she had crossed aboard the *Caroline*. If she *could* get away, where would she go?

She couldn't get away. The warrior's breath stirred her hair; his legs gripped the horse only inches from hers. Her cheek still cried to fit itself to his chest once more. She ignored that urge and sat up straighter than ever. If they didn't kill her when they got to wherever they were going, then she would escape.

Finally they stopped and came together in a milling crowd, slipping down from the horses to pull out rawhide bags from their packs, to look into mirrors and refresh the hideous war paint on themselves and their ponies. "Her" warrior didn't dismount.

"What are they doing?" she asked, suddenly desperate to hear the sound of his voice—and the sound of her own language—in this eerie, savage dawn.

"Painting their brave deeds on their horses," he said, shortly, as if his mind was busy on another subject entirely.

Probably on whether to give her to the coarse-featured man on the dun.

Restless with fear, she moved numbly, all at once feeling terribly light-headed since the motion of the horse had stopped.

A moment later, as if at a silent signal, the others all mounted again. Someone behind Jennie left the group, galloping past her toward the south, and her gaze followed him. Smoke from several fires hung above the next rise of land. That must be their village.

They rode straight toward it, and as soon as they'd topped the knoll, the camp spread out before Jennie's eyes: many, many tipis scattered along a creek that flowed through a natural valley.

The dogs began barking. The warrior who'd ridden ahead to announce their coming came galloping back to join the others, and the next moment the village came alive with people swarming out of their tents, hastily throwing on clothes, running to meet them.

"Li-li-li-li!" Dozens of high-pitched women's voices repeated the sound over and over, a trilling, joyous victory cry.

More singing, with other words, began, and then people on foot, men, women, and children, were surrounding the returning horses, calling and reaching out to touch their heroes.

They reached out to touch Jennie as well. Yelling at her in words she couldn't understand, but in derisive tones that she could, the women pinched and poked, hit her legs with their hands and with switches, slapped her with something metal that felt like the flat of a knife.

Their faces and their cruel hands melted into a blur before her eyes. Instinctively she shrank back against the warrior who had carried her so far, into his arms which now formed a perverse sort of refuge.

But they weren't. They weren't a refuge at all! She jerked herself up to sit away from him again. He wasn't her protector. He was the one who'd brought her to this terrible fate, whatever it proved to be!

"Tell them to get away from me or I'll kick them in the face!" she shouted at him. "Tell them, now!"

She glared down into the strange brown faces and kicked out, hard, at the next woman who raised a hand to hit her. Another woman saw that, and raised her voice in a high cry, pointing at Jennie.

"*You're* telling them," he said, into her ear. "You do not even need to know the language."

Her fury flared stronger than her fear at the casual unconcern in his tone. "I'll make the lot of you wish you'd never seen me!" she shouted, kicking with her other foot at a bitter-looking girl wielding a long switch. "You should not have brought me here!"

"I'm sure she agrees with you," he said with infuriating imperturbability when Jennie's bare toes connected with the frowning girl's wrist, and her switch dropped beneath the feet of the crowd. Several people jeered and laughed, and her captor's low chuckle sounded again in her ear.

She hated him! How could he—*someone who spoke her language, for Heaven's sake!*—bring her into this torment?

The acrid smell of smoke floated on the air, dogs

swirled and barked around the horses' feet, and
more people, it seemed like hundreds more people, pushed toward her. Jennie stiffened her
shoulders. She would not let them see that she
was afraid. She would not.

And somehow, strangely, the screaming fear
pumping through her veins gave her the power
to be brave. She lifted her chin to show all the
Comanches how courageous she was, and when
she felt her hair brush against the warrior's chest,
she made her spine into an iron rod. He, most of
all, should know that she came from a proud people.

He rode over to a tipi on the near side of the
camp and stopped.

Jennie's stubborn seat collapsed, her body
swayed. After all those endless hours of riding,
they had reached this destination, but it felt as if
she were still moving.

Dimly she became aware that a dozen or so of
the women had stayed with them, gathering
around the warrior's horse. For one hostile moment she felt their eyes on her, heard their voices
chattering insults, high and shrill.

Then they faded out of her senses and there
was only the warrior who had carried her to this
place. Without her knowing he had moved, he
was on the ground.

Now he was lifting her off the horse. She made
one feeble attempt to push him away, but her
bones had gone to jelly. There was no way she
could dismount by herself. She would fall. She
would simply crumple up and tumble down to
the ground, lie there, and never move again.

His warm, hard hands, their touch familiar to
her now, picked her up and set her feet onto the
earth again.

She would escape, she promised herself silently, even as she leaned desperately into the support he gave her. Her bare toes gripped the worn grass in front of the tipi, fighting to find a hold so she could stand on her own. As soon as she got the chance, she would escape.

She got her balance and pulled away from him.

"You won't keep me here," she said, defiantly, and stood back and wrenched her aching neck upward to look him in the eye.

The group of women understood her tone if not the words. A speculative murmur rose from them. Jennie glimpsed several of them edging around the horse for a better view of her and the warrior. She kept her eyes fixed on her captor, but she spoke loudly enough for them to hear her hostile tone.

"You took me," she told him, staring straight into his black eyes. "But you can't keep me."

When they killed her, she would have her pride. Trammel had taken that away from her, and she would never relinquish it again.

"I will run . . ." she vowed, and started to say, *back to my people,* but her voice caught in her throat. She didn't know if she had any people. Rowan's Fort was burning, Mama and Papa probably were dead. But she finished fiercely, anyway, "To Texas!"

The Comanche listened and kept looking at her. He didn't change expressions beneath his war paint, but quick approval flashed in his eyes, just for an instant. He searched her face, carefully, as if he wanted to make sure that she meant what she'd said.

Jennie held her challenging pose, chin up, back straight, although every inch of her body had begun to tremble with fatigue.

Then all the watching women vanished and there was only the two of them, connected, as they had been during that first moment on his horse, by the look passing between them.

He accepted her challenge and threw out another one of his own.

"I will keep you," he vowed.

As his voice sang its way into her veins and his gaze dropped to her breasts, she remembered his other vow, the one that he would make her say, "please."

His unsmiling eyes lingered on her breasts, then looked her thoroughly up and down, from her hair to her bare toes.

For the first time in all the long, wild hours just past, Jennie became mindful of the fact that she was wearing nothing but the thin, torn nightgown. A sudden heat rushed to her cheeks, but she held her head high and refused to look down.

The muscles of his massive shoulders gleamed in the sunlight. His wide chest barely moved with the slowness of his breath. His eyes had gone blacker than ever as they traveled over her, but brighter somehow, as if reflected in a fire.

They made something contract deep inside her. She tried to ignore the strange, stirring feeling and did her best to stare him down.

Finally he gave her an almost imperceptible nod. Then he turned and shouted, "Sanah!"

An old woman appeared at the flap of the tipi. He barked more words to her, some sort of orders. He looked at Jennie again.

"You need garments," he said, "and rest and food before you try to run."

Jennie stood, staring, as he made one imperious gesture from the old woman to her, took the bridle of the spotted horse, and led him away.

When he disappeared down the crooked path that ran between the tipis, she couldn't stop watching for him to turn and come back. Suddenly she wanted to run after him instead of away from him as she had promised. He was abandoning her!

But he wasn't her friend who had traveled with her on a long journey. He had snatched her up and carried her off. He was her mortal enemy.

Lost for direction, she turned to the old woman he'd called Sanah.

The group of chattering women, which had earlier seemed to vanish, were suddenly crowded again at her back.

The old woman glared at her out of eyes bright as a bird's, her gnarled hand still holding back the flap of the tipi. Finally she let it drop and took several surprisingly brisk steps toward Jennie.

Sanah called out a command, and in a flash the women had surrounded Jennie.

Her throat went dry as paper. Her heart leaped and began beating harder and faster; she tried to turn and push through the crush of women, but they formed an impenetrable wall.

Then they had hold of her; their relentless hands were all over her, hurting her, taking her prisoner yet again. She kicked and screamed as they dragged her away from the old woman's tipi.

Her mind plunged into action and began to race, as if thinking could save her. Was this the custom, then? Did the women kill the women captives? Was that the order that the warrior had given to Sanah?

No, she thought, as her feet went out from under her and the women half dragged, half carried her along. He had promised to keep her, and he had meant what he said. She had seen the look in his eyes. He had not told Sanah to kill her.

She wanted to scream that at them, but her lips and her tongue had frozen. She could do nothing, nothing to save herself, no more than she'd been able to do to save Mama and Papa.

They stopped, finally, and, handling her roughly, set Jennie into a standing position in a wide, cleared place, surrounded by tipis, near a fire. A *large* fire, burning beneath an iron kettle hung on a tripod.

Did they intend to throw her into it?

Without tying her to a pole like in the horrible tales about captives she'd heard at the fort?

Despite the coppery taste of fear on her tongue, the smell of cooking meat brought saliva into her mouth. Her stomach clenched in upon itself. No. Surely they wouldn't throw her into the fire and ruin their breakfast.

But as soon as she'd thought it, a sudden push sent her staggering toward the pot of stew, bubbling over the flames. Her face came so close to it that its vapors steamed her cheeks. She righted herself just in time.

Her tormentors laughed and jeered louder. The sound roared in Jennie's ears, drowning out every thought of caution. She pivoted to face them.

A girl, long black hair swinging, bent over, scooped up some dirt, spit into it twice, and threw it at Jennie.

It hit her on the cheek.

The insult of it knocked the rest of the fear out of her, sent it fleeing before the white-hot anger that bubbled up in her veins. She rushed at the girl, reaching with both hands for the mane of her hair.

"You'd better be hiding your own face!" Jennie

shouted, noticing, even in her shaking fury, that her tormentor was very young, extremely beautiful, and a full head taller than she. ''Because I aim to dirty it for you, like you did mine. I'll scrub it into the very ground itself!''

The girl blocked Jennie's hands with her arms at first, but every motion sent her loose hair swirling about her, and Jennie grabbed hold of it. The girl kicked out, but Jennie wouldn't let go, pulling with all her might as her opponent twisted and turned to find Jennie's arms with her hands. Her nails dug in, scratching deep from shoulder to elbow.

Jennie jerked her off balance just as her enemy's foot hooked her ankle, and they went down in a frenzied, tangled mass, both screaming and yelling.

Above their noise, Jennie could hear a great cry from the crowd of women, then many, many separate calls and shouts. They would kill her, but first she would show them what the Irish were made of!

She was on the girl, slapping and hitting her, *beating* her with all the horror and fear of the past day and night surging into her muscles like a bursting of joy. By Heaven, here was one Comanche who would remember her, then!

The girl fought like a wild thing, biting and scratching. Jennie held her down for a moment or two, but the Comanche used her greater weight to flip Jennie over and put herself on top. She landed on her with such force that the air went whooshing from Jennie's lungs.

The world went black.

Windrider stretched out on his bed robes, freshly spread and smoothed by Kukapu, Ten

Bears' wife number two. She had placed them farther from the side of the tipi than his mother always did—the thought made him incredibly sad.

His mother. She was riding in the Spirit Land on a journey he could not share.

He had avenged her death. There was nothing else he could do.

Kukapu entered his lodge, now carrying a bowl of steaming stew, but he waved her away. A day of sleep before the night's Victory Dance enticed him more now than food. He would eat when he awakened.

He closed his eyes and let his arms fall to his sides. They felt strangely empty now, without the soft body of the small white woman to hold.

The image of that body, so small and delicately boned, so slender at the hip yet so lushly full at the breast, floated onto the dark nothingness of his eyelids. When he had snatched her up and onto his horse, he had tried to tell himself that one so small was a child who could be trained to become one of the *Nermernuh*. But he knew that wasn't so. He had seen her bathing in the river at dawn.

And he had seen her standing straight and proud to defy him in front of Sanah's lodge. He could have stayed there and looked at her all day—she was so different, so fascinating with all that spirit, which was as fiery as her incredible hair, living in such a small body. Looking at her not only stirred his loins, but his mind as well.

He should never have even thought of keeping her—she might creep into his heart.

But what would he do with her?

Give her to Mopai to replace his daughter, She Blushes, as he had planned when he first took her?

Or give her to Ten Bears to replace his wife, She Blushes, as Ten Bears had suggested the minute he saw her?

Either gift would bring Windrider more power among The People, more influence to bear when the time came for him and Ten Bears to make another leadership decision together. Either gift would bring him much praise and esteem at tonight's Victory Dance.

But both gifts somehow stuck in his throat.

He turned onto his side and nestled his cheek into the folded buffalo robe that he used for a pillow. He grinned to himself.

She was a little she-panther, that one, making a public vow to run away. She hadn't pleaded with him. No, the small woman with the hair like a red flower possessed much courage.

Drowsiness had almost guided him into sleep when laughing voices outside his lodge jerked him back to wakefulness.

"The red-haired captive is a fighter," a woman called to someone. "She pulled Breaks Something to the ground by her hair. Come and help us find out how truly brave she is."

Windrider rolled out of the bed and onto his feet in one swift motion. He would kill that Sanah, old as she was! Hadn't he told her to give the girl food and rest?

The next thing Jennie knew, she was on her feet again, each of her arms held in the paralyzing grip of a stout Comanche woman. The girl she had fought was screaming in her face.

Jennie shook her hair out of her eyes and tried to shout back, but she could only gasp. She hadn't recovered enough breath to speak.

The girl slapped her.

Jennie jerked both her arms as hard as she could, but she hadn't a shred of a chance of pulling them free. She kicked out, but the girl jumped back too quickly for her to land a blow.

"Coward!" she croaked. "Three against one! Turn me loose and fight fair!"

A finger of fear traced a path down her backbone.

The women *were* going to kill her. They had intended to do so from the instant they'd surrounded her at Sanah's tipi.

She hated them. They were ganged up on her like a pack of dogs around a wounded calf.

"Sanah!"

The angry shout broke apart the semicircle of taunting faces and turned the hateful girl around. The women immediately fell silent.

The Comanche warrior who had captured her strode toward her. The one who had gotten her into this.

Suddenly she hated him more than she hated the women. She hated him with every fiber of her being, with all her heart and her soul. Even if that hatred *would* send her soul straight to hell.

Even if his face, washed clean of the terrifying war paint, *was* the most arrestingly handsome she had ever seen on a man.

His cheekbones stood high and prominent beneath his copper-colored skin. His piercing black eyes flashed. His strong jaw stood out square and hard, as if he were clenching his teeth, its muscle working in and out. His nostrils flared, he was so angry.

He brushed the dirt-throwing girl aside and barked an order. The women dropped their hands from Jennie's arms.

She hated him. But she couldn't stop looking at him.

His black hair fell back from his forehead in a sensuous line like the swoop of a hawk's wing.

Sanah stepped out of the group of women with movements slow and deliberate, as if to say that she didn't care whether the man was angry or not. He spoke to her sharply, without even glancing her way. His eyes were on Jennie.

Sanah answered with a long tirade to which he didn't respond.

One gesture and the women stepped away from Jennie's sides. He stood in front of her, close enough to touch.

Jennie swayed on her feet. *What was going to happen now?*

His big hands gripped both her arms. They felt familiar and strong. Her dizziness receded.

"They were trying to kill me," she gasped.

"No," he snorted angrily, "but they anger me so, I wish to kill *them.*"

He turned and began leading her away from the women.

"Stupid ones. They are worse than young braves, too full of themselves to do what the War Chief tells them."

Sanah stepped into their path.

Again, she loosed a torrent of words at Jennie's warrior, shaking her fist in the air.

He answered briefly, leveling his fierce gaze on her, then, slowly, he turned it on the others standing closest by. He raised his free hand and brushed it across the top of Jennie's hair.

"*Kohtoo Topusana,*" he said. When she looked up at him in surprise, he translated. "Fire Flower. Your name."

He took her away from them then, with the girl

who had thrown dirt in Jennie's face sending her a look of terrible evil, and Sanah spitting more harsh words at their backs. He lifted her feet almost off the ground with his one hand clenched around her upper arm, and led her away from the fire and in among the tipis that surrounded it.

"What was Sanah saying?" Jennie asked hoarsely. Her throat felt too dry to speak.

"Bad things will happen to me," he said. "Because I order them to stop the old custom. Testing the courage of captives."

He grinned at her then, actually grinned, like a mischievous boy who had done something he shouldn't.

Again, Jennie found herself unable to look away from him. The absolute power of his hard-angled face, with its aristocratic nose and chiseled chin, changed to pure charm when he smiled.

His lips were full and extremely sensual, curving over straight, white teeth.

"I *never* follow old customs, Sanah says."

Jennie stared harder at him. He must be the rebel among his people as she was in hers! Could that be true of a Comanche warrior?

"Is she right?" she asked, wishing as she spoke that she knew what the custom was between a warrior and his captive.

He raised one black eyebrow and threw her a sharp glance. "I do as I please," he replied.

"What did you say to Sanah?"

"Bad things will happen to *her* because she did not obey my commands when I left you at her lodge. A woman is to obey a warrior at all times, no matter how old and respected she is."

That was no different from the customs of her own people, Jennie thought. Evidently *all* men everywhere expected women to obey them promptly and without question.

A woman didn't have a chance of a choice no matter where she lived.

She realized that she was taking Sanah's side in this matter and shook her head wryly. And after the old woman had thrown her to the wolves!

One wolf, in particular, that hated Jennie with a passion.

"Who is that girl who was hitting me?"

"She is called Breaks Something."

His tone said the girl was entirely unimportant.

As, indeed, she suddenly seemed to Jennie as the dizziness hit her again. The whole fight faded away like a bad dream as she let her mind float away and her tired body take over. He led her past the last tipi, out of the camp and into the tall, cool grass.

Its blades reached to her knees, wiping her legs with the wetness of the morning's dew. Feeling its moisture against her skin made her tongue go dry as a desert.

"I need water," she said, and stumbled from fatigue, her muscles and bones starting to cry for rest and for food as well. "A drink."

"*Paa,*" he answered. "Water."

"*Paa,*" he said again, and with a commanding motion of his free hand, made her know that she should repeat the word.

She could barely speak, she was so tired, and he was insisting that she learn a new language! She shook her head, but finally, as he kept the silence, she ran her tongue over her parched lips and said, "*Paa.*"

Her toe caught on a clump of grass and she stumbled again.

The warrior swept her up into his sinewy arms and began to run, carrying her down a gentle slope in the land. Being cradled in his embrace felt eerily intimate and closer to the rightness of things than any other experience in this strange, threatening world. Instinctively her hand went to his shoulder, clinging to the huge, hard bulge of the muscles there, although there was no need. He ran so smoothly, held her so surely in his effortless strength, that she stayed steady as the sun.

"I can walk," she murmured, but so softly, only she could hear. The palm of her hand flattened itself against his warm skin.

He ran into the shade of some cottonwood trees and knelt down beside a shallow-running stream.

"Drink," he said, gently lowering her to sit on the ground beside him. He scooped up a double handful of the clear water and brought it to her mouth.

Jennie bent over his huge palms and drank. The cold water shocked all her senses: It smelled of clean rocks, it sounded like a song running along in its bed, it tasted better than honey. Greedily she drank every drop, until her lips brushed the roughness of his hands.

Callused palms, hardened skin. They laid a different taste on her tongue, one as agreeably sweet as that of the water.

She lifted her head.

He was looking at her.

"Windrider," he said, touching himself lightly in the middle of his chest.

Jennie couldn't look away from the dark intensity of his eyes. She made the same gesture as he.

"Jennie."

"Jen-nie."

He smiled at her again, and her treacherous heart turned over.

He reached out to gently touch her hair, curling at her cheek. *"Kohtoo Topusana,"* he said, "Fire Flower."

She smiled, too.

"My red hair brings me a Comanche name?"

He shook his head. "Your great courage brings Comanche name."

His eyes smiled into hers. They caught glints of the sunlight. His hair shone in it, too, with blue lights because it was so black. A rawhide thong binding one long lock was its only ornament now.

The wind stirred it, swinging the ends against his wide collarbone, trailing them into the hollows on each side of his huge neck. Her fingertips tingled to touch him there.

They looked at each other.

"How do you know my language?" she asked, at last.

"Trade," he answered. "With Texans."

Texans.

Her world turned cold. He had done a lot more than trade with the Texans.

Windrider, her enemy.

Chapter 5

How *could* she have such feelings about him? She must be crazed, berserk, a completely unnatural girl.

Great courage indeed! If there was a scrap of courage, a shred of loyalty to her parents, in her soul, she would snatch the knife he wore in the beaded sheath tied at his waist and plunge it into his heart. She ought to do *something*.

But she only turned away and leaned toward the creek, dipping up more water, this time with her own shaking hands, dropping her face into it to drink, glad of a reason to hide her eyes.

This unwonted sensation of being drawn to this savage was surely an aberration of her feelings born of bewilderment, caused by the horror she'd just been through. She'd not succumb to it again. All her energy must go into making a plan to escape.

That's what she could do for Mama and Papa. Escape. Maybe they were still alive.

A shaking urgency ran along the tips of her nerves. She needed to find food and something to carry water in. Then she would figure out how to get away from him. She didn't need to take the time to sleep before she went; she had slept on the way here.

He spoke again in his musical voice. *"Tuhk-aru,"* he said, *"eat."*

Just the word brought back the smell of that bubbling kettle of meat stew. Her stomach growled.

"Yes, eat," she said, and pushed up with her hands against the sandy bank of the creek until she could stand on her trembling legs. She would escape, she would tell the Texas authorities what had happened at Rowan's Fort.

She would eat all she could of the food he gave her and ask for more, she thought, as she and Windrider turned away from the noisy stream. The second helping, she would hide for her journey.

Surely she could steal a bag to carry it in, plus a water container. Maybe from his lodge, if he took her there. The important thing now was to remember who and what he was, and not to trust him.

The sunlight poured hot down onto her head as they walked farther and farther from the shade of the cottonwoods, and her dizziness threatened to return. With each step, she placed her feet with great care, so as not to stumble. He *must* not pick her up again, must not touch her at all.

The Fire Flower shook off his steadying hand as Windrider strode a bit ahead of her to show the way, yet close enough to catch her if she should falter again.

Too bad the white women were always so fragile and weak, he thought. This one had the spirit

of a mountain cougar. What a shame that her
body wasn't as strong as it was beautiful!

Her mind was quick, though. She would learn
the language fast. She could be an interesting
companion.

"Brother! We must talk!"

The sound of Ten Bears' voice jerked Windrider's
thoughts away from the girl. He strode toward them
on his short, slightly bowed legs, every step proclaiming his consuming purpose.

"Tonight at the Victory Dance you will give this
girl to me," he said.

He glanced at her with that greedy gleam in his
eye that Windrider hated. It changed to the domineering glare of the older brother giving orders
to the younger one as he looked at Windrider
again.

"There is much talk in the village that you will
give her to Mopai, but I warn you now not to let
them push you to it. Mopai's uncle, Brown Robe,
would take such a gesture as appeasement of him.
It will make him harder for us to control in Council."

"This is the first I know that *we* are working
together in Council," Windrider snapped. For
that one, quick instant of anger, he did not care
how much he might damage their shaky truce.
"You oppose me always."

"Not true, dear brother!" Ten Bears cried, his
high-pitched tones changing as he fought for just
the right sound of sincerity. "You forget that we
are men now, and no longer childish rivals."

"No, Ten Bears," Windrider said, his voice low
and level, "*you* forget. Not all women who draw
both your gaze and mine belong to you by rights.
With this one I'll do as I please."

Ten Bears' broad face flushed. "Think about

what I say," he said. "I *am* older and wiser than you."

"And you are more of an old woman nag and a whining complainer than I," Windrider retorted. "From the minute you laid eyes on me with this girl in front of me in my saddle, you have nagged and moaned incessantly that she should belong to you. Enough!"

Ten Bears' whole face contorted in fury. He turned his back and stalked away toward the creek.

Jennie followed on even shakier legs as Windrider started off again toward the camp. That short, squatty warrior was still determined to have her; she knew it as well as if the entire argument she had just witnessed had been conducted in English.

She shivered. His narrow, hot eyes held no real warmth; they froze her wherever they touched her. Windrider had sent him away, but next time he might give in. As soon as she ate, she *had* to escape!

As soon as she recovered some energy. Maybe she *did* need some rest. Even with the adrenaline of her disgust and fear of the broad-faced man who rode the dun horse, her body kept threatening to simply collapse on the ground. Standing still in the sun, even for that short while, had been a mistake.

At least the excitement of the morning had lessened, she thought, as they approached the village again. She heard calm voices floating out from inside some of the tipis. The camp still buzzed with excitement, some women were still singing, but the high edge of hysterical welcome for the returning warriors was gone.

Only two women remained in the large, open area where Windrider had come to rescue her. They looked completely peaceful now, stirring the pot of stew while several dogs sat to one side, tongues hanging, hoping for scraps of meat. A group of children played nearby with a stick and a rock.

Jennie walked just behind Windrider, holding her head high, blinking against the sunlight. Her eyes threatened to close completely, just for an instant.

She forced them to fly wide open. She didn't need any more sleep. All she needed was food to quiet her complaining stomach, then she would think what to do.

Windrider said something to the women at the fire, and Jennie started toward them, breathing in the fragrant, meaty aroma that floated from the pot. However, Windrider veered off to the left. Her stomach lurched in disappointment, but she went with him.

He strode between two lodges, and as she followed, the cook fire disappeared from her view. Still, he *had* promised to feed her.

He took her to a painted tipi standing away from the others, on the outermost rim of the camp. His black and white horse stood beside it, tied to a staked rope. The horse watched them approach.

Jennie returned his curious look. She thought vaguely of going to him, of touching him and getting to know his personality after so many long hours on his back, but her leg muscles didn't have the strength to carry her the extra steps. They were going looser by the moment, reaching for sleep, while her stomach still cried for food.

Windrider, several steps ahead of her, stopped

and opened the door flap of one of the lodges. The outside wall of this far tipi was painted with red circles and blue waving lines, with horses dancing all the way around it, horses of every color. Was this where he lived?

He bent and entered the tipi, holding the flap open from inside. Jennie followed him in, then stood still for a moment, surprised by the lovely light that filled the round room. It was sunlight, she realized, filtering through the limpid translucence of the tipi's hide walls.

It washed over everything—the decorations painted on the wall's low lining, the parfleches and bags trimmed with beads and pieces of fur, the weapons hanging from pegs on the poles. The sweet smell of woodsmoke rose from a small fire enclosed by a ring of stones in the middle of the floor.

Windrider motioned that she should go to the left, all the way around to a spot almost opposite the door.

"Sit," he said, and gestured toward a woven backrest supported by three short poles. He moved to the right around the tipi's circle, stepped behind her, and took the seat directly across from the door opening.

Jennie's knees wobbled. She touched the tightly stretched skin wall for balance, then let herself sink down. She leaned back and, surprised at how comfortable it was, let her whole body rock into it.

Only her stomach couldn't relax.

"Where is the food?" she asked.

"Coming."

Then, suddenly, her fatigue was greater than her hunger. Every muscle in her body ached; she lifted her hand, although it felt heavy as stone, and rubbed at her shoulder, the one that the hateful girl had battered against the ground. She felt absolutely raw all over, as if she had been peeled.

"Would they have killed me?" she blurted. "If you hadn't come right then?"

"No. It was a test, as Sanah said. A test of courage."

The sunlight, even strained through the skin of the wall, had the power to turn his copper-colored face to a molten gold. He was beautiful.

She glanced down at the pile of robes beside her, reached out and touched them with her hand. But even their unbelievable softness couldn't distract her senses. Her stubborn eyes lifted to find his face.

She felt that new twinge again at the woman-core of her.

Never had she seen a man so well made and handsome. That was the reason she couldn't stop looking at him.

And he had saved her from the women. Yes, that was the reason her gaze clung to him.

A shadow fell over the open doorway, then a woman came in, followed immediately by another. The first carried a steaming bowl of food. She was about the age of Jennie's mother, but instead of being thin and worn, she was rotund.

She stopped in front of Jennie, who held out her hands for the bowl. The woman kept it, and then, to Jennie's amazement, dipped her fingers into it.

Jennie stared at her, dazed. Was this another kind of test or torment? Was the woman going to eat this food while Jennie watched?

No. She brought out a small piece of meat, turned around, and solemnly laid it on the fire. It sizzled, sending even more good odors floating into Jennie's nostrils, making saliva run into her mouth, and her limbs tremble.

"Why did she do that?" she cried, still reaching out with both hands to take the bowl.

"Hukiyani feeds the fire to say thank you for the food."

The woman was smiling now, giving her the bowl.

Shakily Jennie filled the horn spoon and brought it to her lips. Hot liquid moved down her throat and into her stomach, carrying the abiding power of fire itself.

She scooped up another bite. It held a morsel of delicious meat and a piece of something that tasted like turnip. Another was onion.

"Slowly," Windrider cautioned.

"Yes," she answered, but the warning was needless because her hands were so shaky, she was forced to go slowly. She forgot he was there, forgot about the women bustling around beside her, forgot everything except the fact that here was food and she would be allowed to eat it in peace.

The women finished whatever they were doing, ducked back out through the door opening, and were gone. Windrider didn't move. He didn't speak.

He didn't even look at Jennie; instead he stared thoughtfully at the painted lining of the lodge as if he had never seen it before.

Jennie ate every bite. Finally, reluctantly, she dropped the spoon into the bowl and set it down on the ground beside her.

Her stomach was full of warm food. Her eyes began to close.

Suddenly Windrider stood in front of her. "Sleep," he said, and she looked where he pointed to the bed robes the woman had spread out beside the wall. Jennie got to her knees and stumbled into them, stretching out onto their softness.

He had shown her nothing but kindness, she thought fuzzily, as he threw a cover over her, something light and made of cloth, not as hot as another of the robes would be.

A jumble of thoughts tumbled in her head just before her eyes fell closed. Windrider. He had given her water and food and a place to sleep, he had saved her from those tormenting women. He had treated her with nothing but kindness.

He had snatched her up and carried her away from her people into an alien world. He had led the raid that had probably killed her papa and mama.

She mustn't trust him. She had to escape.

She would not rest until she had escaped. She had already slept enough. She would not rest. She would not.

She was asleep before Windrider left the lodge.

"It is good," Ten Bears proclaimed, staring at the dance pole the people had erected in the center of the village. "We will bind the girl and she will stand there." He pointed to a spot between the pole and the fire.

"We will not bind her," Windrider said. "There is no need to bring her here at all. She sleeps."

The words popped out of his mouth before he thought, and he bit his tongue, wishing he could bring them back. The four or five other men who stood nearby turned to look at him. They drifted closer.

"Another custom not worth keeping, eh, Windrider?'' asked the elderly one called Brown Robe, shaking his dry gourd dance rattle impatiently as he spoke. "First no testing of captives, and now no display of them?''

"Next Windrider will have no traditions at all,'' jeered Tall Otter.

"Perhaps he should go live with the Kiowa if he can no longer abide by the customs of the *Nermernuh*,'' said Tatseni.

The harsh judgment in his words and his voice shocked them all into silence. It fell above and around their small group like a trader's pot turned over them. Outside it, the sounds of the drums and the singing kept on.

Tatseni, too, was old, like Brown Robe, and much respected. When he spoke, most of The People listened.

But Yellowfish, too, was old and respected.

"Customs are made by a Council of men,'' he said mildly, but carefully loud so that all would hear, "men who have different ways of thinking. Always, we *Nermernuh* value each one for his difference.''

Half Horse, Windrider's father and Yellowfish's friend since childhood, grunted agreement. "Well spoken,'' he said.

Someone behind Windrider said, "Yes!''

Ten Bears snorted in disgust, but Windrider knew he would say nothing. He would not contradict his father, and besides, it was a disgrace for family dissension to come out in public. That was the reason, too, that Half Horse would say no more in Windrider's defense: He tried never to take sides in the running battle for power between his two sons.

Windrider kept his face still as stone, staring straight ahead, refusing to respond to his critics, even when he felt all eyes upon him. But inside his body, his blood warmed in gratitude to Yellowfish and to his father, even while he heaved a great sigh.

If only the *Nermernuh* had a Great Chief whose word was law, and everyone did as he said without question, like Brave Dog of the Kiowa, instead of this loose organization where each one tried to put in his say, and most had to agree before anything was done!

However, that was not so. The *Nermernuh* moved camp and made war and did trading and raiding as individuals or together after a persuading Council. If he, Windrider, angered very many of the respected men in the band, they would throw their influence to Ten Bears each time a decision had to be made.

Windrider could not let that happen. He could not let The People be put in danger or led into poorly chosen campsites or cheated in unwise trading by his moody, self-centered brother.

And he himself would not live as a powerless follower of the ungenerous Ten Bears.

On the other hand, he also would not permit Ten Bears to drive him away from his family to go live with another band, to make him leave his old father, Half Horse, and his dear nephew, Eagle Tail Feather. To make him never again see his good friend Yellowfish and his laughing, helpful wife, Hukiyani.

No. He would hold his temper and his friends. Windrider would hold his own.

He nodded thoughtfully. "I will bring the white captive to display," he said. "But Windrider possesses much *puha*. The power of his medicine spirit, the wind. His captives do not need to be bound."

* * *

The chanting, singing dancers swirled in Jennie's blurring vision like witches in a nightmare. Evil witches.

Evil witches bent on killing her.

The blaze of the huge fire lit their faces and caught in their glittering eyes as they stepped toward her and then back, toward her and back, to the hynoptic beat of the drums. They came a little bit closer each time, a human chain tightening and tightening around her, soon to choke the life out of her.

Her body stood rigid, her back stiff, and she looked straight at the ones directly in front of her, but not because she was so brave. She couldn't, absolutely could not, move.

Terror held her paralyzed. If Windrider was in that weaving, gliding line of dancers, he would see that he was wrong about her courage.

Just as she had been wrong about his kindness.

Her skin contracted beneath the soft doeskin of the new dress he had given her. He had brought it into the tipi at dusk, making the woman who had woken her wait outside.

"They will take you to the creek to help you bathe," he had said. The caress of his voice had created a tingling along her nerves that drove away the last of her sleep.

She stretched, pushed her hair from her eyes, and looked at him, sitting cross-legged in front of her bed. He held the dress by the shoulders, its fringes swinging, its beautiful beaded trim catching the low light of his tipi's fire.

"You will wear this," he said, "to stand on display at the Victory Dance."

"I don't understand," she murmured, trying to

force her mind to hear the words instead of letting her body simply listen to the sound of him.

"Captives must be viewed by all The People," he said, his voice dropping into the kindest of tones. "They must stand inside the circle while we dance in victory. You need do no more than that. And you must not fear. No one will harm you."

She had believed him.

He had lied.

They carried weapons, these terrible witch/dancers. They threatened her with them every time they came close.

And every time they came closer and closer.

The rhythm and the steps of the dance would bring them all the way to her soon—very, very soon—and the threats would become an attack. They would kill her.

How, in the name of all that was holy, could any human being behave so treacherously to another? He had touched her hair and given her a Comanche name, for God's sake! He had given her water and food and sleep and had brought women to bathe her and dress her in new, fancy clothes.

He had been a gorgeous, commanding man to her, a man who had stirred an awful attraction in her, a feeling stronger than any she had ever felt before toward a man. But she had not even been a person to him, much less a woman.

She had been nothing but a sacrifice he prepared for the ceremony!

That hurt so much, deep inside her, that tears somehow tried to come out of her dry panic. Her throat closed against them.

Well, what did you expect, Jeneen Mary Sigourney O'Bannion? a small, sarcastic voice inside her asked. *You knew he was your enemy, even when you somehow, stupidly, thought he was acting like a friend.*

The sound of the drums changed—the players beat them harder. And faster.

The dancers came in closer.

To think that she would die here, and now, after surviving so much!

They moved back, then danced in closer still.

One of them shuffled and glided even nearer to Jennie. It was a woman, bending and swaying, constantly dancing to the incessant beat, raising and lowering a weapon in her hand. Her face wore streaks of red and black paint.

It was the girl who had fought with her, the one called Breaks Something!

Fear fingered its way up Jennie's arms beneath her soft buckskin sleeves, lightly brushing her skin in one spot and then in another like the long Indian fringes that touched her helpless hands. She felt it move over her bruised and battered body with a detached amazement. How could she possibly feel any more fear?

Yet she did. It crawled up and up, then out onto her shoulders like a thousand tiny snakes, and made the hairs on the back of her neck stand up.

Her scalp tingled and burned. Her skin tightened, all over her body, as if trying to shrink her until she became invisible. Her legs trembled from the screaming of her instincts that she should break and run.

The crowd shouted and cheered. Breaks Something danced closer and closer.

Jennie stared at her, stupefied.

She kept coming. She danced in close and raised the weapon high.

Jennie's arms flew up to protect her face.

Breaks Something laughed—a high, taunting screech of wild laughter—and struck at Jennie, pantomiming a blow to the heart, then caught Jennie's hair in one hand and pretended to scalp her. Panic helped Jennie jerk free.

The girl danced in place, right in front of Jennie. She brandished her weapon high above her head, threatening her again and again.

Jennie's legs trembled, listening to her instincts as they screamed for her to run past the girl, race away.

But she held her ground. She dug in her heels and stared straight into the hateful eyes glittering amidst the red and black paint.

For a fear-filled eternity, with the drums beating in the background, Breaks Something menaced her. Jennie's look never wavered. Her body never moved.

Finally Breaks Something shook the weapon directly in her face.

It was not a weapon at all, but a dried gourd, a rattle shaker to accompany the dance.

Then Breaks Something danced away, stepping backward in rhythm to rejoin the line, jeering and calling in a high, scornful voice, pointing to her unharmed prey.

Jennie's legs went so weak, they shook beneath her. She longed to let go, to collapse on the ground. To lie there and beat the earth with her fists and scream up to heaven, *Help me get free! God, are you watching?*

But she locked her knees into stiffness and set her shoulders straight. She would die proud, she would. She would not show one more scrap of fear to that vicious little bitch!

The drums stopped. The line of dancers went

still and soundless. The fire popped and crackled; its heat bit at Jennie's back.

She waited for an arrow to fly into her heart from out of the darkness. For a thrown lance. For another lone dancer, a warrior with a real tomahawk this time.

The drumbeats started up again with a great burst of new power, a deep, elemental thrumming that arose from the very heart of the earth itself. It set the dancers into motion once more; they flung up their arms and slid their feet to the rhythm.

Directly in front of her, their line broke in two and left a gap of dark night. The light from the fire couldn't reach it; she couldn't see what was coming.

A new dancer burst out of the blackness, whirling and circling, hurtling through the night toward the light and the fire. The brilliance caught on his bronze body with each turn he made, then flared again in the wild, flashing colors of the feathers he wore.

Windrider.

She knew him in spite of the bustles of feathers and streaks of paint on his skin; she knew him by the strength and the grace of his movements alone.

His toes reached for the ground, caressed it, then took it, carrying him around and around into the bright glare of the fire. Carrying him inevitably toward her.

His knees lifted and straightened, again and again.

He was an inexorable whirlwind, a bronze-flashing hurricane, his arms upraised for him to rule the world. His wrists wore wide cuffs of glittering silver, his ankles were circled by bracelets of bells. Their jingling rose sharp over the dull sounds of the drums, faster and faster as he lifted his legs high and stomped each foot, his muscular torso rising and then falling to the demands of the rhythm, turning, turning, always in perfect circles of power.

He was almost close enough to touch, and then he was gone, whirling away from her and closer to the fire. But not before his eyes had met hers.

That one look merged her spirit with her body again.

The shine of the fire made his powerful chest even broader, his shoulders more muscled than any other man's as he danced on and on in full frenzy. Red paint, yellow and blue paint, gleamed on his coppery skin, drawn in designs of circles and stripes, with a handprint flexing on the unbridled strength of his upper arm.

Jennie's body began to breathe again, began to feel.

Thongs crossed just beneath the biggest muscles of his chest and across his flat abdomen over his scrap of a breechclout, thongs that held the bustles of undulating feathers—the huge one in the middle of his powerful back, the smaller one centered on his sensuous buttocks.. Feathers of every vibrant color in the world.

His hair, shining and black, swinging down and then back from each side of his face as he tossed his head to the rhythm, held the only white feathers he wore. They gleamed in the light of the flames. His body glistened with sweat.

The throats of the dancers in the line suddenly sent out a high, piercing song. Everyone shuffled in place, keeping the huge circle that surrounded the fire, everyone clapping hands to the beat of the song. To the rhythm of the revolving, spell-binding moments that Windrider made.

He chose one spot and whirled there, reached to his belt and untied a circle of bells, raised it high in one hand. He brought it down on the side of his thigh.

That gave his feet wings. They became a blur as he flew faster and higher, twirling in spiraling gyrations, bending and turning, raising his magnificent body and twisting it in movements that sent the bells shaking and the feathers swirling beneath his arching back. He could bend over backward so low that they brushed the ground.

Then he straightened and, shaking and dancing, bent the other way. The rainbow of feathers surrounded his body with powerful shiftings of shadows and light.

His marvelous body. It called to Jennie's own in a way she'd never known, *never*—before the dawn had opened the night and shown her this lord of the plains.

His body absorbed and reflected the flames, toyed with them. It used an exquisite magic that knew no bounds to take dominion over the fire.

He danced around its perimeter to embrace it, wheeled and spun into its blaze and out again to love it, darted and whorled to play with it, took out its soul, held it to him, and spiraled up and away from them all, into the very vortex of the wind. Into the sky itself.

Then he straightened and sent his toes deep to take root in the ground, willing it to hold him while he pivoted into a blur, a circling column of white and red and blue and yellow and green and black and copper, spinning so fast, it could never stop.

Until it did.

The drums and the singers fell silent.
Windrider stood still as a tree.

The Fire Flower's face, a pale heart floating in
the bright air, was the first thing he saw.

"A gift!" a voice called from the line of dancers. "Gifts from the great warrior Windrider, who
brings a white captive to our camp!"

Cheers and yells of assent met the cry.

"Make a gift of the captive!" a piercing voice
shouted and the yelling became a roar.

Windrider's stomach tied itself into a hard knot.
No. The Fire Flower belonged to him.

He strode toward her with long, jingling steps.
He had captured her; she was his to do with as
he pleased.

But from the corner of his eye he saw the circle
of dancers sag and break into pieces. People
drifted closer in toward him, calling and talking
to him and one another.

They had much to celebrate at this Victory
Dance, the exhilarating dancing that he had just
done—the best of his life, and they knew it—plus
the victorious attack on the fort, with not one Comanche killed. Yet he ignored them all.

He reached the Fire Flower, looked down into
her eyes, flashing green and bright in the light
from the fire.

For a long moment they looked at each other.

"You have shown great courage once again,"
he said. "Greater courage than any white-eye The
People ever had as captive."

A flame of happiness, bright and hot as one
from the victory fire, leapt into her face. A flame
of hope that flared, then burned steady with a
glow that poured pink life into her pale skin.

A man's voice shouted, loud, and she turned to see him, moving with a zestful grace so free of fear that it made Windrider smile. A few words of praise from him had given her this touching confidence.

"Generous gifts are in order from our great dancer," Tatseni proclaimed, "from our great warrior who has brought us a captive."

Everyone cheered and applauded.

The knot in Windrider's gut slipped a notch tighter. His smile left him.

"He is known as a generous man!" Tatseni concluded.

That tied the knot even harder.

No greater compliment could be given him. He was expected to live up to his reputation.

Sure enough, the prominent old man Brown Robe raised his hands high for silence, and when he had it, chimed in. "A gift of the captive to Mopai would be most seemly," he said. "For Mopai has lost his only daughter to the raping, killing white men."

For one fleeting moment Windrider felt a great relief, in spite of the truth of Ten Bears' warning about appearing to try to curry favor with Brown Robe. That truly was the best disposition he could make of his captive.

Mopai was his great friend; no one could ever treat a captive with more kindness than he and his wife, Numu. In that lodge the Fire Flower would be a daughter, not a wife.

He clenched his jaw at the thought. The white girl was getting beneath his skin too much! Thoughts of her had darted in and out of his head all day, no matter where he had been or what he had been doing. No woman was that important.

And that dancing! The best dancing he had ever

done in all his life had happened because of her. To show off for her.

"Mopai!" someone else shouted. "Give the captive to Mopai!"

Windrider turned to face the people of his band and opened his mouth. With only a few words he could make the girl safe with Mopai, and in addition, he could recoup the public opinion he had lost over the lack of tradition he had shown in dealing with her.

He would need that sorely the next time he and Ten Bears came head to head.

All these thoughts flashed through his mind as he moved his gaze over the faces of the crowd.

Yes. He would give the Fire Flower to Mopai and be rid of the irritation of thinking of her.

But Ten Bears stepped forward.

"I have lost a wife," he yelled in his shrill, overbearing way. "A wife is more of a loss than a daughter. Besides, I gave Mopai fifty horses for his daughter, and it is not my fault that he has gambled them away. Windrider should be a big-hearted leader and give the girl to me."

A great swelling of agreement rose up. Generosity was a quality almost as much prized as bravery among all the people of the far-flung bands of the *Nermernuh*. Windrider was known for both. That was much of the reason that people followed him.

He looked around to see that the calls for him to give the Fire Flower to Ten Bears came from almost all the people. The silly girl Breaks Something was calling loudest of all.

Windrider's teeth gritted together; he felt the muscles in his jaws clench. Ten Bears, ever the greedy, domineering, jealous older brother, had challenged him for Fire Flower by the first look he'd ever given her.

Well, by the Sun Father, he would not have her. This time Windrider, not Ten Bears, would keep the woman.

He lifted his hand and laid it on Fire Flower's shoulder.

"The fire-haired white woman belongs to me," he said loudly, berating himself for a fool while he said it.

It would be utterly foolish to keep her, drawn to her as he was. He was drawn to her, but he could not ever love her. He could not ever love any woman as he had loved She Blushes, and he did not want to—that had brought such grief as he could not bear again. Yet he would not ever take as wife a woman whom he did not love.

Confusion ruled his heart as a great gasp of shock rippled through The People. They had been expecting his usual generosity. And so had he.

The old, traditional men of power would remember this the next time he tried to persuade them to do a thing and Ten Bears spoke for its opposite.

This decision could, in time, make Ten Bears the peace chief. It could mean danger and death for his people.

So he tried to soften the blow and divert them.

"I need her to do the work and take care of my lodge," he said. "For I will not ask Ten Bears to send his wives to do it anymore."

The ripple of shock widened and deepened.

"Such a public display of brotherly squabbling!" one woman hissed.

Ten Bears' face grew as red as the paint he wore, as red as the fire at the edge of Windrider's vision.

"You had better think more of keeping peace in your family and in your camp than of a woman!" he snapped.

Then he stepped right up into Windrider's face. In a contemptuous tone he finished, "*Little* Brother!"

The insult set Windrider's blood to boiling, but beneath its heat, deep in his bones, pricked a sharp knife of doubt. Of impending doom.

He tried to avert it.

"*Na?raiboo?*," he said, firmly, staring rudely into Ten Bears' furious face as he did so.

The Fire Flower touched his arm. Her fingers felt cold, and when he looked down at her, he saw all the joy had fled from her face.

"Who *is* that man?" she asked, her voice trembling.

"My brother, Ten Bears."

Her face went white as frost. "Your *brother*! How can that be?"

"I myself have wondered many times," he said, bitterly.

"I know he wants me. What did you tell him?"

"That you will stay in my lodge as *na?raiboo?.*"

"What does that mean?" She sounded almost frantic now, as the voices of the people began to rise behind her.

Windrider knew the gossip about the rivalry of Half Horse's sons was beginning all over again. It would be growing like a hill of stinging ants. He would have to work, and work some more, to keep his influence strong.

Windrider looked up and glared at his brother again, frowning, thinking, looking for the English word.

At last he found it.

"*Na?raiboo?.* Slave," he said.

Chapter 6

Windrider strode straight into the crowd, forcing it to part before him, never loosening his grip on Jennie's arm. Dazed, she stumbled beside him away from the heat of the fire, past the curious stares of dozens of eyes, out of range of the buzzing of excited chatter. He said nothing, but under the noise of his hard, jingling footsteps, his rich voice repeated over and over again in her head.

Slave. Slave.

And now he was dragging her away from everyone, away from the light, to have her to himself alone in the night.

Shades of Trammel Nordstrom! *God in Heaven, are you there?*

Well, if God didn't strike this arrogant barbarian dead before he raped her, she would. She hadn't gone through all the horror of the past two days just to end up right back where she started!

Desperate rebellion rose up inside, strong enough to choke her. It pushed words from her mouth.

"Slave or no, don't try to take me to your bed," she said, trying to jerk her arm from his relentless

103

fingers. "Before I am a slave in that way, I will kill you or myself."

"You will submit to whatever I say!"

He didn't slow his step.

"I will *not*!" she cried, and before she knew she would do it, she twisted to face him, lunging for the knife he wore tied to his breechclout.

He caught her hand with his free one in a move fast as the striking of a snake.

"Quiet!"

His tone was so dangerous, she snapped her mouth shut. He didn't let go of her arm or her other hand; he hauled her, helpless, through the dark alleys between the empty lodges at a pace that made her run to keep up.

Finally they reached his lodge with its painted horses prancing silently around its circle in the night. Behind them, far behind, the drums and the singing had started again.

He thrust her ahead of him into his tipi. There was no light and no fire; she could only hear and feel him beside her, snorting with disgust, filling the place with his anger.

Abruptly he let go of her arm. Staggering a little, she put out her hand. It touched the slanting hide wall, her foot caught on something she couldn't see, and she went down on her knees onto the bed robes where she'd spent the day sleeping.

"I meant what I said!" she cried frantically, as if he had pushed her there, as if he were forcing himself upon her. "Never again will a man take my body!"

The last words came out high-pitched and shrill, so much so, they shocked her. She must be climbing toward the edge of hysteria.

She clamped her lips together to hold back a scream.

Silence fell.

"Calm yourself," he said roughly.

Jennie bit her bottom lip until she tasted blood and felt around her with both hands for a weapon, trying desperately to remember what she had seen there in the daylight, aching to visualize the bow and arrows, the lance, in their places on the poles. Her memory refused to work.

She tried to quiet her panic so she could think. Right now, at this moment, she couldn't get to a weapon if she knew where it was in the dark. Windrider stood over her, snorting like an angry bull.

Then she felt an emptiness where he had been, heard the bells tinkle on his ankles. With a short, jangled noise, each set of them fell silent. He must have taken them off.

She heard scrabbling noises, as if he were looking for something, then, as her eyes grew accustomed to the darkness and learned to use the moonlight that filtered through the walls, she saw his tall form go still as he found whatever it was that he wanted.

He stood up and turned toward her.

She tensed, trapping what little breath there was in her body. Was he going to tie her? Lash her to the tent poles? Again she slid her hands over the robes and groped for the wall, trying to find something she could use for protection.

He walked back around the perimeter of the tipi, but he stopped before he came to her. The door opening, only two or three feet from where she sat, was still open. More moonlight poured through it and showed her the woven horse halter hanging over his bare shoulder.

The feathers bristled on his back. He untied the thongs that held them and hung them carefully on one of the poles.

She could smell the sweat on his skin.

"I will take no one for *kwuhu*, wife," he said harshly, "without *kamakuru*, love. And I will never love a woman who would kill herself rather than to lie with me."

He went out then, letting the flap fall closed behind him as a signal that no one was to enter. All the camp would respect that; the Fire Flower would be unharmed.

But before he walked away to go and catch his horse, to rush through the night where he could ride out his anger, where he could see the sky and feel the wind, he turned and spoke to the wall of his tipi, to the paintings of his war deeds and horse-stealing raids that shone in the dark on the outside of it. To the untamed woman inside. To himself.

"To bring you to my bed robes is the last thing I want," he lied.

Then Jennie sensed that he was gone. She listened to hear him walking away with that long, languorous stride of his, the graceful step of a prowling big cat, but she heard nothing. He didn't make a sound.

Her shoulders sagged and she used the last of her strength to draw up her knees so she could rest her forehead against them. Wrung-out from the depths of her emotions, she sat there, utterly spent, for a long, long time, her eyes tightly closed against the new reality of her life.

Nevertheless, on the backs of their lids she could still see Windrider, stepping and whirling, dancing, dancing in victory.

* * *

The next morning, Jennie woke to find herself still alone. And a stranger to her own body.

It hurt in every muscle and pore in a thousand different ways from the scrapes, pinches, blows, and poundings, from holding herself still as a statue while on display at the dance, not to mention from riding horseback for so many miles. That had made her bottom incredibly sore, even if Windrider had held her part of the time in his arms.

Windrider.

First her captor, then her . . . what? Companion? Almost friend? Savior?

Now her *master*. He had saved her life to make her his slave.

The thought brought bile rising into her throat.

She scrambled to her feet, smoothing down the skirt of the new buckskin dress. Now was her chance. She might not get another for a long time.

There was enough light in the tipi to see the shape of objects, but not colors, and she tried to remember what bags she had seen where. So much of the time that she'd spent in the lodge had been while she slept, and during the short period she'd been awake last evening before the dance, the two women who had helped her bathe and dress had taken almost all of her attention.

But she had noticed a strange-looking container with animal feet on the bottom and a strap for carrying. It hung on the pole nearest her bed. She took it, trying to avoid touching its hooves, and a soft bag, its sides covered with thick beadwork that felt both rough and smooth under her fingertips.

The two bags bumped her on each side as she crept to the door flap and opened it.

Evidently the whole camp slept. Not even the

dogs were stirring. Everyone was exhausted, no doubt, from the revelry of the night before.

So she ducked out beneath the flap and ran on silent, moccasined feet toward the creek. It was good she had slept in her clothes; she didn't even have to take time to dress.

Last night, near the spot where the women had bathed her, she'd noticed a tree hanging with blue berries. One of them had eaten a handful as they walked, so they weren't poisonous. She would fill the beaded bag with them, and the other with water. That would get her to Texas.

She ran faster. The stiff deer-foot or elk-foot or whatever kind of bag it was banged against her hip. No telling what water carried in it would taste like, but she couldn't worry about that now.

She held it to her side and ran harder, gritting her teeth against the pain. Now she had ridden a horse, although not alone, and she knew she could do it. The Comanche had a whole herd of horses around here somewhere—she would catch one and ride east.

It was that way, where the horizon was lighter, just ready to turn pink from the sun.

Suddenly she began to shiver, shaking all over, although she wouldn't let it stop her from running. A weird sense of traveling through time, of living through the very same moments all over again, washed over her. Big goose bumps popped out on her arms. It was as if she were trapped in this one thing—trying to escape—doomed to attempt it forever.

She set her jaw harder. Well, this time she wouldn't fail.

Thirst tightened her throat, and she headed down to the edge of the creek. She would drink and fill the water bag first, then pick the berries.

Jennie's feet carried her straight to the spot where Windrider had brought her the day before, but she pushed that memory out of her head as she knelt and scooped up a double handful of the sweet water. It hit her stomach with a cold shock that somehow soothed it; she threw herself prone to drink more.

Finally she sat up, wiped her mouth on her long-fringed sleeve, and took the elk-foot bag in both hands. She dipped it into the creek.

Suddenly she froze. She could feel someone's eyes on her, the feeling too strong to be denied. Somebody was here. Somebody was watching her.

Jennie's fingers convulsed on the top of the bag. She drew it up out of the water, closed its lid, slid its strap onto her shoulder. She grabbed the beaded bag, stood up, and turned around, all in one quick motion.

Her green eyes, wide with fear, met black ones, sparkling with frank curiosity. Childish curiosity.

It was a boy, ten years old or so. Jennie drew in a long, shaky breath of relief.

Then she held it. The boy wasn't very old, but he was stocky and strong, almost as tall as she was, and he wore a bow and a quiver of arrows slung over his shoulder. His feet clung lightly to the side of the grass-covered slope, ready to run.

He could shoot her or spread the alarm. He could have Windrider and the whole village down on her before she even sighted the horse herd.

He grinned at her, yet his eyes were watchful.

Her heart fell. She'd never get away now. She had failed again.

She shifted the strap of the heavy bag on her

shoulder. It didn't help. Every shred of her being hurt even harder now, now that her hope was gone.

What would they do to her for trying to escape? Windrider was furious with her already, and Breaks Something would delight in half killing her if he turned her over to the women for punishment.

She forced her lips to curve in a smile.

"Water," she said conversationally, gesturing toward the bag hanging at her hip. "I only came to the creek to get some water."

He couldn't understand her words, of course, but perhaps the offhand tone would allay his suspicions.

The boy smiled back, but neither the wariness nor the curiosity left his dark eyes.

"For-get," he said, in halting English, "fill o-ther bag." His gaze touched the beaded bag, hanging empty at her other side.

Jennie stared at him. Surprise drove away her apprehension for an instant.

"Good heavens!" she blurted. "Does half the tribe speak English?"

His eyes twinkled even brighter. They told her he was trying to figure out what she'd said.

"Me," he said finally, touching a quick finger to his chest, "my *ara?*. Un-cle. Windrider." He shrugged. "O-ther maybe some."

So. He was Windrider's nephew. Windrider helped him learn English.

And, like his uncle, the child was a charmer when he smiled. One fast hope flashed through her, the hope that she might talk him into helping her escape, then, as fast as it had come, it died.

His voice had filled with such pride when he

spoke Windrider's name! Of course, he would be loyal to his uncle.

So Jennie trudged up the gentle hill toward him, the water bag hanging heavy as her heart.

"Why aren't you sleeping, like the rest of the village?" she asked.

When he had arranged the English words in his mind, he said, "I am like my un-cle. Dancing doesn't make me . . . tired."

Jennie smiled at that, in spite of the tears of disappointment crowding into her eyes.

"What is your name?"

"I am called Eagle Tail Feather."

"Well, then, Eagle Tail Feather, let's take this water back to camp."

They walked, with Eagle Tail Feather in front of her, but obviously aware of where she was every minute, back to the village. It, like Jennie's spirits, had changed considerably in the few minutes that had passed since she had run from Windrider's lodge. The dogs were up, snuffling and barking. A scattering of sleepy women were outside their lodges, building up their cook fires.

And Windrider was back.

He stood outside his tipi, brushing the black and white horse. He heard them coming and looked up to watch them walk toward him.

Jennie thought she saw a flash of welcome in his dark eyes as they touched her face, but then his gaze flicked to his nephew and to the empty beaded bag on her shoulder. She knew, as well as if he had accused her with words, that he knew she had tried to run away.

His eyes didn't give her a clue as to what he might do about that. He simply glanced at the heavy water bag and turned back to the horse.

His manner said, *Good. You are working, as a good slave should.*

The inherent arrogance of the gesture blew a hot wind of anger across the icy reaches of her fear. What did she care what they did to her? She would rather die than live as a slave.

She walked straight up to him and pulled the bag around in front of her with both hands. "Yes," she said, sarcastically. "You can see that I'm doing my slave work."

Windrider completely ignored her, but the horse turned his head and stuck his soft muzzle toward her, nostrils flaring to see who she was. And what she carried.

He nudged at the bag; some of the water splashed out onto his nose. He jumped back.

Jennie jumped, too. He was so big, so quick-moving!

Windrider chuckled, but there was no amusement in the sound. "You should learn about horses before you try to run away. It will take many suns if you're walking to Texas."

"I'll walk it rather than be a slave!" Jennie said.

At her elbow, Eagle Tail Feather gave a small, involuntary gasp at her effrontery. On the opposite side of the horse, Windrider shrugged.

He moved back in perfect concert with the animal's restless sidestep, although Jennie hadn't sensed that the horse was about to move again. He settled down, and Windrider stepped in closer as he did so, reading his intentions apparently by instinct.

Envy prickled in Jennie's heart, strong enough to distract her for a moment from her plight. Oh, to be able to communicate like that with such a noble beast!

But Windrider's next words jarred her attention back to her situation.

"So this is the way you repay my hospitality," he growled. "I invite the displeasure of my brother and of The People to protect you, and you try to run away."

Quick fear at his tone and then pure fury at his words rushed through her.

"I'm supposed to thank you for your *hospitality*?" she flared. "After you've snatched me up and carried me off against my will to let me get beat half to death, put me on display like an animal, and then made me your *slave*?"

Her face, with its pale heart shape like a redbud's leaf, held his gaze and wouldn't let it go.

Until he saw her high, round breasts, rising and falling fast with the force of her fury. They drew a man's eyes, and held them like a fire in the winter's cold.

They caused a tightening in his loins.

And that angered him. He felt the betrayal of his body as it yearned to take this woman. He wanted her more than he had ever wanted any other one.

He forced his eyes to let go of her, dropped them, and deliberately fixed his gaze on Echo's spotted withers.

"Did you not believe me when I said I will not take your body?" he rasped. "Is that thought so repulsive to you that you would die lost on the plains instead?"

Jennie stared at him.

"No-o-o," she said, slowly, nonplussed by the question.

He shot her a quick look, one so hard, it almost knocked her down.

"I believed you!" she said, her voice rising.

From the corner of her eye, she noticed Eagle Tail Feather glancing toward the women at the cook fires farther down the alleyway. She didn't care who heard her. She was past caring.

"I need to be free!" she cried. "I was running away because you said I am your slave!"

She jerked her spine straight and herself up to her full five feet two inches. "I'll die lost on the plains any day before I'll be anybody's slave!"

Windrider flashed her another disgusted look, but he didn't answer. He dropped the handful of grass he was using to wipe the sweat off the horse and jerked a clean bunch out of the ground. He stood up and started grooming the paint's hind-quarters.

Slowly, slowly, the spotted horse stuck his nose out and touched Jennie's bag of water once again. The same thing happened as before—water splashed onto his nose, he jumped, she jumped, and Windrider moved gracefully out of the way, not even interrupting the grooming.

Such a look of mischief came into the horse's eye that, in spite of her agony, Jennie laughed out loud.

Eagle Tail Feather laughed, too.

Windrider glanced up and growled a repri-mand in Comanche. The horse stood still after that, but he kept his ears pricked toward Jennie and, after a moment, gradually started moving his muzzle toward the water bag again.

Eagle Tail Feather offhandedly wandered a little distance away, throwing a stick for one of the dogs to fetch, as if to say that he was not a part of such foolishness. He had just removed himself when the loose lid flopped completely open and water sloshed everywhere again.

"Get that away from him," Windrider said, harshly.

"But he's thirsty!" Jennie protested. By heaven, if she couldn't run away, she'd rebel. She had meant what she said, even if Windrider had ignored it. She was nobody's slave.

A trace of amusement crept into Windrider's deep voice. "Echo is a Trickster, like Coyote. He has just drunk from the creek."

"Maybe he didn't drink enough."

She held out her hand and touched the velvet nose.

"Don't argue," Windrider snapped, angry again. "I know him far better than you do. Go. Use that water to cook my breakfast."

"Not now!" Jennie shot back. She stroked the soft nose again. "I've never petted a horse before, only a pony."

Windrider's gaze flew to her face. His hand went still on the clump of dried grass he was using to remove the sweat.

"Never? You never . . . petted a horse?" he repeated, wondering if he had misunderstood the English words.

The Fire Flower nodded. He had heard right.

"Why not?" he asked.

"I was never close enough to one," she said, giving him only a quick glance before she looked back at Echo. She watched her own hand sliding over his glossy hide as if that increased her pleasure in giving the caress.

Windrider watched them both. Echo leaned into the Fire Flower's touch; he bent his neck to nuzzle her shoulder.

Normally he would not have done so with anyone else but Windrider. Normally Windrider

would not have permitted anyone else to handle
his horse.

But, to his consternation, he had no desire to
stop this budding friendship. How could he be
that heartless after hearing what she just said?

He puzzled over the English words again and
again.

She had never been close to a horse. But she
loved horses, and horses loved her. That much
was perfectly plain.

She had never touched them?

Windrider tried to imagine such a strange state
of affairs. Perhaps white women were not allowed to own horses. But they rode them. He had
seen them ride sometimes at trade meets and on
the trail.

"Your father's horses," he said, "you rode
without touching, without . . . petting . . . making friends with them?"

"My father had no horses. Only an ox to pull
his plow and his cart."

"You rode your brothers' horses?"

Her eyes filled with quick tears.

"No. They had none. No one in my family had
horses to ride."

Windrider dropped the new bunch of dried
grass beside the old one and stepped to Echo's
head to look at the Fire Flower in view of this
news. She had had enough to eat; her enormous
green eyes, heavily fringed with gleaming dark
lashes, held much light, her skin was beautiful,
her hair shone with good health. She was extraor-
dinarily small, true, but her bone structure was
delicate. There was enough flesh on them to make
perfect curves in all the right places. And she had
enough strength to be extremely high-spirited.

What a miracle for one growing up in such

astounding poverty! It was hard to believe—an entire family that did not own, had never owned, even one horse!

Echo edged closer to the Fire Flower; her hand moved over his neck and up onto the swell of his big stallion's jaw in a gentle caress.

A sudden jealous desire stirred within Windrider, beneath the deep sympathy he was feeling. His own skin tingled, wanting to feel that touch.

Wanting that same bemused, approving look that glazed her eyes when she looked at the horse to be turned on him, instead.

He blurted, "I will teach you to ride."

The words, unexpected to both of them, made her hand go still.

"You *will*?"

She took a step toward him. Her eyes, deep as green valleys, opened so wide in her surprise that he felt as if he were sliding into them off the side of a mountain.

They looked like stars made of shimmering leaves. No, they shone like pools of clear water, pure and necessary, ready to give life to those who drank from them.

They were filled with happiness for the first time since he'd known her.

But it was her rich, lush mouth that sent the quickening blood rushing into his manhood. Her lips parted in delight, the pink tip of her tongue peeking from between her white teeth, made him feel he'd fallen into a fire.

"I will work for you as payment for the lessons," Jennie told him, speaking quickly, her voice dancing with excitement. "Instead of being your slave."

At first the words meant nothing; he didn't hear them, he was watching her lips move, imagining how they would taste in kissing like the Spanish women had taught him.

"Is it a bargain?" she asked, clutching the water bag to her with one hand, and reaching back to the horse again with the other. "You gave me a Comanche name because you say I have much courage. A person of much courage should not be called slave!"

He watched the flush of earnestness climb up her pale cheeks. She refused to be called slave, this small Fire Flower, even though he held the very breath of her life in his hands. Never had he seen a woman so infinitely stubborn—if he refused her bargain, she would probably attack him with her bare hands, the way she had when he caught her.

He grinned at the memory. "You are a warrior woman," he said. *"Na?raiboo?* no more. I accept your bargain."

Her face lit up like a torch in the night and she whirled where she stood to throw both her slender arms around Echo's neck. Water flew out of the bag as it swung toward Windrider, drenching his legs and feet.

He hardly noticed—he could feel nothing on the outside because he was fighting so hard to comprehend the mix of feelings attacking him on the inside. It was good that he had not kissed her—but oh, how he wished he had—such a thing might have led him to break his promise that he would not take her body.

Yet he didn't really want her; most of what he felt for her was simply pity, pity for how poor her life had been.

Except for his appreciation of her spirited bravery.

That was it. He had only agreed to her bargain because of her courage.

True courage always should have its reward.

By the time they walked out to where the boys and the Mexican head herder were holding the horses, Windrider had almost convinced himself that he was teaching her to ride because of his own, eccentric attraction to the other strange human beings of the world. Much to Ten Bears' disgust, he had always been filled with curiosity about the Spanish, the French, the Comancheros, the Texans. That was all this was, his interest in this small white woman. He had simply never known another like her.

But when she stopped in her tracks at her first sight of the hundreds of horses spread out over the prairie before them, when she drew in her breath in a great, shuddering sigh and gazed at them with eyes full of love, he had to admit to himself the truth. This tiny Texas woman with the magnificent hair and the fascinating face made him feel even more alive somehow, like a vision from his medicine spirit, the wind.

"Comanches have so many horses to ride!" the Fire Flower said, flashing him a smile like a sunrise.

His heart lifted, his lips curved in an answering smile. She would be like a small boy to teach about the horses, he thought. As eager as a child of six years to ride hanging from the side of her mount at a gallop, leaning down to pick up a "wounded" fellow warrior. Well, riding and war games were what he would teach her.

For if he ever began to teach her what could be between a man and a woman when they lay in the bed robes together, he would put himself in such danger that no hard-riding warrior could save him.

"How do you choose?" she was asking, her voice rising with the excitement of actually being able to do such a thing. "There are so many of them, and they are all beautiful!"

Windrider laughed. The wind was fingering the curls in her hair, Father Sun was pouring heat and color over the earth, the horses were grazing in peace.

"First, choose one of your own, not someone else's," he said. "Then, choose for what you want to do."

"But you want to ride! You can ride them all, can't you?"

"Some are very fast, for racing, for wagering, for raiding. Some are agile for games and for war. Some have great endurance, for long travels in hardship. Choose for what you want to do."

Jennie thought her heart would burst with wanting them all.

"I want to gallop, free as the wind! I want to fly across the plains going wherever I wish, whenever I wish it! I want to ride to the top of that hill, there, and see the whole world!"

Windrider laughed again. Laughter bubbled in him, up from inside him like music, this sun, for the first time since he and Ten Bears had found their mother's and She Blushes' bodies.

"You shall gallop," he said. "But first you walk."

He took her in closer to the herd then, past the curious looks of the herders, whom Jennie hardly noticed. All she could see was the horses, grazing together, yet apart, for a mile or more, peacefully drifting along, moving in unison somehow, but slowly, slowly, slow as the flow of a late-summer stream.

Her eyes strained to gather in every color. Red, gray, white, brown, black, yellow, silver, black and white spotted, red and white, brown and white, dark yellow and white, solid pale gold, hues bright and muted, bluish mottled tones, dappled red that washed to palest pink, every color in existence shone there, scattered like living stars thrown across a sky of green grass from the hand of a careless, lavishly generous God.

"How will I ever know?" she asked, in a voice that wouldn't sound above a whisper. "How will I know which one I should ride?"

"The wind will tell us," Windrider answered, but he was already looking at the herd in a different way. His eyes had narrowed, his hand had gripped her arm as if to feel some sort of vibration from her.

He led her into the thick of them, keeping her close to his side. Jennie's movements fell into the rhythm of his, becoming as easy, as attuned to the day, as those of the horses themselves. The smells of the marvelous big bodies being warmed by the sun drifted into her nostrils. She breathed it in, filled herself with it. She belonged with them, with horses. Always, instinctively, she had known that.

Windrider signaled with a tightening of his fingers. Jennie looked at him, followed his gaze to a shining red-coated horse, one that seemed, somehow, to her unpracticed eye, even more beautiful than the others.

"That one," he said. "Stay still; I will catch her."

The word "catch" was the wrong one, Jennie thought. He simply walked up to the mare—it must be a mare, for he had said 'her'—and, when she lifted her head to look at him, put his arm around her neck. He slipped the braided bridle from his shoulder onto her head and led her through the others, still grazing, back to Jennie.

"She's the best of them all," she blurted, holding out both hands to the mare, her pulse pounding with a newfound, nearly overwhelming loyalty.

"Surely she's one of the best," Windrider agreed, and stopped the mare right in front of her. "You two get acquainted. Share your breath."

He placed his face near the red mare's muzzle to show Jennie what to do, and she did it, touching the soft nose with her own, mingling her excited, shallow breaths with the deep, curious ones of the horse.

"You smell of grass," Jennie murmured, taking the velvety nose in both hands to rub its fascinating smoothness with the tips of her fingers. "Of grass and sunshine!"

"And she rides like the wind," Windrider said. "Come and find out."

He went to the mare's side and bent over to cup his hand for Jennie to step into.

Blood roaring in her ears, hands going cold with excitement, Jennie slipped the toe of her moccasin, damp from the morning dew, into the warm, firm stirrup of Windrider's hand. He lifted her like a feather up onto the horse.

The skirt of her buckskin dress was soft, but not wide; it slid halfway up her thighs. She didn't appear to notice, so taken was she with the feel of being on the horse.

But Windrider could not help but notice. Any more than he could help laying his hand on her smooth leg. To put it in the right position for riding, of course.

He tucked the other around the firm curve of her bottom to show her how to sit a horse.

And to satisfy the thrumming urge surging into his palms. He could no more have denied it than he could have sprouted the wings of an eagle and flown into the air.

Her skin felt more wonderful than that on a foal's muzzle; her small hips fit exactly into his hand.

The Fire Flower looked down at him, her cheeks blushing red.

He looked back at her. Heat flamed between them, fast and high, like a prairie fire.

He ripped his gaze from hers and turned to look for the herders.

''Echo,'' he shouted, and made the sign for them to bring him his horse.

He must remember his vow. He must not forget it.

All he would teach to the Fire Flower was how to ride.

Chapter 7

Windrider's hands on her melted that moment and stopped time from moving. She felt as if she wore no clothes, as if only the dancing sunlight and the vibrant, tingling air touched her skin, along with his strong hands.

The sunlight, the air, and Windrider. The broad sky and the endless, undulating land wrapped them all into a sparkling new world created to hold her and Windrider and this herd of light-limbed horses, drifting like colored leaves across the green valley. Horses, and more horses, taking crisp bites of the grass and swishing their graceful tails.

Yet the hot magic of Windrider's hands suffused it all.

She looked down and found him looking up at her again. His eyes had softened from their usual black color to a burning brown.

His long hair, midnight black in the bright sunlight of early morning, parted to fall before and behind his shining bronze shoulders. Sweat broke out on her palms.

Because she could remember how those shoulders felt beneath her arms. Their muscular contours flowed like liquid, warmed like fire.

He turned her loose, except for keeping hold of her mount's rein, and the horse moved faster beneath her; Jennie clasped the mare close with her bare legs. Windrider led them out of the herd.

As soon as there was open space around them, Jennie called to him, "Give me the rein. I can do this."

He shot her a quick glance over his shoulder.

"You can ride, you can fight," he called back as he trotted ahead of the mare, still holding her rein, taking her farther from the other horses. "You are Texas Woman Warrior."

"I'm not a Texan!" Jennie announced grandly from her perch. Being on horseback made her feel as if she were a queen on a throne, even though Windrider hadn't obeyed her order. "I am Irish!"

He reached a flat, open space where the grass had been mostly eaten down, and brought the horse to a halt. He reached to his belt for a long braided-hair rope and tied the end of it to the red mare's halter.

"What is I-rish?" he asked.

"I come from Ireland, a country far away, across the ocean."

"Like the Spanish?"

"It's the same ocean," she said, suddenly at a loss to explain such distances, another world.

She couldn't even conceive of it for herself, she suddenly realized. No place existed for her at this moment except this new ocean of grass and horses, this green sea of the rolling plains beneath its enormous sky.

And no person existed but this copper-skinned man, his strong fingers as deft and beguiling on the rope and the horse as they had been on her body.

As if by witchery, he attached one rope to the other before she could blink.

Then he was back there beside her again. His hard, vigorous fingertips touched her leg.

"Sit straight," he said, making a commanding, vertical motion. "But loose. Feel the horse."

He stepped back and made a kissing sound, letting the length of the rope play out from his hand. The mare moved in a circle in a faster gait than she had previously done. Jennie bounced once, twice, and her legs convulsed around the horse to keep her from falling, then her body relaxed to the rhythm. Her thighs relaxed, then tightened, then relaxed and molded their muscles to the powerful, warm ones moving beneath her. All of her body fitted itself to the inevitable way that the mare moved, and the wind lifted her hair and brushed against her face. They cut a swath through the bright, beaming sunshine.

Jennie had only one thought. Now she knew the reason she had always loved horses: She had been born to ride.

Windrider's smile was already there to meet hers as she came around the circle in front of him again. "*Aimi?aru,* trot," he called.

"*Aimi?aru,*" Jennie said, and the mare twitched her ears back to listen. She kept her steady pace.

Two more times they came around, then Windrider called, "*Wahkami?aru,* lope!"

Jennie repeated the order, and her mount lifted her into a smooth, rocking gait that brought the warm air rushing faster against her face and the blood rising in her veins like a song. Now she truly *was* floating, and nothing could ever bring her down.

She didn't slow the mare even when one of the herders appeared with Echo, and Windrider sprang onto his back. He rode alongside Jennie, controlling the black and white horse without a bridle or rein, signaling him only with the barest movements of his legs. She watched in awe until his occasional touches to correct the way she sat fixed her attention back on her own riding. Those touches and the approving smile and nod he flashed at her connected them more surely than the rope he still held.

It was as if she had found two new friends in one morning, she thought, Windrider and the mare. No, three, counting Echo. *Three* friends when, since the death of her siblings, she'd never even had one.

And none of her siblings, not even Brianna, had ever really understood her, she mused. Not the way this man and this mare and this stallion did. All of them knew what she was going to do, which way she was going to move, before she did it.

Friends.

Could it be possible to be both friends and enemies? She could see, plain as the small red ears on the mare, flicking back and forth to listen for Jennie's voice, that Windrider was getting great pleasure from her happiness in learning to ride. Somehow, instinctively, he knew that it gratified a great need in her.

No one in her family had ever acknowledged that.

The thought threatened to bring the past rushing back.

Jennie pushed it away and took a deep, shaking breath of the glittering, sun-sweetened air. It raced through her body like a bracing gulp of wine. She wouldn't think anymore. She would simply *live*, live in this present moment forever.

Never, ever, did she want this to end. When she was on horseback, she was in another skin.

Finally, though, Windrider slowed his horse, and the mare matched his new pace, although he had long since given Jennie the rope he had held.

"No!" Jennie called across the small space between them. "Let's keep on riding!"

"No!" he mocked, grinning at her. "I am hungry. I want to collect my part of the bargain."

"No, you don't!" she said blithely, her high spirits bubbling off her tongue. "I'm not a good cook."

He laughed as the horses broke from a trot down into a walk.

"Very well," he said. "I will eat at Hukiyani's fire and give *her* your lessons in riding. You can carry the water and cut the wood and walk on your own two feet!"

"Never!" Jennie declared. "If I must cook in order to ride, you will eat burned meat and flat bread!"

"Bread? Only the white-eyes and the Wichitas with their earthen ovens have bread. The People do not."

"No bread?"

Bur she couldn't feel dismay or even much interest in that news. Who cared if there was no bread and no ovens? Who wanted to eat when there were horses to ride?

Windrider dismounted. Jennie, although her limbs were weak from so much riding and her muscles were already beginning to protest their unaccustomed use, refused to follow. She stretched out along the neck of her mount, hugging and patting the red mare.

"She's such a good girl!" she said, as Windrider

slipped the rawhide bridle off Echo and onto his shoulder. "I love her."

The mare turned her head toward Jennie as if she understood the words.

"She loves you, too," Windrider said. "She likes to listen to you, to do some work with you instead of nothing but play."

"What's her name?" Jennie asked, reluctantly throwing her tired, trembling leg over the mare's back and sliding to the ground, heedless of the sweaty hide against her new dress.

"She has no name."

"Why not?"

He ignored the question and made a sign that Jennie should remove the mare's bridle.

She went to her mount's head. "Why not?" she demanded, nodding toward his horse. "*He* is called Echo. She should have a name, too."

"No one has ridden her enough to give her a name," he said, abruptly. All the warmth went out of his face. He shot her a look that was almost a glare. "No one rides her anymore."

Jennie watched him from the corner of her eye as she slipped the strip of rawhide from the mare's mouth. Suddenly her stomach was a roiling mass of strange, new feelings. Disappointment first, at Windrider's sudden, inexplicable coldness. Jealousy second, that someone else had ever ridden the mare at all.

But that was insane, she lectured herself. Of course, someone must have ridden her! Otherwise, she would have been too wild for Jennie to ride.

"She's a good horse," she said, stepping back to look at the mare, walking slowly around to look at her from all angles.

Windrider chuckled, but the sound only tried to be mirthful. It fell far short.

"Now the Woman Warrior knows horses," he said. The words sounded like criticism, a taunting of the passion he had spent all morning approving and understanding in her.

Jennie whirled to look at him, her fists on her hips. "Well?" she challenged. "She *is* good, isn't she?"

"One of the best I own."

"Then why don't you ride her?"

"Men don't ride mares!" he said.

Jennie's heart leapt. Perhaps she could be the only one to ride the red mare! That would almost make her belong to her. At least she could *pretend* that she had a horse of her own.

"Who was the person who rode her before me?"

His face closed to her, his jaw tightened. "The Third Wife of Ten Bears," he said, avoiding She Blushes' name as was the custom when speaking of the dead. "A few times only."

He turned away.

He squatted down and, the muscles across his wide shoulders rippling like the tall grass blowing in the sunlight, snatched up a handful of grass and walked over to Echo. His back to Jennie, he began to rub it over the horse's gently heaving sides.

Jennie watched him for a while, but he didn't turn back to her, didn't glance at her, didn't speak to her. He acted as if she didn't exist.

The red mare nudged her nose into Jennie's back.

Jennie squatted as she had seen Windrider do, and pulled up two handfuls of grass. She stood and began rubbing the mare, but her eyes kept straying to Windrider's set back.

He made her furious. Why did he have to act like this and ruin the whole wonderful morning?

Well, no matter how he was acting, she had to know about this horse, whether she could pretend she was hers.

"Why doesn't the Third Wife of Ten Bears ride this mare anymore?"

He whirled on his heel to look at her. His eyes glittered with a cold feeling that could only be named hate.

"Because she has gone to the Spirit World," he said, each word grating out separately from between his clenched teeth.

His gaze threatened to freeze her.

"Now you go. Go and cook my food."

Jennie let the wads of grass drop from her suddenly nerveless fingers.

A slave. She was a slave, Windrider was her Comanche captor, no matter how many bargains she made, no matter how many riding lessons he gave her. He had seemed to be her friend—all morning long he had fed her that fantasy—but he had not forgotten that in reality he was her master.

When, yet again, the fire Jennie had laid so carefully between two logs outside Windrider's lodge refused to burn, she sank back onto her heels in despair. The fire wouldn't burn like the ones the other women had at their tipis, the tripod wiggled and swayed as if it would drop the kettle at any moment, the foods she had found in pots and bags inside the lodge were unfamiliar to her.

She took a deep breath, leaned forward, and tried again, stirring the old, dead coals and the new, tiny flickers of flame for the hundredth time, blowing on them and carefully adding more small sticks and dried buffalo chips, praying that they would catch so she could cook the finely ground substance she planned to drop into the water if she ever, indeed, did persuade it to boil. She also prayed that it was really cornmeal as she had assumed. All she wanted now was for things to go smoothly, for Windrider to eat without incident and go leave her alone.

Alone to explore and to learn and to start making the stash of supplies she would need to escape. How could she ever have thought, just a short time ago, that she wanted simply to live in the present? She was a slave and a captive whether she bore the name or not. How stupid she'd been, how naive, to try and bargain that away when Windrider held all power over her, and she had nothing to barter with in the first place!

Well, she could be just as treacherous as he. He had falsely pretended to be interested in her as a person, so she would behave falsely to him. She was through being stupid and naive.

She would please him so that he would continue to teach her to ride; she would ask questions and appear to be learning every skill in order to do his work well when actually she would be tricking him into teaching her what she needed to know to survive when she left him! It would serve him right!

She bent even closer to the feeble fire. She blew on it again, but too hard this time, and the sparks that had come to life died out.

"Blast it all!" she cried, and sat up, pounding

her fists against the ground, shaking her hair back out of her face so she could look around for help. But who would help her? The Comanche women hated her.

And they were busy with their own lives. Every lodge had breakfast cooking; the smells of stewing meat wafted on every warm breeze that touched her face. Every dog and every child was outside playing, barking, laughing, shouting, while waiting to eat. Only the warriors and older men were not much in evidence.

They, no doubt, were still lying abed, waiting for their slave-wives to serve them. Well, that was one thing she could be thankful for. She didn't have to serve Windrider in bed as wife.

Two lodges over, across the space that gave Windrider his privacy from the rest of the camp, the woman who had brought her that first bowl of food, the one called Hukiyani, emerged from her lodge. She turned her head and looked straight at Jennie.

Her fire burned merrily, her kettle hung securely above it.

She smiled. Jennie smiled back. Hukiyani had helped her bathe and dress last night, too, and had been unfailingly cheerful and kind.

"Hukiyani, would you help me?" Jennie called.

The woman smiled even more broadly at the sound of her name and started toward Jennie. Once at Jennie's cook fire, she motioned for Jennie to help, to do as she directed, and, using a sign language that made her meanings perfectly clear, she soon had the fire going and the water boiling in the pot. When, at her direction, Jennie began stirring the meal into it, she beamed at her with such a proud smile that Jennie couldn't help but be proud, too.

Windrider might have battered her feelings into the ground, but at least one of these people seemed to like her. She wanted to teach her, too. While they worked, Hukiyani named the fire, the tripod, the kettle, the food, in Comanche. Jennie repeated all the words and remembered about half of them. Knowing the language might help her escape. Knowing about the food certainly would.

Glancing down, Jennie realized with a little shiver of shock that the implement she held in her hand was a bone, polished from long use. Her fingers loosened and tried to drop it, but she forced them to grip it again. She would be tough, she thought, tough enough to escape and survive.

To do so, she would have to hold all her emotions in check. That included every feeling that Windrider might arouse in her, all that disappointment and anger.

And the attraction, her tiny voice of honesty shouted from the back of her mind. *Don't forget the attraction.*

That, too. *Any* emotion toward Windrider would only cloud her thinking as she made her plans to escape.

Hukiyani squatted beside the foodstuffs that Jennie had brought out of the lodge, took a knife from the sheath at her waist, and began slicing a hard substance packed into a casing like a sausage. She called it pemmican, beaming at Jennie when she indicated that was a word she had heard before.

Hukiyani had just finished showing Jennie how to lay the slices out neatly on a large leaf when Windrider stalked up to loom over them. He didn't speak to either of them, he simply stood for a moment, then strode to a place in the shade thrown by his tipi and sat down, cross-legged, on the ground.

Like the arrogant master he was, watching the slaves at work!

As remote as if he'd never smiled at her, never touched her, never looked in her eyes to share her joy as she learned to ride! Resentment rose in her like a river in flood, washing away all her resolutions to have no feelings toward him.

She might as well have resolved not to feel the warmth when she stood in the sunlight. His very *presence* set her teeth on edge.

"Your food is ready," she said, tightly. "One breakfast for one riding lesson; I believe that was our bargain?"

Hukiyani shot her a questioning glance, but Windrider appeared not to even hear her. He stared past them both, off into the far distance.

Hukiyani touched Jennie's arm to bring her mind back to her task, directed her in using a wooden paddle to scoop out the mush into dishes made of bark, added slices of the pemmican on the side. She turned and fed the fire a bit of the dried meat, then indicated that Jennie should take food to Windrider.

Stiffly Jennie crossed the small space, stepped around the end of the fire-logs, and held it out to him. Without looking up, he took it.

Hukiyani motioned Jennie back to her side and tugged at her to sit down in front of the other bowl, across the fire from Windrider. She said, "*Tuhkaru*," which Jennie recognized as the word Windrider had used the day before when he urged her to eat.

Yesterday. He had brought her here just yesterday.

Shock numbed her as she picked up a slice of

pemmican to use to scoop up her mush as Windrider was doing. Was this really only the second day she had been here? How in the name of Heaven had he caused so many contradictory, bone-deep emotions in her in so short a time?

Well, no more. She would feel nothing toward him anymore, nothing except "good riddance." She took a bite of her food to start building her strength.

The pemmican was delicious! It was sweet and tart at once on her tongue, with the light, bursting flavors of berries and honey combined with the heavier, smoked one of the meat. She put aside the mush and quickly ate two slices of it as if it were candy. She would take a bag of it when she left here.

"This is wonderful!" she said to Hukiyani. "Do sit down and have some!"

Windrider still didn't look at her, but he spoke gruffly, evidently repeating the invitation in Comanche, because Hukiyani filled a bowl, took some slices of the dried meat for herself, and sat down beside Jennie, beaming at her with friendliness. Jennie tremulously smiled back, thinking how truly likable the woman was.

But she wouldn't let *that* emotion stand in her way, either. The cold hurt of Windrider's sudden change sat like a rock on her heart. She would not make friends with anyone here, she would simply learn everything she could from Hukiyani. The woman's skills might be key to the success of her getting away.

Windrider finished eating, dropped his empty bowl to the ground, flexed his long, burnished thigh muscles, rose in one motion, and ducked into his lodge. A moment later he came out with two bows and a quiver of arrows. He walked rapidly toward the open prairie without looking at them, without saying a word.

Jennie stared after him, the bitter, rank fury filling her veins in spite of every resolve she had made.

After that beautiful ride this morning, she *was* nothing but a slave! And he was acting just like Trammel!

Scalding tears stung her eyes.

Furiously she turned on the innocent Hukiyani.

"Do all men eat their food like pigs and never say one word of thanks to the women who worked so hard to cook it?" she demanded, almost shouting.

She leapt to her feet and stood over the amazed woman, her fists on her hips. "And do they all just turn their backs and walk off without one word of good-bye to people who, a few minutes earlier, they treated like friends?"

Her face was getting hot as the cook fire; she knew she was flushed red as her hair, but she didn't care.

And she didn't care that Windrider wasn't her friend, she thought wildly. It was being treated like dirt after she'd worked so hard to serve a man for the second time in her life—like a bad dream she'd had before. It made something snap inside her.

Even overbearing Papa had always thanked Mama for every meal when he got up to leave the table.

She stamped her foot. "It makes me so mad!" she cried, the sight of Hukiyani's worried face blurring from the tears that had begun to swim on her lashes. "It makes me furious. I won't be treated that way anymore, I just won't!"

Hukiyani scrambled to her feet, making calming noises, reaching to pat Jennie's arm, trying her best to soothe her. She looked down the alleyway between the lodges and called to someone.

"I can't do it!" Jennie cried, forgetting that the woman didn't know what she was saying. "I can't pretend to try to please him and let him walk all over my feelings, no matter what he does to me! I *won't* live like this again, I *can't*, not even for a little while!"

Eagle Tail Feather materialized at her elbow.

His sudden appearance surprised Jennie into silence for a moment, in which Hukiyani spoke to him rapidly. He listened, then, his brow furrowed in concentration, he turned to Jennie.

"An-gry," he said. "Hukiyani say . . . why?"

"Because Windrider didn't say 'thank you'!"

That sounded foolish suddenly, and weak. Jennie blushed harder. She was having a full-fledged temper tantrum, acting younger than this child who was translating the words of her fit!

She tried again, her tears flowing in earnest now.

"Because Windrider didn't say 'good-bye'!"

A flash of amusement—and of sympathy—showed in Eagle Tail Feather's face, but he smoothed it into a noncommittal expression and spoke to Hukiyani.

She, too, looked at Jennie calmly, but Jennie could sense that her worry was dissolving. Her bubbling laughter was very near the surface and her eyes showed amazement. She gave Jennie a pat and a sympathetic, very indulgent, smile.

Jennie stared at her in horror. Oh no! Hukiyani was thinking that she had become so attached to Windrider that she was crying for him to return!

Chagrined, wiping at her streaming eyes with

both hands, Jennie turned and dashed across the short space into the refuge of Windrider's lodge. Dear Lord, she had never been so embarrassed in her life! Would Hukiyani and Eagle Tail Feather tell this to Windrider?

"My uncle. He come . . . back," Eagle Tail Feather said from behind her. "This sun. Perhaps."

His voice vibrated with sympathy and assurance, as if he were comforting a small child. Jennie whirled to face him.

Hukiyani stood directly behind him, her hands on his shoulders. Both their round faces were struggling between amusement and sympathy, reassurance and laughter.

"I have to *do* something before he comes back!" Jennie cried, desperate to make them understand that she wasn't weeping for him to return. "Something to show him that I'm not his slave! I'm no more important to him than that . . . parfleche thrown over there on that woodpile!"

She flung out her hand and pointed at the painted bag, lying on a heap of carelessly piled firewood. It was quite beautiful, with a design of bear's paws and triangles in deep shades of blue and yellow.

Frantic to move, wild to do *something*, Jennie scrambled to her feet again.

"See?" she cried. "He doesn't take care of any *thing*, much less of people! This is so beautiful, it should be hung up to look at, like a picture!"

While Eagle Tail Feather translated, Jennie ran to a pole beside the door and hung the painted bag on a peg. She stepped back to look at it.

"There!" she said. "Isn't that better?"

And in that moment she knew what it was she could do.

And by the name of Saint Patrick and the memory of her awful days and nights with Trammel, she would do it, too. She would not live another day being oppressed by a man just because he was bigger and stronger and more powerful than she.

Windrider had brought her to this Comanche tipi, and it was where she had to live until she could escape. But in the meantime, she would live here as a *person*, or Windrider could kill her now.

Windrider moved quickly and silently, on the hunt for game, willing meat to come to him. And willing the plains to swallow him up. He stepped as carefully as if he were slipping up on a big elk or a rare white buffalo, even though he knew full well that he was the hunted, that his feelings had set out to stalk him.

Why in the name of the Sun Father had he ever put the Fire Flower on that red dun mare, anyway?

His special spirit, The Wind, bowed the tall grasses over in front of him, lifted them again, then came whistling past his ear.

Because The Wind had led them to that horse, and that horse only, with Windrider's hand around the Fire Flower's arm.

Windrider pushed that truth away, tried to talk himself out of believing it.

No. He had loved She Blushes so much, he had been trying to bring her back from the Spirit Land. He had caught the mare out of his aching love and need for She Blushes still to be there, waiting to mount her, ready to ride out on the few innocent excursions they had had.

He felt the old bitter disgust with himself twist in his gut. She Blushes had always insisted that

Eagle Tail Feather and one of his friends, or a group of the young girls, should come, too, so there would be no question of propriety. He shouldn't have listened to her. When they had known Ten Bears would never offer her to Wind-drider, he should have ignored the custom of the *Nermernuh* that the warrior must wait for the woman to come to him. He should have run away with her, should have taken her right out from under Ten Bears' nose and gone to live with another band.

Because she was the only woman he would ever love. She had been sweet and gentle, nurturing and helpful, besides being beautiful. She Blushes was everything a woman should be. He had loved her with all of his heart. He would never love anyone else.

All during the morning and until Sun Father had slipped halfway down the sky in the afternoon, until Windrider reentered the camp with the carcass of an elk slung over his shoulder and two rabbits tied at his waist, he relived his precious memories of She Blushes. He tried to recall her face.

Instead, over and over again, it was the pale, heart-shaped face of the Fire Flower that kept coming into his mind.

Hitting the elk with the fourth arrow he had shot had been a simple gift from the Earth Mother—the first three arrows had flown into the empty air like blind bats from a cave, useless because the Fire Flower's face, instead of the game, had filled his eye. It was enough to make him completely ashamed of himself. Had he no loyalty?

Had his feelings for She Blushes been so weak, so transient, that they had left him already? He would not permit that to happen, for if he did, who would remember her, who would love her?

Certainly not Ten Bears. Ten Bears had never loved her at all. He would never have given fifty horses for her if Windrider hadn't been planning to marry her himself when he could get enough horses.

He shrugged the string of his bow farther back onto his shoulder and strode through the crowd of barking dogs and shouting children who had run out to greet him, smiling at them, touching their hair without really seeing them, either. No, he thought, he would not let the feelings of caring for the white girl come into his heart.

The wind swirled down the open way between the tipis, lifted his hair away from his face. It whispered into his ear again.

He had started teaching the Fire Flower the language and the customs as soon as she was here in the village. He had danced for her. He had taught her to ride.

Windrider refused to listen.

Yes, he would keep her in his lodge. To do his work, that was all.

And to keep her from Ten Bears, to show the camp that Windrider would not be intimidated. "Little Brother" indeed!

Chapter 8

Jennie's hands froze on the rawhide cords she was tying. They held the rolled-up sides of the tipi two feet or so off the ground, letting the breeze whirl into the lodge and around her. It carried Windrider's voice to her.

He spoke again, just outside the lodge.

"*Parua*," he said, "elk."

Jennie listened. What was he *doing*? Giving English lessons?

Hukiyani's calm, good-humored tones repeated, "Elk."

Jennie smiled. Bless her. Hukiyani wanted to learn to communicate better with the hysterical Fire Flower.

But the thought couldn't hold her attention. As she looked around Windrider's tipi, apprehension welled up in her, so sharp and overwhelming, it made her shiver. What had she *done*?

Her temper fit was gone now, and Windrider was here. Trammel's beefy face, red and frowning, was suddenly as close as the thin strips of leather tangled in her fingers. She could hear his flat, oppressive voice commanding, "Put it all back where it was."

She glanced quickly around at the things she

had moved in Windrider's tipi. She *wouldn't* put it all back!

Windrider spoke once more, closer to her, in response to a child's shrill question. Jennie twisted to look at the door opening.

He stepped into the tipi.

His dark gaze touched her briefly, then flicked over the lodge.

Jennie stared at him.

She *couldn't* put it all back. If she did, if she let him bully her the way Trammel had done, she would never be a real person again.

If only he hadn't come in when she was kneeling here on her bed robes like some humble supplicant! She forced her fingers to finish tying the knots and scrambled to her feet.

She made herself stand very straight and face him. If he ordered her to return everything to its original place, she would run away, this minute, unprepared for survival or not. He could beat her senseless, but she would not move one beaded bag, one cooking utensil. Not one.

Finally he spoke. "Nice," he said, his deep tones rumbling in the confines of the skin walls. "More space for visitors."

Utter astonishment took the strength from her legs.

He walked around the circle to the right, the way he always entered the tipi, carefully looking at every change she had made.

"The parfleches are now easy to choose," he said, gesturing toward the buckskin bags she had hung like pictures on the different lodge poles.

The praise sent energy surging through her; she took a step toward him as if he had tugged on her hand. Then she stopped.

God in Heaven, how could this man do this to

her? He jerked her from the depths of despair to the heights of happiness with a word, with a glance! Just because he had understood how she felt about the horses didn't mean that she should give him such power over her!

His sharp glance shot to the backrest he had used the brief time he had been in the lodge with her and the stack of robes folded behind it.

"Good," he said, "not to move my bed. The bed of the lodge owner has always place of honor across from door."

Jennie watched him. His high cheekbones, all the chiseled angles of his face, caught the glow of the sunlight that poured through the walls. He truly was handsome beyond belief, especially with that look of approval for her in his eyes.

She couldn't, she could *not*, put too much stock in that. She mustn't let herself think it made him her friend.

"Hukiyani told me," she said.

His gaze went immediately to the other bed robes, the ones she had been using. She had moved them from the place beside his to a spot much nearer the door, where only the firewood stood between her and the opening. But he didn't comment on that.

"Hukiyani told you with signs?"

"Yes. And your nephew translated, too."

A small smile curved the corners of his sensual mouth; for an instant Jennie's breath stopped. She braced her heart against that crooked, charming grin of his.

He grew solemn again, giving only a little shrug and a shake of his head. "Those two," he said, "always in mischief."

He circled the tipi, his gaze touching his war lance, his other bows, the quivers of arrows hang-

ing by loops on the skin walls. She had let them
be, too.

But his drum sat in a new place with its sticks
crossed beside it, and one fringed bag, beautifully
beaded in brilliant colors, she had hung on the
pole over his bed. All the cooking utensils and the
foodstuffs, the tools and the firewood, she had
moved and arranged more neatly.

Would those please him, also?

She made herself take a deep, rasping breath.
She hadn't done all this to please him—she had
done it to please herself, to make a statement!
She didn't care whether she pleased him or not.

But when he nodded his acceptance at last, she
felt a smile spring to her lips.

"Look nice, Fire Flower," he said.

"I'm glad you like it, Windrider."

Her soft voice turned him on his heel.

Her face blazed like a star with happiness. With
the pleasure that his words had brought. Sympathy twisted in him, as it had done when she'd
told him that her family owned no horses. Hadn't
anyone ever praised her before?

"You did well," he said again.

Her smile grew brighter, like dawn coming on
a misty morning, filling the tipi with light. Because of what *he* had said.

Such power lured his soul. He took a step toward her.

He looked again to her bed robes, now put
away from his, then back to his own and the place
where hers used to be.

"Did Hukiyani not tell you also that the place
of honor for guests is the one to the left of mine?
The one on my heart side?"

She shook her head, her smile changing to a
frown of puzzlement as she took in his words.

"Well, it is," he said, in a light, teasing tone, wanting to see her smile again. "I put you there, but you have moved out of it to be closer to the door."

He stepped around the fire pit and walked slowly toward her. When he spoke, he put a deep fierceness into his tone.

"Are you telling me again that you are going to run away?"

Her startled look told him she thought his anger might be real. He stood directly in front of her and waited for her answer.

The Fire Flower looked at him straight. Her deep green eyes, her spring-grass-in-the-sunshine-beautiful eyes, blazed up into his, fringed by curling dark lashes. Long lashes that he yearned to brush with his fingertips.

No, with his lips. He wanted to close her eyes and cover her eyelids with kisses.

She tossed back her hair and tilted her chin. He felt himself smile inside. Always full of spirit, this small one. He was enjoying teasing her no end.

"I will run when I am on horseback, not when I am in my bed," she replied, her light voice full of fierceness, too, in return.

He wanted to laugh, to laugh out loud with the sheer joy of being with her, of getting to know her brave self. But he only cocked his head to one side, letting her know he would hear more.

"You should have thought of that when you started teaching me about the horses," she went on. "Didn't you think I would run away when you showed me how to ride?"

Then her lushly curved lips lifted at the corners in the ghost of a smile, and he saw that she'd known all along that he was jesting. He grinned back at her.

"No," he said, and let his voice drop to a low tone, speaking in a slow rhythm that betrayed exactly what he was feeling. "I knew then that you would want to stay."

The pulse at the base of her smooth, pale throat fluttered hard, like the feathered fan of a war dancer.

And, oh, calling to his hands like the song of the wind—her high, rounded breasts rose and fell with her deepening breath.

He would go mad if he didn't touch them.

If he didn't cup them into his palms where they would fill up his hands exactly. If he didn't reach with his thumbs to find their budding tips . . .

But he wouldn't. He would not force himself onto her as his captive. He would treat her as one of The People and not approach her until she gave him a sign.

Sweat broke out on the edge of his brow. His loins ached as his manhood swelled.

He at least had to kiss her. It would only worsen every one of his yearnings to take her, but he could not walk out of this lodge without that to remember.

A kiss between a man and a woman did not always mean they had to do more. According to the Spanish women who had taught him this strange custom of kissing, that was true.

He lifted his hands, their palms burning for the soft shape of her breasts, for the smooth sensation of her bare skin, and placed them on her dress-covered shoulders instead. On the fragile bones of her small shoulders, forever squared bravely against the world.

He bent his head, buried his face for a heartbeat in the floating, fragrant cloud of her hair. Then, with a groan and the sliding caress of his cheek against hers, he gathered her up in the crook of his arm and covered her mouth with his.

Her eyes flared wide; she made a little whimpering sound. He pulled her closer into his embrace, his lids drifted closed, and he heard and saw no more. He could only feel, as raw and fresh as if he had never kissed before, the tingling thrill from the heat, from the silkiness, of her mouth.

And he could taste. He could taste the honey of her mouth, hot and fresh as from a newly robbed summer hive. Her lips met his with a sweetness that sent a trembling along his spine, moving tentatively, then more surely, to accept and finally to return the slow, burning kiss.

He ran the tip of his tongue along the seam of them, asking gently to be let in, and she parted them slowly, almost in wonder, as if she, too, had never done such a thing until now. Then her tongue drifted to meet his, touched to welcome him. They twined together then, clinging and letting go, then coming back to meet again and again as if one could not exist without the other.

The passioned kiss lasted until, without his permission, his hands moved over her back and down the delicious tunnel of her spine to cradle her small bottom and crush her against him. The feel of his hard manhood made her gasp.

The fitful sound, the sudden stiffening of her body, brought him back to his senses. Still, it took two more long heartbeats before he could force himself to break away from the deep-drawn pleasure.

He kept his gaze locked with hers for a long, breathless time. Admonitions to himself beat in his head like a singer's drum.

He must not impose himself upon a captive. For the sake of his warrior's pride, he must wait

for her, as for any woman, to come to his bed.
He must put his mind on something else.

He tore his eyes away from hers and glanced
around the tipi once more.

"*Ura*," he said, "thank you." He peeled his
hands away from her body to gesture around the
circle of his tipi. "For this work. Thank you."

Then he made himself turn and go out, his own
words echoing in his head.

Thank you for what?

For destroying, with one shining, joyous look,
with one sweet, hot response to a kiss, his resolve
to leave her alone.

For a long time Jennie stood where he'd left
her, stunned by his kiss. The heat of it still burned
her lips, the shape of his mouth shaped hers yet.

Her heart beat hard enough to smother her; her
arms hung so empty, they could never be filled.
Except by Windrider.

The rich tones of his voice lingered in the lodge
to stroke her skin and please her ears. The place
of honor for guests? She moved out of it?

His *heart* side? He had *put* her there?

By his heart side.

And she was stunned by his other words. *Thank
you!* Windrider had thanked her for being her own
bold self, for rearranging his tipi and putting
things where *she* wanted them!

Of all the reactions she had thought he might
have to her handiwork, she had never imagined
this one!

Quickly, unbelievingly, she relived everything
that he had said and done from the moment he
returned to the tipi, savoring his approval of her
decisions, of her taste. Her thoughts slowed and
lingered over his teasing about her moving her

bed and what it meant. Then they stopped completely, remembering one line over and over, hearing exactly the way his deep voice had said it.

I knew then that you would want to stay.

He had sounded very sure, very satisfied. Did her rearranging the tipi have some significance in Comanche culture that she didn't understand? Had it signaled him that she had truly moved in and permanently settled herself?

Had she inadvertently assumed the position of his . . . wife?

Was that the reason he had kissed her?

What, exactly, had he been thanking her for?

"Kohtoo Topusana!"

Hukiyani's voice floated in through the door opening; Jennie whirled to see her round, excited face framed there.

"Elk!" she said, beaming, beckoning to Jennie to come with her. "Windrider! Elk!"

Hukiyani was so proud of speaking in English that Jennie smiled back at her in spite of these new questions burning holes in her brain, and the weak feeling in her legs that threatened to send her crashing to the ground.

"*Tumaramiitu,*" Hukiyani said, her smile changing into a mournful frown because her English vocabulary had run out. With gestures, she indicated that the word meant that she wanted Jennie to join her.

Jennie moved slowly, still dazed by her speculations. Hukiyani reached in, grabbed her hand, and pulled her out the door.

She chattered eagerly in the Comanche tongue, throwing in the English word "elk" from time to time, holding to Jennie's arm, leading her around to the side of the lodge where a group of excited boys were playing with their bows and arrows, pretending to shoot at the elk, which was already hanging, tied by its hind feet, from the branch of one of the large trees. As it twisted slowly in the slight breeze, Jennie saw that its body cavity had been gutted and cleaned. It was huge; its rack of horns was nearly as wide as Jennie was tall, its body so long that the antlers almost brushed the ground. Windrider and Hukiyani's husband, Yellowfish, sat on their haunches a few yards away, in the late afternoon shade of some other trees, with their backs to the tipi wall, smoking and watching the children.

"Windrider," Hukiyani said, practicing her English again. "Elk."

She pointed and pantomimed the fact that this was Windrider's kill.

Then, pointing to the carcass and to the soft dress that Jennie wore, she picked up a fold of the skirt in her fingers, dropped it, and rubbed their tips against her cheek to sign how soft it was. She pointed to Jennie and to the elk again.

Jennie stared at her, horror drowning out the whole complicated mass of emotions swirling inside her. Surely Hukiyani didn't expect her to skin this animal and make a dress! Hukiyani had taught her how to do other chores, but this one she *couldn't* learn!

Hukiyani had a great deal more to say. She led Jennie to each side of the animal, pointing and chattering, then she opened a pouch hanging at her waist and took out a sharp knife. To Jennie's profound relief, the older woman went to work skinning the elk herself, gesturing that Jennie should cook the two rabbits, which were already skinned and gutted and lying on one of the logs that enclosed the coals of the cook fire.

Heaving a great sigh of relief, Jennie went to the fire and squatted down to begin the task of starting it up again. She would drag out the task of cooking the rabbits until they were charred to a crisp, if necessary. Anything to keep from getting a lesson in how to skin an elk, with Windrider sitting there watching her every move!

But he wasn't watching her. Some other men joined him and Yellowfish, and when she stole a glance in that direction, she saw that Windrider was completely immersed in conversation. If he thought she had taken on the role of his wife or his companion or volunteer servant or whatever, he wasn't very excited about it.

If only she *knew*, if only she could ask Hukiyani the importance of what she'd done, maybe this tingling in every nerve in her body would calm down! She glanced up from the stubborn coals to the older woman, efficiently busy with her knife. Wouldn't Hukiyani have explained at the time if Jennie had been inadvertently making some statement by rearranging the lodge? She *had* told her to leave Windrider's bed where it was, after all!

Hukiyani moved back and forth between her task and Jennie's, demonstrating how to fix the meat on the spit and set the sticks to hold it. Her chin-length black hair, parted in the middle, swung back and forth as she moved, sometimes hiding her face. But she brushed it away every time she looked at Jennie, and her eyes twinkled warmly.

Jennie smiled back at her. Just being with Hukiyani made her feel calmer.

As Jennie finished adding kindling to the fire, the murmur of the men's low voices stopped.

She looked up. Ten Bears was walking down the path between the tipis; as she watched, he veered off his course and strode toward her on his short, bowed legs. Even though Yellowfish called a greeting to him, his gaze met Jennie's instead. He coveted her, it said, coveted her in a purely impersonal way.

A shiver ran through her, inside, and she stiffened so it wouldn't show.

That was the same look he always gave her. She wished she never had to see him again.

"*Tumaramiitu*," Windrider called, as his brother came closer.

The rich sound of his voice drew Ten Bears' eyes.

And Jennie's, too. That was the same word Hukiyani had used to urge Jennie out of the tipi. Windrider must be asking his brother to join him and his friends. Surprised, Jennie watched them covertly, thinking how generous of him the invitation was, considering the acrimonious exchange between them at the Victory Dance.

But Ten Bears obviously was not so eager to make peace. His low brows pulled more tightly together, his sullen face grew darker, and he refused Windrider's invitation in such a snarling tone that several of the men glanced up in sharp appraisal.

Ten Bears glared from one disapproving tribal member to another, then stalked on his way, sending a contemptuous parting glance at his brother.

Windrider's face filled, just for an instant, with a look of such mixed hurt and love that Jennie's heart broke for him. How sad to have a brother alive, right there, and have such trouble between you! Even from across the space that separated her from him, his anguish felt palpable enough for her to touch.

Windrider loved his brother. He wanted to be friends with him again. That message was so clear in his eyes that he might as well have leapt to his feet and shouted the words at Ten Bears' stiff, departing back.

The group of men resumed their quiet conversation, accompanied by the calm, rhythmic motions of filling and smoking their pipes. Jennie bent her head over her work, turning the meat on the spit. Their voices hummed and blended. She wondered if they mentioned Ten Bears, if they took sides in the brothers' dispute.

The flames now leaping up to cook the rabbits blurred with her sudden tears. Trouble separating brothers was a terrible waste—she would give anything if even one of her brothers or sisters could still be alive to argue with her. She would make peace in an instant and forever keep it that way.

A touch on her shoulder jerked her from her musings and made her jump half out of her skin. Hukiyani squatted beside her, took her arm, turned her around so that their backs were to the men.

Hukiyani cut her eyes toward Windrider, then looked significantly in the direction Ten Bears had gone. She shook her head, making the clucking, reproachful noise that Jennie had often heard from her mother—that sound of displeasure which must be the same among wise women everywhere.

Drawing her fingers down her cheeks like falling tears, Hukiyani frowned and wagged her head again as if to say there was nothing anyone could do.

"Windrider," she said, in her proud English. Then she passed her work-hardened hand through the air from Jennie's heart to hers and said, *"Kwuhu,"* pointing in the direction of Ten Bears.

Jennie concentrated, realizing she had heard the word from Windrider. Then she remembered. *I will take no one for* kwuhu, *wife.*

The wife of Ten Bears? The *Third* Wife of Ten Bears? The only other person who had ridden the bright red dun mare? Was Hukiyani saying that Windrider had loved her, loved his brother's wife?

"Windrider?" Jennie blurted, trying to keep her voice to a whisper. She made the sign from one heart to another as Hukiyani had done. *"Kwuhu* Ten Bears?"

"Windrider," Hukiyani whispered back in a flat tone of finality, repeating the sign. *"Kwuhu."* She inclined her head toward the spot where Ten Bears had last been.

Windrider had been in love with Ten Bears' wife!

No wonder the mention of her this morning had made him turn so strange!

A new, undefined feeling stabbed through Jennie.

Hukiyani set her face blank as a mask. She closed her eyes with her fingers and sat very still. She held her breath.

Jennie stared at her.

Dead. She was saying, as Windrider had done, that Ten Bears' wife, the one Windrider loved, was dead, gone to the Spirit World.

Ten Bears' wife was dead, but Windrider still loved her.

That must be true, or he would not have behaved in such an unreasonable way when he'd mentioned that the woman also had ridden the red mare.

A strange, quick happiness brushed her heart. At least he hadn't spoken so callously this morning because of Jennie herself! He *hadn't* simply been treating her as a slave!

Then her spirit plummeted. She *was* something more than a chore-woman to Windrider, but that something wasn't necessarily a friend or a companion.

She was a prize to keep from his brother.

The woman Windrider loved had belonged to Ten Bears. Now a woman whom Ten Bears wanted belonged to Windrider.

Wild, scattered thoughts scrambled around in her head.

Windrider had publicly refused to give her up, so he would never do so, surely. Yet he wanted peace with his brother, so he might.

What would happen to her?

As if she could feel Jennie's turmoil, Hukiyani reached over and patted her on the arm, for all the world just as her mother would have done. Jennie turned and smiled at her gratefully, looking at the kind, round face through eyes too desperately dry to cry as she wished she could do.

She put both hands on the spit and began slowly turning the meat, hardly smelling the delicious aromas that rose from the juice dripping, sizzling, into the fire. It didn't matter, she told herself fiercely.

Not even Windrider's kiss mattered.

He hadn't been kissing her, Jennie O'Bannion. He had been kissing the woman Ten Bears wanted.

Immediately she fought to erase all the disturbing emotions that the thought of the kiss had stirred. On top of them, a sharp, sick feeling of disappointment rose in her.

She gritted her teeth. What she had to do was *think*, not feel, if she ever hoped to escape from this nightmare.

None of these relationships in this Comanche camp had anything to do with her at all. Soon she would be on her way back to Texas. Perhaps she would find Mama there, still alive.

That's what she needed to think about: her Mama alive and waiting for her, not some dead Comanche woman she had never seen. As long as he kept her away from Ten Bears, Windrider could love that woman forever and it would make no difference to Jennie.

That night, as she lay huddled in her bed robes against the cool April air, Jennie's mind wouldn't stay on her mother and Texas. It clung stubbornly to Windrider and where he would sleep when he finally came home.

Surely he wouldn't come to her bed. After all, he had sworn last night that he never would sleep with someone who would rather kill herself first!

But . . . had he rescinded that vow when he kissed her?

Had *she* rescinded that vow by rearranging his house?

She turned over restlessly and clenched her fists until her nails cut into her palms. If only she could communicate well enough with Hukiyani to ask her! But she would never want Eagle Tail Feather involved in this, for he would tell his uncle.

I knew that you would want to stay.

Those words, and the look he had given her when he said them, tortured her memory.

And so did the stirring sight of him riding as if he were one with the horse, so did the magic touch of his hand as she rode beside him on the red mare.

And the melodious sound of his intimate, teasing tone as he called her "Texas Woman Warrior."

And the masculine, musky scent of him as he bent close to place her hands on her reins.

But those were nothing to the profound wash of sensual impressions that flowed through her when she remembered his kiss. It made her muscles move and twitch, restless to get her up, carry her out of the lonely tipi, out to find Windrider wherever he was and repeat the kiss over and over again.

Made her wish that he *would* come to her bed. No matter if it *was* just to have her when Ten Bears couldn't.

That unbidden thought shocked her into stillness.

She stiffened in disgust with herself and flopped her protesting body over to lie on her stomach instead of letting herself get up. She must be losing her mind!

The sound of Windrider's voice floated in through the walls of the tipi, rolled down to the ground now to keep out the night breeze. Evidently he was still sitting outside where she had seen him when she came in, two lodges down the way, still talking with the men he'd smoked with all through the late afternoon and the supper preparations. They had moved to the new spot after they'd all eaten, the same loosely knit group except for the addition of Ten Bears.

He was the reason Jennie had come inside and gone to bed so early. As she'd finished cleaning up the dishes with Hukiyani, Ten Bears had wandered back into the vicinity and sat down with the men, but his eyes had strayed over and over again to gaze in Jennie's direction.

There was no reason that she could see that he should join the group then, after refusing so hatefully earlier in the evening. The only difference was that this time, as far as she could tell, nobody had invited him. Perhaps Ten Bears always did the opposite of what others expected.

Jennie pressed her face and body more tightly to the bed, reached down with both hands, and pulled the covers up over her shoulders. Even that warmth, though, couldn't keep her from shivering.

The question that had hung in the back of her mind from the moment she'd seen Ten Bears sit down cross-legged in the same group with Windrider came leaping forward to taunt her. What if the brothers began to talk to each other? What if they made peace?

What would happen to her then?

The fear held her in its cold grip for a long minute, until Windrider's musical voice sounded once more.

It was as warm as his strong hands on her as he showed her how to sit the horse. Warm as his smile, his wonderful, unexpected smile that caused a singular, new melting in the deepest part of her.

Warm as his vulnerable look of love for his brother.

Obviously his feelings ran deep, Windrider's. As deep as his body was strong.

What had she been like, that woman whom Windrider loved?

And how had she felt about him?

Had she, Third Wife of Ten Bears or no, ever shared Windrider's bed?

The next morning, Windrider got up and went out, early, while the Fire Flower slept. Last night she had been awake—he had known it from the stillness in the tipi, from the silence of her breathing—when he came in and lay down in his bed robes. And that had been very late—Mother Moon had already started on her downward path.

He had stayed outside, talking and smoking for so long, because Ten Bears had joined them. He said little of importance directly to Windrider, or to anyone else for that matter, but his presence was meant as an apology for his earlier rudeness, and everyone knew that. Yellowfish welcomed Ten Bears, helped smooth the way for the brothers to speak peacefully, and Windrider felt grateful to him.

Keen regret twisted his gut. Before he and Ten Bears had found the bodies of their mother and She Blushes, they had overcome so much of their enmity! Now it had reclaimed them like a strike of lightning—and over a woman again!

Ten Bears *did* want her—the lust had been strong in his face yesterday—but he wanted the victory of his will over his brother's even more. Windrider set his jaw. He would get neither.

The thigh-deep grass washed his legs with dew. He strode faster, enjoying the cool wetness slick against his skin, and silently thanked the Moon Mother for the moisture. He would ride the buckskin stallion this morning. On such a day a man ought to ride fast and far, as far as the red buttes to the north and west, and that young horse was one that needed such work to strengthen his lungs and his heart.

Windrider took a long, deep breath of the splendid morning and blew the tension out of his body along with it. On such a day a man should ride alone to rest his spirit.

But when the herder brought the buckskin to him, the red dun mare voluntarily came along. She nosed at him, looked around behind him, as if asking where was the girl to ride her.

On such a day a man should see bright happiness.

Before he would let himself think, he called to one of the boys who helped the herder, sent him to the camp to get the Fire Flower.

"It is to flaunt her to Ten Bears, to make him know Windrider is not *Little* Brother," he muttered to the buckskin as he cinched his blanket pad onto him. "That is all."

But when she came into view, running toward the herd, wearing the bridle she had used the day before over her shoulder, its rein flapping behind her and her hair burning in the air like a flame in the wind, he admitted the truth in his heart. It was so he could see her face full of passion for the horses and wonder how it would look filled with passion for him.

He *would* try to make her give him a sign, he *would* take her to his bed if he could, he thought, as she ran nearer and nearer. But he would remain loyal to the memory of She Blushes. He would bed this beautiful white girl, but he would not let himself love her.

"Are you waiting for me?" she cried, and his foolish heart leapt out of his chest and into his throat.

But then it fell into his moccasins. She ran past

him to the mare and threw her arms around the
filly's neck. "I think you are, I think you are."

He watched her press her pale cheek to the
mare's gleaming skin, watched her blazing hair
blend with the same-color mane. Watched her
dazzling eyes close in bliss.

It was good that she had this connection with
this horse, he thought. The presence of the mare
with this girl would always remind him how
painful loving could be. Perhaps *that* was the reason his medicine spirit, The Wind, had put these
two red-haired ones together.

So he would not let himself love her.

Windrider had been waiting for her, too. Jennie
could tell by the way he had raised his head from
the work of fastening his cinch and watched her
run out to the herd.

He gave no sign that her rearranging his lodge
had changed anything between them.

He hadn't come to her bed, so she must not
have done anything untoward. He hadn't given
her to Ten Bears, so she must be safe.

He had sent for her to ride, on a day so mar-
velously beautiful that it must be full of magic.
That was the act of a friend.

She slid both hands over the wonderful, shiny
warmth of the horse's hide, loving the feel of it,
watching the small ears twitch back and forth to
hear her crooning endearments. Drawing in deep
breaths, she gloried in the already familiar, indi-
vidual scent of the mare. She smelled different,
much more delicate than Echo did.

"Ready to ride?" Windrider asked.

"Yes!"

Jennie slipped one arm around the dun mare's
neck and the braided-rawhide bridle off her own
shoulder. The horse stood like a dream and stuck

her nose into the loop. The next instant Jennie was on her back, her heart thrilling, for she had been too quick for Windrider to help her.

She needed no help. She was mounted. She was independent. She was invincible.

She was free.

Jennie let the muscles of her thighs mold themselves to those of the horse's sides as she began to move; she felt for the mare's mood through her mouth and the connection of the rein. Jennie could tell the mare was happy. Happy and ready to run.

"*Aimi?aru,*" Windrider said, and Jennie realized that he was now mounted, too.

"*Aimi?aru,*" she repeated to the little red dun, and rode her away from the herd at a trot, pleased that she had remembered the meaning of the Comanche word.

Outside the herd, she took the mare into a big circle. From a distance Windrider occasionally called a change of pace or a word of praise. He was a part of the day, a creature of the prairie sent to make her one, too.

She lifted her face to the wind and flew into it. The fleet, little red dun blew over the rolling plains, her feet dipping into the deep grass up and down, faster and faster. This mare could carry Jennie straight up to heaven.

When she had a bit more practice in riding.

Jennie slipped a bit on the mare's sleek back as the speed increased even more, so she pulled on the rein and eased her into a circle, sitting back and saying, "Easy, now, girl, easy now."

The muscles of her buttocks and legs must get used to this unaccustomed work; her whole body must practice balance. But it wouldn't take long because, from now on, she would spend most of every single day learning this skill!

Windrider rode the yellow horse across the green space between them. Jennie wheeled her mount and pulled her down to go even slower, thrilling inside when the mare obeyed her so readily. They trotted to meet him.

"You are a wonderful horse trainer!" she called. "She does everything I say."

"That's because you and that red mare belong together," he called, over the muted sounds of the two horses' hooves. His dark eyes smiled at both of them. "Your spirits talk to each other. You even match in the color of your hair."

He flashed her that sensuous smile.

"Fire Flower, the mare is yours."

Jennie sat back and down so suddenly that the mare came to a stop.

A horse of her own! She had a horse of her own!

Tears stung in her throat, blurred her vision. She blinked. When she opened her eyes, the whole expanse of the prairie sprang at her, brilliant and bright, green and gray sprinkled with dew in the pink and yellow light of the climbing sun.

But it was Windrider's face, filled with happiness for her, that held her gaze still. *I know exactly how you feel*, his eyes were saying. *I am so glad to make you this gift.*

He was giving her a glimpse into his soul.

She answered him in that same, silent way. *Thank you.*

The look held for several long heartbeats.

Then Jennie gasped for her breath, and the spring scent of the plains filled her lungs.

"I'll ride her down to those trees," she said,

pointing into the distance, her words hoarse with joyful gratitude, knowing that Windrider could hear it. "Just the two of us, me and Spirit Talker. That's her name."

"*Mukwooru*," he translated, knowing that the way he spoke the name told the Fire Flower how welcome she was to the gift. "It is right. My medicine spirit says so. Go, now."

The Fire Flower flashed that bright smile at him, lifted one hand high in a jubilant wave, and whirled her mare's head to the west. They trotted, then lifted into a lope to float across the rolling grassland.

Windrider sat, unable to take his eyes from her, mesmerized by the sight of her lithe body fitted so surely to the mare. Her flaming head was thrown back in undisguised happiness, her long, slender neck drew a creamy line of pure delight against the blue sky.

As he watched, her confident seat wavered a bit and she lifted one arm, fast, to regain her balance. Perhaps he should go with her—she was still such a new rider.

But the Fire Flower sensed the spirit of this day like one of The People, and she deserved to ride alone with her mare. She would be all right—she rode like one of The People, too.

She had the natural seat of a born horse-woman, she knew instinctively what other whites took months to learn.

He watched until they disappeared over a rise, then turned the buckskin in the opposite direction.

If the Fire Flower *did* have any trouble, the mare would come back to the herd.

Chapter 9

Jennie started for the trees, but halfway there, decided they were too tame a destination; too close, too confining, too much down in a valley. Spirit Talker moved beneath her like one of the horses in her old dream. She would go farther, faster, higher.

She laid the rein against her neck, still not believing that she, Jennie O'Bannion, could control such a magnificent creature, but the mare responded like magic. She swung away from her course.

"To the sky, Spirit Talker," Jennie murmured, and bent forward to caress the silky neck.

At the same instant the mare lifted into a gallop, Jennie remembered that leaning forward meant go faster. She slipped a little, just at first, but she found her balance again and clasped her legs tighter. Her heart swelled with such happiness, she thought it would burst.

This mare was hers! This mare was hers!

The whole world passed by them in a blur; soon all of it would disappear. She and this mare would fly to the top of it and over the edge.

The wind tangled her hair and whipped it against her face; it urged them to race the heat from the sun. The earth beneath Spirit Talker's feet helped them, too, rolling and rising, lifting them ever upward.

A delicious thrill shivered through her. This mare belonged to her, Jennie O'Bannion. She owned a horse!

Then they hit the top, the very top of the highest hill in the plains. The green land fell down and away to lie quiet around the horse's hooves; the blue sky took them in and surrounded them. Jennie pulled on the reins and sat back; the mare dropped into a slow lope, trotted, then stopped.

She stood, blowing a bit, but with her head up, looking everywhere.

"I love you," Jennie said, the words bursting from her on her own short breath, short from excitement as much as from the long ride. "I love you, sweet Spirit Talker."

Neither of them could keep still. No other person, no other horse, was in sight in any direction.

The wildflowers, thick in some places, thinner in others, dancing among the grasses, lured them to come along. Their lavish colors, blue, orange, red, purple, yellow, white, shouted at them from the quiet greens of the grass, calling them down off the hillside to the west and into infinity.

Jennie had to search for the word Windrider had taught her the day before, and in a moment it came. *"Miaru!"* she cried. "Go!"

At the sound of the word and the touch of the rein, Spirit whirled on one hind foot and they dashed downhill, with the grasses cut by her feet smelling like wine and the crisp air going to Jennie's head like a swallow of whiskey.

The mare's sleek sides fitted against Jennie's legs warm as a caress; her ears flicked back and

forth to listen for her voice. They were friends.
Jennie had her horse *and* a friend.

The whole day, the whole brilliant, beautiful
day, the entire endless expanse of the wonderful
plains, intoxicated her. She was drunk with it,
drunk as a lord.

Jennie had no idea how long or how far she had
ridden, but the brightness of the wildflowers was
blurring before the wind-whipped tears in her
eyes, and the sun's heat was beating down on her
back, when Spirit Talker began to slow. The filly
fell into a steady trot heading up the side of a hill
crowned with a stand of small, gnarled trees.

When Jennie loosened her hold, the mare took
her head, dropped it, and began to graze, picking
among the clumps of grass that grew more
sparsely here. Deliciously tired from the ride, Jennie relaxed and stretched out along her warm,
sweaty back. She closed her eyes against the blue
infinity of the sky.

Its space wasn't what she wanted anymore, not
now. Now she wanted the solid earth and its stillness, the warm, good body of her own horse beneath her, and quiet time so that she could really
get to know her.

"Mukwooru, Spirit Talker, friend of mine," she
crooned, delighting in the thought that the mare
was hers.

And, equally so, in the knowledge that she
could ride. She truly could ride, after a lifetime of
waiting!

She delighted in letting her body move to the
rhythm of the mare's slow grazing, in rubbing her
shoulders with the soft heels of her moccasins and
her hot sides with the palms of her hands. The
mare snuffled and swished her tail.

The reins dropped from Jennie's fingers. She

caught one with her leg and held it against the mare's side, but she let the other one fall. Every inch of Spirit Talker's body said she wasn't going anywhere for a while.

Jennie opened her eyes. The sky still shone blue, but a paler shade now, bleached by the yellow of the sun. The few, straggling clouds, almost invisible, floated far away and got lost in its vastness.

She turned her head so her cheek lay against Spirit Talker. Her hair made a pillow for it, but the warm power of the mare soaked through it and into her in an instant. Her gaze wandered lazily.

This hill was steeper than the knoll they'd climbed earlier; the grass here grew thinner by far. That didn't discourage Spirit Talker, though; she went after it greedily, drifting toward a spot where it was thicker on the other side of some rocks.

The mare belonged to her! The delicious thought thrilled Jennie all over again. She struggled to sit up, forcing her tired muscles, protesting after such unaccustomed use, to move so that she could look at her miraculous possession.

Before Jennie had her balance, Spirit Talker stiffened and threw up her head. Jennie managed to gain her seat just as Spirit Talker took a step forward, ears pricked, eyes fixed on a spot at the top of the hill.

Jennie stopped breathing. Was someone there?

Fear washed through her and she laid her hands on the mare again, weaving one into her mane to help her hold on if need be. They were both tired, yes, but they could still run.

A high, screaming whinny came crashing through the air, through the trees, through the peace of the day. It rang once against the rocky hillside, then again. There was no sound of hooves, no sign of any horse but Spirit Talker.

The call came once more, echoing, like the cry of a ghost horse.

Spirit Talker leapt forward, jerking Jennie off to one side in the first instant. She arched her back, gave one high, bucking leap, and tore free. Jennie hit the ground before she had fully realized the mare was going to throw her.

Then Spirit Talker was gone, her beautiful body plunging past Jennie's dazed eyes like a race-horse. She was *gone*!

And fast. Faster than Jennie could believe, the mare galloped up onto the hard-packed earth beneath the trees, her hooves thumping against it, ringing now and then against a rock, dropped over the crest of the hill, and disappeared.

Jennie scrambled to her feet and chased after her, her calls rising to screams, her throat going raw with panic. She strained to get a glimpse of her, running faster than she had ever thought that she could, even if she weren't exhausted and stunned by her fall, but by the time she reached the top of the hill, there was no bright red dun horse in sight, nor any ghost horse, either.

She staggered into one of the twisted trees, grabbed its rough branch in both her trembling arms, and burst into tears. They blurred her sight, but they didn't distort it completely; she pressed her cheek against the trunk and kept on looking down into the rough valleys below while she cried.

Nothing. No Spirit Talker.

The wind was strong on the top of the hill; it picked up a handful of dirt and swirled it into her eyes. She bent her head, wiped them on her sleeve, then looked again.

Maybe there. Maybe that was a cloud of dust, just a puff of it, in that direction. To the right of those other trees straggling in ragged bunches along what must be a canyon at the foot of the hill.

She wiped her eyes again and started down the side of the hill opposite to the one she had climbed. She must find the mare. There was nothing else to do but find the mare.

Spirit Talker was the fulfillment of all her dreams, and the reality of her had to last longer than a few short minutes.

And Windrider!

He would be *so* disappointed in her skills with the horse! He would regret having given her to Jennie!

The irony of that worry struck her so hard that she bit her lip as she ran. Why was she concerned about what Windrider would think?

She ought to be worried that her means of escape from Windrider was gone. But not once in this whole, wonderful morning of freedom, not even after knowing she had a horse of her own and the skill to ride it, had the idea of running away from the Comanches entered her head.

The thought chilled her. She must be losing her mind.

But she couldn't think about that now. She'd *never* be able to escape if she didn't get Spirit Talker back, for Windrider certainly would never trust her with a second horse.

Jennie ran until she couldn't. Her lungs tightened until she couldn't draw a deep breath. Her legs burned until she couldn't move them and sudden sharp pains stabbed her in the side. Finally she staggered to a stop.

But her eyes kept on moving, scanning the plains in every direction. There was not a horse in sight.

Jennie stared until her eyes blurred and teared, while the pulse in her temple slowed back to its normal pace and the stitch of pain faded from her side. She picked up her feet and started walking again.

But on the second step, her foot came down on a stone and she slipped, twisting hard, bringing her ankle bone all the way to the ground. She cried out and dropped down into a helpless heap.

Jennie sat with her knees drawn up, holding her hurt ankle with both hands, growing thirstier and thirstier. Her head felt light enough to float off her body, but she didn't want food. *Water.*

Soon she must have water.

Some of the pain left her ankle. Exhaustion dragged her shoulders down. She dropped her head onto her knees and let it take her.

When she woke, her mouth and throat felt filled with cotton. The sun was marching steadily down toward the horizon, although it was a long time yet until dark.

There was still light enough to find water—if she only knew where to look!

She stood up, holding her arms out to balance her, dreading to put weight on her throbbing ankle. Gradually she did so. It was painful, but not unbearably so. She looked off to the east, in the direction of the Comanche camp, now out of her sight, hours of long riding away. If only she had been with them long enough to learn how to find water. If only she could get back to them now!

If only Windrider would come this way and find her! Had he gone back to camp from his ride?

Nothing moved, not in any direction she looked.

Jennie's heart began to pound out of her chest. The only landmark she remembered was the faint knot of trees that huddled at the top of the hill quite a ways behind her. That was the place where she had lost Spirit Talker.

She turned around and took a faltering step toward it. Maybe Spirit Talker would come back to her there. Perhaps she had run for a while with the mysterious horse that had lured her away, then returned to the small grove of trees to wait for Jennie.

Surely the horse knew that Jennie was looking for her. Hadn't Windrider said that their spirits talked to each other?

Tears sprang to her eyes and she blinked them back, wondering as she hobbled on how tears could come out of a body so parched and dry. If she didn't find the mare before dark, she would start walking back to the village as soon as the sun came up tomorrow. She would find Windrider, and he would find Spirit Talker for her. He would. Hadn't he said she was one of the best horses in his herd?

But before then, somehow, she had to have water.

Her ankle hurt only enough to slow her down, not nearly enough to stop her, and she trudged steadily toward the trees on the hilltop. She had no other destination. None that she could hope to reach before dark.

She racked her mind to remember the way she had come. Had there been any sign of water anywhere?

She forced one foot to step in front of the other for what seemed an age, fighting her tired muscles that steadily cried out for her to stop. She kept going until her ankle was hurting too much to bear her weight and she was staggering from the dizziness caused by her thirst.

Then a blur of movement in the brush up ahead caught her eye, and her heart stopped. Spirit Talker? Could it be?

She shaded her eyes with her hand and squinted, almost falling forward as she tried to walk faster.

No. It was several animals, not horses. Deer?

Yes. A dozen or so of the fleet creatures darted out of the trees growing at the foot of the hill where she had lost her mare. Jennie watched them vanish as quickly as her mare had done. She kept walking, kept churning up the dust, kept trying to think. Something about them was significant.

She forced her tired brain to stop its screaming for her to sit down long enough to *think*.

At the fort, when the families had gathered to have meat parceled out to them, hadn't the men who brought in the game talked about wild animals going to water holes? They said they went at dawn and at dusk. Yes. Dawn and dusk.

Water holes. There might be water there, in that canyon, where the deer had just come out! She set her jaw against the pain and began to run.

Two rabbits scattered out of the close-growing trees as she came crashing into them. She licked her dry lips and drove on through the brush, pushing it away from her with both arms until she could see the small pool of clear water, part of a shallow, rocky creek.

Jennie ran to it, fell flat on her belly, and drank.

She turned her face sideways, pressed her cheek to the warm rocks, and let the cool water settle in her suddenly churning stomach. Then she turned back and drank some more of it. It filled her emptiness, healed her dry lips, washed the dryness from her mouth and her bones. She lay there beside it, occasionally drinking more, until dusk.

Then she sat up and looked around her, peering through the straggling branches at the last streaks of purple and red in the darkening sky. She couldn't stay here any longer—no telling what creatures might come to share the water.

Besides, if Spirit Talker did come back for her, she would come to the top of this hill where she had left her. Jennie took another long drink, wishing that she had something to carry water in, and made her tired body get up and move.

She wouldn't be far from the water, she comforted herself, and in the daylight tomorrow she'd find *something* to carry it in. She climbed fast, to try to beat the darkness, her feet and hands scrabbling among the rocks and into the dirt to pull her upward, up the west side to the top of the hill.

A long, unearthly howl pierced the night. Jennie stopped in her tracks, just inside the protection of the small, scrawny trees. The sound had come from in front of her.

A wolf? A panther, maybe? Bears didn't howl, did they?

A bear had been seen near the fort not long before the O'Bannions' arrival.

An answering, ululating wail rose into the air, from behind Jennie this time.

The darkness thickened, closed around her like a shroud.

She would die out here alone, she thought, torn

to pieces by wild animals. After all she'd been through: the cholera, the sorrow, the horrible overland journey, the nightmare of Trammel, the unspeakable shock of being taken captive, the loss of her parents. Now she would die.

A quick, rustling noise traveled over the hard-packed earth to her left, coming straight at her.

She let out a whimper and ran for the tree that she'd clung to when she cried for Spirit Talker. Her ankle pained her wildly now. Sweat popped out on her face.

She gritted her teeth, grabbed the tree, and hid behind it, her arms trembling with exhaustion, too weak to try to climb it. She wished with all her heart that they had never left Ireland.

She wished the Comanches had never attacked the fort.

She wished Windrider were here.

A new baying cry tore through the night; before it was over, a closer scratching, scrambling sound alarmed her. Frantically she clasped the trunk of the tree with both exhausted arms as if she were about to blow away in a wind.

If only she could build a fire! Didn't fires keep wild animals away? But she had no way to start one and no fuel to keep it going.

She had no weapon, either, not even the knife that Comanche women carried for skinning small game.

The stones. Her only defense on this godforsaken knoll of land, alone in the dark, was rocks. She peered through the night, looking to see where the larger ones lay, judging how far she must go from her tree refuge to get them.

One thing to be thankful for was the rising moon. At least this wouldn't be a completely dark night.

Fighting the frantic fear that beat in her veins, threatening always to turn into panic, Jennie pried her fingers loose from the rough bark and darted to the stones she could see, holding her breath when she felt into the shadows near them for more. She brought them back and stacked them in a pile.

By the time she had finished, the moonlight had grown bright. It showed she had gathered them all.

And a pitiful pile it was. No more than seven stones, none bigger than her clenched fist.

She collapsed beside them, her back against the tree's trunk, one last rock in her hand. If she survived until morning, she would find the Comanche camp again. She would find something to carry water in. She would find Spirit Talker.

If she could survive this night, she could do anything.

The yelping howls of the coyotes—or were they wolves?—gradually died away. The wind rose a little and sighed through the branches above her head. It moved them back and forth in a peaceful rhythm.

Her body greedily began to relax and rest. Her eyelids burned and ached to close.

She let them.

A chilling cry pierced the darkness.

Her muscles froze to her bones, then melted away in an inextinguishable fire of fear. The moonlight played along the thin, twisty branches, dancing from one leaf to another in the faint breeze. Lower down, in the deep shadow at the edge of the grass, something glinted in the dark. Something moved.

Her heart leapt out of her body. She threw the stone.

It struck, then the world went silent. Not even the wind stirred.

Her empty hand stayed in the air, uselessly poised to throw again. Would it attack her in revenge, whatever it was? Would she die now, alone, in a place that had no name?

The silence and the stillness stretched on. Nothing moved, not the leaves, not the air, not her breath.

She had to do something. If she didn't, this fear would consume her. She took a stone in each hand and struggled to her feet, lurching into her limping run, setting her jaw against the stabbing pain.

Then came a quick, flashing feeling that she'd chosen the wrong direction. Before she could turn, before she could think, something, *someone*, grabbed her from behind and pinned her arms to her sides.

A brand-new panic, overwhelming in its intensity, burst into her blood, drawing strength she didn't know she had from every screaming nerve in her body. She shrieked like a banshee, kicking backward with the foot that wasn't hurt, striking at her captor with the rocks although she could barely move her hands.

"The I-rish Woman Warrior," a low voice growled in her ear. "Trying to kill her enemies with pebbles."

Windrider.

Sweet relief poured through her, washing away her fear, making her dizzy as the thirst had done, rising like a sudden fever all through her veins. She sagged backward into him; her cheek landed against the smooth skin inside his upper arm.

It felt like satin underlaid with ropes of iron.

It felt safe.

She dragged in a long, shaky breath of the masculine, musky scent that was only his.

He crossed his arms over her and held her back tight against him.

"Fire Flower," he said. His voice vibrated with relief.

Her fingers went limp, her weapon-rocks dropped at her feet.

"Windrider! Thank God in Heaven!"

Her trembling voice chimed in his ears like the song of a bird. She twisted to face him, heedlessly rubbing her breasts against his chest like a seductive woman, then burrowing deep into the safety of his embrace like a terrified child, throwing her arms around his neck to press herself closer and closer.

Her hair brushed his face, a sweet-smelling cloud, then it was her mouth. Her mouth on his.

He braced his legs and gathered her to him, wanting her honey, wanting to taste her and feel her and explore all of her mouth with his tongue.

She whimpered a little in the back of her throat. He crushed her closer, harder, but she felt so small, so easily broken, that he loosened his hold. His arms stayed around her, though, twining, and his legs slid farther apart so he could bring her entirely into the shelter of his body.

So he could feel the soft flatness of her belly against the hard shaft of his manhood as he had longed to do again since the time he'd kissed her.

That part of him, the man-part, reached for her as his arms had done. She made the juices spring up and flow from the center of him like warmth beaming out from the Sun Father's heart.

The hot, smooth haven of his lips made Jennie know that she was found, but in the next instant the tip of his tongue touched hers, and again, she was lost.

She fell into the abyss of delight, hurtling through the night as if she'd slipped from the face of a cliff. The power of his brawny chest had pushed her over it.

Yet his wide shoulders were all that kept her from crashing into pieces at the bottom. His muscles roping beneath her arms, with the cool of the night air sheening the warmth of his skin, were what held her up. He was what she should cling to. He was all she had, all she needed.

He gave her moisture and warmth, water and fire.

The kiss blazed, melted them together. He thrust his hand into her hair, cradled her head in its huge strength, and her mouth fell completely open to his.

She dissolved into the profligate abandon he created in her, new wanton feelings that opened into infinity and let her fall through dark, sparkling space. She tightened her arms around the muscular column of his neck and held on to it for her life.

An incoherent sound of pleasure burst from somewhere deep within her. His tongue pushed deeper into her mouth, twining with hers, thrilling it beyond thought, then pulling away. His lips lifted—almost, not quite, letting hers go—and then slanted across them again, hard, in a way so ravenous, yet so fulfilling, that it made her mind disappear.

His kiss was all she knew, all she wanted to know.

But he broke it at last.

He still held her, though. His eyes burned down into hers through the pale moonlight.

Her head, cupped in his hand, felt too dizzy to move.

She gasped for a breath, helpless as a little girl overcome with wonder.

So *this* was what it meant to be a woman!

A woman held, kissed by a man. It wasn't always an awful, repulsive thing as it had been with Trammel; it could be enjoyable, exciting, enticing.

It could be marvelous—this free-floating fancy, this deep-swirling delight, this *closeness* with a man!

"How can this be?" she whispered, completely astonished. "Kissing . . . I didn't know that a kiss could be . . . such a pleasure."

"Ah," he said, and gave her that knowing grin that held all the mischief in the world, "it depends on who it is that you will kiss."

She hardly heard him. She lifted her hand and touched his curving lips. They were so warm and sensual that they fascinated her fingertips. She traced the wide line of his mouth.

"Me," he said, "I like to kiss my little runaway."

It took an instant for the word to sink in.

Runaway?

Then, in one great rush, it exploded in her head.

She was his captive!

Still. Even though he had just set all her senses free.

And that was exactly the peril. Trammel had gotten power over her through financial support and his physical strength.

But Windrider could own her for sure and forever because he had the power to make her own body betray her.

He could make it cry out for him, no matter

what the cost to her freedom. As it was doing at this very instant.

That thought sent a wild fear zigzagging through her, a terror stronger than that of dying of thirst or being eaten by wild animals or being burned at the stake by Comanches challenged by captives who tried to run away.

And with the terror came hot anger at herself.

She pushed at him, both hands against his chest, frantic to get away from the continuous, passionate thrill of his touch. Somehow, crazily enough, it was still firing her senses in spite of all the opposing emotions rushing through her.

She had started it! Why had she ever kissed him like that?

"I told you I only wanted to ride alone for a while! Why did you think I was running away?"

Another feeling, a sharp disappointment, stabbed her, too, cutting through her fear.

"Don't you know me any better than that?" she cried, the words slipping out between her trembling lips, bruised by his kiss. "After we said more with our eyes than with words when you gave Spirit Talker to me?"

She hit at his chest with both fists, but she might as well have been pounding at the rock face of a mountain.

He kept his hands locked behind her, hot and hard against the small of her back.

"*I* did not think so," he said, still smiling. "But when I came back to the camp after my own long ride on the buckskin, most of the village, except for your friend, Hukiyani, told me you must have run away."

She arched her spine to push against his hands, but that did her no good. It only brought the tips of her breasts brushing against his bare chest.

Jennie retreated, but the brief touch had already opened a brand-new, deeply shocking desire inside her, a yawning, open need that threatened to swallow the chaos of her thoughts.

It made her long for his mouth again. Made her *desperate* for his kiss.

"Turn me *loose!*" she cried. "Get your hands off me!"

Her traitorous body screamed just as loudly for him to hold her closer.

His fingers burned their shape into her as if the soft deerskin dress were not even there.

"Breaks Something, especially, believes that you have repaid my gift of a fine horse by taking it and running away."

Jennie threw back her head and glared up at him.

His eyes glinted into hers from the shadows. The moonlight slashed across the lower part of his face, making his white teeth shine between his parted lips, showing her that his smile had turned to a grin of pure bedevilment.

He was enjoying this; he loved watching her get angrier and angrier, like a small boy teasing his sister, she thought suddenly. That realization sent a mixture of relief and frustration surging through her.

He *didn't* believe that she ran away. He wasn't angry or planning to punish her. He was teasing her as one of her brothers would have done.

Still, it made her furious.

His wolfish grin broadened.

"Breaks Something says she saw you steal a water bag and some provisions," he said.

"Breaks Something lies!" she shouted, even while she tried to stop herself, even while she knew that was exactly the reaction he expected and wanted. "You know that! She lies all the time and she hates me! You know that, too!"

He shook his head in mock disbelief, still grinning.

He tightened his fingers on her waist, loosened them, and slid his hands down to rest on her hipbones. She was small, her frame delicate as a fawn's. He could crush her bones with one squeeze.

But not her spirit.

Her green eyes flashed lightning that told him that.

He could never crush her spirit, and neither could anyone else. She was magnificent, this green-eyed, fire-haired woman!

"I may be white, Windrider," she said, fiercely, "but I am becoming one of The People. You teach me to ride, Hukiyani teaches me much. I will learn to survive like a Comanche."

His heart jumped, leapt into his throat like a bird rising to fly.

She wanted to become one of The People! She planned to become Comanche!

She drew herself to her small height proudly, full of dignity, even though she stood within the cage of his hands.

"But I don't know enough yet," she said. "I must learn more before I can hope to find water, find the way, and reach Texas alone. Breaks Something underestimates me if she thinks I don't know that. I would *never* be so foolish as to run away now!"

Those words shot the bird of his heart. It fell to the ground.

Even his relief at finding her safe couldn't revive it. The homesickness was working in her. She would go back to her people someday.

Chapter 10

~~~~~~~ᗧᗤ~~~~~~~

He let his arms fall away from her.

A terrible sense of loss shook Jennie. When the night breeze hit her body, every place that Windrider's warm touch had just been, she felt hollow inside, like an empty keg bobbing on the cold ocean. Every hurt, every bruise on her body, leapt to aching life; knives of pain stabbed into her sprained ankle. She didn't have the strength to stand up anymore.

She jerked away from him and, tilting precariously to favor her injury, started back to her tree, stepping with a piteous, hobbling limp.

With a rough sound of disgust, he stepped to her and took her by the arms.

"Rest your leg," he growled, in a voice so harsh, she hardly knew it as his. "I'll carry you."

"You will *not!*"

She struggled so sharply to keep her feet on the ground that he let her, but still he steadied her, leading her back to the small, gnarled post oak that now, strangely, felt like home to her.

She tried to hold her body away from him, tried to make it as wooden as that tree beneath his touch.

"*Sutenapu!*" he muttered. "Stubborn person! Sit! I'll bring you water and food."

"*Sutenapu,* yourself!" she cried. "I can take care of myself!"

He snorted at that idea and left her.

She had to believe that, she thought, as she mulishly stayed on her feet by holding on to a branch of the tree with both hands. She had to believe that. All she needed was a few more weeks of watching and learning, then she'd be ready to get on her horse and ride for Texas.

If she had a horse.

The tearing despair of having Spirit Talker run right through her hands ripped her apart again. Oh, dear Lord! She had to persuade him to find the filly for her. *That* was all she had to do.

That and to remember never to kiss him again.

When he had completely disappeared into the darkness that lay at the bottom of the hill, she turned loose of the branch and lowered herself painfully to sit on the ground at the base of the trunk. She had to get a grip on her tongue, too, she thought. If she wanted him to find her horse, she'd better stop threatening to run away.

He came back almost immediately, emerging silently from the dark into the mottled moonlight at the top of the hill, leading Echo and another horse. Without a word, he tied them to trees.

When he had taken two bundles from their packs and walked over to her, he spoke in that same rough voice.

"So you lost the red filly."

Jennie reached with both hands for the water pouch.

"She left me. A ghost horse called—I couldn't see it *anywhere*—and she ran right out of my hands."

She drank, directly from the pouch, which he opened for her.

"You shouldn't have tried to follow her," he said harshly, dropping down to sit cross-legged beside her to open a packet of food. "I have hundreds of horses."

She flung up her head to stare at him as if he had slapped her. She thrust the pouch back at him with shaking hands.

"Well, *I* only have one! And even if you gave me another, it wouldn't be the same. *You* know that—you said you put me on Spirit Talker because our spirits could talk to each other!"

"No matter. No horse is worth your life!" he growled. "I could've been a panther sneaking up on you, or a Lipan Apache or even an Osage, far from home."

"I'm not afraid of panthers or Lipan Apaches or Osages, either," she shouted, her temper flaring, her heart dropping even deeper into disappointment at his change of attitude about Spirit Talker. "And that reminds me—why did you sneak up on me like that? That was not necessary and it was not fair!"

"To teach you this very thing, that you could be dead right now. Next time you lose your horse, walk toward camp, not away."

"There won't be a next time. I'll catch her and teach her never to go away from me again!"

"Ah!" he said, sarcastically, "Horse-Trainer Woman."

She put her fists on her hips and leaned toward him.

"I'm *not* walking away from my horse!"

"And I'm *not* going chasing her and you any farther! It's almost time to move camp again. I won't leave Ten Bears alone to lead the band."

They glared at each other.

"Then give me the supplies you have here and I'll go after her alone! I know where there's water, and if I have something to carry it in, I can go a long ways."

He made a rude sound of contempt.

"You wouldn't last one sun," he said, with biting sureness. "You wouldn't even catch sight of that mare."

"I would so! Try me and see!"

His eyes glittered angrily into hers from the shadows.

Finally they spoke at the same time.

"*Sutenapu!*"

The jointly spoken epithet surprised them both so much that they burst into laughter. When it had died away, she reached for the water pouch again, and he gave it. When she had drunk, he took out the pemmican and offered it.

"Windrider," she begged as she took a slice, "please help me find Spirit Talker. She's my horse, the only one I want."

The sweet pleading in her voice made their gazes lock again.

Now he couldn't look anywhere but at her. Her enormous eyes shone with tears; more of them trembled on her lashes in the moonlight.

He needed to wipe them away. He needed to fold her into his arms and comfort her.

He needed to kiss that tender mouth again.

His mind reached for the barriers that She Blushes had caused him to build, but he couldn't find them. He searched for the hurt, for the fury, that the Fire Flower had created in him only moments past. He couldn't find them, either.

He drew in a deep breath, and surprising himself as much as he did her, he said, "At first light.

But we cannot spend many suns away from the band.''

He made a motion that meant she should eat. She took a bite, then shook her head.

"Let's go as soon as we rest a minute," she said, stubbornly. "Please? Maybe at night we can see the ghost horse."

He made an impatient sound.

"Your ghost horse is a wild stallion who has stolen many mares," he said. "He will let us see him day *or* night—it's catching him that will be the challenge. Many good horsemen have tried and failed."

The Fire Flower leaned forward. She brushed back the hair from her face, the pemmican fallen into her lap, forgotten. The moonlight washed her pale features, gleamed deep in the silvery green of her eyes. The low ache began again in his loins.

"Maybe we won't have to catch *him*," she said, speaking as quietly as if the horse could hear her. "Only the Spirit Talker. If we see them and I call to her, my spirit will be calling to hers."

"But he will be calling her, too, and the call of a stallion to a mare is the strongest of all."

Those words pounded in his ears like the beating of a war drum while he persuaded her that the search would go much faster in the Sun Father's light, while he told her of the different methods of catching wild horses, while he warned her that two people only, and one of them inexperienced with horses, wild or not, most likely could not rob the wily stallion of his newest prize.

Those words roared in his head like the thundering of a herd of buffalo when he spread out the sleeping robes he always carried on the trail and lay down on them.

But when the Fire Flower fell suddenly asleep,

exhausted, and he rose on his elbow to look at her, lying so still in the blankets he'd brought to keep her from the night's chill, those words changed to the bright, floating notes of a cottonwood flute.

The call of the stallion to the mare was the strongest of all.

His heart came back to life again, fluttered its wings, and flew great, leaping circles around in his breast.

The Fire Flower would come if he called. If he taught her the pleasures of his bed and his body, she would stay with the *Nermernuh* when he gave her the choice of going back to her people.

Look at the great value she had placed on the gift that he gave her.

Look at the way she had kissed him!

A shrill, sharp sound tore Jennie from sleep. She awoke completely in that instant.

The cry came again. High and strident, it reached out of the night to jerk her and Windrider out of their blankets, to set them scrambling to their feet.

"There's your ghost horse," he said.

Echo and the spare mount began to answer, their voices desperate, full of longing to be as free as their wild brother.

Jennie stood beside Windrider, shivering in the sudden chill of the after-midnight wind, staring with him out across the pale prairie. She had no idea of the direction of the far-resounding call; it bounced off the rocks and the hills, floated in the air with the moon's beams. It seemed to come from everywhere at once.

She narrowed her eyes, still accustomed to the

dark of sleep, and peered into the flood of bright moonlight.

"Is Spirit Talker with him?"

"*Ke-tsuwihnu*, no doubt. She's new. He probably hasn't yet put her into his herd."

Echo whinnied again.

Windrider said, "Good that our mounts are not mares—they would already be gone."

Jennie parted her lips to answer, but then she saw the horses. Every word left her tongue, every thought left her brain.

They floated along the high ridge, apparently without touching their feet to the ground, their stiffened tails rippling like banners against the sky. Their long manes whipped in the wind. The wild stallion, dazzling white as a winter frost, flew along the crest of the rise, keeping just ahead of the bright, dancing flame that was Spirit Talker.

Halfway across the hill, the stallion glided to a stop, Spirit Talker moving like a shadow at his side. Both of them turned to look across the valley at Windrider and Jennie.

The wild horse and the tame one stood still as sculptures, one made of ice, the other of fire. Bathed in the radiance of the bright, late night moonlight, they stopped Jennie's breath in her throat.

The white stallion threw up his head and whinnied once, his tone high and triumphant. His jubilance echoed loud and long across the wide plains before it finally died away. He stood then, looking slowly around, reigning over all that had heard him, holding the night in the thrall of his silence.

He sent out his call once more, and Jennie felt its power. The challenge of it sounded across the whole world this time—wild enough, magic enough, to reach both of the oceans and Ireland itself. When his echoes had faded, he wheeled and was flying again, racing along the rim of the earth, Spirit Talker staying close by his side.

They disappeared downhill, plunged into the darkness, and were gone.

Jennie couldn't move, couldn't look away from the place where such beauty had been, although she knew they wouldn't return.

Finally she and Windrider turned to look at each other. Neither one of them could speak.

An uncontrollable fit of shivering took hold of her. Windrider put his arm around her and walked her back to the bed robes, both of them stumbling a little, even in the bright moonlight, because the horses still filled their eyes.

They sat down cross-legged, facing each other, and Windrider reached with both hands to pull the striped trade blanket up around Jennie's shoulders. She leaned back a little so that his fingers wouldn't brush her skin, but she could feel them anyway, through the cloth, throbbing with a powerful purpose, pulsating with desire.

Yet not necessarily for her. His relentless gaze pierced the far distance.

Then it swung back to her.

"So," he said, "how can we reclaim your mare?"

His eyes gleamed; they shone with the fierceness of the stallion's challenge.

"I don't know," she said fervently, leaning forward so fast that the covering slipped off her trembling arms. She crossed them over her chest and jerked it back up, fast, before he could place it around her again. "But I know we'll do it."

He threw back his head and shouted with laughter.

"Horse-Catcher Woman!" he said, and shook both fists in the air in that powerful gesture she loved. The magnificent muscles that crossed his chest rippled in the moonlight. The tips of her breasts hardened, tingled with the desire to touch him again, and to have him touch her.

"And we'll catch the Wild White One, too!"

She stared at him, surprised by that, steeling her heart against a hard twinge of regret. It would be terrible to take the magnificent stallion from the wild. Yet . . .

"He would be marvelous to ride."

She barely breathed the words, partly because the idea was too new and bold to grasp, partly because the touch of her dress on her breasts as she looked at Windrider had become torture. But she couldn't ever let him hold her again.

Never. It gave him too much power.

She would have to learn to live with this long-ing. She would have to put her mind solely on this horse hunt.

"The stallion has told us he cannot be caught," Windrider said, "and that he will not give up the mare. Did you not hear him?"

"He does not know *us*," she said intensely, leaning even closer to him, her cheeks blushing with passion to the color of the catclaw tree's flower.

He looked at her, wished he could devour her with his eyes, with his hands, with his mouth. She was wonderful, this stubborn, determined, small person! So open to the spirits of the horses and the earth itself. If only she would be open to him!

She caused such happiness to rise in him that his fun-loving side took him. He grinned at her.

"You think that when he knows us, he will sit

and smoke with us and talk to us? We will bargain and he will finally trade back what he has taken?''

She laughed. ''Yes!'' she cried. ''For we are two who can talk to horses!''

That childish confidence made his smile widen. ''Ah!'' he said. ''The Fire Flower, The I-rish Woman Warrior. The Horse-Catcher Woman. Have you a plan to introduce us to the Wild White One?''

''Windrider, War Chief of The People, Great Horseman,'' she answered, mocking his singsong tone, flashing him a new, mischievous grin that twisted his heart. ''Hukiyani says you are a *great* horseman. *You* will introduce me to the wild stallion.''

I will introduce you to loving a man.

He reached for her then, took her face in his hands.

Her skin felt smooth as a foal's muzzle to the tips of his fingers; her fragrant hair floated like thistledown on the backs of his hands. But he lost both sensations in the heat of her mouth.

Lips slightly parted, it met his halfway.

And set him on fire.

Flames leapt in his loins, lit like sparks in the grass blown on the wind. He forgot about the stallion, forgot about catching him. Because she lifted her hand and touched him on the neck.

Because she came to him sweet as Cross Timbers honey, pliant as a willow's wand. She brushed the tip of her tongue to his.

He took it, he entwined it with his, he drew her lips beneath his slowly, to savor the seduction. He lost himself in the taste of her.

He let his hands slip from her hair, over the wings of her shoulders and down onto her back, pushing the blanket down and away. The supple elk-hide of her dress couldn't keep the heat of her skin away from his palms—he slid them around beneath her arms and cupped both her breasts.

She broke away.

"Don't, please *don't*," she begged, in a tone so husky with desire that he lifted one hand to bring her back to him.

She evaded him.

"No!" she cried. "Don't, Windrider!"

Then he saw the fear in her eyes.

It doused the fire in him, quick as a sudden rain.

She Blushes used to look at him that way.

Afraid, she was always afraid.

And now he saw that same fear glistening in the Fire Flower's eyes.

She wasn't afraid of panthers of Lipan Apaches or Osage, but she was afraid of him. No, she was afraid of lying with him.

A hard determination formed within him, created a rigid cocoon around his thoughts of seducing her into choosing to become *Nermernuh*. He would erase that terror, he swore by the Sun Father. He would make this woman look at him with those enormous green eyes overflowing not with cold fear, but with hot desire, as She Blushes had done.

But this time it would all end differently.

The Fire Flower would come into his arms and let him make love to her all night long. And she would make love to him.

She would choose him, choose to stay with him.

This time it would all end differently.

And this hunt for the horses would give him the time alone with her to teach her to want him.

He forced his mouth out of the set lines of angry disappointment and smiled at her.

Then the smile became truly tender. Her face had gone white as the moonlight. She snatched up the blanket and wrapped it around her, up to her neck, her arms crossed to protect her beautiful breasts.

He was such a fool! He should go slowly with her. She was very young. Probably she had never known a man before.

"Do not be afraid," he said, reaching, very gently, to tuck a tendril of her curling hair behind her ear. "You said you never knew kissing could be such a pleasure? My hands on your body, my man-part inside you, will pleasure you, too, when you let go of your fear."

The deep, rich tones of his voice hung between them on the pale night air.

Jennie clamped her trembling lips against the cry that threatened to spring from them.

Your hands on my body have already pleasured me! I have no fear! I want to feel them again!

But much as she wanted it, she would not let the words pass. She would not let him have this double power over her that would take away what little freedom of mind she had.

They looked at each other.

The moonlight traced the chiseled features of his face—strong, slightly hooked nose that could only be called aristocratic, high cheekbones, arched brow bones, hard jaw—but it left his eyes in shadow. Oh, how she longed to see them burning into hers again!

Panic pulsed in her throat, panic that she would lean toward him, into his arms again.

She had to think. She had to say something.

But the only thing that came to her tongue was, *I'm not afraid. Show me those other pleasures. Now.*

He waited, watching her as if he knew that was what she'd say. But much as she wanted to, she didn't speak.

She had longed all her life for her freedom, and if she ever had him once, the bondage of wanting him always might be too strong for her ever to break.

Finally, restlessly, he moved, rolled the soles of his feet flat against the ground, and got up.

"I will make medicine," he said. "To bring the horses to us."

Jennie scrambled to her feet, too, unwilling to be away from him, unwilling to be left out of any part of their task. Windrider indicated with a sharp gesture of his hand that she should stay.

Reluctantly she obeyed.

"I want to help, too," she called as he strode toward the supplies he had unloaded and piled neatly beneath the tree. "I want to be your partner in this hunt!"

"You will be," Windrider called back.

And you will be my partner in my bed, he thought as he walked away from her.

Soon he returned, carrying his rope and the beaded skin bag in which he kept his pipe and tobacco.

"This medicine is for before a raid," he said. "But it will work for this horse hunt."

He stood in front of her, quite near her as he formed a loop in the rope, lifted it, and whirled it over his head. The massive muscles in his arms and shoulders rippled, catching the gleam of the moonlight. They seemed to dance, moving effortlessly as the wind, but the sound the rope made as it cut through the air told the power they wielded. Jennie caught the unique scent of his skin and his hair, his dried sweat and the horses, his tobacco and his cedary breath.

Slowly, settling with the gradual grace of a floating feather, the rope came closer and closer to earth, touching it at last. It dropped and lay against the ground in a large circle that enclosed both Jennie and Windrider.

"Sit," he said, and she did so, facing him, both sitting with their legs crossed as they had done before.

He opened the beaded bag.

They sat in silence while Windrider took out his pipe and tobacco, filled the bowl, and lit it. The breeze picked up and played in Jennie's hair. From somewhere not too far away came the same wild, wolfish cry that had frightened her so before.

She shivered, but not from fear this time. She lifted her face to the night wind and watched Windrider, who sat very still. Windrider had come out to find her. Now she wasn't afraid of anything.

She spoke, hardly knowing what she said, reaching for words to put up as a wall between this moment and the one in which he had kissed her. The one in which he had cradled her breasts with hands so hard and sure that they had seemed to be coming home.

"We should name him," she blurted. "The Wild White One."

Windrider nodded, and pulled on his pipe. He sat as still as if she had just said her part in a foreordained ritual.

"Do it," he said.

"But . . . I don't have the language! It must be

a beautiful word, one as beautiful as he is, in the
tongue of The People!''

''Does it matter what the word *means*?'' Windrider asked dryly, taking another pull on his pipe.

She laughed. ''Of course!'' she said, looking
around her, searching. ''Oh, perhaps it could be
the word for moonlight. He looked as if he were
made out of moonlight!''

''Sister Moon, Mother Moon, she is woman,''
he said. ''The White One is a great warrior.''

''Women can be warriors, too!''

She sounded so fierce, he had to smile. ''You
are,'' he agreed. ''I-rish Woman Warrior.''

The Fire Flower smiled back, and Windrider
clenched his fists to keep his hands on his pipe
and away from her.

''How about Robe-on-His-Back?'' he asked.
''Perhaps he wears the moonlight as a coat.''

She frowned a bit. ''Is it a beautiful word?''

''*Kwahira*,'' he said.

''It is beautiful. *Kwahira*.'' She tried the word
on her tongue.

Windrider looked at her, a long, straight glance
that touched something deep in the core of her,
pulled her to attention, attached her to him from
her soul to his.

She held the gaze steady as he took a long draw
on the pipe, until he turned away to look up at
the sky. He blew smoke at the moon.

He spoke in a reverent, reverberating tone, in
the language of The People. Then he fell silent for
a long time. He blew the smoke upward again.

''Windrider . . .''

Jennie barely breathed his name, reluctant to
break the spell, but yearning, needing to be included.

He understood.

"Mother Moon," he said, "if it be your will, let this rope take many horses. Let this rope take the wild white stallion. Let this rope take Kwahira."

Jennie shook back her hair, looked up at the moon, took a long, shaky breath, and said, "Mother Moon, let this rope take Spirit Talker."

Once more Windrider sent smoke wafting toward the silent, shining moon. He repeated both pleas in both tongues.

Then he stood up, coiled the rope into his hand, and put his pipe to one side to burn itself out.

"Tomorrow at sunset," he said. "We will have our horses."

The next day at sunset Jennie lay along the neck of the spare horse, who was called *Esatai*, Little Wolf. Through the scraggly stand of cottonwood trees that hid them, she peered at the pool of water that she had drunk from the day before. Esatai's body heat soaked through her dress and made her feel she had a fever; his mane hairs stuck and scratched her skin on the outside while her nerves thrummed and prickled on the inside.

If she did everything right, she would soon have her horse again! And Windrider would have the white stallion.

She took a deep breath of the dusky evening air.

It would be a sin to take the stallion, he was so free!

Yet it was clear that the sight of him had set a fire of determination blazing in Windrider, it had put a wanting in his heart to lay his hands on the Wild White One like the yearning she had in her own for the touch of Windrider's hand. And his mouth.

The thought made her suddenly restless.

Heedless of the warning he'd drilled into her to be perfectly still and quiet, she sat up and rubbed at her swollen ankle. She had to remember why she was here, she lectured herself. It was to get back her horse so she didn't have to walk anymore, so she could ride her own horse and someday escape.

But at this moment, all she could imagine was running to, not away from, Windrider, begging to feel his hands cradling her breasts.

She made a little sound of disgust, a reprimand to herself, but Esatai thought it was for him. He moved forward a step, closer to the pool, which Windrider had told her was fed by the only underground spring in a wide stretch of dry country.

"Whoa!" she whispered, wracking her brain for the Comanche word, working with her hands and her legs and her seat to keep him from going any farther.

Surely the wild horse and Spirit Talker would come to drink soon. Windrider had sworn that they would. They didn't want to disturb the horses while they were drinking, he had said—they wanted their bellies completely full so that their legs would be slow when they commenced to run.

Just the memory of his voice telling her all that made her shiver.

With the excitement of such an adventure and of getting her horse back, she told herself. Not because Windrider was her partner in the endeavor.

To wrench her mind away from the memories of his mouth on hers, she tried to remember every word of the orders he'd given her.

Ride out of the ambush calling to Spirit Talker, he had told her, keep her and Kwahira looking at Jennie during that first, flying moment before the wild one would know that Echo was carrying Windrider toward him from the opposite direction. Ride straight at the stallion to turn him closer to the rope if need be. Stay as close—

The sudden sound of pounding hooves froze the instructions in her brain and her hands in Little Wolf's mane. Without warning, a terrible need to draw in a deep breath seized her throat and her chest, but she held the one she had instead, scared that any sound from her would send Little Wolf crashing out of their hiding place too soon.

The approaching hoofbeats changed in loudness and texture as the horses dashed across the edge of the hard plain and onto the softer ground by the pool. Jennie strained her eyes, staring beneath and through the low, leafy limbs of the trees, praying that she could do everything right.

The horrible thought flitted through her mind that these horses might not be Kwahira and Spirit Talker, but then, in the next instant, she saw that they were. They must be. Four shining red legs followed four gleaming white ones into the shallow edge of the pool.

Two beautiful heads, one white and one red, dropped down to smell and blow at the water, then they buried their muzzles in it and began to drink. For an endless time they drank, pulling the cooling liquid in, then raising their heads to look around before drinking again.

Finally, the third time they lifted their heads, Jennie managed to let out her breath and silently draw in a new one. In preparation for the charge.

Sure enough, after only one more dip into the water, a playful shaking of his head and rinsing of his mouth, the white one turned and started out of the pool, walking at a leisurely pace back the way they had come. Spirit Talker followed.

Jennie let them take a few steps on their way, as Windrider had told her, then she made the kissing sound, the signal to go, that he always used, and sent Little Wolf forward. She bent low on his neck to avoid the reaching limbs of the trees, calling, "Mukwooru! Spirit Talker! Come to me!"

She got one sharp glimpse of the two of them stopped in their tracks, heads thrown up, turned toward her in surprise, then the whole world became a flying blur. A scrap of Windrider's order to "ride straight toward him" darted through her head, then it and every logical thought was gone. She stayed on Little Wolf's back purely by instinct as he thundered toward the white and red streaks, she clung to his mane with both hands while he raced alongside.

Then she sensed and heard the whine of the rope through the air, and she glimpsed the jerking of Kwahira against the restraint. Little Wolf came down to a trot, and through the swirling dust Jennie could see Spirit Talker circling behind the faltering stallion.

He reared, in midstride it seemed, and Jennie's heart stopped in her chest. His forefeet struck at the rope, each strike looking, in her swirling vision, dangerously close, then closer still, to Windrider. The stallion screamed his protest in a voice meant to tear the sky in two.

Then Spirit Talker was screaming, too, looking back at Jennie one time before she ran heavily after Kwahira, who dropped to the ground and took off in a charging run. Little Wolf stayed alongside, changing from gallop to lope to a trot as

Echo's fresh strength and the belly full of water worked together to slow the white stallion down. They all fell into a walk.

He fought, but his native craftiness and his physical condition momentarily tamed his instinct for freedom. He could do nothing at the moment, his great, rolling eyes, showing white at the edges, told them both.

But just wait, shouted his huge, flaring nostrils and the proud lift of his perfectly formed head. Just wait.

The first chance he got, he would be gone.

Windrider, too, saw the gauntlet go down. Grinning fiercely at the challenge, he gave a great cry of victory, whirled Echo, drew the rope tight across his thigh, and brought both horses thundering in a huge, dusty circle. Little Wolf and Jennie stayed out of their way, turning with them into the whirling dust, away from the open country and back toward the holding pen Windrider had shown her, the one his band of the People had built long ago near the watering place.

With every step they took toward it, Kwahira let them know that this was the only time they would ever lead him anywhere. He tried to break away once more, but the rope wouldn't give, and Windrider's great strength and skill, combined with Echo's, held him. He came with them, swinging his head from time to time to see if Spirit Talker followed.

Windrider turned to look for Jennie, his eyes flashing like beacons through the flying dust.

"We did it!" he yelled. "Horse-Catcher Woman, my partner. We caught the Wild White One!"

Jennie heard every word, even through the noise of the horses' thudding hooves. And even through the fast-coming dusk, she clearly saw the triumphant jubilance in his face.

It looked so brilliantly joyful, his face looked so incredibly handsome and happy, that at that moment she didn't care *whose* freedom it had cost.

Chapter 11

Once Echo had led Kwahira into the tiny box canyon that The People used for a horse trap and Spirit Talker followed, Jennie raced to shut the gate behind them. Joy beat in her veins like the thunder of galloping hooves.

They had done it, she and Windrider! She had her own horse again! Spirit Talker was back.

She sent Esatai pacing up and down outside the barrier so she could see the mare through the stacked logs. Jennie called to her, but the mare didn't answer. She ran into the shadows of the rock walls at the back of the pen.

At the front of it, Echo and Kwahira performed a dueling dance. Kwahira glowed like a moving light in the deepening dusk, evading Windrider's hand reaching to pull the loosened loop from his neck. At last he dropped his head at the same moment Windrider shook the rope. It dropped off and the wild horse was free.

No, he wasn't, and he knew it.

Jennie stopped Little Wolf to watch him. The stallion stood still, looking furtively from side to side with his head halfway to the ground. Windrider turned Echo and walked away from him, pulling up the rope and coiling it into his hand as if the wild horse didn't exist. Spirit Talker whinnied.

Kwahira didn't move, didn't raise his head.

A terrible, fearful restlessness moved in Jennie's soul, mixed itself with the elation of their victory. She turned Little Wolf, kicked her heels into his sides, and trotted up to the gate. At that moment she could not have said whether she intended to open it for Windrider or for the captive Kwahira.

Another glance at the beaten stallion made her sick to her stomach.

"We should have left him alone!" she called to Windrider. "We should have roped Spirit Talker and left the stallion alone!"

"Never!" he called back, wheeling Echo to ride toward the gate. "It took great luck to catch him, and the help of Mother Moon and The Wind."

He rode Echo out through the gate at that moment and flashed her that grin of his that never failed to stop her heart. His teeth and his eyes gleamed in the fast-falling darkness, his powerful thigh muscles caught the last of the light as he urged Echo sideways to the gate and leaned to fasten it.

"So!" he said, and his low voice carried like music across the short distance that separated them. "We have done it, Horse-Catcher Woman! We are partners with much *puha*, much power, indeed!"

He was so tall, so sure of himself, so arrogantly victorious looming over her, close beside her now, his well-strung saddle muscles making him one being with the horse he rode.

His flashing eyes, his low-pitched voice full of intimacy, making him one being with her.

"Windrider and the Fire Flower! We are the

best hunters of all The People, we catch the wild horses that cannot be caught!''

He set Echo to circling Little Wolf in a twirling dance, whipping his head around to keep his eyes on hers. His slanted smile set her woman's core aflame with desire, just as his kisses had done.

No, this wanting was stronger.

It made the tips of her breasts hard and took away her breath.

It burst into blossom and grew big enough in one heartbeat to overpower her excitement, her worry for the stallion and the happiness about her mare. It blotted them all out and left nothing but a great ache that cried to be filled.

Her fingers went limp on her reins. Her legs tensed against Little Wolf's sides.

Echo came circling closer.

"Dismount," Windrider called. "Let's stake these mounts and go look at our new ones."

Jennie, her gaze arrested by his face, nodded dumbly. But she couldn't dismount.

Her arms ached to reach out and touch him. Her lips tingled to press against his skin. To taste his mouth.

Windrider stepped off Echo and snaked out his arm to sweep her off Little Wolf. He pulled her against him with a strong, quick squeeze of victory.

"Ten Bears will be jealous," he said, and for one confusing moment she thought he was speaking of her. But he strode toward the holding pen, keeping her close to him in the growing dusk, his sharp gaze looking for Kwahira.

"Many of The People have tried to capture the Wild White One and failed," he said, the celebration of victory vibrating in his voice, "but we have done it, you and me!''

He gave her that long, straight look again, and she felt that his soul was connected to hers. His smile illuminated the whole valley in spite of the fast-falling darkness. She wanted to walk into his arms.

She wanted it all the while they peered at the two captured horses through the failing light, as Spirit Talker ignored their calls, and Windrider assured Jennie that the filly probably would come to her in the morning. She wanted it even more as they prepared their camp near the rocky stream flowing out of the rough hills that held the small box canyon, while they ate the sweet, cold pemmican and agreed not to bother to build a fire.

Windrider felt it, too, Jennie thought suddenly, as she opened the packs he had brought and began to spread their blankets beneath the stars. He was standing still, watching her through the darkness.

She knelt there, her hands flat on the soft wool where she'd smoothed it out, and looked back at him.

"Enough," he said, his voice a rich rumbling in the night. "We can share."

He came to her then, his steps not making a sound, yet the power of his presence was stronger than a shout. Jennie turned to face him as he knelt beside her.

He took her shoulders into his big hands. Pulsating heat flowed out of his fingertips and into her blood.

"We share this blanket as we share the capture of the horses," he said. "You rode bravely to go full out so soon after you have learned to sit a horse."

"I am Warrior Woman," she teased, her voice a husky whisper. "I ride like a warrior."

He leaned forward and took her mouth with his. His lips were hot and sure.

He held them gently still for one long, sweet heartbeat, then he cupped her head in both hands and deepened the kiss, pushing against her lips with the tip of his tongue.

She parted them for him, the hot coals of wanting leaping into flames in her blood.

He made an incoherent, joyful sound and pulled her completely into his arms, stretching out onto the blanket, rolling onto his back as he drew her down on top of him.

The feel of her tight-budded breasts, reaching for him through the thin, smoked skin of her dress, surged through his blood with the lust of a war cry. He set both his hands on her rib cage and held her a little bit away from him, so she would brush against his naked chest in a delicious torture.

She whimpered with sharp pleasure, deep in her throat, and edged the tiniest bit closer to make the contact between them exactly perfect. She tore her mouth away from his and took his face in both hands, turning his head so she could place slow, biting kisses along the line of his jaw.

"Windrider," she said, and the word was the most feathery of whispers, so lost was her voice in feeling his touch. "Never . . . never . . . have I ever felt such . . . a pleasure."

"You said that . . . before," he managed to say, teasing her, even as her words melted the core of him and poured it into his manhood.

With a rough growl, he turned onto his side and fumbled with the fringed bottom of her blouse, slid it up and over her head in one catlike motion, completely forgetting any need not to scare her as he laid her on her back and bent his head to take one of her freed breasts into his mouth.

A sensation sweet beyond bearing shot through Jennie's body. It flashed through her veins like lightning in every direction at once, it raged there like a storm rampant, blowing away her muscles, her mind, her will, and her breath.

Yet it gave her a heart reborn.

And an open wanting that only Windrider could fill.

She stroked both her hands over the hard, moving muscles of his back, swept them in from the incredible width of his shoulders to the firm narrowness of his waist, sent her fingers trailing down the fascinating hollow of his spine where it led beneath his breechclout. But she was careful, always careful, never to move so much or so fast that he would take away his magic tongue, his suckling lips.

Jennie slipped her hands underneath his scrap of a garment and cupped his curved, muscular buttocks. Suddenly she had no more strength. Her hands dropped away and she lay helplessly still, lost in the sparkling feelings he was giving, giving back to him with her heart.

Then the fire surged into her hands and drove them up and over the jutting bones of his hips, over his flat stomach, down to the hard, throbbing shaft of his manhood. The shock of it, the iron-hardness covered by satin skin, the alluring newness of its incredible heat to her palm, stopped her hand.

What was she doing? What in this world was she doing?

She was not married to him! What was she thinking? This couldn't be right!

But had it been right when Trammel took her body?

A small, shameless, troublemaking voice shouted the question from somewhere inside her. She *had* been married to him.

The very word "marriage" recalled the raid on the fort, filled her head with the sound of the ululating war cry soaring from a hundred throats. It brought back the sight of the river of mounted Comanches flowing in through the open gates, it re-created the smells of the fire.

This was Windrider she lay with. *Windrider, War Chief of the Comanche.*

The Comanche who had raided the fort and killed her parents.

She placed both her hands on his chest and pushed him away, her whole body suddenly gone as stiff as the gesture it took to set herself free.

He let go of her. Unlike Trammel, Windrider didn't roll over and crush her to the ground with his big body, he didn't lock her into helplessness with his strong hands and legs. He didn't lash at her with his voice or curse her. He simply let go.

Jennie lay still, her heart pounding, her hands splayed palms-down against the ground.

Windrider didn't reach for her again, except with his voice.

"Fire Flower?"

He voice was harsh and ragged, but still he didn't move. He didn't come after her.

Relief and a sudden, overwhelming gratitude rose in Jennie, filling her up with tears, pulling the rigidness out of her bones. She let her eyelids close against the dark.

"Fire Flower. What is wrong?"

The words came out of his throat slowly, every one of them hurting. Hurting his pride, as his manhood was hurting.

His blood rose higher, now hot with anger and

shame as well as with wanting this woman. In one swift motion he sat up, very straight, and crossed his legs firmly beneath him in spite of the fact that his whole body was still stiff with desire.

What was he doing? *Begging* her?

He was Windrider, War Chief of The People! He did not beg women for their favors. Especially not fearful women. He clamped his lips shut.

Jennie opened her eyes and sat up as he did, although not in defense, for the fear had gone when he didn't force her. Now she felt shame for leading him on.

And also regret that she had stopped him; desire still burned in her blood.

And more shame for ever lying with him, ever kissing him, when his people had done such terrible things to hers.

The opposing feelings warred in her, threatening to rip her apart.

She fumbled for her blouse and put it back on, forcing her hands and arms to pick it up, to find the sleeves, in spite of their trembling weakness. Her own touch felt strange to her against her breasts and on her stomach, everywhere Windrider's hands and mouth had been.

The very *night* now felt strange to her, the formidable hugeness of the land around her, the clouds scudding back and forth to cover the moon. The wind lifted out of the west, carrying more of the lonely howls that had frightened her before.

She was lost again, in the dark, far from home.

"We are enemies," she blurted, "and we always will be!"

Pain pulsated in her words. Windrider listened to it linger on the air like the scent of the faraway mountains, like the dusty smell of the rocky hills and the fragrance of the shallow water. The Fire Flower was hurting, just as he was.

And that made his anger dissolve, made him want her more than ever.

"Before the Sun Father went to his bed robes," he said, slowly, trying to feel his way into her heart to find what was troubling her, "when we caught the horses, we were partners, not enemies."

"I remembered the attack on the fort."

There wasn't enough starshine to see her face, and only a sliver of Mother Moon was peeking out from the clouds. But the flatness of her voice told him everything. He *was* her enemy.

He made his hands into fists and silently hit the ground. Was she one of those who never forgot, never forgave?

He ached to touch her. But that might make things worse.

"The raid on the fort is done," he said. "It can't be changed."

"No more than we can change who we are," she said, in her stubborn tone. "We will always be enemies."

"Not always!" he said, harshly. "When the fighting is over, enemies sometimes become friends."

Wasn't that just like an overbearing man, contradicting her, telling her that black was white? Men were all alike!

Even as she had the thought, the little voice of truth inside her insisted that it wasn't so. Wasn't Windrider *talking* to her, trying to understand her feelings, as Trammel never had?

She said it anyway.

"*Men and women* can never be friends."

Ah! Windrider thought. So that was the way the

land lay. It had been the memory of a *man* that had come to tear her from his arms.

He drew in a long breath, the tightness in his muscles flowed away. Memories could hold much *puha*—he knew that as well as anybody—but the memory of another man he could overcome. He could wipe it from her mind.

"There was a man who—" he searched his mind for the English word—*"tsaka?uhru*, betrayed you?"

A fierce new jealousy twisted his heart. "A man you . . . loved?"

Yet how could that be? She had seemed so new to the pleasures that he gave her.

She whipped her head around; her eyes flashed at him in the darkness.

"No!"

The wind carried the truth into his head then, brought it riding into his ears on the high, lonesome howl of a wolf calling to his pack.

"Was there a man who . . . did not *pahna?aitu*, treat you with respect?"

She froze, then lifted her chin pridefully. He glimpsed the gleam of tears in her eyes.

"Yes," she whispered, at last.

The one pitiful word, so soft that it barely reached his ears, roused his fury. Some cruel white fool had hurt her, had made her afraid to lie with a man.

I will find him and kill him, he thought. Then he realized that the devil probably was dead already. Had more than likely died in the raid on the fort.

The high, howling call of the wolf came again; then, just as it died out, came an answer.

The Fire Flower sat so still that the hurting vibrated out through her skin and into the air between them. Windrider's arms ached to draw her to him, to wrap around her and hold her safe.

That protective instinct purified the desire he felt for her, made it leap higher like fed flames, made it burn from the inside out until every inch of his skin yearned to feel hers rub against it again.

He waited.

"He . . . forced himself on me," she said, in a soft, broken voice. Then it hardened and rose higher with each word. "He forced himself *into* me, and there was nothing I could do to stop him!"

"That is not the way of The People," Windrider said, using his gentlest tones to stroke her as he wished he could do with his hand. "We let the woman make the advances. If she is interested, she comes to the man's bed or she lets him know with words and glances that he should speak to her father."

"That seems strange," she said, shakily. "When Sanah disobeyed you, you said the women are to do as the men tell them."

"In most things. But in this, the woman comes to the man so as not to risk a warrior's pride."

"You mean . . . if he went to her and she did not want him, she could turn him away?"

"Yes. And that would bring him much shame."

He drew in a long, rough breath and promised, "I will wait for you to come to me, Fire Flower. When you are ready."

Panic, unreasoning fear like the cut of a mountain cat's claws, swiped at him. With She Blushes, he had waited too long. Now it was forever too late.

No matter the custom, he should have risked his pride, he should have simply taken her, made such love to her that the pleasure of it would have tied her to him. And that is what he should do with this beautiful Fire Flower. He should never have let her pull away!

But now, with her, also, it was too late. He had given his word.

So he stayed where he was, his throat tight, his heart thundering with the half-deadly longing.

"I want to forget I was ever . . . introduced to him!" she said, brokenly, unable to say that she had been married to Trammel when, in her heart, she had not. "I want to forget he ever existed!"

The wolves' howls came again, in chorus now, and closer. He should go and check the stake ropes of Echo and Esatai.

But he sat looking down at her, at her head bent into her hands, her hair bright somehow, even in the darkness. He reached out and touched one of her curls.

"I am not that man."

The flat statement, made in his deep, rich voice, tugged at her heart.

She wanted to turn to him, to reach up and slide her arms around his neck and lift her mouth to his again. She wanted him to slip her blouse off as he had done before and take up where he had left off. She wanted him to make love to her in such a new, precious way that she would know for sure and forever that what he had just said was true.

But then she would want him forever. And a person couldn't keep anyone or anything forever. Hadn't she already lost every single person she had ever loved?

"I'll see to the horses," he said, his voice suddenly gone hard and raspy. "The wolves' howling may spook them."

He got to his feet in that miraculous, flowing motion of his and added, ''Spread the other bed robes near these. The wolves won't attack people, but you might be afraid.''

Jennie did as he said, thankful to have something to do, some use for her arms and her legs that would work off the terrible tension without carrying her running to twine them around him. She made two beds, a distance apart, about the same length as two of Windrider's long strides.

Then she lay down in hers and prayed that the good Lord would give her sleep so she wouldn't think any more about her family or Trammel, so she wouldn't feel any more sorrow. So she wouldn't want Windrider.

He came back and, without a word, lay down in his robes. As far as she could tell, he slept.

But she lay awake, suddenly aware that, in her own way, she was as trapped as Kwahira in the canyon catch pen. Trapped by her past, which had stopped her from lying with Windrider, trapped by the fact they were enemies.

Trapped in her own bed when she wanted to be in his.

Jennie woke to the sound of Kwahira's hooves. At first she couldn't identify the continuous, rhythmic sound, but when she realized it was hoofbeats, she rose up and peered through the faint, very earliest light of the morning. Glimpses of his silvery body flashed at her through the woven brush barrier of the gate. Her eyes could barely follow the pale sightings, he moved so fast.

He didn't whinny or call, he made no noise at all except the desperate, determined, rapid thudding of his feet striking the hard ground. His tension filled the entire prairie and all the sky, the bend in the shallow river, the copse of cottonwood trees; it reverberated from the sheer rock faces of the canyon cliffs that formed the pen.

Jennie sat up and looked at Windrider. He didn't move. Apparently he was still asleep.

His face was turned away from her, away from the pale early daylight; his head was pillowed on his folded arm, his hair spread like a black silk fan across his back.

He didn't even hear the poor, frantic creature!

She threw back her cover, jumped up, and ran toward the pen. Kwahira's feet hadn't faltered, hadn't slowed, hadn't stopped.

They beat out a tragic, jarring prayer, begging release from an unendurable condition. No, they demanded it, pounded the breast of Mother Earth, trying to get her attention. Jennie stuck her moccasined toes into the holes in the gate and climbed up to look at him.

And Spirit Talker! What was she doing?

The mare huddled in one corner at the back of the pen, a red blur in the predawn shadows. The stallion ran ceaselessly around the perimeter of the pen, his head high, his eyes rolling at Jennie when he saw her, but his voice silent, too proud to plead.

He passed right beneath her. His coat was wringing wet in places, his chest was nearly black with sweat. Jennie could smell it. And she could smell his fear.

She watched him make one more circle; then, as he rushed past Spirit Talker and toward Jennie again, she stiffened her arms and pushed herself backward, jumping down to the ground in one leap. She ran to the braided horsehair rope and cottonwood stick that made up the fastener to the gate that closed off the mouth of the box canyon. Her fingers didn't even tremble when she slipped the stick through the loop and swung the gate open.

Kwahira ran through the space without hesitation, as if he had known all along it would be there for him. He gave Jennie a glance with one great, rolling eye, his gaze meeting hers for an instant. His look exhilarated her, but it was so fleeting, she almost felt she imagined it. His nostrils were trembling, gaping open for air, then he was galloping past her, his head high into the wind, his mane whipping his neck, his back stretched flat to run.

She kept her eyes fixed on the stallion until he was out of her sight, until his white flowing tail vanished into the gray morning prairie like a wisp of smoke disappearing into the sky.

Then, a deep-souled feeling of satisfaction surging through her, she stepped into the pen and pulled the gate closed behind her, calling for Spirit Talker. At least she would have her horse, she would have one friend in the world.

The mare was already running flat out for the gate, the place where the stallion had left her. She circled and pawed when she found it was closed, but then she snorted at Jennie's outstretched hand and gradually came down to a stop.

Jennie threw her arms around her neck and pressed her cheek to the silky hide, pushing the scratchy mane out of the way.

"Don't you be mad at me, too," she pleaded. "You know he had to be free. He was miserable, Spirit Talker!"

Spirit Talker muttered an answer deep in her throat, a sound that could have been agreement or not.

Jennie hugged her tighter.

What would Windrider do?

"Surely he'll understand," she murmured to the mare. "*He* roams the plains free as the wind, he knows how good that feels!"

She could convince him that it was only right to turn the stallion loose, she thought. He could be very understanding when he wanted to. Look at the way he had treated her last night—he had wanted to hear about her feelings, he hadn't forced her to do anything. Why, he had been trying to get to know her, as she had once tried to get to know Trammel!

The filly jerked, threw up her head beneath Jennie's arms. She pulled away and saw the mare prick her ears, then she heard what the mare had heard first.

Terrible screams tearing the air, far in the distance. Shrill, frantic shrieks of pure horror, pleas for help.

The piteous, unearthly sounds of a panicked horse.

Jennie knew that with a dead certainty, although she'd never heard it before. Then, with a dreadful chill that penetrated every bone in her body, she pinpointed the direction of the nightmare noise.

It came from the same way Kwahira had gone!

Jennie stood looking that way, but seeing only the pale, empty prairie stretching before her in the early morning light.

Kwahira! Oh, dear God, what was wrong? What had she done by turning him loose?

The next instant the mare's ears swiveled to the

gate and Jennie turned, still holding on to her, to see Windrider throwing himself over the woven brush barrier. In a blur of quick tears, she saw that he wore his lasso over one shoulder, his bow and quiver over the other, that he held a scrap of bridle in his hand as he came. And only an instant earlier, he had been sound asleep!

"Let me have her," he ordered, in an urgent voice that vibrated with anger.

He was keeping it calm so as not to spook Muk-wooru, Jennie knew, but she wished he would yell his fury at her. That would be easier to take than the disdainful look in his eyes.

"No. I'm going, too!"

"You'll slow me down. Get out of my way!"

She slipped back to Spirit Talker's side, clutched her mane with both hands, and, bouncing a little to get momentum, mounted.

Windrider was upon them before she could find her seat, slipping the loop of the simplest Comanche bridle over the mare's lower lip as he ran to her side.

"Get down, I said. Let me have her!"

Jennie locked her legs against the mare, expecting any second for him to drag her off onto the ground, and he grasped her arm for an instant, his muscles flexed to do it, but he didn't. He flashed her a look of pure scorn and leapt up behind her.

"You let him out," he said, spitting the words out one at a time from between his clenched teeth. "I saw you."

She set her own jaw. She couldn't bear his censure. Not now, without knowing what terrible consequences her action had brought to the stallion. She had done what she had to do at the time.

"Go get Echo!" she shouted at him, even though he already had the filly moving. "Get your own horse and let me ride mine! Men don't ride mares, remember?"

"When there is danger and the mare is closest, they do," he yelled back.

He shoved the gate open with his foot, and put them through it, already galloping, before she could recover her breath.

He kept one arm around Jennie to hold on to the rein, an arm as hard and unforgiving as if it were made of iron. She couldn't even imagine how it had felt around her in a caress, couldn't even remember his embrace. His face looked carved from granite.

She tangled her fingers in Spirit Talker's mane and thought of Kwahira. That *had* been his voice. She knew it from the night before last when he had challenged them in the moonlight.

Windrider bent over to urge the mare for more speed, his implacable body forcing Jennie's to bend, too. She couldn't breathe, she was being squeezed to death.

She closed her eyes. The wind was whipping her hair into them until they filled with tears, anyway; the dawn wasn't yet strong enough to throw enough light to see, the dust was a torment.

But mostly she closed them because the sight of Kwahira, hurt, would break her heart.

The look in Windrider's eyes already had.

But turning the stallion loose hadn't been wrong! She had only given him back his freedom, which he had had for years. He had lived free for years; he should know how to take care of himself!

She wanted to yell that at Windrider, but she

couldn't talk, and at this speed, he couldn't hear her.

After an age of hurtling straight through the cool air without being able to draw enough of it into her lungs, Jennie felt Spirit Talker start uphill, heard her hooves striking against rocks. Then she slid to a sudden stop and tried to back up. Jennie opened her eyes and sat up straight as soon as Windrider did.

His hard thigh muscles flexed against Jennie's legs and he drove the filly forward against her will, around a bend in the dry creek bed full of rocks, up into a gash in the earth of the plains that ended at a low mesa wall. He let her slow, dropped the rein across her withers, started pouring a series of harsh cries from his throat.

The scared scream of the wild horse came again, reverberating, echoing, against rocks and the earth, and the sky, too, it seemed, so close and so loud that it made Jennie's first full new breath stick in her throat.

He slipped his bow off his shoulder and an arrow from the quiver while Jennie tried to take in what her eyes were telling her.

"Wolves!" she breathed.

Kwahira was rearing, his white body clear and sharp as a painting against the backdrop of brown earth now that the sun was giving more light to the land, standing on his hind feet like a great, dramatic statue. But he was obviously made of flesh—blood ran in narrow, ruby red streams down his chest.

The big, gray-brown bodies on the ground held Jennie's gaze; they swirled and then scattered beneath the onslaught of a human voice. One, the one closest to Kwahira with its mouth snarling open, dropped to the ground as she watched, impaled on an arrow.

She hadn't even felt Windrider move.

The stallion crashed down to rest for a moment. Windrider leaped from Spirit Talker's back to go to him; the mare whinnied and danced, shying from the wolves.

Jennie managed to keep her seat. She had calmed her mount just a little when Kwahira rose into the air once more, pawing and snorting at the scent of the man. Windrider slowed his movements, became a quiet shadow, waiting for him to come down again.

Kwahira's big body landed with a thud, and Jennie saw that his heaving sides shone iron gray with sweat, poured sweat, three times as much as he had had on him when he was running in the pen. This was dripping, falling onto the dry ground in huge, splattering drops. Windrider slipped to each side of him, staying ten feet or so out, to look him over.

Kwahira squealed and reared again, and for the first time, Jennie noticed that one hind leg was set far behind the other, apparently caught among the rocks. It was a miracle that he didn't rip it off, rearing like that!

Windrider saw it, too.

He went closer on that side, crouching next to the mesa wall to see what held the hoof. His nearness sent Kwahira into a panic once more. The stallion struck sideways at Windrider with one forefoot, then dropped heavily down, all the way to one knee, then struggled up to stand on all four legs, all of them shaking, trembling with fear and fatigue. His nostrils stretched to the tearing point to try to draw in enough air to fill his heart-girth.

Windrider looked up and pierced Jennie with his eyes as mercilessly as he had shot the arrow through the wolf lying dead at his feet.

"*Now* he is caught," he said, "because you turned him out to the wolves."

Chapter 12

"I *didn't* turn him out to the wolves! I only gave him his freedom!"

"When you knew how much I wanted him. After I worked so hard to catch him."

"So did I! You said it yourself—you couldn't have caught him if I hadn't helped!"

Jennie threw her leg over Spirit Talker's withers and slid down to stand unsteadily on the ground. "He was miserable, Windrider. He was running and grieving himself to death! I couldn't bear to keep him cooped up a minute longer."

"You couldn't bear it," he mocked her. "The horse was *mine*."

"He was mine, too," she said, giving him a straight, steady look.

"And now he belongs to the buzzards."

She glanced to the sky, then took a step toward him. "What are you talking about, the buzzards?"

"His leg," he snapped at her, turning away to look at Kwahira again. "He turned to fight off the wolves and stepped into the place where the water comes out of the earth when it rains. Rocks slid down while he struggled. If he pulls it out, he will break it."

Goose bumps broke out on Jennie's arms.

"Then we'll help him! We'll move the rocks and get it out!"

Windrider dismissed the idea with one sharp gesture.

"You can see he is against the wall of earth. There is no room."

Jennie wanted to run across in front of Kwahira to look more closely, but she forced herself to walk, to move slowly enough not to startle the stallion into struggling again. She crouched and peered at his trapped foot as Windrider had done.

"I can get to it," she said. "I'm small."

Windrider was staring at the horse. He didn't even flick her a glance.

"You'd be crushed."

"I would not! I can climb right down behind him and—"

"And have him rear again and mash you between him and the mesa."

"No, he won't."

Jennie stood up and looked at Windrider's set, furious face. "You'll be at his head, talking to him."

He whirled around to meet her gaze.

"*Talking* . . ."

"And holding his front feet together with your rope. He wouldn't try to rear without them loose to balance with, would he?"

They both looked at Kwahira, who stared back, sides trembling, huge eyes rolling until the whites gleamed, his muzzle dripping foam. He wasted no energy on a squeal, but he gave a vicious swipe at the rocks with his right forefoot.

"He might," Windrider said. "The wolves panicked him into running into this trap, and his blood's still full of fear. He might do anything."

"Where are the wolves now?"

"Probably circling out there, watching. They fear people."

"I can free this horse, and I'm the only one who can," Jennie said, keeping her voice steadily confident in spite of her heart's racketing in her chest. She had learned that much since she'd been with the Comanche. They didn't respect modesty, they respected confidence and courage.

She must retain Windrider's respect so he would help her.

Without looking at him again, she bent and pulled her calf-length skirt up between her legs to free them, tucked the bottom fringes firmly in at her waist, and began inching higher up onto the slanting earth wall, keeping her back to it, digging in her heels to hold her upright in the crumbling dry dirt, pushing into it with her fingers, too, for balance. She started making her way toward the rear of the horse. Kwahira swung his head toward her and kept it there, fixing her with one disastrously suspicious eye.

Jennie pretended not to see it. She pretended Windrider wasn't there, either.

She pretended that she was alone, on a hillside in Ireland, although the early morning breeze was carrying the smells of sagebrush and faraway pines instead of the fragrance of the sea, and the air she took in in shallow gulps was as dry as the earth in her hands instead of filled with bounteous moisture. She was Jennie O'Bannion before any of the bad things had happened. She was Jennie O'Bannion, ready for adventure, and she could do anything.

She had no idea how long it took her, but too soon her feet were reaching for purchase in the deeper slant at the narrow head of the draw. She began working her way down, straight down toward the powerful hindquarters of the wild horse. She tried to go slowly, so as not to loosen more rocks, she tried talking to him, low and gentle, so as not to surprise him.

It took all the strength she had, for she wanted to fling herself headlong at the rocks and get this over and done. But she had to do it right. If she couldn't save this horse, Windrider would always look at her with that scorn in his eyes.

Rocks cut through her moccasins and she flinched, but she didn't stop, didn't let herself hurry. She didn't let herself look to see what Windrider was doing. She had said she would do this and she had to do it, with help or without.

She kept talking softly, inching her way down and down, then she began to slide, straight toward Kwahira's trapped foot. Windrider's voice came from nowhere, low and urgent.

"Be ready to scramble back uphill when he blows out of there."

Her heart soared.

Now he believed that she *could* save the stallion. She spared one quick glance. He *was* holding his feet as she'd suggested!

Kwahira shuddered when she stopped, wedged so close between him and the earth that her face was almost touching his sweating hide. She tilted her head sideways so her hair wouldn't brush against him, and balancing herself with one foot on each side of the pile of rocks, she began to lift them away from his hock.

She had no breath to keep talking to him, so Windrider took up the rhythmic crooning in his own language. Some of the rocks clung to the slope when she set them aside, but others rolled underneath the stallion, and there was nothing she could do to stop them. Kwahira only trembled.

"A horse usually kicks straight backward," Windrider said, softly. "And there is no room for you to get to his side. When he is free, go up the mesa wall as fast as you can."

"You told me that," she managed to say. "He won't kick. He knows I'm helping him."

She reached the last rock, a big one, and pulled it away from the battered, shaking leg.

It was buried hock-deep in the ground.

"It's at such an angle," she said, staring at it in horror, "that he can't—"

But the next instant the stallion jerked free, lurching back toward her so close that his tail scraped her face and his bulk pressed her, for one terrifying instant, back into the earth.

"Get away!" Windrider called, the urgency in his voice like a physical blow, then he was clicking to the stallion.

The huge weight of the horse lifted, moving forward, and Jennie stood up, gasping to draw all the air into her lungs that she could hold. Her gaze dropped to Kwahira's bruised and bleeding hock. He put his full weight on it.

"It isn't broken!" she called, forgetting to keep her voice low and calm. "Oh, Windrider, he'll be all right!"

"He may back up—get yourself out of that trap!" Windrider ordered, but Kwahira let himself be led another few awkward steps forward, farther away from her.

Windrider crouched and, in a motion so fast, Jennie couldn't see how he did it, twisted his rope into hobbles around both Kwahira's forefeet. The long end, he brought up and threw over the stallion's neck.

Jennie stood stunned.

"We just freed him!" she cried. "Now you're trussing him up like a dead fowl! He'll go crazy and *really* break his leg now!"

She followed the horse, impotent fury rising in her throat. "And after I risked my life to prevent that very thing!"

Windrider shot her a murderous glance.

"You risked your life when you let him out of the pen. That was the act of an enemy."

He turned his back to her and began leading Kwahira downhill, out of the gully. Even seeing that the hobbles were loose enough for him to walk gave Jennie no comfort. She glared at Windrider's broad, muscled back and went after him.

"You have no mercy in you at all!" she cried, driven to challenge his anger toward her. Even risking her life to save Kwahira's had not redeemed her terrible sin of setting him free!

"That horse would have grieved himself to death. He was in misery!"

Windrider didn't turn around, didn't answer. Jennie kept after him, but he was walking faster to reach Spirit Talker's side.

Her hands started trembling and her head went dizzy.

"He would have *run* himself to death!"

"So," Windrider said, throwing the words at her over his shoulder, "you gave him to the wolves to save him."

Her disappointment, her fury, grew.

"I didn't know that the wolves were so close!"

"You heard them howling before you went to sleep."

"You said they wouldn't attack us!" she said, through clenched teeth. "And I didn't know that they would chase Kwahira."

He took hold of Spirit Talker's rein.

"So," he said again, in that superior, arrogant tone that she hated, "you don't know enough about life in the Comancheria to handle the horses. Wolves will attack them, but usually not people. Horses will run from wolves."

"Well, you don't know enough about anybody else's feelings to be a companion to people *or* horses, and you don't care!" she yelled at him, walking faster, ignoring the bruising assaults of the rocks through her moccasins.

Her feet were being pushed along by the storm of sickening disappointment gathering in her heart. It threatened to smother her. Even if they *had* caught this wild horse and then rescued him together, they weren't partners at all.

They really *were* enemies!

"You've always been free to do exactly whatever you pleased, whenever you pleased!" she raved. "You don't know what it's like to be trapped and bossed around and oppressed and never have one word of say about where you go or what you do."

She tore her gaze from Windrider's implacable back and glanced at Kwahira. Her setting him free hadn't caused him any permanent damage. He continued to pick his way along, blood dripping from the cut of a sharp-edged rock on his hock and a little more from the scratches on his chest now and again, yes, but it wasn't pouring. It would soon stop.

"He isn't badly hurt," she challenged. "*I* saved him from death. *You* were going to leave him for the buzzards."

Windrider led the little procession out of the ravine and onto the prairie. Once in the grass, he turned and fixed his eyes on Kwahira as if Jennie were not even there, as if she'd never said anything. Spirit Talker dipped her head and cropped off a bite of grass.

Kwahira threw up his head and searched in every direction with his eyes and ears, his nostrils testing the wind. He turned and, for one luminous instant, met Jennie's gaze. Then he dropped his muzzle into the grass and began to graze.

"See!" she said fiercely. "He has just thanked me for saving his life. And he isn't hurt, not really!"

Windrider, who was removing the braided rawhide loop from Spirit Talker's mouth, threw Jennie another of his disdainful glances. "He wouldn't be hurt at all if you hadn't been sneaking around trying to injure me, *your enemy*!"

There was a definite tinge of pain beneath the sarcasm in that last word, but Jennie didn't have time to think about it. What he had said was so amazing, it absorbed all her attention.

"Trying to injure you!" she exclaimed, taking two steps toward him through the rippling, thigh-high grass. "I wasn't trying to injure *you*. I only knew that I had helped cause Kwahira's misery—that agony was on my head."

Windrider expanded the loop of her bridle and slipped it over Spirit Talker's neck. He looked at Jennie again, very briefly, but long enough for her to glimpse appraisal beneath his anger this time.

The glance lessened *her* anger, shot hope into her veins again. Maybe she could make him understand.

She took another step toward him, but he held out his hand as a signal she should stop, and with his eyes, indicated the horses. She stood still and lowered her voice, but she couldn't keep back her words anymore than she could dam the raw feelings pouring through her.

"I have felt that very same way that Kwahira did in the catch pen," she said, as Windrider took the end of the mare's rein and moved through the waving grass as silently as a breath of breeze toward Kwahira. "All my life I've been trapped and penned up, forced to stay when I wanted to go, forced to do what someone else told me when I wanted adventure and freedom. I have never had any freedom at all, Windrider, not even free use of my time!"

He didn't look at her, didn't answer. Crooning in Comanche, his voice so gentle and soft that it brought tears to her eyes, he drifted near enough to Kwahira to take the rope from his neck and tie the end of it to Spirit Talker's rein. The horses looked at each other, then went back to the grass.

Windrider watched them for a moment, then he turned and strode silently toward Jennie, parting the tall grass with his powerful, bare thighs as he came.

"I didn't turn him out to hurt you," she said, lifting her swimming eyes to meet his. "I did it to keep from causing any creature the same pain that I have suffered. I've never had my freedom, Windrider, and I couldn't bear to be the cause of Kwahira losing his."

He stopped in front of her and looked down into her face. He was silent, his heartbreakingly handsome face quiet and still, as if he was thinking about what she had just said.

"Kwahira will have freedom with me," he said. "Freedom to raid and to ride the warpath, to race across the plains toward the sky."

"That isn't freedom! He'll be doing what *you*

want when he has been accustomed to being a king!"

"He has been accustomed to fighting all his own battles, too," Windrider said. "If we had not been here, the wolves would have killed him."

"He could break a wolf's head open with one kick from his hoof."

"He could. But horses protect themselves by fleeing. Kwahira ran into a trap, so he had to turn and fight. There were too many wolves."

"I don't care," she said, stubbornly setting her fists on her hips. "I still think he would have died in that pen before he would have let you tame him."

"No. Many wild horses act like that at first. Then they learn to enjoy the companionship of a man."

His dark eyes gleamed.

The sunlight poured across his wide chest. It gathered in golden pools in the hollows on each side of his collarbone. His skin would be warm as melted butter.

"You could learn that same lesson, Fire Flower."

He smiled and her heart turned over.

But her old fears were too strong.

"No. I want my freedom."

"Everyone must have friends—I must give in sometimes to Ten Bears and the elders, or I must live alone. Complete freedom isn't always good. Ask Kwahira."

"That was an accident. He has lived a long time free without help from a man."

Windrider put both hands on her shoulders and ran his hands down her arms. She shivered, fighting the thrill of it.

"On this sun he got help from a woman," he

said, "from a brave Woman Warrior. My heart filled my mouth when you vanished behind him, Fire Flower."

His fingertips brushed the insides of her wrists, opened her hands and claimed them, tantalizing her palms with a touch as light as the wings of a butterfly. A touch that made her throat go tight with a sudden, fierce longing for more.

He cared about her! He had been afraid she'd be hurt!

But she already knew that. His voice, when he had warned her to get out of Kwahira's way, had been unmistakably anxious.

Now it was intimately melodious.

"Kwahira and I are now friends," he coaxed. "You and Kwahira are friends. It is time for you and me, the old enemies, to be friends."

"How can that be?" she said, tilting her head so that she could see the sunlight slant across his face. His powerful, high-cheekboned face. "You do not forgive me for turning out the stallion."

"I do forgive you," he said, and his eyes on hers warmed until they were the color of melted chocolate. "Because you explain. That was the act of a *tahkapu*, a poor person—one who had in her life no horses and no freedom."

His hands gave her his strength to cling to.

His smile gave her his confidence to share.

But it was the understanding look, the respect in his eyes, that tore her heart loose from its moorings and gave it wings. Even though he was a man, he had actually been listening to her! He was a man and he had heard her, he understood her feelings!

"I will give you both," he said.

He was a man and she loved him.

Jennie's heart quit beating. She stood very still

and listened to those words in her head, over and over again.

She loved him, and that was the truth.

Such a look came into the Fire Flower's eyes that Windrider felt a catch in his heart. He felt bathed in cool water. He felt wrapped in soft fur.

He ought to give her her freedom.

He had just told her he would, and she had believed him. He ought to tell her she could go or stay, that he would take her back to Texas if that was what she chose.

But not yet.

"Kohtoo Topusana," he said, and he turned loose of her hands and opened his arms. "Let me show you what we can share now we are enemies no more."

Jennie walked into his embrace. Into his kiss.

She wrapped her bare legs around his, brought her fingers into his hair to cup his head in her hands, melted her breasts to his chest. That kiss held the power of the sun, the magic of the moon.

It held all the longing of a high, lonesome wind, a crying, a call from his heart to hers.

It sent his hungry hands over the wings of her shoulders, underneath her loose blouse to caress the skin of her back, drew them down, starving, to cradle the curves of her bottom in his palms.

It lifted her up against him. Against his hard manhood, sweet and hot.

It made her hands ache to close around it again.

It made her whole body want his, even more desperately than she had wanted him the night before.

What did it matter if they were not married? What earthly difference did it make? She loved him.

Life was short; she could have died today, be-

tween Kwahira and the ungiving earth. She, or
he, could die tomorrow, suddenly, the way her
other loved ones had done.

And she loved him.

She melded her body against his, slid her
sweating palms down over the massive muscles
of his neck and along the tops of his shoulders,
trailed her fingers down the fascinating power of
his arms.

A low moan came from his throat, a sigh of
satisfaction too long denied.

She moved herself higher against him, wrapped
her arms tight around his neck, tore her lips from
his and buried them in the hollow of his shoulder, tasting with her lips and her tongue, desperate for the very essence of him.

His skin was like sugar, no, like salt on a tart
apple—sweet and sour and deliciously refreshing.
It cooled the scorching bruises his lips had made
on hers.

He spread his big hand across the back of her
neck, thrust his fingers into her hair, and held her
searching mouth against him.

"Kohtoo Topusana," he murmured, his voice
low and rhythmic as if he were beginning a song.
"Come with me. Come with me."

But he didn't move from that spot.

He bent and pressed his face to hers, using his
chin to push back her tumbling hair. His other
hand still cupped her hips against him.

"My skin needs your skin," he said, rubbing
his cheek against her forehead, "as much as my
heart needs your heart."

The simple statement shattered any last reserve
that might have been lingering in her.

"I need you, too, Windrider," she murmured.
"I need you, too."

But those were not the words that danced on her tongue, trying to leap out into life in the air.

She opened her eyes and looked beyond Windrider's bronze-colored shoulder to see the green earth and the blue sky and the white horse and the red one. She listened to and felt the wind. But nothing changed, not even the heat in her cheeks cooled in the breeze.

Those same words kept crying to be spoken.

They came spinning out of her mouth. "I love you, Windrider."

He listened. He went perfectly still.

Then he slid his hands up the sides of her body and held it firm, leaning her backward so they could look into each other's faces. His pupils darkened to black, changed to glittering midnight bits of coal; they turned into stars. She thought they would blind her, she thought they would burn all the breath from her body.

His thumb tilted her chin. His lips brushed hers and he whispered against them, "Come with me."

He gathered her into his arms and held her close against his thundering heart.

I love you, Windrider.

The words twined themselves in and out of his ears, in and out of his stunned mind. The Fire Flower loved him!

This time she wouldn't push him away.

Mother Earth, warm and welcoming, caressed his feet through the soles of his moccasins, carried them a short way through the grass. Then she drew them down to her breast and they were falling—into a bed of wildflowers and onto each other.

He found the Fire Flower's mouth again, possessed it with his. The crushed flowers filled the air with their tingling scent; broken stems grazed the skin on his arms.

Then her soft hands slipped beneath his breechclout, and after that, he could feel nothing but the sweet torture they caused. She arched her back to bring herself against him; his blood roared in his ears.

Willing. She was warm and willing at last, the beautiful Flower of Fire.

"Windrider," she murmured, breathlessly, when she had pulled her lips slightly away, when she had lifted her hands to leave his loins bereft while she stroked back his hair. "The . . . horses . . ."

He tried to answer, but he lifted her higher against him instead, his mouth searching for the swelling tip of her breast, then caressing it through the thin elkskin that both revealed and concealed how much she was wanting him.

She was no longer afraid to lie with a man. She wasn't afraid to lie with *him*.

And she was thinking of his feelings, wanting him not to lose the stallion again.

The thought gave him such *puha*, he felt he could fly.

That realization brought him such tenderness, brought him as much medicine as the Sun Father and the Mother Earth could give. Added to that of his guardian spirit, The Wind.

At that moment the horses could have run all the way to the high plains of the Llano Estacado and he wouldn't have cared.

He tried to take his mouth away from her body to reassure her, but he couldn't. Only for quick words between kisses.

"Tied together . . . the mare will . . . stay . . ."

He had worked his way around to the side of

her breast, to the delicious, sweet bareness showing through between the strips of rawhide that
held the front to the back. He kissed it, then lifted
his head to *look*, simply look at the silvery white
skin shining between the crisscrossed pattern of
the laces.

The sight fired his blood. He groaned, grasped
the poncho shirt, and pulled it up over her head,
wadding it with one hand to make her a pillow
while he dropped his face to her skin again,
mouth closed to brush back and forth, back and
forth, nostrils flared to breathe in the fresh, clean
scent of her.

Her soft hand brushed back his hair from his
ear and traced a circle around it.

He moaned, deep in his throat, as his mouth
fell open against her. His fingers found the thongs
that held her skirt together and untied them.

The crush of cloth fell away.

And left her body bare, a treasure under his
hands.

Smooth, her skin so very smooth and fine and
warm in the sunlight, her flat belly so porten-
tously vulnerable.

He sat up then, and spread the skirt out beneath her to make her a bed; he knelt between
her legs and looked at her, at her tousled, bright
hair and her deep green eyes, heavy with the haze
of desire.

They smiled at him. They told him that she
loved him.

They tore a mighty hole deep in his soul. A
place where only she could live.

He placed one hand on each side of her, palms
flat in the rioting orange and blue blossoms—none
of them, not all of them together, so resplendent

as this woman/girl who loved him—set his knees, leaned forward, and kissed her on the belly.

The sweet shock of it shot all the way through Jennie.

The tip of his tongue sent a lifting into her veins like the thrill of a horse beneath her, floating into a lope. It took her fast up and into the sun-sweetened air, then it was moving, and his lips were nipping at her, trailing a zigzag path lower and lower toward the woman-part of her, now crying with need.

His mouth brushed her there, then it came homing back to hers and met her open lips at the same instant the hard shaft of his manhood entered her begging body.

Windrider lifted her from the earth more surely than Kwahira had raced with Spirit Talker off the hilltop, with an awe-inspiring power, a magic so sheer and wild that she left the ground to float through the sky as the horses had done in the moonlight.

With the ancient authority of the dream she used to delight in, the blissful dream where she rode all the horses in the world.

He moved her with a primal rhythm that gathered strength on top of strength in long, sure strokes like the majestic stride of the stallion. It melted her body into the earth with the pleasure but carried her out of it with the joy. It made her a spirit that flew through the sky.

One spirit with Windrider.

Racing headlong toward the heavens and through them out into a wild, glorious infinity of wind, light, and stars.

Chapter 13

They lay still as midnight in the sweet-smelling seduction of the summer morning, unwilling to move so much as a breath apart. Jennie dropped a light kiss in the hollow of Windrider's throat, then onto his mouth, stretching up to reach it, delighting in the thrill of her skin sliding against his.

He gave a great, shuddering sigh and wrapped her closer into his arms.

He tasted of salt and sunlight and sweet grass, of the spicy scents of the flowers that made them a bed.

Their marriage bed.

She opened her eyes and waited, but the twinge of guilt never came. She loved this man. It was as right for her to share his bed as it had been wrong for her to share Trammel's.

He tightened one massive arm around her as if she had spoken the thought aloud.

"You are wonderful, Windrider," she said.

He chuckled, deep in his throat, a sound happy and rich as water running over rocks in a stream.

"Of course I am wonderful. I am Windrider, War Chief of the Comanche. I am the man who holds the Fire Flower in his arms!"

She laughed, too, and said, dryly, "I have noticed that modesty is not rampant among The People, especially not among the warriors."

He drew back and fixed her with a quizzical look.

"What is mo-des-ty?"

"Humbleness. Not bragging on oneself."

He squinted at her, deepening the small lines at the corners of his dark eyes, making her reach up to smooth them away.

"We have no such word in the language of the *Nermernuh*," he declared. "Among us, it is good to brag. *If* what one says is true."

"And what *you* say is always true, isn't it?" she teased, looking into his eyes, which were smiling now, trailing her fingertips along the line of his hair to the high, chiseled bone of his cheek.

Say you love me.

The words sprang to the tip of her tongue, but she bit them back.

"It is," he said, and now his lips were smiling, too, their corners lifting in sensual curves that drew her hand from his cheekbone to trace their shape instead. "And I can prove it."

He nipped gently at her exploring fingers.

"I told you the horses would stay with us, did I not?" he said, his lazy smile changing into his mischievous grin.

Jennie turned her head quickly to look, her heart suddenly thudding. She had forgotten all about the horses!

They lifted their heads from the grass, almost in unison, to look back at her. The rope stretched between them like a yoke, but neither seemed to be aware of it. The blood had dried on Kwahira's chest.

She swung her eyes back to Windrider.

"Yes, you did," she said, meeting his grin with one of her own. "How did you know?"

"I possess much *puha*," he said, mocking her light, teasing tone. "I also told these flowers to make us a bed and the birds to sing for us."

Sure enough, the light, trilling song of a lark, probably a meadowlark like those she had seen at the fort, came tripping to Jennie's ears on the breeze.

Windrider threw back his head and laughed, a deep, rumbling laugh so full of pleasure that it warmed her blood like a flame.

"Of course, I believe you," she teased. "Because you already told me that you always tell the truth."

He glanced toward the heavens, then raised up onto his elbow and looked straight into Jennie's eyes with such heat in his steady gaze that it melted her bones.

"Do you believe that I told Father Sun to reach the high peak of his journey as a blessing while we are here together?" he asked, still jesting, yet with a hard edge of seriousness, even a reverence in his tone, that shook her.

"Yes," she said, her face and her voice going suddenly solemn as a vow. "And before Father Sun starts his journey downward, I want you to hold me again."

He folded her closer into his arms, chuckling, nuzzling his smooth lips into her hair to kiss her ear.

"I am holding you," he said. "I have been holding you ever since we lay down."

"No, I mean really *hold* me," she said, and threw her leg over his to show him what she meant.

Jennie thought of that look many times during the intimate days that followed, but he never gave it to her again. He gave her laughter and loving and more pleasure, she was sure, than ever before had been between a woman and a man. He gave her Mother Earth and Father Sun and Mother Moon, with the stories about them, he gave her the great, wild world of life in Comancheria with its immense, far-reaching sky and rolling, never-ending land, with its blackberry bushes and sagebrush, purple coneflowers and prairie clover, its cottonwood trees and its willows, the black haws and hackberries and the hard, gnarly ones called Osage orange. He continued to give her a new, musical language with its whispered vowels. He gave her the skills to survive as she helped him find food for their fire, for they did everything together, unable to bear to be parted during all of those magnificent days.

And he gave her horses.

Earlier he had taught her to ride, yes, and he had given her Spirit Talker for her own, but on the endless plains, with only the two of them to break and train Kwahira, he made her the horsewoman she had always been in her dreams. They worked as partners in every stage of his care and training, from gathering the plants and making salve to rub onto his wounds that first day they took him back to their camping place by the catch pen, to the day after that when they kept him moving around the inside of that pen, driving him on every time he ran from them until, at long last, he wanted to stop, until he turned his hind end to the fence and his head to the warrior, until he walked up to Windrider, lowered his head, and thrust his muzzle into his hand.

The horse had sorely tried his patience, had

kept him standing in the sun for endless hours, had acted as if he had forgotten his docile behavior and his gratitude of the day before when they saved his life. But when he came to him, Windrider lifted his other hand and stroked the graceful white neck, now dark gray with sweat, in a gesture so gentle, it brought tears to Jennie's eyes.

Windrider the War Chief, yes. But he had an understanding tenderness unlike any other man.

The sun was almost down, and they had all walked slowly together to the river, where she and Windrider had rubbed Kwahira's sweaty back with double handfuls of sand. Then, in the slanting, crimson light of the setting sun, they had strapped on a saddle-pad and had ridden, first Windrider with his long legs shining like burnished copper against Kwahira's white sides, his hips never moving from the seat he had taken.

Her eyes had filled with tears again, from what cause, she did not exactly know. She had blinked them away to watch the warrior and the horse, to imprint on her memory the sight of them cutting such a swath through the belly-deep grass, Windrider's hair flowing loose from its tie-band, its long, black weight lifting and falling on the wind.

Soon they cantered back to her. Windrider leaped down and put Jennie in his place as if it were only her right. She had turned the stallion's head toward the sunset, which was gilding the whole world now with crimson, and he had taken her floating west at a gallop through the shimmering light. Never, ever, had she felt such a thrill.

Except in making love with Windrider.

One day, after they had camped alone by the river for more than ten suns, Windrider woke when the Sun Father did. He lay still and stared into the red dawning, smelling the fresh morning as it came. He had no desire to move.

His throat tightened, hard, as he realized why. It was time, past time, for them to go back to The People.

The hurting of his heart was gone now, cauterized and healed by the fire of the Fire Flower, asleep at this moment in his arms. Since they had been camped here in this place, he had not wakened one single morning with the memory of She Blushes on his mind. He never would again.

Instead, every morning for the rest of his life, until an enemy's arrow or a buffalo's horn or the simple weight of his years took his spirit out of his body, he would wake with the thought of the Fire Flower in his heart. At that instant he prayed to Sun Father and Moon Mother, to his guardian spirit, The Wind, that on every one of those mornings she also would be in his arms.

Without her, nothing would be good for him. The grasses wouldn't whisper messages when the breeze blew through them, the horses wouldn't ride with the speed of the wind, the sun wouldn't warm him. Without her, he might as well be already gone into the Land of the Dead.

Fear, swift as a coyote, clutched in his chest.

Had lying with him, living with him, made her want to stay? She had said that she loved him. But when he gave her her choice, would she choose him or her people?

He tightened his arms around her waist and pulled her back against the front of him, curving his knees behind hers to mold their two bodies together. He buried his face in the thick curls of her hair.

"Kohtoo Topusana," he whispered.

She slept on.

"Fire Flower," he said, and ran his fingers down her bare arm.

She twisted in his embrace and opened her eyes, huge green eyes glazed with dreams. Yet immediately they filled with love for him.

"I'm glad you are the woman in my lodge," he told her. She smiled sweetly, sleepily, but he knew she was hardly aware of what he had said.

The coyote fear clawed at his heart again and, this time, tore it to pieces.

"You belong to me now, Kohtoo Topusana," he said, more loudly than he had intended. He heard his voice go harsh with fear, but he couldn't stop that, either. "You are mine! When we return to camp today, remember that!"

Jennie's warm body shivered with a sudden chill.

His?

Her hazy mind began to work.

She belonged to him? The way she had belonged to Papa and then to Trammel?

No. Never, ever, again would she let any man claim she was his, a possession to do with as he pleased.

"What in the world has come over you?" she cried, starting to struggle to get up and away from him. "I thought we were partners!"

A deeper panic began to run in her veins. Had he, in preparation for going back to The People, reverted to the idea that he was her master and she, his slave? Had he treated her as his equal only because they were all this way out here, alone?

And from what he had just said, this dream of a magic time was ending today!

"What do you mean I *belong* to you?"

The shaking disgust in her voice obscured the meanings of the English words for him. The fading of the love from her eyes pulled his panic out into the open, sent it leaping across the roiling whirlpool of his gut from the rock of one memory to another. Going nowhere.

He could think of no reason, none, that she should turn from fire to ice in the space of one heartbeat.

Setting his jaw, he clenched his fist against her flat stomach to keep her close, but she stiffened her body all up and down, made it stiff as a tree. She twisted out of his embrace to lie on her back.

"Go that far and no farther," he growled, planting his hand on the ground at her side, arching one arm over her to keep her beside him.

Jennie opened her mouth, then closed it. Was he losing his mind?

She stared up into his implacable face, one side framed by the white feathers in his hair, and a sudden realization swept over her, searing hot as the sun shining in her face. Her hand reached for something to cling to and found only hard ground.

She, Jennie O'Bannion, was one small being lying prone and helpless under this huge expanse of sky, naked and weaponless beneath the hard body of a man, a wild Comanche, whom she didn't know at all. She was thousands of miles from anyone who knew her and light-years away from anyone who cared how she fared. He could do anything to her.

She closed her eyes. That idea was too ridiculous, too melodramatic, to be countenanced after the closeness they had had for all of these days. *She* was the one losing her mind!

"I told you how much I need my freedom,"

she said, opening her eyes, smiling at him, looking for the Windrider she knew. "I belong only to myself."

"I thought you had learned complete freedom is not always good," he said, sternly, but a hint of his old smile answered hers. "People need each other. That is why The People live in bands. That is why Ten Bears and I work at getting along, for the good of all the camp, so our one band won't split into two."

"I belong to no man, as slave, chore-woman, or wife."

He felt his smile grow until it covered his face. *Wife. She had said wife.*

She put her hand on his fist, slipped it up onto his wrist, even though it was too big for her fingers to close around. His pulse beat beneath her thumb like a wild thing.

He was the same old Windrider whom she loved, the same Windrider whose blood ran hot at her touch.

Wasn't he?

"You would be my wife?"

His tone was light, with a trace of laughter. He had become his old teasing self again.

Except for a vibration, a tension she couldn't put a name to that was woven in the web of his words.

She answered in a tone just as light as his.

"*That* could split the band in two," she said. "Ten Bears might be resentful."

"Don't worry about that," he said, unclenching his fist, setting her free as he swiftly sat up. He grinned that mischievous grin of his. "Ten Bears can be soothed. It's a custom for brothers to share their wives."

Of course, he could never share the Fire Flower. Never.

But she didn't know that. She sat up so fast, she bumped her head against his, grabbing for their cover-robe, leaning away from him as if touching him were the last thing in the world she wanted.

Shock, unutterable shock, turned Jennie as cold as a winter wind. How could he *say* such a thing, how could he *think* it after the days and nights they'd just had?

"You're a savage!" she cried, clutching the robe to her breasts, scrambling to get up and away from him.

The epithet struck at his heart like an enemy's arrow. Once, then again.

"You're a primitive savage to say such a thing! To have such a repulsive idea, after what we've just shared!"

She believed that—she was staring at him as if he were a monster. She didn't love him. She never had loved him, or she wouldn't be saying these things now.

She didn't love him.

"You're right," he shouted, rising with full dignity to his feet, "marrying with you wouldn't be worth the trouble it would cause with Ten Bears. Because I *couldn't* share you, no matter what claim he makes!"

How could she think he would give her to his brother, whom she loathed? Didn't she know him any better than that?

He clenched his fists and beat them on the muscles of his thighs.

"The very custom is barbaric! You are all barbarians, all of you! Savage barbarians who killed my parents!" she cried, using one trembling hand to brush the hair back out of her eyes, the other keeping the robe against her, between them, as she stepped forward to say her piece right into his face.

"You and your murdering warriors came pouring in through the gates of the fort, with innocent people in there asleep—"

"*Innocent* people!" he roared. "No! *Guilty* people! Murderers themselves! My mother and the Third Wife of Ten Bears, two of the truly good persons who ever lived, were stolen from their berry picking and raped and ravaged and *shot dead* by those innocent people. Maybe your father was one of those who spilled their blood!"

Jennie took a step back, clutching the robe so hard, her fingernails dug into her chest. The image he conjured made her stomach roll. Memories that now seemed from an age in the past came back to her, snatches of talk in those rough strangers' voices.

So that was the business they had had with Comanche women.

She shook her head slowly, back and forth. Behind her, in the pen, Kwahira whinnied. Spirit Talker answered. They sounded a thousand miles away.

"No. *No*," she said. "My papa was an overbearing dictator to women sometimes, but he would never be a party to such a terrible thing. Neither would anyone else at the fort. The men who did it were wanderers who ran to the fort for shelter."

He cocked his head and stared at her through narrowed eyes.

"It's true," she said, her lips going stiff with remembering the killers sitting at her table, sleeping in the next room from her and Trammel.

"Their names were Digger and Nate. That's all I know about them."

He glared at her fiercely.

"Then how do you know they did the killings?"

"I heard them talking—just bits of conversation that I didn't understand at the time—about Comanches and how the woman maybe put a curse on them, how she fought them."

Sudden tears glistened in his eyes.

And stung in hers.

He gave a short nod, and she knew he believed her. "That would have been my mother putting a curse on them. Fighting them."

Finally he spoke, his voice rough with grief.

"I'm sorry about your family," he said. "But the white eyes have no place on the plains. They were not born to this land. It belongs to us."

They. Us.

Killings and rapings and shootings and burnings between *them* and *us*.

Jennie turned from him, looked wildly from side to side, hurting so much, she could hardly see the copse of cottonwood trees by the river, the red cliffs of the canyon in the sunrise.

How could she ever have thought that she and Windrider could love each other?

He set his face hard as the rocks beneath the stream.

"They should stay at *their* home," he said.

She clutched the robe tighter, with both hands.

"Then why did you bring me here?" she cried. "Why didn't you leave me at home? I never asked to come with you! Take me back!"

His face darkened with prideful fury.

"I will do that!" he said. "I will take you to Texas!"

* * *

They rode east, the spare horses following. Windrider sent Kwahira out a little ahead, and Jennie held Spirit Talker another length behind that. She kept her eyes away from Windrider's symmetrical, bare back, swept them over the horizon, searching for landmarks.

If only she could rip her stubborn mind from its agony, as well! He was gone from her. He would never hold her again.

The thought made her heart shatter into a thousand pieces.

She took a long, shaky breath. She *would* survive, she would survive all of this.

But what would she do, where would she go, when they reached Texas?

The fort was ashes. If her parents had somehow lived through the raid, they could be anywhere, maybe even on a ship headed back to Ireland.

Her mind escaped, began to imagine Ireland ahead, there, on the eastern horizon. She would ride up the fenced, winding lane through the mist of an early morning and into the yard of the thatched tenant cottage. Mama and Papa and all her brothers and sisters would come swarming out the door calling her name; she would get down from her horse and run into their arms.

The sun was straight overhead when she realized that they were no longer riding due east; their tracks were making a definite angle to the north. She clucked to Spirit Talker and rode faster to catch up to Windrider.

"We're heading too far north," she said, observing the Comanche custom, which the two of them usually ignored, of not looking the other person directly in the eye. She *couldn't* look into his face. She would either burst into tears or leap from her horse to his and scratch him to pieces.

"Texas is that way," she added, pointing.

"Texas is everywhere," he said, sourly, and kept on riding without even turning his head.

"Talk riddles all you want," she snapped, "but you promised to take me to Texas, and you aren't doing it. You're heading the wrong way!"

"I will take you to Texas or I will send you with my Spanish trader friend, Oñate. But not this sun. I have been gone so many suns already that Ten Bears will be thinking he is Great Chief of all the *Nermernuh*."

That brought her eyes to his face, glued her gaze to it.

"You're taking me back to The People?"

Her voice rose and cracked with incredulity as her mind raced to understand it.

He had intended this ever since they started out! He had let her think she was going to Texas when she wasn't!

Well, why should that surprise her? she thought bitterly. He had let her think he cared for her, perhaps even loved her, when he didn't.

"This isn't the way to your people's camp, either," she said stubbornly. "I may be a white-eyes, but I know that much!"

"Camp has moved," he said, shortly. "We have been away for many suns. Long before this sun, that camping place got dirty. Ten Bears chose a new one and moved it."

She turned Spirit Talker's head away from Kwahira, wheeled her around, and rode her back to the place where they'd been in the little procession, all the while glaring at Windrider's back, welcoming the fury that was rising to glue her heart back together. She ought to take Little Wolf with his load of supplies and just ride away, head straight east and go to Texas on her own.

Windrider would do nothing to stop her. He obviously didn't care if she lived or died.

All morning he had talked of nothing but how much power Ten Bears must be getting in his absence. He had promised to take her to Texas, but he was taking her back to the village. He was a treacherous person, a liar who couldn't be trusted.

She turned around and looked at Little Wolf, thought about which supplies she had packed on him that morning, but finally she kept Spirit Talker on course, following Kwahira. Texas seemed farther away than Ireland and as foreign to her now, more so, than the Comanche camp. At least she would have Hukiyani. *Hukiyani* wouldn't lie to her.

They rode around a grassy, rolling hill and into a draw that led toward a stand of hackberries and elms. Just as they reached the cool shade of the trees, her small voice of truth finally reached her.

Windrider hadn't lied to her, either. Not about this trip, anyway. He had never said *when* he would take her to Texas.

They sighted the smoke from the fires of the camp just before daylight started fading to dusk. Windrider had gone straight to it, up the valley of a shallow river to the new spot where The People had camped in the kind of place they liked, along a stream in open timber. To the west of camp, on the grassy plain, the enormous, magical horse herd grazed.

A movement near it caught Jennie's eye and she smiled. One of the herdboys had seen them and was going to spread the news.

The fragrant smells of sweet woodsmoke and spicy stew floated out from the fires as they rode up to the camp, and Jennie closed her eyes to draw them in. Somehow it seemed that it smelled like home.

Men, women, children, and dogs ran out to greet them, calling and chattering. Eagle Tail Father ran by Spirit Talker and touched Jennie on the foot, calling up to her, "Hel-lo, Kohtoo Topusana!" before he raced on through the crowd to greet his beloved uncle. Just that quick glimpse of the excitement sparkling in his dark eyes made her smile.

Then, somehow, in all the frenzy, Jennie was off Spirit Talker, onto the ground, and folded into Hukiyani's arms. The rotund woman squeezed her, twice, hard, then pulled back and looked at her, studying her from top to toe. She nodded, beamed a beatific smile, and hugged Jennie again, making her bobbed hair swing madly forward and back, pouring a steady murmur of Comanche into her ear.

Jennie laughed, in spite of the ache in her heart. This was a real homecoming!

Then they both turned to see Windrider leap to the ground and throw his rein to Eagle Tail Feather, whose face was shining like the sun from such an honor.

"Thank you, My Uncle," he said loudly, looking around to make sure that all the other boys saw and envied him.

Jennie thought, with sudden surprise, that he had grown several inches since she last saw him.

"Does this mean you are sharing your new horse with me?" the boy asked boldly, a bubbling chuckle in his voice.

A great shout of laughter went up. It wrapped

them all in warmth like a blanket around their shoulders, and Jennie was included, because after her language lessons from Windrider, she understood every word.

Her eyes flew to Windrider's chiseled face, then she felt the sting of tears. What an irony! She felt completely a part of the tribe now, but she would never be close to him again. She stood very still, unable to look away from him, caught in her haunting memories of the days and nights just past.

The entire tribe, it seemed, had gathered around Windrider and the great white Kwahira, the legendary wild horse that only their legendary War Chief could capture and tame, everyone jostling to see him and touch him. *She would never touch Windrider again.*

He would never touch her.

Windrider nodded assent to Eagle Tail Feather. The boy bent at the waist, still carefully holding the horse, and did a few circling steps of the Victory Dance, lifting the rein to dance under it. The cheers and laughter rolled out again in a great wave of sound.

Hukiyani took Jennie's hand in a remorseless grip. It made Jennie's gaze swing away from Windrider at last to fasten on her earnest face. She wasn't smiling now. Her small, dark eyes flicked back and forth between Jennie and Windrider, her brow wrinkled in a frown.

"There is anger between you?" she asked. "After such a long time alone on the plains?"

Again, Jennie understood every word of the Comanche. But she didn't answer. She couldn't.

Suddenly Hukiyani plunged into the melee, badgering and pushing a path open for them, relentlessly puling Jennie behind her. Jennie came

willingly enough, until she saw that Hukiyani
would not stop until she had reached Windrider.

"No!" she called. "Hukiyani, no!"

But the words did no more good than did digging her heels into the ground. Hukiyani's greater
weight carried her along like a feather, and the
noise and confusion were too great for Jennie's
shouts to be heard. Hukiyani reached her goal and
tapped firmly on Windrider's shoulder.

He turned from the horse and looked down at
them. Jennie stared past him at Kwahira.

Hukiyani spoke loudly, pouring out the words
in a spate of Comanche, and several people
nearby stopped talking to listen. Windrider went
very still, but when Jennie glanced at him, his
face showed no emotion.

Hukiyani's hand touched Jennie's arm, then
made a quick gesture toward Windrider. She was
asking him to translate.

For a moment he said nothing.

Then he looked at Jennie and, in his rich voice,
said, "I have a surprise for you, Kohtoo Topusana. You will become a true member of the *Nermernuh*. You will be one of The People. You will
be adopted into this band, welcome to live in any
lodge in this camp."

Stunned, Jennie stared at him, forgetting for a
fleeting second that the words came, not from
him, but from Hukiyani. She whirled to look at
the woman, but her sparkling black eyes were
fixed on Windrider, her round face flushed dark
with excitement. She spoke again, fast, too fast
for Jennie to catch even one Comanche word.

"We are glad you are with us," Windrider
translated woodenly, "and that you are alive after
being lost. Kohtoo Topusana, you are too dear to
be kept as a captive. Tomorrow, when the Sun

Father comes again, we will smoke and say the
words to make you *Nermernuh*. After that, you
may go to any tipi you choose.''

Hukiyani winked and smiled, looking from Jennie to Windrider and back again, nodding as if to
say that everyone knew, of course, that Jennie
would stay with him. She crossed her arms across
her ample bosom and made a low clucking sound,
as if to say that now everything would be all right.

Jennie stood staring from one of them to the
other, completely overwhelmed, drowning in the
maelstrom of conflicting emotions churning inside her. Tears sprang to her eyes, she was so
touched by what Hukiyani had said, by her wanting Jennie to be adopted into The People.

But she wanted to throw herself facedown and
scream and cry and beat her fists against the
ground. *Windrider* did not want her here.

Yet she must speak quietly. This was an honor
that Hukiyani was conferring, in public, with a
face full of love.

It would break Jennie's heart all over again to
see the sad disappointment replace that love and
excitement, but she had no choice. It wouldn't be
right not to tell Hukiyani the truth.

Jennie opened her mouth to speak, but the feelings flooding through her washed away every
word of her new language. She could barely find
the English to say what she wanted to say.

''Tell her I am greatly honored,'' Jennie said at
last, looking straight at Windrider, speaking
through lips gone stiff with pain. ''And I am as
greatly sorry to disappoint her. But I cannot accept the adoption. I have chosen to return to
Texas.''

He spoke.

She longed to shut her eyes then, not to look,

not to see the hurt come in and darken Hukiyani's face. But she was Kohtoo Topusana, too brave to be kept as a captive. She owed it to Hukiyani to try to let her know how much she hated to reject this gift.

As Windrider translated, she reached for both Hukiyani's hands and looked straight at her, trying to say with her eyes all that she felt in her heart. But the happy excitement stayed on Hukiyani's face!

When Windrider had finished translating, she ripped her hands out of Jennie's grip, threw her arms around her, and hugged her harder than she ever had before. Over her plump shoulder, Jennie's bewildered gaze flew to Windrider.

Obviously he had not translated correctly. Other people were gathering closer, patting her and making congratulatory noises. Eagle Tail Feather jumped onto Kwahira and called down to Jennie, grinning, one fist raised in victory, the other hand holding firmly to the legendary stallion's rein.

He chanted, "Kohtoo Topusana! Kohtoo Topusana! You will be *Nermernuh*! You will be of The People!"

Windrider's closed face told her nothing, but his hooded dark eyes met hers.

She opened her mouth to call to him—she must make him correct this immediately. Why, she couldn't let this dear woman adopt her into the tribe when she would deliberately leave it so soon! That would be as awful a treachery as what Windrider had done to her.

But no words would come from her mouth. Her body, as traitorous as Windrider, relaxed into the warmth of Hukiyani's motherly one, and her lips returned the smiles of The People.

Chapter 14

Jennie turned over in her bed robes for the hundredth time and opened her eyes. Dimly she could see the tipi poles slanting up to the smoke hole far above her. It felt strange to be inside after so many nights in the open.

But that wasn't the reason she lay sleepless. And having ridden hard all day wasn't the reason she felt a weird sensation as if she were still moving, unable to stop, unable to draw a deep, peaceful breath.

The itching restlessness pulled at her until she got up and went to kneel at the lodge's entrance, lifted the door-flap, and peered out at the camp, which was washed in a dim, pale moonlight. The fires burned low; a few people moved in the spaces between the lodges, but not many.

Windrider was still in the Council meeting, no doubt—Ten Bears' tipi, rolled up around the edges, showed the faint glow of a fire and the shapes of many bodies.

Somewhere nearby a dog snuffled in his sleep, and Kwahira, tied to his stake rope just to the side of the lodge, stopped grazing, threw up his head, and rumbled a warning deep in his throat. Jennie smiled. The next dog- or wolflike creature to attack him would feel the force of his hooves, whether horses were instinctively flight creatures or not.

A woman moved into Jennie's line of sight, walking gracefully between the lodges, carrying something in both hands. Her movements looked like Breaks Something's flowing glide. She stopped at Ten Bears' lodge and went in, suddenly awkward in trying to manage her burden and lift the door-flap at the same time.

Jennie felt a bitter smile touch her lips. Breaks Something had wangled the task of bringing food to the Council members—for a chance to see Windrider, no doubt. Well, Breaks Something could have him!

She turned, left the doorway, and threw herself back onto her bed. Hukiyani had told her at supper that the Council was to meet that night about something important, but not about Jennie's adoption. Everyone had already agreed on that, she'd said. The People loved her.

"The People have much love for the Fire Flower," Yellowfish had assented, nodding vigorously. "They know that the Fire Flower has much courage, as much as any warrior." He stopped and smiled. "She must tell us again the story of Kwahira and the wolves."

"You might let her eat her supper first, Silly Old Man," Hukiyani had answered. "The child has had nothing to eat except her own cooking for many, many suns."

All of them around the fire, Jennie included, laughed loudly at that.

"Ah! I thought Windrider looked as thin as a stick," Yellowfish joked, and the laughter grew even warmer. "Now, girl, you learn from Hukiyani to cook and you can make him fat."

He winked one hawklike eye and drew his wide lips down into a wry grin.

Jennie had no trouble in understanding his meaning, just as she had every Comanche word. Nor did she miss a single one of the significant looks that passed between the rotund older woman and her husband. How embarrassing! Evidently they had decided that she and Windrider were now a couple, no longer master and slave. How embarrassing if the whole camp had gotten that impression!

She followed Hukiyani to the cook fire and helped her dish up the stew, leaning close to speak privately to her.

"May I stay here tonight, please?" she asked. "With you in your tipi?"

"A captive must stay in her master's lodge," Hukiyani answered, fixing Jennie with a stern look from the corner of her eye. "After the ceremony tomorrow, you will no longer be captive, you will be *Nermernuh*. Then you may go where you please."

She dipped a bone ladle into the delicious-smelling broth, filled a wooden bowl, and handed it to Jennie.

"You would miss your War Chief, your great horse catcher," she murmured, smiling. "Soon, you will see, the anger will pass."

But it wouldn't.

Jennie had known that the minute Hukiyani had said it, and she knew it now. So why hadn't she told her and the fun-loving old Yellowfish, made them understand that she couldn't be adopted, that, as soon as possible, she was going back to Texas?

That question had been torturing her all evening long, all through the long dinner with its

endless eating and storytelling, all through the
unpacking of hers and Windrider's gear and arranging it in his lodge. But the other question tor-
mented her even more.

Why hadn't Windrider told the whole tribe Jennie
was planning to leave? Why had he mistranslated
her words?

Her heart caught in her throat. Could it be that
he was trying to keep her here because, as his
body had told her so many times, he did love her?

No. He didn't love her.

Not after the way he had looked at her when
she called him a savage. He had agreed in a heartbeat to take her to Texas.

She closed her eyes against that memory and
drifted, willing her mind to take her away into the
wonderful days they had had just before their awful fight. Lost in that fantasy, she hovered between daydreams and night dreams of Windrider
until some slight movement, some sense that
someone was there with her in the lodge, brought
her instantly alert.

The air moved, a slight rustling sound floated
to her from Windrider's bed robes.

"Windrider?"

She sat up and cleared her throat, trying to rid
her voice of its trembling. Trying to rid her heart
of its forlorn bit of hope.

"Why didn't you tell Hukiyani what I really
said?"

"Why didn't *you*?"

The hard edge in his voice cut the hope to
shreds and shattered the last vestiges of her
dreams.

"I didn't want to make a liar out of the great
hero, catcher of the famous wild stallion," she

shot back sarcastically. "That would disappoint The People."

"You are most thoughtful."

He spoke with a flat finality, as if her question were not still hanging between them, there in the air.

He made a great fuss about arranging his robes. She peered through the darkness at his big, supple body, at his movements outlined in the moonlight that filtered through the hide walls.

"Don't you go to sleep without answering my question!" she cried, going up onto her knees. "Talk to me! Were you telling the truth when you said you would take me to Texas?"

With a great sigh of annoyance, he said, "Yes. Now I must sleep."

Anger boiled in her, pulled her toward him, even though she couldn't see his face at all. She clenched her fists and hit them against the robes beneath her.

"Then why are you letting poor, trusting Hukiyani hold a ceremony to make me a Comanche? She'll be so disappointed when I go away!"

"It's best that you become *Nermernuh.*"

"*Why?* You tell me why!"

"To make it harder for Ten Bears to get you."

For one shining moment, the hope sprang to life again inside her. It dragged her heart, pounding hard, up into her throat.

He did care about her—he wanted to keep her for himself!

"You will no longer be a captive that my brother can ask for," he said, "to taunt my lack of generosity."

Her stupid heart fell from her throat into the ground.

"What in the name of Saint Patrick does Ten

Bears have to do with this?'' she cried, trying not to understand, truly furiously hurting now. ''You have ruined my honor because of something about Ten Bears?''

''You could have saved your own honor,'' he said shortly.

She chose to ignore that.

''Ten Bears! Ten Bears! It's always Ten Bears! I'd be halfway to Texas by now if you hadn't had to rush back to battle with Ten Bears!''

''Texas! Texas! It's always Texas!'' he mocked her.

He raised up on one elbow and said, in a low, biting tone, ''I promised to take you to Texas, and I will. But not now. Now there is danger, and I must have power to influence my brother and others—for the good of The People.''

''What kind of danger?''

''The Texan Rangers. Many of them, riding together. Looking for the band of *Nermernuh* that burned the fort.''

''So what does that have to do with whether I am a captive or a member of the band?''

Her voice was shaking again and she swallowed hard, trying to control it. Trying not to think what would happen if the Rangers found The People.

''We will have to make many decisions,'' he said, quick passion flowing into his voice. ''I need no cries and shouts from Ten Bears about my stinginess in keeping you from him or from Mopai. My power to persuade The People, it is crucial now.''

It was true, then. She *was* nothing but a pawn to him, a pawn in the eternal political games that he played with his brother. He didn't love her, and he never had.

She would hold him to his promise. She would make him take her to Texas.

Windrider set his jaw and turned onto his side to face the wall away from her. If she spoke again, he would refuse to answer. He would send her from the lodge if she did not keep quiet so he could consider the Council news about the Rangers.

She kept quiet. Soon her breathing changed from fast and shallow, angry, to slow and deep in the darkness.

He listened. Could she have fallen asleep so quickly? His mouth twisted in irony at the thought. Why not? If her heart, which he had thought was loyal and loving—hadn't she *told* him that she loved him?—was hard enough for her to call him a savage and demand to leave him because his people had taken a revenge on the fort, which was nothing but the way of the world, then it was hard enough for her to fight with him one minute and go to sleep the next.

He squeezed his eyes more tightly closed against the image of her curving white body against the dark buffalo robes. She could sleep in them alone from now on, for all he cared. If the joy and the passion they had found when they shared a bed meant nothing to her, then so be it.

But the thought of never holding her again made him empty, made his body go hollow with loneliness, made his mind go barren of every thought but the Fire Flower. He fought to drive her out of it, to think about the pale-eyed Rangers camped out there on the prairie this very night, hunting this band of people he loved, eager for their blood.

He must think about that and about how to

manage Ten Bears instead of about this woman. No woman was worth risking the lives of The People.

But before he succeeded in banishing her from his mind, he had another passing thought. Another night, when his anger with her had passed, he might hold her and make love to her again just to remind her of what she was giving up. He would still have her right here, living in his lodge. Hukiyani's adoption ceremony wouldn't change that.

The next afternoon, Jennie sat in the place of honored guest in Hukiyani's tipi. The sides had been rolled up so that the whole camp could hear the proceedings of her adoption ceremony, recited by Windrider's and Ten Bears' father, Half Horse. His voice was low and firm, like Windrider's, and he had smiled at her twice, yet his eyes held the most sorrowful expression she had ever seen. Now he simply sat, looking at her, waiting for Windrider to finish translating the last formal, poetic words that made her a member of the band. One of The People.

"Now we will go out together," he said, when he had finished. "And you will greet your new brothers and sisters."

Hukiyani stood up, motioned to Jennie to rise, and led the way outside into the open space at the center of this camp. The warriors, the elders who sat on the Council, and the women important enough to have been invited inside followed them out into the bright sunlight.

Jennie had expected the memories of the Victory Dance to haunt her as she stood on display again in the middle of the whole band, but this campsite was very different from that first one.

Here a rough circle of berry-laden hackberries surrounded the community space, trees that held out their arms and offered their fruit to everyone. Behind them, the fast-running river talked.

That and the breeze moving in the trees were the only sounds. Even the children were quiet, intimidated by the large gathering and the air of solemnity.

Half Horse wrapped his blanket around his age-bent body, walked slowly, with great dignity, to Jennie, and lifted his hand to hold it over her head. His deep voice, speaking in Comanche, carried over the entire camp.

Then Windrider's, like an echo, repeating in English.

"Welcome to The People," he said. "You are one of us. From the time of this sun, for as long as the grass grows and the water flows, you are called Kohtoo Topusana."

"Kohtoo Topusana!" The high, uncertain tones of a very young child repeated the words. A light chuckle raced through the crowd in answer, but it quickly hushed.

Looks of curiosity flashed from face to face. Jennie knew everyone was waiting for the most interesting part of the ceremony, the question.

Half Horse lowered his hand, walked to a position facing Jennie, fixed her with his sad, wise eyes, and asked it.

Windrider translated, "Little Sister, Kohtoo Topusana. In which lodge of this camp of the Antelope Band of the Comanche do you choose to live? Which warrior do you choose as your protector?"

Jennie slowly raised her eyes to meet his. His face was fixed into an uncaring mask, the same look it had taken on when she had called him a savage.

She turned away, searching for Hukiyani. The older woman stood beside Yellowfish, to Jennie's right, watching her, smiling, looking from Jennie to Windrider as Jennie opened her mouth to answer.

"I choose to live in Hukiyani's lodge," Jennie said, clearly. "I choose Yellowfish as my protector."

She repeated her choice in the formal Comanche phrases that Eagle Tail Feather had taught her this morning.

The boy had kept her secret well, as she had asked him to—a great whisper of surprise, a sound like a wind, swept over the camp.

She dared to look at Windrider. For one flashing instant, his eyes blazed brilliant with hurt and shock. Eagle Tail Feather had not told him, either, although he must have been sorely tempted.

Everyone gathered around them then, as they had done the day before when the two of them had come home. The press of bodies kept Windrider near her, but he turned his eyes away.

And his heart. She had driven it away with her words.

He had not been happy to be rid of her, not at all.

Jennie stood frozen, trying to comprehend it. He had wanted her to stay with him; his look in that one vulnerable instant had told her that. *Did* he care for her, after all?

Oh, Lord, what had she done?

Then Hukiyani had her by the arm, and Jennie turned to look into her round face, suffused at once by happiness and dismay. Behind them, around them, calls and greetings came from everywhere.

Yellowfish appeared at Jennie's side and greeted her, smiling and frowning at the same time, it seemed.

"So, Windrider!" came an old man's teasing voice from out of the crowd. "Who will do your chores now?"

"*I* will," a woman's light voice came back in answer. Jennie looked toward the sound. Sure enough. Breaks Something was smiling at Windrider, cutting her sharp eyes at Jennie.

Another, younger male voice taunted, "Ho, Windrider, can't keep your woman?"

Windrider acted as if he hadn't heard any of them, turned, and pushed his way out of the crush. Jennie's heart started beating so wildly, she thought it would tear a hole through her chest. She wished she hadn't known enough Comanche to understand the gibes.

She had made him lose face; this would give an advantage to Ten Bears somehow, and she was sorry.

But suddenly her heart filled with grim satisfaction. That flash of disappointment and hurt she had seen in Windrider's eyes had not been because he cared for her, but because her leaving him made him lose a point in the game. Made him lose his pawn.

Hukiyani pulled on Jennie's hand and began moving. Gratefully Jennie followed her to Windrider's lodge, gathered her few possessions, and took them to Hukiyani's.

"No big fire . . . this dark . . . go down," the tagalong Eagle Tail Feather said. "Ran-gers."

"No . . . dance," Hukiyani agreed.

Thank God, Jennie thought. All she wanted
was to be alone.

But once Jennie had put her things away, Hukiyani motioned her to a backrest, and Eagle Tail
Feather to another. Then she proceeded to
roundly scold them both.

The boy used his few English words, Hukiyani
said "Windrider" in English no less than a hundred times, it seemed; Jennie understood most of
the Comanche words, and when the older woman
finally ran out of breath, Jennie knew exactly what
it was she had done. She had insulted Windrider
to his face and in public by leaving his lodge.

"I'm not sorry!" she cried, in full rebellion. "It
serves him right. He certainly doesn't worry about
my feelings any!"

Hukiyani answered with a piercing look, a disgusted shake of her head, and a spate of words
and signs that Eagle Tail Feather translated as
"Feast. To honor . . . Kohtoo Topusana. Before
Father Sun go. Dress."

Regret seized Jennie in its sharp teeth and
shook her hard. Windrider would have to come
to the celebration or lose *more* face; he would have
to endure more taunts and teasing. How would
this effect his "power to persuade the people"?

Had she inadvertently given an advantage to
Ten Bears that would place the band in danger?

Somehow Jennie was able to keep moving. She
bathed, dressed in the finely beaded and quilled
new dress that Hukiyani gave her, walked
through the crowd, sat in the place of honor, and
pretended to eat, to enjoy the feast. Windrider
never so much as looked in her direction.

He sat with Ten Bears and the rest of the Council as the long afternoon passed, in a tight knot of
men gathered off to one side for privacy, smoking

and talking as much as they ate. At one point, Windrider stood and spoke to the rest of them for several minutes. At another time, Ten Bears did the same.

Jennie watched, praying silently that, whatever the question was, Windrider's answer would win.

Dusk fell. The moon rose, silvering the fading light, blotting out the small cook fires that the women were banking for concealment in the darkness. Later on, the dark would be deep—this was only a quarter moon, not a full one like the magic moon of that first night she and Windrider had been alone.

A sudden feeling of pure desolation swept through Jennie.

She turned to Hukiyani.

"Could I go now," she whispered, "back to your tipi?"

Hukiyani nodded, but Jennie didn't move. Because suddenly Windrider's rich voice filled the night.

Jennie went still as the tree trunk at her back.

He was to her left, out in the open circle formed by the whispering leaves of the trees. He wasn't looking at her—if he were, she would feel his gaze touch her flesh like the pressure of his fingertips.

The sound of his voice came again, strong as the call of a bugle this time. Shouting Comanche words that Jennie well understood.

"We ride!"

A great chorus of agreement rose from dozens of throats, and many, more than a dozen, young men sprang to their feet. Windrider pointed to one of them, then another, and another.

Everyone waited; Jennie held her breath. But that was all. He turned away.

Those three men ran for their tipis, their equipment, for their horses.

Windrider faded into the shadows.

Her heart tripped. Her throat closed, hard and tight. He was riding out, right now, into the deepening night. To attack the Rangers?

With only three men to help him?

Oh, dear Lord, he might be killed!

Jennie forgot her desire to go back to the tipi, and began circulating through the restless camp instead, staying right beside Hukiyani until they had learned what Windrider had persuaded the Council to do. Windrider was leading a few men on a pretend raid to lure the Rangers completely out of the Big Turtle Creek country, the others told them. Ten Bears and all the other warriors were staying to defend the camp. The raiders were taking many extra horses and riding past the Rangers' camp toward the east so that the Texans would follow, thinking to prevent a large war party from raiding a white-eyes settlement.

Ten Bears had argued for war, for attacking the Rangers while they slept.

Windrider had warned that, if they did that, there would be massive retaliations all over the plains against innocent bands of The People, for the Texan Ranges were a different breed of pale eyes. They never forgave and they never gave up.

Jennie walked away from Hukiyani, moving blindly toward the river. She needed to be outside and alone, under the huge sky filled with stars, smelling the sweet grass and tasting the wind. Listening to the wind.

A few minutes later, they were gone. She knew it, although she had never heard so much as one hoof strike the ground.

* * *

The sun came up and bore down on the camp like an oppressing hand. For an eternity, for an age. Until finally it went down again. It did that four times, and still Windrider did not return.

The Rangers had been camped a long way off, the scouts had said, and they, like The People, moved often. Windrider would have to find them. And then he would lure them far, far away, all the way up to the Cross Timbers if they would follow. Windrider might be away until Mother Moon was full again.

Jennie kept to herself one day, making Hukiyani crazy with worry by riding Spirit Talker for miles out from the camp alone, and the next, she stuck to her foster mother's side like a sticker-burr. The next, she rode alone again. She couldn't decide what she wanted, where she wanted to be, but wherever she was, she kept an eye on the eastern horizon across the wide creek. This was her chance to escape, she told herself, each time Spirit Talker carried her miles away from the camp. But always she had the mare carry her back again.

On the fifth day that Windrider had been gone, she went for a long ride to the east, the way he would probably return, but she saw no sign of approaching riders. When she returned, she trotted her mare right on past the horse herd and into the tipis strung out along the Big Turtle Creek.

Several children, swimming and playing games in the water, called and waved to her. The rest of the camp lay drowsy and quiet in the midsummer heat.

Jennie waved back, but she didn't slow down, not even when Eagle Tail Feather called that he would take care of her horse for her. She rode all the way up to Hukiyani's lodge.

"*Pia*, Mother!" she called.

Hukiyani stuck her round face out the door opening.

Jennie recited her request in Comanche, as she'd been rehearsing all the way back to the camp.

"May I tie my mare here tonight? She will keep me company."

Hukiyani looked at her and frowned.

Jennie frowned, too. Did she not understand her? Had she used the wrong words?

But then the plump woman answered, "You may tie your mare here."

Her gaze flicked from Jennie to a spot just behind her.

Jennie's arms broke out in goose bumps. Was it Windrider? Had he and his men ridden in from another direction while she had been gone?

She tightened her legs against Spirit Talker's sweaty sides and turned her around.

But Hukiyani was only looking at Yellowfish and a man sitting in the shade of Yellowfish's lodge, smoking and talking. Then Jennie saw that the man was Ten Bears.

A finger of foreboding traced its way down her spine.

She turned the mare's head to Hukiyani's lodge again and got off on the side away from the men.

"What is it, *Pia*?"

Hukiyani motioned for her to come inside.

Jennie tethered the mare temporarily to a lodgepole, as Hukiyani, casting one last, sharp look at the men, withdrew from the door.

"I will return to rub you down," Jennie promised Spirit Talker, stopping to touch her nose before she went into the tipi. "You must only wait for a moment."

Hukiyani gave Jennie a piercing look, too. Then she started speaking before she even finished pouring her a drink of water from the bladder bag hanging on the pole.

"This is the second time he has come to talk with Yellowfish," she hissed, almost in a whisper, and Jennie looked around to see if someone else was there.

No, they were alone.

"Ten Bears?"

"Yes. He comes to ask how many horses for you."

Jennie stared at her as she took the wooden bowl of water in both hands. She heard the words, but they went past her ears. Somehow her mind couldn't snag them and bring them in.

Hukiyani clucked her tongue impatiently and took a step toward her. In her own language and with signs, she said, "He comes to ask my husband how many horses he will take for you to be new Third Wife to Ten Bears."

Jennie turned the bowl toward her, missed her mouth, and spilled every drop of the water down the front of her dress. It ran over it, onto the ends of the fringes, and down the skin of her bare legs like rivers of tears.

"No! No, it cannot be!"

She thought she had shouted, but she barely breathed the words.

"No," she said, more loudly. "Tell them, *Pia*! Please. Never could I be wife to Ten Bears!"

"I have *told* my husband," she snapped, casting a bitter glance at the wall as if Yellowfish could see her scorn through it. "He will not listen, because he loves many horses and he is too old to raid for them."

"But Windrider could give him many horses!"

Jennie blurted, then bit her lips for what she had just said.

And to stop what she wanted to say. *Windrider!* her heart was screaming inside her. *It's Windrider's wife I should be!*

"I told him that, too," Hukiyani sighed and said. "But he says that will never be. You chose not to live in Windrider's lodge. You made him lose face in front of all the camp."

The breeze blew in beneath the rolled-up sides of the tipi and cooled the water on Jennie's legs. A puddle was forming in each of her low-cut moccasins.

Hukiyani's voice sounded so flat, so final, that it made Jennie's very bones go cold.

She loved Windrider. That was why she couldn't sleep, couldn't eat, why she was so restless, she couldn't stand to be trapped in her own skin.

But Windrider was gone, and she had no idea when he would come back. Perhaps never.

Even if he came back today, he wouldn't claim her. He was absolutely, scornfully, furious with her. He cared nothing for her. He never had.

That will never be. Yellowfish was right.

"My husband is right in another thing he says," Hukiyani said.

It took a moment for Jennie to realize that her foster mother wasn't simply agreeing with her thoughts.

"What thing?" she managed to say, although her lips would barely move.

"Yellowfish has lived too many winters to be your protector. You are headstrong and ride out alone when you know there are Rangers. Hard, dangerous times will come. So will the cold moons, the hungry moons."

There was grudging acceptance, and yes, now a hint of approval in her tone.

"Yellowfish loves you, Daughter, as well as horses. Ten Bears can take care of you. He is not a bad man."

The agreement was already made, Jennie realized. A feeling of dreadful foreboding dragged the strength from her limbs. *That* was what the dear woman was trying to tell her.

All Ten Bears and Yellowfish were doing now was haggling over the price.

Her price. She would be bought and sold like any other possession.

She had only *thought* she was a prisoner in Trammel's house and in Windrider's lodge as his slave. Now she would be in Ten Bears' lodge or alone on the plains, running away.

With Windrider forever in her heart.

Now she was a captive.

Chapter 15

The next three days were the most miserable Jennie had ever known. She had never lost all courage before, not even in the worst times. Why had she now? She had a horse of her own and the knowledge to survive and the instinctive sense of direction to take her to Texas. So why didn't she climb onto her mare, ride her out to the east again, and never come back?

Time was growing short. Ten Bears pressed his suit daily, steadily raising the number of horses he offered to Yellowfish, until Jennie began cherishing each moment that she remained in Hukiyani's lodge. She hollowed out a space among the heavier buffalo robes Hukiyani kept for winter use and started a cache of supplies she would need on the trail. She would run soon. Truly she would.

But not before she saw Windrider once more.

She stopped with her hands tangled in the fastener of the parfleche she was hiding, trying to keep her wild imagination from leaping ahead of that one small admission of truth. But it began rolling out the fantasy scenes that she saw in her head every night before and after she went to sleep, the dreams that kept her from losing her mind.

Windrider, safe and unwounded, thundering into camp at the head of his men and many horses. He would bring Kwahira sliding to a stop, and when all the camp ran to meet him, his piercing eyes would immediately find Jennie in the crowd. He'd leap off his horse, gather her into his arms, and begin striding toward his lodge, shouting to Ten Bears and Yellowfish (when they objected) that he would pay a thousand horses, two thousand, but never would he give up the Fire Flower.

"Kohtoo Topusana?"

Jennie whirled to face the voice, almost convinced by her vision that it must belong to Windrider. It was only after she realized it was Hukiyani's that she noticed she still held the parfleche with both hands in front of her.

Hukiyani glanced at it, but said nothing.

"Ten Bears offers so many horses, my husband cannot stop smiling," she said. "They have smoked on it."

Jennie wheeled around and stuffed the parfleche back into its hiding place, knowing, even with her back to Hukiyani, that she had guessed its purpose.

"When will he bring the horses?"

Her voice sounded so muffled, so dead, that she wouldn't have known she had spoken if it hadn't hurt her lips and her tongue to form the words.

"Before Father Sun leaves us."

Jennie heard her move, felt her come closer. Work-worn fingers touched her arm, stony and gentle at the same time like her mother, Kathleen's.

Then Hukiyani's hand was on her shoulder, urging her to turn. Slowly Jennie swung around to look at her.

It was so Hukiyani could use signs as well as words. Even though Jennie had a great deal of Comanche by now, Hukiyani was taking no chances on her misunderstanding this comforting thought.

"Sometimes the husband does not come to his new wife's lodge for a long time after he brings the horses to her father. Sometimes a sun or two rises and sets or an even longer time goes by."

Then Hukiyani's smile faded into a look so sympathetic, it brought tears into Jennie's eyes. The motherly woman opened her arms and folded her into them.

Jennie cried her heart out while Hukiyani stroked her hair and murmured an unending litany of ways that Ten Bears could protect and take care of her. She reminded her that she would be nearby, that their days together need not change, and that Ten Bears already had two other wives to help with the work. She even remembered to say that Half Horse and his sons and their wives pitched their tipis near hers and Yellowfish's in every camp.

Then she switched to an even more cheerful tone.

"The Fire Flower, Yellowfish, and Ten Bears will be told of in legends," she said. "Never has any woman brought the great price of one hundred horses!"

She patted Jennie's back.

"The women will be coming soon to set up your new lodge, daughter," she said, "very near to mine. And we will help you bathe and dress."

Jennie understood everything she said, but the

one bit of information that gave her true hope was the first. Maybe Ten Bears would decide to wait, hoping to let Windrider see him go to his new wife's lodge, or her come to his! Maybe his other wives would be jealous and keep him at home.

Yet she dared not take that chance. She couldn't get away from Hukiyani or the other women now, but when she was alone in her new lodge, she would escape at dusk. During the time Ten Bears' other wives were serving his supper.

She stopped crying. Hukiyani took her by the shoulders and held her away to look at her, just as Kathleen would have done.

A horrifying sensation swept over Jennie, the feeling that all this had happened before. And *that* time, she had hated herself for waiting too long to run.

She shook herself free of the thought. She wasn't waiting too long this time. She was going tonight.

Even if Windrider didn't return.

She pushed that thought away, too. She would think about nothing but slipping her cache in among her other things and moving it with her into the new lodge. Her life depended on that—and on Spirit Talker.

The women came then, many of the same ones who had frightened her so that first day, she was sure, although the only faces she remembered from then were Sanah's and Breaks Something's. Today they laughed and chattered instead of taunting her, and somehow, strangely, their murmuring voices made her feel calmer.

They took her outside, down the creek a little way almost to the bend in the stream, and sat her down in the shade of a cottonwood tree. They used horses to pull in a set of new lodgepoles and brought skins already sewn into a tipi to put over them.

Jennie watched as they built her new home for her, its white hides stretched firm, its brown poles tied at the top, the tipi blending into the landscape as if it had always been there. It looked peaceful and charming in between two of the larger trees, a spot with some privacy, but still in sight of several lodges, including Hukiyani's.

And Yellowfish's. Tears sprang to her eyes. She hated feeling so much resentment for that old man whom she had always liked. She must try to remember that he wasn't acting only out of greed—he was trying to make sure she had someone to hunt food for her and to protect her.

She blinked to clear her vision. The best thing about the location of her new lodge was that it could make escape easier—she wouldn't have to pass any other tipis on the way to the horse herd and Spirit Talker. It would be sad to leave many of the members of the band, especially Hukiyani and little Eagle Tail Feather, but she'd do it and not look back.

"Now," Hukiyani said, taking Jennie's arm after the builders had shown her everything about her new tipi. "It is time for you to bathe and dress. He will be bringing the horses soon."

Jennie leaned close to her ear. "You said he might not come to me tonight, *Pia*."

"He might not. But you must be ready."

She would be ready, Jennie swore to herself as the frolicking women led her to the river, stripped off her blouse and skirt, and began to bathe her. Ready to run.

Jennie let them pour cool water over her skin. She let them bend her over and wash her hair without being conscious of their matter-of-fact fingers against her face and on her scalp. She wouldn't let herself feel anything at all, she thought, not anymore, not until she was far, far away from this camp.

They took her back to the tipi and dressed her in the good beaded dress that Hukiyani had given her. Then they moved around the lodge, laughing and chattering as they handled everything, making sure that all Jennie needed had been brought from Hukiyani's and was in order.

Then Breaks Something, who appeared to be the happiest person of all about the upcoming wedding, broke Jennie's control. She almost cried out as she watched Breaks Something smooth out the bed robes again and again and pause with her hand on the backrest folded near the bed.

Jennie held her breath. If Breaks Something found the parfleche, looked into it, she was lost!

But the girl moved on to set the trade pots more evenly inside one another. Hukiyani straightened the rocks around the fire pit and started a fire, then she gave the signal for all of them to leave. She was the last to go out.

Without a word, she hugged Jennie and left her.

Jennie dropped the flap behind her, turned, and ran to the backrest, shoving it to one side to get to the parfleche. Soon, very soon, Ten Bears would drive the horses to Yellowfish. Dusk was almost here. In the dim light, during the commotion, she would slip out beneath the back wall of her lodge and be gone.

"Li-li-li," the trilling women's voices began, just outside the walls, then they rose even higher in celebration, "Li-li-li." They went on and on, rising and falling, as sounds of excitement sprang up all over camp.

Jennie froze, listening.

The children were running, shouting. Above the din, Jennie heard the thunder of a hundred horses' hooves rumbling into the village.

The back of her head burned with tension. She must get out of here! The herdboys and Ten Bears were bringing the horses splashing through the creek just on the other side of her walls, taking them to Yellowfish. At any moment after that, Ten Bears could come to her.

She slipped the strap of the painted bag over her shoulder and turned toward the door, her blood going colder with each step she took. She opened the flap and peeked out.

Yellowfish's lodge looked as if it were floating in a sea of color, a sea of horses. Gray, red, spotted, black, dun, yellow, their colors blended, then separated, then flowed back together as they milled around the tipi. They were relatively quiet, though, Jennie thought, considering the excitement crackling in the very air over the rare size of the herd. It looked as if every person in camp was gathering out there to watch Yellowfish accept his price for her.

She dropped the door-covering and turned, started toward the back of the tipi. Father Sun was going down. Everyone was busy, no one was thinking of her. This was her chance.

Before she could move, a vibration surged from the ground through the sole of her moccasin, into her foot and up her leg. A harder tremor came through her other foot, and in the same instant she realized the whole ground was shaking, she heard again the roaring of hooves. A child's high voice pierced the walls of the tipi, a little girl forgetting herself in the excitement piling upon excitement.

"The warriors have come back!" she shrieked. "They bring many horses!"

Windrider!

For that one, glorious moment, as Jennie dashed across the tipi to throw herself out through the door, everything else washed from her mind. He was back! Windrider had returned, alive!

And in time to save her!

She ran through the village, past the half of the tipis strung out to the south of the central meeting grounds, into the stream of bright-eyed people torn between wanting to see the warriors come in and wanting to finish the uncompleted drama in front of Yellowfish's lodge. The herders had no choice, they had to stay and ride around and around Ten Bears' horses to hold them against the lure of many others galloping in.

Jennie's mind raced as fast as her feet. As soon as Windrider heard about Ten Bears buying her, he would stop the whole transaction. After all, she thought, with a terrible twinge of bitterness, wasn't she the pawn between them?

Visions of his face flashed in her memory: the hurt in his face when she called him a savage, the shock in his eyes when she said she had chosen to live with Hukiyani. The mask he had worn at her adoption feast when he had never once looked in her direction, as if she didn't exist.

The love in his look when he had held her in his arms.

Her bitterness melted, right then, in the heat of her blood.

Windrider would save her.

She ran with the others to the center of the village, then stopped, surprised to see that the war-

riors were returning from the west. In a cloud of
dust.

A doubt squeezed her heart—what if Windrider
wasn't among them? What if . . .

But then the evening breeze opened a path and
she saw him.

He was unmistakable, even in the haze that
hung in the air against the sunset sky.

He rode closer and closer, coming fast, very
fast, at the head of a huge herd of horses, his
body a dark, proud silhouette that left no doubt
who was chief of the men driving the animals behind him. Kwahira raced beneath him, his eyes
flashing rings that shone as white as his hide
through the red dust.

Kwahira's forefeet reached the shallow western
bank of the creek, pulled him down it; Windrider
turned and signaled to the others to hold the
horses there. Already small boys on horseback
were appearing from nowhere, racing to go hold
that herd.

The stallion flew across the creek, barely touching the water, then Windrider was sliding into the
center of camp, into a circle of his rejoicing people, sitting the stallion so magnificently that sweat
broke out in the palms of Jennie's hands. He was
directly in front of her.

His dark eyes found her, before the horse had
even stopped moving, their piercing gaze shining
into her through the fog of swirling dust. He
searched for her, he picked her out of the crowd,
and then he looked away.

That was all.

After that, his gaze swung past her as if she
had been a rock or a tree.

He raised one fist high as he spun Kwahira to

a stop. The wide cuff of silver around his wrist flashed bright in a ray of the dying sun.

"We have lured the Rangers out of the Big Turtle Creek country!" he shouted, in the same confident, singsong tone Jennie remembered from what seemed a lifetime ago. "All the way back to the white-eyes settlements!"

"After that, we rode west again to raid our enemies, the Lipan Apaches. You see we have relieved them of many, many horses!"

The excited camp erupted into exuberant cheers. The people swirled in closer around Windrider and Kwahira, who towered above them, lording it over first one segment of the crowd, then whirling to face another. But Windrider never looked at Jennie again.

A layer of lighter red dust lay along his cheekbones and surrounded his eyes, making the edges of them startling white and the pupils dark and wild. His bare upper body, too, wore a coat made of dust, but it did no more to cover the rippling contours of his hard muscles than it obscured the chiseled shapes of the bones in his face.

His teeth made a bright slash in the red, with his sensual lips drawn back in a predatory grin. His lips. His lips that could melt her right into the ground.

She stood there for a long time, her gaze stubbornly clinging to his incredible face, while her heart turned to hard, cold stone. And her mind cried for her to turn and run. Back to her lodge.

To get her supplies. And then run to the horse herd.

But still she stood there.

Finally Windrider swung down from Kwahira and disappeared into the crowd.

Jennie stayed where she was. She stood there

until The People had scattered, some following
Windrider, some splashing across the creek to his
horse herd, some gathering around the men who
had ridden with him, some drifting back to Yellowfish's lodge—and Ten Bears' hundred horses.

Ten Bears!

Windrider would never save her from Ten
Bears. And, by the pride of the Irish, she would
never ask him!

Jennie forced her body to turn, her legs to carry
her back the way she had come. She even managed to run, but she couldn't feel her feet hit the
ground. All she could feel was a great hollow in
her middle, in her very soul, a hole where her
heart and her stomach and her courage used to
be. A hole big enough for the wind to blow
through.

She loved him. And he would never love her.

All she wanted now was to go so far away, she
would never see him again.

But Hukiyani was waiting outside Jennie's tipi.
When she saw her sitting there, cross-legged on
the ground beside the door-flap, Jennie slowed
her pace and tried to smile.

"*Pia*," she said, when she'd reached her. "You
have come to visit my new home."

"*Petu*, Daughter," Hukiyani agreed. "I have
come to visit you." She nodded toward the tipi
behind her. "I have fed the fire in your new
home."

"Thank you, *Pia*."

She patted the space beside her, and Jennie reluctantly dropped into it, although her nerves
were screaming for her to run. Hukiyani made
small, social talk until Jennie began thinking,
wildly, of taking her foster mother into her confidence. She bit her tongue just in time.

Jennie tried every distraction she could think of, but the woman would *not* go away and let her make good her escape. She sat there until the light was failing badly, until full dark had fallen all along the eastern horizon, until Yellowfish had accepted Ten Bears' horses and sent them back out to the band's horse herd, until the excitement from that and from Windrider's arrival had channeled itself into the building of a huge fire of celebration, safe to have now that the Rangers were gone.

She sat there until the stars came out.

The good thing was that Ten Bears didn't come to her. He was nowhere in sight.

Thank God for Windrider's arrival in that way. The two brothers were talking, Hukiyani said. Perhaps the Council would meet. Perhaps Ten Bears would forget all about her for days.

But perhaps he would not.

"Don't you want to go to the celebration, *Pia*?" Jennie finally asked. "Yellowfish will want to share his joy in his many horses with you."

Hukiyani nodded slowly and turned her head to peer toward her husband's lodge through the dusk.

Jennie held her breath.

Finally the older woman nodded again. "I go," she said, gave Jennie's hand a squeeze, got up, and left her.

The instant she had disappeared into the shadows, Jennie scrambled up and went inside the lodge. She wanted to change into her more familiar blouse and skirt, but she only grabbed them instead and stuffed them into the parfleche on top

of the leaves that wrapped her dried jerky, pemmican, and fruit.

She looked over her shoulder to spot the
bladder-bag full of water that one of the women
had carried in, and saw it in the pale glow of her
fire. Hurry. She had to hurry.

She snatched up the bladder-bag and tucked it
under her arm, slipped the parfleche onto her
other shoulder by its strap, and rushed to the back
of the tipi, the side nearest the creek. She got
down on her knees and rolled up the flap. She
tied it.

A hard breeze hit her, blowing all through the
lodge. Behind her, the door opening had lifted,
too.

She was too late.

Her hands clutching the heavy parfleche like a
weapon, she stood up and whirled to see who it
was. Hukiyani's head popped in. She was smiling.

"Get ready," she whispered. "Your husband
is here."

Jennie turned to stone. Ten Bears. Oh, dear
Lord, how could she bear it? How could she let
him use her as Trammel had done?

"Thank you, *Pia*," she whispered, her jaw feeling so fragile that she thought it might break. All
her bones were made of glass, she could not
move. Yet she *must* move—she had to run!

She felt her nostrils flare, trying to keep back
terrified tears. She waved her foster mother good-
bye.

But Hukiyani stayed where she was, smiling.
Still smiling.

A helpless fury filled Jennie.

Then Hukiyani was gone and the door-flap
stood open.

Jennie's legs sagged beneath her. She'd never make it if she tried to run now.

Too late. She had waited too late.

She let the parfleche and the water bag drop to the floor; she turned away from them, fell to her knees, and hid her face in her hands. Ten Bears taking her body as Trammel had done would kill her spirit forever.

Because when Trammel had taken her, she had never known the miracle of lying with a man whom she loved. Then, all those eons ago in that other country, she had not been in love with Windrider.

Suddenly someone was there.

She hadn't really heard a noise, yet without warning, she sensed that the lodge was filled with another presence.

She didn't look up, didn't even breathe.

The flap to the door opening dropped closed. Its soft swishing sound said there would be no escape.

She raised her head, drew in a deep, trembling breath, and turned to face her husband.

For one stunned moment, her blood stopped flowing. Then her heart filled and let it rush like a waterfall, bubbling and singing, spilling over the hard edge of her despair into a river wild with happiness.

Windrider. He had come to her!

He was beautifully clean, his hair still wet.

And the look in his eyes was as different from the last time she'd seen him as if the dust had been washed from them, too. His coppery skin, always warm with sheer life, picked up the gleam of the fire. On the high planes of his face, it danced.

In the same rhythm as her heart.

She leapt to her feet and ran to him, flew, into his arms. He crushed her in his embrace, drove his fingers into her hair and held her to him.

"You came to me!" she marveled, then the miracle of it struck her numb. Her body melted into the haven of his.

"I wanted to see your new lodge."

His voice was the old teasing one, calm and playful; his big hands stayed steady as they began to caress her hair. But somewhere, beneath the iron-hardness of the muscles of her arms tight against her back, deep in the broad chest that cradled her cheek, she could sense a trembling.

"*I* wanted to see *you*," she said, winding her arms more securely around his waist.

"It doesn't seem so," he drawled. "The last time you threw yourself into my arms, you gave me a kiss."

"A bribe to persuade you to find my lost horse," she teased in return, barely finishing the last word before he brought his mouth down hard on hers.

His lips were smooth, hot, sure. *Real*, better by far than she had dreamed them!

Familiar. Oh, dear Lord, how had she lived all those long days and nights without this?

His tongue traced the line of her lips, then breached it, gentle only at that very first instant, then fierce with a power like fire at midnight, keeping her whole body suspended in air while something moved deep within her.

A hunger. A need so strong that it shook her soul.

He broke the kiss before that need was filled, long before.

She uttered an incoherent sound of protest, a whimper deep in her throat.

"I want you in my hands," he muttered hoarsely, hungrily running his palms over her arms, her waist, her hips, "without this dress, on the bed robes."

But he couldn't let her go. He tucked her closer to him, drawing her whole body into the curve of his legs, his arms, fitting it to the sinuous shape of his torso.

"I still can't believe that it's you," Jennie said, huskily. She shivered, remembering. "After the way you didn't even look at me when you first rode in."

"That was before your foster mother told me," he said, nuzzling his lips into her hair to kiss her ear.

"Told you what?"

"That you would have run away long since, but you were waiting for me to come back."

"That Hukiyani . . ."

His lips moved from her ear down the side of her neck. She caught her breath with the sensual pleasure it sent shimmering through her, and gasped, "So that's why she delayed me so long!"

"Long enough for me to say the magic medicine words to Yellowfish," he murmured.

He lingered at the spot he had just kissed, brushing his lips back and forth, just grazing her now sensitive skin, warming it with his cedar-scented breath. Her whole body went weak in his arms.

His scent, his heat, his charming voice, the feel of his hard muscles beneath his smooth skin, fogged her mind like a mist. Yet she had to know. Hukiyani had said, "Your husband is here."

"What were the magic medicine words?"

"Twice . . . as . . . many . . . horses," he said, between the tiny, thrilling kisses he placed, deliberately, carefully, down the side of her neck and onto the curve of her collarbone.

She laughed, little sounds of pure joy bubbling out of her throat; she tilted her head to catch his in the hollow of her shoulder.

"You are wonderful and wise," she said, "Windrider, War Chief of the Comanche."

"Of course I am wonderful," he muttered, and, with one last flick of his tongue against her skin, pulled his mouth free so he could straighten. He swept her feet off the ground.

"And I am wise, for I am the one who holds the Fire Flower in my arms!"

A teasing retort about bragging tried to form on her tongue, but instead, she said, "I love you. Windrider, War Chief of the Comanche, I love you."

Gratitude and pleasure, happiness and satisfaction, melded into a dark growl that came from his throat. It sent a victorious thrill into her blood, through her bones.

It destroyed all her need to use words. She would never need words again.

All she would ever need was her fingertips to trace the beloved bones of his face, her lips to follow her fingers over them and down to his mouth while he carried her with swift, sure steps around the circle of the fire.

But soon, by the time he reached the bed robes and knelt to lay her down, she needed more.

She needed Windrider to fill her.

To her hunger-glazed eyes, he was mostly a shadow, hovering close and dark between her and the dying fire, but to her hands he was real, real and solid as the earth itself. And powerful as the wind.

She slid her palms over the taut muscles of his

back as his hands reached for the fringed hem of her dress, brought it up over her head and off her as if it had never been. She reached for his breechclout.

He wore his medicine bag, as usual, and another, slightly larger one, tied to his waistband, but they didn't delay her desperate fingers. Nothing could. She found the knot and untied it in an instant, let the scrap of clothing fall away.

"Ah, Fire Flower," he said, in a voice turned harsh and raw with his passion, "I have missed you so!"

That confession took them faster into the dark pleasures of the night, into each other, than Kwahira or any horse they ever rode. She pulled him down on top of her, he slipped one muscled thigh, then both, between her slender ones, she stretched her back flat against the infinite, heavy softness of the buffalo robes. His hard, incredible silkiness drove into her.

The fire's faint crackling went quiet. The earth held them still in her cradle. Outside the wall, the creek stopped its chattering flow. The night breeze quit blowing straight over the plains; it soughed through the opening at the bottom of the tipi's walls and swirled around them, only them, picked them up on its swift-rushing wings.

Windrider held her, he filled her, and as Jennie's high, hopeful voice called his name, the Spirit Wind brought them in a wild, whirling rush ever deeper into that heart of the earth. Deeper into the heart of each other.

Windrider woke when Father Sun climbed high enough to stroke the lodge with long, hot fingers. His arms tightened around the Fire Flower, brought her hip tighter against his thigh.

But he couldn't lie still, he had to wake her. He had to see the happiness in her eyes when he gave her his gift.

Without letting a light-beam of space come between them, he reached for the fringed bag tied to his breechclout. Awkwardly, without lifting her fiery head from his arm, he brought his hands together, untied the bag, spread its drawstrings apart, and pulled out the combs.

Then, his heart feeling already lonesome, just with the act of turning her loose, he separated from her. He laid her head gently onto the bed and sat up, rubbing the silver combs against the robes to make them gleam, holding them up to see them catch the light.

He combed back the Fire Flower's beautiful hair on one side and fixed one of the ornaments into its thickness just above her ear, then turned her head so he could do the same on the other side.

She never stirred, her sleep was so deep.

He sat there, cross-legged, and looked at her. She was the most beautiful being he had ever seen. And the combs made her more so. He had known that the silver nestled in her red curls would be as pleasing to the eye as a white eagle against the blue sky.

He reached for the bag again, took out the mirror.

"Kohtoo Topusana?" he murmured, bending to drop a kiss onto the tip of her nose. "Wake up and see your gift I have brought."

She opened her eyes at once, coming fully awake at the first sound of his voice.

He held the shell-handled mirror in front of her.

Her huge green eyes widened, began to dance like a child's. Her breath caught in a great gasp.

"They're beautiful!" she cried. "Oh, Windrider, they make *me* beautiful, too! Thank you!"

She leaned forward and dropped a quick kiss on his fingers that held the mirror. It set a coal of desire burning on that spot, but she was already looking at herself again, touching the combs with quick, soft adjustments.

"Where did you get them?" she cried. "I have never, ever, had such a generous gift! Whenever I am not wearing them, I'll keep them in my medicine bag, close to my heart!"

"I traded five horses to Oñate for them," he said. "On the way home with the Lipan horses, we saw him at a trade rendezvous with some Kiowa. I told him these combs would look like sparks in the fire of your hair."

She closed her soft hand around his, brought the mirror down to lie on the bed.

Jennie's mind raced to take it all in. He had been buying her a present during the very time she had been thinking he would never forgive her for leaving his lodge!

"You talked to Oñate about me?"

How could the look in her eyes be serious and laughing at the same time? But it was.

"Yes."

"You were confident in your charms, as usual," she said, pulling up a robe to hold against her naked self, "to buy me a present after leaving without even saying good bye."

"You first left me," he said.

For a long moment her solemn look held, with the smile completely gone.

Her heart went out of her body. Was he not going to forgive her, after all?

"But now we both are here," he said, gently. "I have come back to find that you stayed with my people, waiting for me. I have come to your lodge to be your husband, and you are my wife.''

Joy began to rise inside her. *I have come to your lodge to be your husband,* he said. He did love her. Even if he hadn't said the words, he did!

''I had a husband once before,'' she said, slowly, ''but I never felt married to him. I do feel married to you, even without a ceremony by a priest.''

''I have heard of a priest,'' he said, glad to have this common ground between them.

''He is a religious leader, a . . . medicine man,'' she said, groping for all the Comanche words she knew. ''You have seen churches?''

''A mission,'' he said, and made gestures to show a steeple with a cross on top. ''And a man in black clothes. Oñate said 'priest.' ''

''Yes,'' she said. ''Catholic, like the ones in Ireland.''

''Oñate said this man tells people what to believe,'' he remarked skeptically, searching her eyes as he twined one finger into her hair. ''But I do not think it could be so.''

''It is true.''

''Grown men? They let him tell them, instead of going on a vision quest to find their own medicine?''

''Yes.''

He shook his head in disbelief at such incomprehensible behavior. Then his eyes narrowed to look into a more important matter.

''I did not know you have a husband,'' he said. ''What is his name?''

''Trammel Nordstrom, the trader at the fort. But he is dead now, I'm sure.''

''I'm sorry. You lost a husband as well as two parents in the raid.''

She was silent.

He bit his tongue, wishing he had not mentioned the parents again.

"Tram-mel Nord-strom," he said, and listened to his own voice go harsh with useless jealousy while the memory of the trader's coarse face came back to his mind. "Did you love him?"

"No."

In that instant he knew that her husband was the man who had hurt her. Fury and hate wiped out the jealousy.

But then she gave him such a look that those bad feelings went away, too. Such a look that told him what she would say before the words fell from her lips.

"I love *you*, Windrider," she said. "I have never loved any man but you."

A happiness rose in him, a singing of his heart that made him want to laugh, to dance, to throw himself onto Kwahira and fly.

With the Fire Flower in his arms.

Jennie watched his face soften, looked deep into his eyes, and waited. But he didn't speak.

Do you love me?

Her impulsive tongue almost asked the question, but she bit it back. He did. He loved her. His body had just told her so as it had so many times out there on the plains.

He had paid twice as many horses as Ten Bears to be her husband, and the way he was looking at her now said it was not just to keep her from his brother.

She held the robe to her breasts with one hand, used the other to pick up the mirror, glanced into it again, tilted her head so the combs could catch the light. But she couldn't relax completely into happiness until she knew.

She put down the mirror and frowned at him.

"What kind of trouble is this going to cause?" she asked. "Our being married, I mean."

He frowned back at her.

"The trouble of having everything always re-arranged in my tipi," he said, gruffly. "And of my wife constantly begging to borrow my best horse, Kwahira, and the trouble of asking poor Hukiyani to cook my meals because my wife is out riding!"

She laughed and pretended to hit him. "I mean with Ten Bears," she said. "I saw Yellowfish send the hundred horses he paid for me out to the herd."

"He was sending them back to Ten Bears after I paid him *two* hundred horses," he growled, and ran the tip of his finger down the curve of her cheek. "Too many horses to drive them into the village. I took Yellowfish out to them, instead."

She gasped. "Windrider! So many horses! I hope you didn't include Kwahira and Echo among them!"

He looked into her eyes, shining at him like stars.

"Even to save you from Ten Bears, I would never do such a foolish deed!" he teased.

"You wouldn't? What a disappointment!"

She gave him an even wider, more mischievous grin. "But then, I must tell you that I would never trade Spirit Talker for you!"

He threw back his head and gave a great, roaring laugh, reaching out with both arms to gather her to him.

"The Fire Flower!" he said. "First Wife to Windrider!"

She slipped out of his grasp.

"*Only* wife to Windrider!" she cried. "Oh,

Windrider, I cannot share you. I never can share you. Never!''

''Do not worry,'' he soothed, pulling her back into his embrace. ''I do not need more wives.''

He matched the green fire in her eyes with his own dark heat as the joy pulsing in his veins came leaping off his tongue.

''I could not satisfy more wives than you,'' he said, bending his head closer and closer to hers, using one hand to hold her near him and the other to pull the robe, little by little, away from the snowy mounds of her breasts.

''You are so full of fire that you take all the juice from me! I am exhausted from our wedding night.''

She was not fooled.

''Ah,'' she said, as his hand slipped beneath her covering and cupped around her breast, making her shiver. ''I can tell how very tired you are.''

Then she reached out and put her hand on him.

He dropped his mouth onto hers with a passion that was fully fresh and wonderfully whole and new.

Chapter 16

A s the long, bright suns went by, slipping away one after the other, Jennie and Windrider left their troublesome questions unspoken. For the sake of the warm, dark nights.

The moon passed from full to new and back to full again.

The band moved once during that time, to an even more beautiful place, a long scattering of cottonwood and aspen trees that grew beside a deep-running creek, one of the headwaters of the river that the Spanish called the Colorado. As far as Jennie could tell, Windrider and Ten Bears together made a mutually agreeable decision to camp there, although it took only two days ride to reach it.

This could not be as far north and west as Windrider had been arguing that they should go to get away from the Rangers, and she wondered, but she didn't question him about it. She didn't want to hear about the politics of leadership or the relationship between the brothers or to think about what dangers might lie in the future. She didn't want to think about the future at all.

There were no more sightings of Rangers, and no sign of buffalo, so the camp settled into a quiet routine. The heat became so fierce during the middle of each day that the women performed only the most essential tasks and the children spent most of their time in the water. When they were not hunting, the men sat in the shade smoking and talking peacefully.

Not even Breaks Something caused any dissension. She acted in an exceptionally friendly way toward Jennie whenever their paths crossed. Hukiyani said that was because Jennie and Windrider were married now, and Breaks Something had given him up.

One morning after they had been camped on Long Tree Creek for six or seven days, Jennie and Windrider went out to the horses, very early, as they always did in the cool of the day. Spirit Talker and Kwahira, inseparable now, were grazing out to one side of the herd.

"They remind me of us," Jennie said, smiling up into her husband's eyes. "We pitched our lodges away from the others, too."

He reached out to touch her face, the silver cones on the saddle he carried jingling like laughter in the wind.

"But you can't say I'm as hardheaded as Kwahira," he said. "I'd never run away from you to fight a pack of wolves all alone."

"Ha!" she scoffed. "Who rode out with only three men to lure six times that many Texas Rangers into chasing them?"

His only answer was a cocky tilt of his head and the lift of one arching black brow.

Jennie made a silly face at him, then looked again at the horses. Kwahira touched his nose to Spirit Talker's back, nibbling at her spine in the signal that she should groom him, too, in return. The mare ignored him.

"Look!" Jennie said. "Spirit Talker isn't a flirt with him the way she usually is."

"But we can't say the same for her owner," Windrider replied smugly, not taking his gaze from Jennie's face to look at the horses.

She picked up the end of her rein and pretended to hit him.

"I'm *not* a flirt," she said, laughing. "You're just conceited. You think you're so handsome, every woman is flirting with you."

"It is true," he said, trying to keep his expression as solemn as his tone of voice.

Jennie laughed again, but she stood on tiptoe to reach his chin, to turn his eyes to the horses.

"Look at them, *please*," she begged, trying to ignore the thrill that tingled through her at the feel of his warm skin and the hard-chiseled bone underneath. "I think my Spirit Talker is acting strange."

As they both looked at the mare, she turned her back on Kwahira and kicked out at him.

"She's never done that!" Jennie cried. "Do you think she's sick?"

Windrider glanced at the horse, then his hot, dark gaze flashed back to Jennie. For an instant she almost forgot what she'd asked him.

"She's not in heat," he said, "that's all. I've watched her during this whole moon and she didn't come in. She carries a foal, so she has no more use for poor Kwahira."

"A *foal*? Really? Spirit Talker will have a baby?"

Windrider laughed at her excitement. "Calm yourself," he said, "it happens all the time."

Jennie shoved the bridle she carried up onto her shoulder so she could grab his arm with both hands. "When?" she demanded. "When will she have it?"

He held up both hands and then one finger. "Eleven. Eleven moons."

"What month will that be? . . . What moon is it now?" she asked, squeezing his arm in excited demand for an answer.

"*Urui mua*," he said, "hot month. July."

"So the foal will come in June!" Jennie said, happily. "What is June in Comanche?"

"*Puhi mua*, leaf month."

Jennie opened her mouth to repeat the words, but the sound of drumming hoofbeats drowned them out. Both she and Windrider whirled in their tracks to see who was coming.

Two horses raced toward the camp, too far away for Jennie to tell even whether anyone rode them or not.

"Our scouts," Windrider said, and she marveled once again at the ability of The People to see far into the distance.

They turned and began to run back to camp, Jennie taking three strides to Windrider's one to remain by his side. They reached the center of the village and the early risers gathering there just before the scouts thundered in.

"*Numu kuhtsu?!*" they shouted. "Buffalo!"

The words hit the walls of the lodges like thrown rocks, bringing dozens of sleepy faces popping out of the tipis, dozens of voices to repeat the magic words. *Numu kuhtsu?!*

As the scouts flung themselves off their mounts, the whole encampment not only came awake but became an anthill of activity.

"The hides will be in their prime!" Hukiyani called, motioning for Jennie to come to her. "Come, daughter! I will share my tools with you!"

Jennie ran to her. Windrider was already mov-

ing toward some men gathering to form a Council
to choose the hunt leader.

"We'll take only what tools we need and the
hunting tipis," the older woman said. "You have
none of that at your lodge anyway. Help us
here."

The contagious excitement beat through Jennie's veins, and she threw herself into the communal preparations. They made her think of
harvest time at home, on the farm in Ireland, with
all her siblings still alive. The thought brought a
grateful joy to mix with her sorrow—once again
she was part of a family.

The Council named Windrider hunt leader, and
he immediately sent runners out to find a location
for the hunting camp. It would be somewhere
near wood and water, Wide Foot, one of Hukiyani's neighbors, told Jennie while the two of
them tied the undercoated skins and the poles and
stakes that constituted a hunting tent onto a tra-
vois. Once the runners had chosen the place, they
would come back for several women to go and
build the drying racks for the meat.

Before noon, all was ready. Windrider,
mounted on Kwahira, led a lightly burdened procession of the camp's able-bodied men and
women mounted for the hunt and leading packhorses and mules to carry the necessary equipment and the hides and meat they would bring
back.

Jennie rode away from the other women to trot
Spirit Talker up beside him, her heart thrumming
in her throat with the excitement of this intriguing
new adventure, her throat tight with anticipation.
And with the question she was bound to ask.

He had to say yes. He just had to.

He threw her a welcoming glance.

"Well?" he asked. "Are you ready for your first big hunt? Is your skinning knife sharp?"

She swallowed hard and gave him her brightest smile.

"No," she said, boldly, "but my horse is fit and ready to run."

He sent her a sharp look, his eyes narrowing.

"You plan to skin the buffalo with a dull knife, while he is alive and running, working from horseback? Have you told the other women of this new custom?"

His wry tone and the vision he created made them both laugh.

"No," she said. "I won't be working at the skinning with the women. I will ride into the herd with you."

She stared straight ahead, between Spirit Talker's dainty red ears, afraid to look at his face.

"I see," he said, drawling the words out thoughtfully. "I must have made a mistake. Somehow I thought that *I* had been chosen leader for this hunt."

"You are hunt leader," she acknowledged, using the same pensive tone. "I say I am going only because I know you are wise and will let me come with you. Spirit Talker and I can help guide the animals underneath a hunter's lance. The People need much meat and many skins."

She looked at him then, with such a sincere look, yet one with such adventurous mischief sparkling in her green eyes, that his heart melted all over again. How could he ever deny her anything?

"The hunt goes too fast, it is too wild for anyone to guide the buffalo," he warned, talking to himself as much as to her. "It is everyone for himself."

"I can ride as well as some warriors," she said. "That is true."

How could he ever ride into a herd of buffalo or anywhere else without her by his side?

"You may come," he said, gruffly, his throat suddenly full.

He cleared it and stared out over the plains, forcing his eyes to pick out the faraway tops of the trees that marked the temporary camp. But immediately his rebellious gaze returned to feast on his treasure, his Fire Flower, close by.

"This hunt will give us the supplies we need for the long ride north," he told her, squelching a small twinge of his conscience as he thought of that journey. "We have agreed to winter with our brothers in the canyon called Palo Duro."

Once the band had moved that far away from Texas, it would be too far to take her back if she should want to go, and he had never done as his honor demanded and formally given her her choice. But there was no need of that.

As soon as she was adopted into the tribe, she was free to come and go as she pleased. She had chosen to stay with his people and wait for him; she had told him she loved him every single day and night since he had become her husband.

She loved him. She would choose to stay with him forever. She cared nothing about going back to her people.

He held Kwahira back and rode exactly beside her, letting his leg brush against hers, meeting her bright, excited gaze with his. She loved him, there was no doubt.

But the memory of her crying, *Take me to Texas!* had never faded completely from his mind. She had said that *after* she had told him the first time that she loved him.

He did not believe that she would ever say it again, but a man could never completely know a woman's heart.

Jennie clutched Spirit Talker's sides closer against her legs as the long semicircle of riders slowly moved toward the top of the low ridge, but she still shivered, anyway. She stuck her feet back into her stirrups, wishing that Windrider hadn't insisted that she use her saddle for the sake of safety—if she were sitting on the mare's bare back, she would feel much warmer.

Yet the predawn air *was* warm, signaling another hot day. It was excitement making her shake and the sweat pop out on her forehead and her palms.

If she could see the buffalo herd in the hazy early grayness, if she could see *anything* down over the edge of the land, she wouldn't be so scared. But all she could see was the nearest riders in a long, curving line of horses, Windrider on Kwahira to her left, moving, like all the others, at a walk.

He appeared to have forgotten all about her.

For the hundredth time, she checked her equipment, the rawhide rope coiled on the flat, spoon-shaped front horn of her saddle, and the twenty-foot-long reins tucked into her belt. She might be able to grab them if she was unseated, Windrider had said, so that Spirit Talker could pull her free of the herd.

She clasped the mare more tightly and settled deeper into her seat. She would stick with her mount no matter what happened, she vowed silently. No matter what.

Jennie touched the small bag beneath her blouse

that held her silver combs. They would bring her luck.

From the corner of her eye she caught a quick movement. Windrider lifted his hand and brought it down in a fast, choppy signal that sent the line of riders flying forward. With no signal from her, Spirit Talker was moving.

Running headlong into the misty early morning, they darted over the ridge and down it, circling around a herd of huge, grazing animals. Jennie could barely see what they looked like, she was moving so fast; all she could tell was that they seemed to be covering the whole face of the earth.

Windrider was there, still not far from her, riding faster and faster. The dull rumbling of the buffalo as they started to run shook the ground. A scent new to her, yet ancient, a musty, old-animal smell that must be the buffalo, rode into her lungs on her every breath, over the smells of early morning air, fresh-broken grass, horses, and leather. A fiery excitement suddenly beat in her blood, melted her skin to Spirit Talker's and her hands to the reins. It burned away her fear.

She rode faster than she ever had before, holding her place in the tightening ring of riders, helping to circle the buffalo as they lumbered into a run. The shaggy bulls took the outside, forcing the cows and calves to the middle. Their heads hung down and their tongues out; their breath rushed in and out of their mouths. They were huge. They filled the world.

Then Spirit Talker, her darling red mare, was shooting into their midst like an arrow, running deliberately into the mass of huge, swirling bodies, racing full tilt through the foggy cloud of dust and haze. Jennie saw nothing but a sea of animals, felt nothing but the powerful horse surging beneath her like another part of herself.

They dodged buffalo and warriors, stabbing horns, flying hooves. They became one creature of instinct, staying out of the path of arrows and lances by the power of their talking spirits, rushing in and out and racing alongside the prey, holding it to a path nearer its hunter in spite of Windrider's saying that it couldn't be done, helping to provide meat and skins for the winter.

Jennie felt a great, jubilant cry tear from her throat, a cry no one could hear through the noise of the herd.

The wind blew across Windrider's face, cleared the dust from his vision in time for him to see the bull he had just shot stagger and fall. He noted the location so he could dress it out later and lifted his eyes and his bow to look for another, turning to look back and see what animals were coming.

His hands froze in midair, his drawn arrow nocked. Kwahira raced on beneath him.

Eagle Tail Feather was caught in a crush of buffalo bulls halfway between him and the middle of the herd. The boy was mounted on his favorite spotted pony, but just barely. He leaned so far out from the horse's rushing body and at such an awkward angle that each moment aboard appeared to be his last.

Windrider's blood rushed to his head with a terrible chill.

The boy had misjudged it all in the heated excitement of his very first hunt—the speed of the buffalo, the weight of his lance, the position he needed to be in to throw it. He would die, right here before his uncle's eyes, falling to his death to be mashed to a pulp beneath ten thousand hooves.

Windrider pressured Kwahira with his knees, instinctively trying to turn him, straining to get to Eagle through the milling mass of terrified animals. But even as he tried, he knew it was hopeless.

The boy was too far away. He could never reach him.

A glimpse of red caught in the corner of his eye. He twisted to see Spirit Talker weaving through the rush of bodies with the Fire Flower on her back, riding as if she had been born one of The People. Her hair had come loose from its wrappings; it flew behind her and whipped around her face like a cloud of fire carried on the wind.

He saw it all in one great, horrifying glimpse; saw her spot Eagle and knew what she would do. The air in his lungs turned to dust.

The Fire Flower was closer to the boy, much closer then Windrider was. She was where *he* ought to be, where he had to be if he were to save the boy.

Why, his heart screamed, why hadn't he made her stay outside the herd with the other women? Now he would have to see them both be killed.

She slid the rope from her saddle horn, and Windrider's heart shouted approval of her quick instincts; then, in the same breath, it plunged into horror again. A buffalo veered away from another, rammed the hindquarters of Eagle's pony with its shoulder. The boy went flying—over the buffalo that had been his target and the one running beside him—to land facedown on top of the rushing herd.

It carried him away, fast as a white-water river, but he fought like a warrior to stay on his hands and knees on top of the furry, shifting backs, to keep away from the lethal lake of horns bobbing up and down around him. He was lurching and rolling, though, his limbs almost out of control, coming closer and closer to a fall to his death beneath the plunging, galloping hooves.

Windrider was too far away. There were too many animals in between.

The Fire Flower hesitated only for the blink of an eye, then she threw her loop, sent it floating out over the cruel horns toward Eagle. The rawhide wasn't long enough, it couldn't reach him; a buffalo would run into it and jerk her off, too.

Windrider turned completely toward her, the horror rising like gorge in his throat.

She lurched forward, driving the tall horn of her saddle into her stomach, almost unhorsed by the pull on her rope. Eagle Tail Feather had caught it.

Then she was sitting back again, secure on the racing filly, her legs clutching firm. Thank the Sun Father for that filly. She compensated for the pressure on the rawhide lifeline, never stumbling, never slowing her pace, keeping her position for the boy crawling, now walking, now leaping over the surging backs of the crowded animals toward safety.

He fell onto the mare behind the saddle and threw his arms around the Fire Flower. She turned to him with a smile like summer sunlight as she looped the length of rope around the horn and let it go.

Windrider's heart filled with such a song of thanks, he thought it would burst.

No, it was *love* that filled it.

In that instant, for the first time in his life, he knew what love was. The love of a man for a woman.

His mother had been right. He never truly had loved She Blushes.

Because he had never *admired* the timid, delicate girl.

The Fire Flower, he admired. The Fire Flower, he loved with a feeling like fire in his heart.

He began angling Kwahira out of the side of the herd, all desire for another kill forgotten. When he had ridden into the open and let the bulls thunder on by, he saw the Fire Flower following his track.

"Uncle! Did you see?" Eagle Tail Feather shouted, leaning toward him, determined to make him hear over the thunder of many hooves. "The Fire Flower saved me! Now she can ride double in the parade for the war path!"

That unexpected remark, added to their joyful relief, set the three of them whooping and shouting with laughter. Jennie twisted in her saddle to throw her arms around the sweaty imp of a boy, but, embarrassed, he slipped from her grasp and dropped off over Spirit Talker's tail to the ground.

"I will find my pony!" he yelled back over his shoulder. "I *will* make my first buffalo kill!"

Jennie watched him go, then turned to Windrider, who had ridden up very close, facing her. She tried, but she couldn't speak. Her breath came in great, shuddering gasps now, shaking her whole body, because she had held it for so long.

No. Because Windrider was looking at her, his face completely open and unguarded.

The herd moved on past them.

The calls of the women as they fell to the butchering rang in the air.

A horse whinnied somewhere nearby, and a bowstring twanged.

Jennie saw none of it.

Windrider sat beside her, their horses touching shoulders, almost as naked as his mount, who wore no saddle to slow him and no bridle or reins to occupy Windrider's hands. He was breathing hard, the muscles of his broad chest rippling in the sunlight which was blazing now, pouring down on them like a blessing.

His hair, black and shining as the wing feathers of a songbird, lifted off his powerful neck and blew gently back and forth in the wind. But it was his face that caught her gaze and held it. He was looking at her with his heart in his eyes.

"I love you, Fire Flower," he said, in English, speaking carefully as if to be sure that she understood. "I've never loved any other woman. None but you."

He leaned toward her then, reaching across Spirit Talker to place his hand on her hipbone, to pull her close and reaffirm his claim. Jennie tilted her body into his.

His touch sang in her veins. Now she knew what happiness was.

His lips took hers with a new heat. It held a melting sureness that satisfied them both somehow, as if sealing an old agreement fast and closed. Yet, even as it finished one thing, it started another. He pulled her closer.

"Fire Flower! Come! Come and help me!"

The shrill call penetrated Jennie's ears, but it wasn't strong enough to break the kiss.

The earsplitting screech came again. "Fire Flower! I need help. This one is for the widows and orphans!"

They broke apart and looked around, his hand still hot on her skin, still refusing to let her go.

In every direction the buffalo lay scattered on the plain, with both women and warriors swarming over them, working madly to prepare the meat. If it was not butchered and cut into strips, laid out on the racks to dry by sundown, it would spoil.

Breaks Something called to Jennie again.

"This one is for the widows and orphans," she repeated. "Ten Bears killed it and gave it to them. Will you help me prepare it?"

She was working alone, just beginning to skin the great bull.

Jennie and Windrider looked at each other and nodded. They would be as generous as Ten Bears to keep good feelings evenly distributed in the camp.

"Help her," Windrider murmured. "And I will kill one more to also give to those lodges who have no hunter."

"All right," Jennie murmured, covering his hand with hers, then running her fingers up along his arm.

"Go, then," he said, smiling at her as he slowly let her go. Her bright gaze, liquid with love for him, drifted longingly to his lips. It made them hurt with hunger for her.

"Tonight we will finish that kiss," he said, "and more. Much more."

He met the farewell touch of her fingers, and she left him to trot Spirit Talker up the side of the small hill to Breaks Something and her work.

Windrider filled his eyes one more time with the sight of her, then whirled Kwahira around and thundered away into the thick of the hunt.

Jennie slid down from her mount and took her skinning knife from its sheath. She had never worked at anything so messy, she soon decided, trying not to be splattered with blood as Breaks

Something finished pulling the entrails from the bull. The girl set aside the heart.

"It is to honor the buffalo and encourage them to multiply," she said, and turned back to cutting out the liver.

She sprinkled it with green bile from the broken gallbladder. "And this is for Ten Bears—we save the liver for the hunter."

Then she slanted her mischievous grin at Jennie. "We can have a taste, though," she said, and sliced off two small portions.

"I . . . I'm not hungry," Jennie said, but Breaks Something held out a share to her, and she knew that to refuse would be to insult her. She didn't want to start all their old trouble all over again.

She took it and made herself bite off a small mouthful.

"Why, it's delicious!" she exclaimed, and quickly ate the rest of her portion.

They set to work in earnest, Jennie watching Breaks Something closely to learn exactly where and when to slice the skin and how to cut the meat away from the bone. It seemed to take forever, the animal was so huge.

Breaks Something finally stretched her arms out, then wiped her hands and her knife on the grass. "Let's rest a little," she said, "then I will take my pony and go for a packhorse. We have butchered a load."

Glad for the respite, Jennie cleaned her hands and knife, too, and stood up. Spirit Talker left off grazing and wandered over to nuzzle her.

"She was a good mount today," Breaks Something said generously. "I watched her running in the herd."

"She *is* good," Jennie answered, rubbing the

mare's soft nose. "I hope her foal that she will have next summer will be as brave as its mother."

"It will be," Breaks Something said. "All of that line of horses the mare is from have much heart."

She walked past Jennie and Spirit Talker then, up over the little rise of ground toward the east, stretching her arms and her legs before remounting her pony. Jennie petted her mare and talked to her until she sensed that Breaks Something had stopped walking and was looking back at them.

But when she glanced up, the girl was holding one hand to shade her eyes against the sun and looking off into the distance again.

"Your husband is way out there signaling to us!" she said, her voice suddenly going loud and tense with excitement.

Puzzled, Jennie said, "But he went that way, to the north, following the buffalo herd, when he left us."

"He circled around to the east!" Breaks Something said. "He is signing. He wants you to come to him."

Jennie got to her feet and went to stand beside Breaks Something, then squatted to wipe off her hands on the grass once more before using them as shade for her eyes.

"Why?" she asked. "Why doesn't he come to me?"

"Perhaps he's found a buffalo calf left behind or something else that you would like to see!"

Jennie lifted her hand to keep out the bright sunlight and stared in that direction, trying to see Windrider.

"My vision still isn't as sharp as yours and the rest of The People's," she muttered, straining her eyes into the morning sun's glare. "But it's better than when I first came."

Then, squinting hard, she made out what Breaks Something was talking about—a tiny horse and rider, moving against the great expanse of the plains. The horse was big and shining white against the green and gray of the grass.

"Go to him!" Breaks Something urged. "I'll find someone else to help me here."

Jennie turned and ran to mount Spirit Talker.

"*Ura*, thank you," she called, and galloped off to meet her love.

Deep down, Breaks Something was a nicer person than she had thought her to be, Jennie thought, as the wind caught her hair and dried the sweat off her face. She could have simply not mentioned seeing Windrider way out there, and Jennie would never have known the difference.

Spirit Talker immediately slowed to a trot, putting her ears back to hear what Jennie would say about that, then keeping them back to say that she didn't really care.

"All right, lovey," Jennie said, leaning over to stroke the mare's neck without taking her eyes off the distant horse and rider. "I know you're tired from such a long, hard run in the hunt. We'll go at a trot, but no slower."

Suddenly anticipation began to beat in her veins.

Windrider. She needed to see Windrider as deeply, as desperately, as if they had been parted for days.

She narrowed her eyes again and tried to see him better. What was he doing so far out here away from everyone else?

The ground rolled then, more than she had realized it would, and she lost sight of him. Spirit Talker picked up to a lope to keep her balance going downhill, slowed again as they crossed, then trotted parallel to the next rise of the land.

Gently Jennie pulled on the rein and set her head directly toward it.

"Oh, no, you don't, you lazy girl," she said, laughing a little. "No taking the easy way out and sneaking back to the herd. Straight up the hill is the quickest way to get you some rest."

She bent over to hug Spirit Talker's sweaty neck. "Because it's the quickest way to Windrider!"

The red dun listened and did as she was told.

Jennie rode up the incline of the knoll and over the top. She lifted the mare into a lope and her hand to shade her eyes again as they hurried down the other side, her eyes roaming the vastness of the plains, searching for Windrider.

Then she saw him.

Was that Windrider?

A bell of alarm began to clang in her mind.

That horse was tall and solid white, true, but he moved with a heavy, lumbering movement at the gallop that looked nothing like Kwahira's fast, floating gait.

The clamor of the alarm bell became a racket of panic, an uproar of blood in her head.

That white horse was not Kwahira!

The man astride wasn't Windrider! He wore a hat—he was a white man!

"No!" she choked, "Whoa, Spirit Talker!"

But the wind carried her weak words away while the mare's loping gait rose and fell, rose and fell, and Jennie sat frozen in her saddle. Her eyes burned. That rider wasn't even alone!

Another one, on a small gray horse that blended in with the grass, galloped beside him. They were racing to meet her.

That thought freed her arms and legs from the grip of her fear. She leaned over Spirit Talker's neck, pulling on the rein with one hand while she pushed against her cheek with the other, desperate to turn her around.

The mare turned, her ears laid back, listening now to Jennie's wild screams. Spirit Talker stretched out and began to run, but in the first stride or two, she used up all she had. The big-hearted filly had no more to give.

Jennie's head felt suddenly so light that it could float off her body. Sweat drenched the palms of her hands. She couldn't bear to beat her mare, yet she took the rein in both hands and hit her in the flanks with the end of it, kicking her sides with both feet.

The horse surged forward in one last try, then stumbled and steadily slowed.

Jennie gritted her teeth hard enough to grind them to powder, but that still wasn't as hard as the feeling filling her heart. Breaks Something truly *was* a cruel, conniving little bitch. She truly *did* hate Jennie—her friendliness had been nothing but a farce.

Switching the end of the reins to hit Spirit Talker on the other flank, Jennie saw from the corner of her eye that the big white horse was looming closer and closer. Its rider was clutching at her. She tried to swerve Spirit Talker away from the man's reaching arm, only to find the one on the gray horse closing in on her there.

One last scream burst from her throat, but neither she nor the mare could do one thing to stop them.

They galloped up even with her on both sides. The one on the white horse stood up in his stirrups and stretched mightily forward.

He caught Spirit Talker by the bridle.

Chapter 17

Jennie called to her, begging for one last burst of speed. The mare shuddered and tried, but she staggered.

"You oughtn't to run from us, ma'am," her captor yelled.

From the other side, his friend shouted, "Stop your horse. We're Texas Rangers!"

It seemed weird to hear fluent English with no accent. Their clothing and boots brushing against her bare legs felt alien to her.

The whole world had gone so strange that Spirit Talker's hooves might as well have been pounding against the dome of the sky as against the floor of the plains. *Nothing* was what Jennie expected.

The Rangers wedged Spirit Talker between their two horses and gradually brought them all to a stop. They stood, shaking, the animals gasping for breath.

Jennie threw her hair back out of her eyes and stared wildly from one white man to the other.

"This is your lucky day, ma'am!" one of them called, shouting as if she were nearly deaf.

She turned her face away from the harsh sound of his voice.

The other man, the one on the white horse, was looking at her with blue eyes full of pity. His hands slid from Spirit Talker's bridle down onto her reins; he gathered them in and looped them around the horn of his saddle.

"Don't holler at her, Rivers," he said, and his voice was low and pleasant, but not as rich as Windrider's. "Can't you see you're scaring her?"

He lifted one hand to the brim of his hat.

"You're a white woman and we're Texas Rangers, Captain Rivers and Captain Gentry," he said, smiling at Jennie. "We're gonna save you. Them savage Comanches been holding you captive, ain't they, ma'am?"

"No! No! They adopted me. I am one of The People! Let me go!"

She leaned forward and held out trembling hands to the kind one in a plea for him to return her reins.

"I want to stay with The People," she said. "The Comanche. I want to stay. Will you please let me go?"

The Ranger only kneed his horse closer to her. When it got close enough for its shoulder to bump Spirit Talker's, the man's big hand closed around Jennie's arm.

Hysteria came screaming into her veins on a wild burst of adrenaline. "Let go of me!" she cried.

She leaned backward in the saddle, hitting and scratching at his hand and arm. "Don't you dare touch me!"

The other man caught her around the shoulders and dragged her, kicking and fighting, off Spirit Talker and onto his horse, in front of his saddle.

"Calm down," he said. "Calm yourself, honey; we ain't gonna hurt you like them savages did."

The prison of his arms shut off all her ability to think, all her hearing, all her reason. She screamed and fought with the last shreds of her strength.

It wasn't enough.

The man on the white horse took her from the other one's arms and put her gently onto the back of his mount.

"Your mare's as worn-out as you are," he murmured kindly as he set her arms into place around his waist. "You just lean your head against my back, now—sorry my shirt's a little sweaty, there—and we'll start on back to San Antonio de Béxar with you, ma'am."

"Yeah," the other man chimed in, riding up close beside them as they turned the horses and headed east. "We'll tell the rest of our company of Rangers where them Comanches are, and they'll take care of them for you."

"That's right," his partner said, his pleasant voice rumbling into her ear through his back where she had dropped her lolling head. "You're free now, ma'am. Free!"

Finally all the words soaked into Jennie's numbed brain. They turned her chilled blood to icy water. She whipped her head up and turned to the man riding beside her.

"No need to tell your other Rangers anything," she croaked, her lips going dry with fear. "The Comanches are far away, a long, long way from here. I rode out of the camp alone and got lost."

He shook his head and flashed her a pitying glance.

"We seen the buffalo hunt from that rimrock over yonder," he said. "We was ridin' closer to get an idea of the size of that Indian band before we fetched the rest of our Ranger company."

"Soon as we saw the color of your hair, we knew you was an escaping captive," the other Ranger rumbled, turning his head to see her. Pity gleamed in his eyes, too.

"I wasn't escaping!" she cried, wishing she could double up her fist and hit him on the shoulder to take that look off his face. But she couldn't. She barely had the strength to talk, the terror held her in such a grip.

"I was tricked," she said, pouring every bit of persuasion into her voice that she could muster. Maybe if she could make them understand, they would let her go.

Maybe she could warn Windrider and Hukiyani and the others. Maybe she could talk these men out of sending a large force against the *Nermernuh.*

"A girl named Breaks Something tricked me, but you don't need to attack her for it. I wasn't escaping. It's all right, really it is. I am not a captive, I am one of The People."

"Lots of captives are confused when they're first rescued," the man on the gray horse said, in a tone so condescending that it made her want to do violence. "Them savage Comanches has put them through so much hell, they don't know their own names, sometimes. "

"No!" Jennie said, her anger bringing new strength to her voice and her limbs. "I'm *not* a captive!"

She turned loose of the Ranger and twisted in her seat to try to find her Spirit Talker. The mare stood in the distance, her sides still heaving, her head hanging nearly to the ground.

Jennie shifted, trying to lift one leg to throw over the white horse's hindquarters so she could slide to the ground.

"I need to get back to my filly," she said, in a tone she tried to make nonchalant. "If you'll just turn me loose, I'll go back to the Comanches. My husband is there. My husband is Windrider, War Chief of the Comanches."

"We've hearda him," the Ranger on the white horse said, slowing his mount so the other one could reach out to hold Jennie's leg in place.

"You stay with us," Rivers said. "Let our buddies follow them Comanches back to their camp, and you start thinking about getting back to civilization."

Jennie slapped at his hand and at the other one's back.

"No!" she screamed. "Don't send the other Rangers to the Comanches! They'll kill them! They might kill Windrider!"

The fear, actually put into words, made her lose all control. She began screaming and sobbing hysterically, fighting again to get away from them, yelling in agony that it would be wrong to kill the Comanches. Finally they stopped talking about the other Rangers, and the man who rode with her pulled her in front of him instead of trusting her to sit behind.

"Go on," he told the other one. "And bring back that Tennessee Walker mare for her to ride. They've tortured this poor girl till she's at the end of her rope."

He held her gently but firmly in his arms and kept them moving east while the other one spun and rode away to the south. Jennie managed to look around the Ranger's arm and watch Spirit Talker while they rode farther and farther from her until she became a motionless speck and then nothing against the distant horizon. She lost all sense of time then, and had no idea how much had passed when the other Ranger returned, leading a tall, black mare.

Jennie fought them again, fought them to the end of her strength, but in the end they set her onto the black and tied her there, took hold of her reins and led her along between them. She finally gave up on trying to use words and gave in to the frantic tears, crying until the cords that bound her hands were soaking wet, but even that did not persuade them. They took her east, always east, at a ground-eating lope.

When Windrider had finished skinning and butchering the last bull he had brought down, he bagged the meat neatly in the hide and stood up to signal for a packhorse to be brought to him. *Ohawunu*, or Yellow Steps, one of the little girls who often tagged admiringly after the Fire Flower, came running with a tall, rawboned mule in tow.

"Take this meat to Old Sanah," he said as wiped his arms and hands clean with big wads of grass. "Tell her it is a peace offering from Windrider."

Chuckling at the memory of the tongue-lashing Sanah had given him the day he had rescued the Fire Flower from the old woman's test of courage, he loaded the gift onto the mule and tied it fast.

"Go, now," he said to the child. "Tell her this meat must be laid out to dry without delay. The bull was overheated with running when I brought him down."

He picked up Ohawunu and set her onto the mule in front of the load. She clutched the rein, kicked the animal in the ribs, and set him trotting back toward the camp.

Windrider whistled for Kwahira, who was keeping watch nearby. He leapt onto the stallion with a motion like the joy leaping in his heart. This hunt would provide much food and shelter for the band, enough so that they could begin to move far away from the Texans.

He would persuade Ten Bears that they should leave as soon as the meat had dried, he thought. But first he would assuage his conscience and his honor by giving the Fire Flower her choice of whether she wanted to stay or go back to her people.

He smiled to himself and patted Kwahira on the neck.

He knew the answer now, for sure. She would choose to stay.

Desire moved through his body as he remembered her face, the look on her beautiful face when he told her he loved her. She loved him, too, too much ever to leave him.

He had killed and butchered three bulls since she had gone to help Breaks Something. No telling where she was working now.

Windrider's eyes scanned the beehive of bodies looking for the Fire Flower as the stallion wove his way through the scattered carcasses that littered the plain, trotted around the people working at butchering and loading the precious meat and skins, and picked the best footing to avoid the blood and mess. Her bright hair always blazed like sunlight among the night-dark heads of The People; he should be able to find her easily.

But he couldn't see her anywhere.

Then, in the middle of a tightly knit group gathered to one side of a huge cow that still had Ten Bears' lance sticking out of its breast, he saw the Spirit Talker. She stood with her head hanging and sides heaving, obviously almost done in.

Quick anger stung him. Where in the world had

the Fire Flower been? She knew better than to push the mare like that after she had run so hard in the hunt!

Then came a shivering fear. His heart jumped and crashed in his chest like a wounded bird, trapped. More important than the mare, where was the Fire Flower now?

He kicked Kwahira into a lope and rode up to the chattering bunch. As he threw his leg over and slid to the ground, Breaks Something picked up Spirit Talker's reins and came toward him.

"I hate to bring you bad news," she said, but the excitement trembling in her voice gave the lie to her words. "The Fire Flower has asked me to return this mare to you."

She handed him the twisted rawhide reins.

Stunned beyond thinking, he reached out and took them.

"Where is the Fire Flower?"

The voice that asked the question was completely unrecognizable, even to himself.

Breaks Something took a deep breath and looked to make sure that she had the attention of everyone standing around.

"When we were butchering the bull that your brother had killed for the widows and orphans," she said, with a gesture that made Windrider notice for the first time that Ten Bears stood, scowling, in the midst of the circle, "we stood up to stretch our arms and rest a bit."

"So?" Windrider prompted impatiently.

"Far, far in the distance we saw two riders," she said, "white-eyes."

The waiting silence that greeted that revelation told him these people had heard this before.

The skin on the back of his neck broke out in a cold sweat.

"And?" he demanded.

"The Fire Flower suddenly decided to leave us. She told me to tell you that she was going back to her own people. She said she would turn the mare loose when she reached the men so that you can have her and the foal she carries. She said to tell you good-bye."

Windrider stared at the girl, trying to take in with his eyes what his ears refused to absorb. Then his eyes moved, slow as turtles in their sockets, and he turned his head to stare at the red filly.

There she stood, living proof of the truth of Breaks Something's disastrous words.

The Fire Flower had left him. And even after he told her that he loved her!

The thought carved the heart out of his body and the flesh off his bones, leaving him a standing skeleton. He no longer had a heart nor a spirit, nor muscles nor skin, yet he hurt more deeply than he would have thought possible to hurt and still breathe.

"Brother."

After a moment, the sound came again. "Brother."

Windrider turned his dull gaze from the mare to Ten Bears.

"Something is wrong with that story," Ten Bears said flatly.

Several people gasped; Breaks Something made a little sound of protest.

Ten Bears ignored them all and took a step toward Windrider, who somehow, through the haze of his pain, saw a gleam of hope in his brother's narrow black eyes. Ten Bears walked to him without breaking eye contact.

He put his hand on Windrider's arm.

"The woman Fire Flower loves you," he said, and his voice held a warmth Windrider hadn't heard there for a very long time. "Just the way she looks at you proves that."

Windrider closed his fist around the reins, willing their roughness to cut through the bigger pain, to make a channel in it for his brother's words to come through.

"This woman loves you more, much more, than my Third Wife who was killed loved you," Ten Bears went on, "and *that* affection was so great that it made me crazy with jealousy."

Windrider stripped the rope through his palm. The channel was open now. His ears were listening. Ten Bears might be right. Surely the Fire Flower did love him.

He called up the vision of her face.

"This despair I feel when I look at you now is worse than that jealousy," Ten Bears said. "I cannot bear to see such pain in my brother's face. You must not become an old grouch like Ten Bears, who has never had a woman, not even any of his wives, love him so much as the Fire Flower loves you."

Those words, crafted and weighted with truth like a perfectly made arrow, flew from Windrider's ears straight into his soul.

He dropped the reins from his hand, turned, and threw both his arms around his brother.

The next morning's sunlight was a slap in Jennie's face. She blinked against its bright heat and slumped deeper into her saddle, trying to slide back into the stupor of despair that had enfolded her all night.

If she were where she ought to be, riding back to the rest of the band from the hunting camp, she thought with a stab of pain so sharp she could almost feel the blood drip from her heart, the sun wouldn't be glaring into her eyes. It would be at her side, on her left hand. Windrider and Kwahira would be on her right.

She dropped her chin into her chest, shook her hair over her face like a curtain, and clung to that image, pretended that that was true. Windrider. She and Windrider were together, riding at the head of the shouting, laughing procession of hunters, leading them back to the main camp of The People with their packhorses loaded with food and shelter, everything they would need to move far to the north and the west.

Out of the reach of the Rangers.

"You want a drink of water, ma'am?"

Jennie closed her eyes and ignored the nudge of the metal canteen against her hand.

"Better drink somethin'," the soft voice urged. "You didn't eat a bite when we camped last night."

She didn't answer.

The pressure of the canteen went away, but the irritating talking didn't.

"Where did the Comanches get you?" the other man asked, calling to her so loudly, she gritted her teeth. "Do you have a family we can take you back to?"

The question made her eyes fly open.

"No!"

She tossed back her hair and turned to glare at him.

"My family is in the Comanche band. Let me go back to them—don't take me anywhere!"

"Indians killed your folks?" the other Ranger asked, his deep voice full of sympathy. "They catch you traveling or was you people setting up a homestead somewhere?''

"We were at Rowan's Fort," she muttered.

"Rowan's Fort!" both men repeated, their voices lifting with new hope of making her happy.

"There was other survivors of that raid," the man on the white horse said encouragingly. "Mostly women and children that slipped through the little door in the fort's wall and run down to hide by the river. You may not've lost all your family, the way you think."

"They walked for days," the other man said. "But most of 'em made it on in to San Antonio de Béxar."

As that news soaked into her numbed brain, a tiny tendril of hope reached out and touched her heart.

"My . . . mother?" she asked, noticing for the first time that her lips were so cracked, she could barely speak. "Kathleen O'Bannion? Was she among them?"

"Don't know, ma'am; I'm sorry," they said, almost in unison.

"We'll find out soon, though," the one on the gray assured her as he pushed the canteen at her again. This time Jennie took it and drank. "Two days from right now we'll find out—if we don't have a horse come up lame or if Rivers here don't get us lost."

Neither disaster came to pass, and the three of them rode into San Antonio late in the morning of the day Ranger Gentry had predicted. Since it was in the heat of noon, the streets were quiet, although a few people stirred.

Jennie sat up straight in her saddle and ran her fingers through her hair, her sore heart suddenly thumping hard against the cautions of her weary mind. She mustn't get her hopes too high; she didn't have the strength to bear another terrible disappointment.

But there was a chance. A chance that, out of all she had lost, she still had her beloved mama.

The Rangers turned at one corner and then at another without hesitation, without even consulting about where they should go.

Finally Jennie asked, ''Where are you taking me?''

''Right here,'' Ranger Gentry said, and turned his horse toward the hitching rail that ran along the side of the dusty street. ''This store belongs to one of the survivors of the Rowan's Fort raid.''

She raised her gaze from the wooden sidewalk to the sign painted on a board that hung over the door.

TRAMMEL NORDSTROM'S MERCANTILE AND EMPORIUM.

Her eyes locked on to the words, bored into them, straining to move the big, bold letters around, to rearrange them into proclaiming a completely different message.

But they stayed in their places, exactly where they were.

TRAMMEL NORDSTROM'S MERCANTILE AND EMPORIUM.

She thought she would die. She wanted to die.

The Rangers had to lift her bodily from the saddle and carry her inside. Neither her arms nor her legs would move.

This was the worst, something inside her kept repeating. This was the very worst she had yet been through, and she had no strength left to face it. She couldn't bear this. She absolutely could not bear it.

The store even had the same smell as the one at the fort, the exact same blend of pickles and coffee and tobacco and lamp oil and leather. It had the harness hanging on the right-hand side the way it had been at the fort.

This was Trammel's store, all right.

Yet it couldn't be true.

"You said *women and children* survived," she blurted, her voice stridently hoarse and trembling. "You didn't say *men!*"

"Two of the men also got away from the Comanches," Ranger Gentry said, removing his hat and hitting it against his leg to remove the dust. "This storekeeper here and his hired hand."

The curtain hanging directly behind the counter moved then and Trammel stepped through the doorway, into the same room with her. The murdering traveler called Nate who had been their guest during that fateful week that now seemed part of another lifetime came close on his heels.

The two saw Jennie and the Rangers and stopped in their tracks.

Her mind screamed at her arms to break free and at her legs to run, but if the Rangers' big hands hadn't been holding her up, she'd have fallen to the floor. She couldn't move, not even to close her eyes against the ghastly sight.

Finally Trammel smiled. He stepped forward and lifted the hinged piece in the top of the counter; he came through it, his bulky body moving as inexorably toward her as if he'd been a charging buffalo.

The screaming in her mind became a frantic shrieking that she thought surely they all could hear, but still she couldn't move.

"My wife," he said. "You men have found my wife."

The Rangers turned her loose and pushed her gently toward him. He reached out and took her by the elbow with fingers that gripped like talons.

Now she knew what captivity was.

Chapter 18

Being so close to Trammel, looking into his mud brown, bloodshot eyes, made Jennie's skin crawl. Yet she couldn't tear her gaze away. Even stranger than finding him alive and still calling her his wife was the fact that he was looking directly at her, as if somehow, during their separation, she had changed from an object into a real person.

"I thought I was a widower," he told her, his heavy voice raw with surprise. "I thought you was dead. You mean to tell me that you've been livin' with them Injuns all this time?"

A sudden thrill rushed through her with those words, a burgeoning excitement that began to chip away at her fear. He was right to look her in the eye—she *had* become a person during these past few months. And he had been right to think that she was dead.

The old Jennie O'Bannion *was* dead; she had changed forever into a much tougher, much stronger woman, a woman who was her own person.

A Jennie O'Bannion who was one of The People. She was a Comanche now.

"Yes," she said, "the Comanches took me and I learned to live."

She threw back her shoulders and pulled her arm from his grasp.

Trammel went stiff with surprise. He stared at her face for a long time as if he were not sure of her identity after all, then he ran his muddy gaze up and down her body. He turned away and looked from one of the Rangers to the other.

"You found her living with the Comanches?" he asked, a new, lascivious tone of curiosity coming into his voice.

"She was riding away from them, from a buffalo hunt—" Captain Gentry began.

Trammel stopped him with an upraised hand.

"Step over here, if you would," he said, "so we can speak in private."

The captain hesitated. "Shouldn't we find a chair for the lady? Can you stand all right, by yourself, ma'am?"

Jennie looked at him, turned her back on Trammel.

"I'm fine, thank you."

And without warning, with a stunning clarity, she knew that was true. She *was* fine. She was alive and she would get through this. She would use this awful experience to make herself even stronger.

And someday, when she was strong enough, she would leave San Antonio and ride out to find The People. She would find Windrider and never be taken from him again.

Instinctively she turned toward the door as the men moved away from her to talk quietly.

But Nate had gone around her somehow. He stood squarely in the open doorway, his shifty eyes sliding all over her, flicking from time to time to Trammel and the Rangers as he listened to them.

". . . have to keep an eye on her . . ."

"Like many prisoners, she's confused, thinks she wants to go back to them savages . . ."

". . . said she has a husband name of Windrider. We know *that* red devil's name . . ."

Running steps and voices outside on the board sidewalk drowned out the soft voices inside the store.

Two children who looked vaguely familiar to Jennie burst in, screaming, "Mrs. Nordstrom, Mrs. Nordstrom, you're saved from the Indians!"

Behind them, their skirts held up in both hands so they could move faster, rushed a half dozen women. The second one she saw was her mother.

An overwhelming wave of joy washed over Jennie, picked her up, and carried her across the short distance into her mother's arms. Her mama was alive! Her mind struggled to take that good news in while her weary body collapsed into Kathleen's comforting, bony embrace.

They never turned loose of each other during all the confusion of greeting the others who had lived through the raid on the fort, the good-byes of the Rangers, and Kathleen's outspoken expressions of gratitude to them. Jennie watched her mother and listened to her in amazement. The shy mama she used to know would barely have murmured her thanks to the strangers, even for reuniting her with her only child.

Mrs. Rowan, who apparently had retained her leadership of the women of the fort, put her arms around Jennie and Kathleen.

"Mr. Nordstrom, let us take Jennie to the boardinghouse," she said, gently. "We'll help her bathe and give her some real clothes, and she and

Mrs. O'Bannion can have a bit of a private reunion, then we'll bring her back to you."

"I've got real clothes in this store, and bathtubs and water, too," Trammel growled. "No wife o' mine is gonna be seen at yore *boardinghouse*!"

"You might as well give up your nasty insinuations and get accustomed to women in business," Mrs. Rowan retorted, her soft voice going hard as his own. "You're in the city, now, Trammel Nordstrom."

"Yore husband must be turnin' over in his grave," Trammel said, hitting his fist on the counter for emphasis. "With you stayin' out here in this Spanish wilderness, leadin' these other ladies astray, when all of you could go back east to live with yore folks."

"These ladies and I prefer to make our own way in San Antonio de Béxar, not to live on the charity of others," Mrs. Rowan said, haughtily, taking a step forward to face him. "And speaking of my husband, he would be appalled to know that the religious fervor that once filled you has been replaced entirely by greed! I don't understand your problem with our boardinghouse—it does not compete with your mercantile."

Trammel's face flushed red with anger.

"If you want t' help my wife bathe and let her visit with her mother, do it here," he snapped. "Otherwise, git back to yore own place."

Mrs. Rowan indicated that the other women should go, so they began shepherding the children out the door while she stayed with Jennie and Kathleen.

"Come this way," Trammel barked then, and they moved toward the door that he and Nate had come through from the back of the store. He turned to look over his shoulder.

"Nate, there's a customer comin'," he said. "Look sharp."

He ushered them into living quarters much larger and nicer than those they'd had at the fort. Dimly Jennie realized that the store, too, although it smelled and was arranged the same as the old one, was much more impressive and ostentatious. Trammel was more interested in earthly things than he used to be.

He stood to one side and stared at them as Kathleen led Jennie to the table, and Mrs. Rowan went to the fire to put water on for tea.

"My wife don't leave this building," he said, each word flat, hard, and heavy as a stone. "I been told by the law that she ain't quite right in the head, and it's my responsibility to watch her. Anybody takes her outta here, I'll have you arrested."

Then he turned and went back into the store.

"He cannot bear the thought that we're making a success of our boardinghouse business," Mrs. Rowan said, bustling around Trammel's large kitchen to find the tea things. "You would think that since the Lord blessed him with his life and his money that he had buried beneath his store at the fort, he could be happy for other people, too."

"Trammel Nordstrom can't bear for women to be happy or to have any power at all," Jennie said. Her knees buckled suddenly, and she dropped into one of the carved oak chairs at the table. "What is all this about a boardinghouse?"

"Mrs. Rowan bought it with money from an inheritance she had in a bank in Pennsylvania," Kathleen said, quickly. "And, Jennie, I'm working for her! I am her assistant manager there and I'm earning my own way!"

She sat down across from Jennie and took both her hands.

"Darlin', we'll try to get you away from Trammel Nordstrom; we'll do *something* to bring you to live with us."

Jennie squeezed her mother's thin fingers, noticing as she did so that Kathleen's hands were trembling as much as her own.

"He would have the law down on you; you heard what he said," Jennie demurred. "He might ruin your business and he might lock me up as truly crazy. Legally, to white men, I am still his wife."

She smiled, trying to steady her head against the dizziness of hunger and exhaustion that threatened her. In spite of all her hardship, though, and the shock of falling back into Trammel's trap, she felt incredibly strong.

"I can take care of myself now," she said. "I'm not the least afraid of Trammel Nordstrom."

"I'm so happy you're alive!" Kathleen said, for the hundredth time. "I've cried meself to sleep over you every single night since the Indians attacked."

Mrs. Rowan bustled toward them with a steaming pot and two mugs for tea. She found a tin of small cakes, too, and opened it.

"I'm going to set up the bathtub; I'm boiling water for Jennie's bath now," she said, pausing to pat each of them on the shoulder. "You two just visit and I'll be back in a bit," she said. "I'll make Trammel give me some clothes for you, too, dear."

She left them.

Jennie stared after her.

"You and Mrs. Rowan have certainly changed," she said, taking the mug of tea her mother poured for her. "You both used to be so shy!"

"Your papa and the Reverend Rowan died in the raid," Kathleen said, dryly, averting her face to pour her own tea.

"Are you saying that you two are better off widows than married?" Jennie teased. "That doesn't sound like the mama I used to know."

"I didn't say that," Kathleen said, giving Jennie's hand a little shake before she passed the tin of tea cakes. "We miss them both terribly. We always will. But fending for ourselves has made us strong."

"It does that," Jennie said, "but sometimes a woman can have a husband as partner and still be strong."

She got up to walk across the room to the basin to wash away the grime of the trail. And to gain some time to get accustomed to the familiar/ strange smells of the cakes and tea before she ate and drank.

Most of all it was to give her a chance to think how to break the news to her mother.

"Mama," she said, turning to look at her mother over her shoulder once she had washed and then found a clean towel. "I have to tell you that you were wrong about a woman's lot. Sometimes a woman *can* marry the man she loves. I did it."

She turned completely around to meet her mother's eyes while she dried her hands. Kathleen stared at her, her faded green eyes wide.

"What do you mean? You . . . aren't speaking of . . . Mr. Nordstrom?"

"No. I married a Comanche warrior, Mama. He is called Windrider and he is my real husband

and my partner. With him I can be myself and I can be free."

A quick happiness, a gleam of victorious approval, flashed in Kathleen's eyes, behind the shock. But then her face clouded with worry as Jennie walked back to her.

"Did he . . . force you, daughter? I'm so sorry . . ."

"Windrider would never force me, Mama, but Trammel did. Windrider lets me be myself, but Trammel won't."

The shocked surprise, the amazement, the quick succession of other emotions that raced across her mother's face, made Jennie laugh again and cling to her hand even harder when she sat down again.

She lowered her voice to a quiet murmur, even though she wanted to shout the words in defiance so Trammel could hear them.

"I vow it right now, Mama," she said, picking up her cup of fragrant tea. "I swear on my life that I'll find Windrider and The People again. I don't care how big Comanchería may be."

"But, Jennie, don't you have to live outside all the time and cook on the ground? Don't you have to scrape skins and use sinews for threads when you sew?"

"Yes," Jennie said, taking hold of the cup with both hands, "and you smell the sweet grass and the faraway pines on the wind, you feel the warm power of your horse pulsing beneath you and see the endless sky stretching over your head. You taste the good, cold water from the creeks and the tangy sweetness of honey from hollow trees. You rest when you're tired and ride when you're rested. You are free, out there with The People, Mama, free!"

She took a great gulp of her tea and fixed her eyes on her mother's astonished face.

"Come with me when I go, Mama! The People would take you in! I'll make all the plans, I'll prepare, and then I'll come for you when I leave Trammel!"

Loneliness filled Kathleen's eyes. "I couldn't do it," she murmured. "I'm too old a woman to get used to living like that. But, oh, Jennie, life is so short. You go. I do want you to be happy!"

The enormity of that sacrifice and of Kathleen's accepting the rightness of Jennie's relationship with Windrider was almost too much to comprehend.

And so was the idea of leaving her darling mama so soon after she'd miraculously found her again.

Jennie leapt up, not caring that her chair fell to the floor with a crash, and ran around the table to her mother.

"Don't think about it now, Mama," Jennie said. "Let's not think about anything now. We're both alive. We're both alive!"

Trammel thought the old O'Bannion woman and the Rowan widow would never leave. Finally, when it was almost dark and time to close the store, he sent Nate to walk them home. Once they had gone, he heard no sound from the living quarters—Jennie was quiet as a sneaking Indian.

That thought just popped into his head, but once it was there, he relished it. Being quiet and sneaky wasn't all she'd learned from them savages.

He finished counting the money he'd taken in that day and put it into the metal box. Tucking it beneath his arm, he strode to the front door, closed and locked it. Nate would stay out drinking, as always, and when he did return, he could use his key.

Trammel turned and started across the creaky floor of the building. There'd be three of them now, in the living quarters back there, and he'd have to keep an eye out for any hanky-panky between Nate and the girl. She'd be accustomed to giving it to any man after being taken by every red barbarian on the plains.

Then the thought soaked into his head and he gave a wry chuckle. Why should he care if Nate used her when all them savages already had? He himself would never touch her again, no matter *what* they had taught her to do. She was filthy now.

He clasped the money box closer to his side and used both hands to close the inside shutters and latch them across each expensive glass window. Then he stood still for a moment in the dimness, thinking of all the implications for his business of having a wife come back from the dead.

Back from being a whore to the Injuns looking strong and healthy and dangerous and beautiful beyond belief.

Already, just in the four or five hours since she'd been here, a dozen or more men had come into the store, their eyes darting furtively to the curtained doorway again and again, buying first one thing and then another while they stalled, wishing to catch a glimpse of her. Them Rangers must've been talking about her in every saloon in town.

And he, Trammel Nordstrom, would be the envy of every man in town! *They* didn't have to know that he wouldn't touch her.

He settled the metal box more firmly into place

in the crook of his arm and strode across the room toward the living quarters. Just think what the traffic into the store would be like when she began working as clerk!

He found her standing at the window in the lamplit kitchen, her profile to the room, her arms crossed beneath her breasts. The tight fit of the dress emphasized them more than the buckskin had done—they looked bigger than he had remembered.

"No sense thinking of going out the window," he said, and stopped still in the doorway to watch her face when she turned to him. "I'd have you caught before you got to the corner."

"I wasn't thinking of going anywhere," she lied, and lifted her chin in her old, stubborn way when she swung around to look him in the eye.

A niggling, uncomfortable feeling worked its way down his spine. That gesture was the same, but somehow she looked even more dangerous when she did that. Being caught by the Indians had changed her in more ways than one.

He shifted the square box in the crook of his elbow so it wasn't poking into the flesh of his arm.

"You jist settle in here and git on back to your chores, come morning," he said, raising his voice to try to make her know that *he* was in control in his own house, as always. "You can watch the store most of the time, but you are never to leave here unless me or Nate goes with you."

Her green eyes went as cold as if she were thinking of killing him dead and cutting out his liver. But that look didn't surprise him half as much as what she said.

"I'll do all my chores except the one in your bed. I sleep alone."

Shock and fury washed over him in a wave that tangled his tongue in his teeth and wouldn't let him speak. He wouldn't touch her—he had already decided that he wouldn't dirty himself—but she didn't know that.

He was the one to tell *her* she wouldn't sleep in his bed.

"I'm not married to you," she went on, in that same, inexorable tone, completely unafraid. "I never was, and I never will be."

She dropped her arms loose to her sides as if she were ready to fight. "I have a Comanche husband I love, and he loves me, so don't *you* dare to touch me, ever again."

Stunned, he stared at her while the blood roared to his head and pounded there like a storm.

The nerve! The unmitigated gall of this little heifer, to tell him, her own *husband*, to keep his hands off her.

"You are *unclean*," he said, very loudly, "eternally unclean because you have lain with those savages. Any *decent* woman would have killed herself first."

That brought an angry flush to her calm face, and he smiled. Good. He would enjoy the struggle it would take to get her whipped back into shape.

"I'll never touch you," he said, roaring each word at her now. "But I'll keep you here, under constant guard, because you belong to me, no matter what you say or what you've done. The law is on my side on that."

She just stood there, without moving at all.

"You and the law can go straight to hell," she said.

And he probably would. Because he was lying, lying through his teeth.

He *did* want her, he wanted her so badly that his groin, his whole body, ached with it. He *had* to have her again.

Before, at the fort, she had been beautiful, yes, but now there was such an air about her, such a sureness, that it was an undisguised challenge to any man. He would never be able to keep his hands off her.

But he wouldn't try it tonight. Not while she was in this mood.

"Remember," he said, pouring all the menacing strength that he could into his voice, "you belong to me, and nobody, not even some sneaking, dog-eating, stinking Indian, takes Trammel Nordstrom's possessions away."

He turned and left her on that last word, with a surge of satisfaction rising up to drown out his frustration. He could do as he pleased with her, he thought, as he pushed into his bedroom and secreted the box of money in a larger box of his clothes. And he'd never have to feel constrained to treat her with the respect due his wife, either, not even in public, since she bore the stigma carried by every returning woman captive.

Jennie began to believe that she had her bluff in on Trammel, that he really would leave her alone.

Or maybe he was staying away because he truly did consider her unclean, she thought, as she turned back the bed in the spare room for the fourth night in a row. According to this thinking, she had lain with a savage, and now she was forever unfit for him to touch.

Her heart lifted. If that was true, she was safe.

She could devote all her thoughts and energy to figuring out how to get away and find Windrider.

In the dark, she changed into the nightgown that Mama had brought her, wishing she could sleep in only her skin as she had done on the plains. But here she didn't have that freedom—it made her feel too vulnerable, too exposed. She buttoned the garment up to the neck and stretched out on the folded blankets, in the closed room that threatened to stifle her breath.

For a moment, images of the long day swam before her—working in the store and trying to ignore all the curious stares, parrying the suggestive remarks of some customers. Then, faint with exhaustion from the unaccustomed nervous tension of it all, she fell quickly and deeply into sleep.

An alien pressure on her breast woke her.

She came instantly awake, crying out in protest, using both hands to try to push it away, struggling to get out from under it and get up.

But Trammel was too much stronger than she.

And too much bigger. He loomed over her like a huge boulder of rock, holding her back flat to the bed.

He pulled at her nipple.

Fear and loathing poured into Jennie's blood in an icy stream, freezing her where she lay. Yet she would die rather than submit to him again.

But she had no weapon.

She would have to use her brain, her cunning, to get his repulsive body away from her.

"You must be forgetting how unclean I am," she said, in a voice so cold and clear that it rang against the walls of the house. "But then, you don't even know the full extent of it."

His clumsy fingers stopped moving.

"I'm carrying a baby," she said, in that same strange tone.

He jerked his hand away.

"A half-Comanche, savage baby."

He made a strangled sound and pushed awkwardly up from his kneeling position to stand on his feet.

"Them filthy, murdering, thieving, *mindless* Indians have ruined you," he said, fairly spitting the words as he towered above her.

She scrambled to her feet, dragging her cover with her, holding it against her breasts.

"*One* of those Indians has more of a brain than you or your stupid hired hand, Nate!" she cried. "It was Nate and Digger who caused every bit of the dying and suffering at the fort—for no reason at all, they raped and killed my husband's mother and his sister-in-law!"

She advanced on him as if she would launch a physical attack. He took a step backward, his face twisted and flushed in the dim moonlight coming through the window.

"There's no hope for you!" he hissed. "If you're gonna have their babies and defend their murders, then there's no hope for you. You'll burn in hell!"

He turned and left her then, rushing from the room as if Windrider and a dozen warriors were after him.

Her knees trembled too much to hold her, so Jennie let them crumple. She sank back down onto her bed, clutching the ragged quilt to her face with both hands.

She would have to run away. Now, after only these few days of seeing Mama for an hour or two each evening.

For Trammel would be back, fumbling at her in her bed. He would force himself on her, once he knew that her claim of carrying Windrider's baby was a lie.

A wracking sob shook her, and she stuffed the quilt into her mouth to hold it back. If only the baby weren't a lie! She would give anything to have a part of Windrider with her right now!

She threw herself prone, facedown, and cried herself sick with hopeless despair. All her whole life, except for those three wonderful full moons as Windrider's wife, she had been plotting to escape. It would never end.

When the tears were all gone, she forced herself to dry her eyes and to think. She had to think of a way to find Half Horse's band of The People, a way to travel all those miles and run into Windrider's arms.

Because there was no way he could come to her. Any Comanche within miles of the outskirts of San Antonio would be shot on sight. People were even more rabid on the subject of Comanches since the raid on Rowan's Fort. Word had spread all over Texas about that.

She rolled onto her back and ran her hands through her hair, pushing it back from her hot face, wishing she could push away just as easily the question that tortured her. Did Windrider even *want* to come to her?

That treacherous Breaks Something probably told him that Jennie rode out to join the Rangers of her own free will.

Jennie bit her bottom lip and narrowed her eyes. Well, the hateful little varmint would not get away with it. She would find someone, *someone*, who could lead her to Windrider, and she would slip away from Trammel and go. But who?

The answer dropped into her head like a gift from God.

Onate. He had traded with Windrider for years. He knew the approximate area where The People would be each season. Even if they had already started for the faraway Staked Plains, he could find them.

Now all she had to do was get word to Oñate.

Holding that thought to her heart, she finally slept.

The next morning she woke obsessed with the idea of finding the Spaniard. She hurried through her chores in the living quarters so she could go into the store as soon as it opened, a complete reversal of the past few days when she had lurked in the back rooms as much as she could to avoid the townspeople's curiosity.

Either Trammel or Nate watched her constantly, but from that day on, she promised herself, she would find a way to talk privately with every one of the traders and suppliers who came into the store. One of them, surely, knew Onate.

"Leave them dishes," Trammel said as he came out of his bedroom with his metal money box in his hands. "You do more good in the store than back here."

Jennie turned to look at him, her hands deep in the dishwater she had just heated over the fire. Her mind whirled. What did he mean, she did more good in the store?

A fearful leap almost took her heart out of her chest. Was this a trick on his part? Had he read the desperate wish in her mind to make contact with someone who could help her? Was he setting a trap?

She puzzled over the remark while she dried her hands, removed her apron, and smoothed back her hair, while she opened the shutters in the store and began dusting off the goods on the shelves. It was not until two bearded settlers came in and asked for twenty feet of rope, a pound of nails, and two sticks of licorice candy that she understood.

Trammel called her to wait on them, although he easily could have done so himself. He kept her standing right in front of them while he told her what to do and how to do it.

Trammel was putting her on display, his exotic, captured wife who claimed a Comanche husband. He was basking in the jealousy of the men who came through the door. Their sexual attraction to her was the undercurrent that had been pulling at her these past few days, and she'd been too lost in her misery to understand.

Most of the men who came in wanted to be in Trammel's place. That was certainly true of these two.

They watched her every move, running their eyes over her as if she were naked. They talked to her and tried to charm her into answering them, into looking at them.

They talked *about* her as if she weren't even there.

"You ever see sich a wild beauty?" one of them asked the other as she turned her back to measure the rope they were buying.

The other said, "Skin the color of honey agin them green eyes and red hair, makes a man think about tastin' some candy."

"I reckon them Injuns done taught her a trick or two."

That voice was Trammel's!

Jennie had to hold on to the counter to keep from whirling around to confront him.

"They learned her to move like a mountain cat when she walks, that's for sure," the first voice said. "That's a whole lotta kitty for you to have in yore bed, Nordstrom. You ever need any help, you jist holler fer me."

Jennie burned to turn and lash the end of the rope across all three of their faces, longed to run past them out the door and keep running until she reached the wide, clean plains. But Trammel would only send the Rangers to bring her back.

She set her jaw, cut the rope, and coiled it.

When she left Trammel, she would do it in such a way that *nobody* could bring her back. Please God in Heaven to send her a messenger to send to Oñate.

Her prayers were answered late that same afternoon, just after Nate had gone on his regular errand to the wagon yard to pick up their freight. A silversmith came in with some bracelets and earrings to sell.

Trammel pushed Jennie forward, as usual, but this man, who spoke with a Spanish accent, seemed hardly to notice her.

"I am called Martín Gutiérrez," he said. "My good customer, Señor José Rodríguez, has suggested that Señor Nordstrom might also display my work in his illustrious establishment."

Jennie looked at him, amused by his cleverness in using the Rodríguez recommendation. Trammel constantly talked about, admired, and competed with the only other general store in town, which belonged to José Rodríguez.

The man spread out his work on the trade cloth

that Trammel placed on the counter, and her amusement changed to excitement.

The engravings on his pieces closely resembled those on her silver combs, which she carried in the medicine bag she wore constantly beneath her dress. Maybe Oñate had bought the combs from this man before he traded them to Windrider!

She could hardly contain herself while the silversmith and Trammel dickered and talked, bargained and argued, but finally Trammel selected several he wanted to buy.

"That's highway robbery!" he protested, when the man named the price. "That's more money than I even keep in this store!"

Gutiérrez held firm, though, mentioning again and again how well his work sold down the street at the establishment of Señor Rodríguez, and Trammel finally went back into the living quarters to get some more money.

Jennie spoke quickly and quietly to the man.

"Do you know a trader named Oñate?"

Startled, the silversmith glanced up from the jewelry he was putting back into his case, the pieces that Trammel hadn't bought.

"*Sí!*" he said. "Yes, I do. Good man, Ysidore Oñate."

Relief like a warm river flowed through her.

"Take him a message from me, please," she begged, the words tumbling from her lips in a hoarse whisper. "Secretly! Don't let Trammel Nordstrom know."

The man went very still, and they both glanced at the doorway through which Trammel had disappeared.

"Tell Oñate that he must come for me," she said. "He must take me to my real husband, Windrider, War Chief of Half Horse's band of the Comanche.''

The man was staring at her, his dark eyes gleaming. He was surprised, yes, the look said. But he was quick. He understood.

"I will tell him."

"Tell him to hurry," she said, just as, from the corner of her eye, she saw Trammel coming back through the door.

"The engraving on these bracelets is beautiful," she said, loud enough for him to hear.

The man nodded and dared to give her a wink. Then he pocketed his money, took up his case, and was gone.

"I want to go visit my mother," Jennie said. "I'll be back before dark."

"You'll go straight to the kitchen and cook my supper," Trammel retorted coldly, flicking his gaze to her face from the money he was counting.

Then he smiled. "I have to hand it to you, wife," he said. "You're some good to me, at least. You've brought in more business than I've done in one week since I set up store in San Antonio."

She simply stared at him, straight into his flat brown eyes, silently calling on God in Heaven to strike him dead.

Finally he said, "Oh, all right. You've earned it. After we eat, I'll send Nate to get your mother, and you can visit with her until bedtime."

Jennie turned and left him then, and went into the kitchen to stir up the fire. A great feeling of victory swept over her in a sudden wave, and she had to catch her tongue between her teeth to keep from singing. She had done it!

The silversmith was a good man. He would not betray her. Soon she would be gone, free of Trammel forever, free of this place.

But after that, the days flowed by, one after another, then another and another, each of them very much the same.

Oñate never came.

Chapter 19

Jennie was behind the counter of the store, pulling bolt after bolt of cloth out of the shelves to show to a woman whom Trammel had introduced (with a fawning politeness that turned Jennie's stomach) as Mrs. Hope, whose husband owned and operated the freight yard, when the sound of a horse dashing up to the sidewalk made all three of them look up from what they were doing.

A slightly built boy, dressed in the white tunic-blouse and pants of a servant, but with a bright sash tied around his waist, ran across the board sidewalk and stood in the open doorway.

"Señor and Señora Rodríguez request the honor of the presence of Mr. and Mrs. Trammel Nordstrom at a masked costume ball on the evening of this Saturday approaching," he recited in heavily Spanish-accented English, standing very straight, the ends of his sashes still swinging. His gaze met Jennie's, then Trammel's, then slid away.

"*Gracias, muchas gracias!*" Trammel boomed, and Jennie's stomach lurched again. He was so impressed with Rodríguez that he was obsequious to the man's servant! "Mr. and Mrs. Nord-

366

strom will be honored to attend. You may inform
your master."

With a small salute, the boy turned and ran
back to his horse.

"Why, then, you'll be coming, too!" Mrs. Hope
exclaimed, giving Jennie a small, tight smile. "I'm
surprised, considering that . . ."

She caught herself and hurried to change her
tack. "That's the ball for which I'm buying this
new dress. The best socials in San Antonio are
given at the Rodríguez villa—it's absolutely fab-
ulous. You'll have a wonderful time!" she bab-
bled.

"She'll meet everyone in town, too," Trammel
chimed in, his heavy voice fairly bubbling with
happiness. "Everyone important in business in
this part of the republic!"

Obviously this was his first invitation to go
there.

Both women glanced at him. His ruddy face
was gleaming.

"That's true," Mrs. Hope said, picking up a
bolt of heavy yellow moiré and shaking it out to
hold up against her. "José Rodríguez's annual
masked ball is *the* social event of the business
community of this town, both Anglo and Spanish. And it's so entertaining to try to recognize
everyone in costume!"

Jennie's blood turned cold. The last desire ever
in her heart was to enter society, any society, and
even worse would be to do so as Trammel's wife.

No, as Trammel's exhibit.

She didn't want to go. She *wouldn't* go.

As if she could read Jennie's mind, Mrs. Hope
said, "Who shall you be for the ball, Mrs. Nordstrom?" She snapped her fingers and beamed as
an idea struck her.

"An Indian squaw! A Comanche! That's a role you could play with a great deal of authority!"

"I wouldn't be playing a role—I *am* a Comanche, one of The People," Jennie said, straightening her back to look the taller woman in the eye. "Do not call me Mrs. Nordstrom."

Mrs. Hope dropped the bolt of fabric onto the counter, spun around with a great swishing of her skirts, and hurried away, trembling with the excitement of having such a juicy tidbit to tell.

Trammel launched his huge bulk at Jennie along the back of the counter with such speed that she thought he would hit her. She braced herself, keeping eye contact with him, feeling around beneath the slick cloth to try to find the scissors to use in defense.

But he struck out only with words.

"Don't you ever, *ever*, do something like that again!" he said, grating each word out from between his teeth. "You not only lost us the sale of that dress, but maybe a great deal more business, too. You *are* Mrs. Nordstrom, and you will damn sure answer to that name!"

"And *you* will answer to the good Lord in Heaven for holding me here against my will and putting me on display like a piece of merchandise to sell!"

"I'll sell you, too, if I please!" he shouted, his lips pale with anger in the ruddy fury of his face. "I'll do whatever I like with you. Now, get yourself a costume for next Friday night and go to that ball. You are my wife and you'll do as say!"

"Your freak, you mean. You only want me there as entertainment, something for the women to watch and whisper about, and the men to lust after!"

"It brings them into the store, don't it?"

His eyes narrowed thoughtfully; the anger left his face.

"That wasn't a half-bad idea for you to go dressed as a Comanche," he said. "Do that."

"I'll do as I please," she snapped back at him, and turned away to go back to her room.

She *would* go to the ball, though, she realized as she pushed through the curtained doorway, but not because Trammel had ordered her. Because Oñate might possibly be there.

As Jennie stepped down from the fancy carriage Trammel had hired for the occasion and onto the polished, flat stones of the Rodríguezes' courtyard, the same wish that had consumed her before her wedding to him attacked her again. She wanted it to be the end of the world.

Even though the tubs and banks of flowers massed along the walls and around the fountain filled the sultry September air with a wonderful perfume, even though there was a string quartet playing sweet, lilting music, it ought to be the end of the world.

Too many people filled the patio, too many eyes were turning to look at her from behind their masks.

Jennie stood still as the stone fountain in the center of the big quadrangle, unable to lift her wooden feet and walk toward the party. She had to force her chest to move in and out, to send air into her lungs.

So many people inside of a house, even inside the walls of the courtyard, would shut her in, smother her. She could not do this.

If only these were The People, surrounded only by the endless sky and the eternal prairie!

A hot knife of longing stabbed into her body

and cut out her heart. If only this were Windrider beside her instead of Trammel!

A slightly built, silver-haired man, dressed in the brilliant, tight pants and short jacket of a toreador's costume, detached himself from a group and strode to meet her. Trammel suddenly loomed at her side, his voice filling with oily respect as he presented the man as Señor Rodriguez.

José Rodriguez greeted Trammel graciously, but he quickly turned from him to take Jennie's hand. He bent over it, kissed it, and when he finished his bow, his eyes, flashing in the holes of his narrow black mask, met hers.

"Señora Nordstrom, *bienvenido!*" he murmured, his low voice singing another melody beneath the notes of the string band. "Welcome. *Mi casa es su casa.*"

Trammel waved at Nate to drive the carriage on to the stables. Then Señora Rodriguez brought her three daughters sweeping up to greet Jennie graciously. Her panic began to subside.

She smiled, she spoke to them, then she ignored Trammel's fingers grasping for her arm and moved ahead of him through the crowd toward the huge doors of the house, flung widely open. They weren't the doors of the chapel at Rowan's Fort; they held hope instead of despair. The rectangle they formed was light instead of dark, lit by hundreds of candles and the bright costumes of the guests already dancing. And instead of grim silence and the unctuous voice of Reverend Rowan, here her ears were filled with music.

She set the half mask closer against her face and touched the high upsweep of her hair. That was another difference, she thought. Trammel was no longer telling her to cover it up in public.

It was her most distinguishing feature, and he wanted her to be recognized tonight.

Well, so did she. That was the reason she had left off the lace mantilla of her Spanish lady's costume. Windrider had told Oñate the color of her hair. She didn't want her hair covered if Oñate was here to see her.

He was here. He had to be here.

She touched the heavily worked edges of the silver combs at her temples. Oñate would recognize them. Oñate was here.

But he was not. Jennie danced with every man who asked her, ignored the stares and the whispers and the constant surveillance of Trammel and Nate. She made polite small talk with her partners, always, always working it around to business and trading and the trader called Oñate. No one knew him.

After an hour of so, when tears of frustration had begun to sting at the corners of her eyes, her host, Señor Rodríguez, stepped up, clicked his heels, bent over her hand, and asked her to dance. Behind him, she glimpsed Trammel's ruddy face beaming at her. He would *really* be watching her now, telling her with his stares and his grimaces that she must further his acquaintance with this important man.

She stared into the Spaniard's handsome face and came within a trice of refusing him. Her lips parted to plead a headache, a need for fresh air, any excuse to wipe that satisfied smile from Trammel's evil mouth.

But there was a gleam, an intensity, in Señor Rodríguez's look that held her tongue still. She gave him her hand.

And immediately wished that she hadn't. As he drew her into his arms, the music ebbed and almost died out into silence, then it rose full and flowing, winding itself into a high, enchanting song with a melody so sweet, it ripped out her heart.

This was a stranger who held her in his embrace. Never, ever again would it be *Windrider's* arms that held her.

Even if she could get out of this town, how could she ever find him?

"Dance me outside, *please*, take me out of here," she blurted, fighting the welling tears. "I feel I'm about to smother."

"This moment, it is done," Señor Rodríguez said, and something knowing in his tone made her tilt her head to look at him.

His sharp gaze was as provocatively unflinching as his voice.

For an instant, it shook her.

Had he misunderstood her intentions? Did he think she wanted to escape the company alone with him in order to have a private tryst?

She searched his face.

No. No, he had no designs on her. But there was *something* secret lurking in his dark eyes.

The music swirled them around and he led her expertly past Trammel, who had gone to stand beside one of the refreshment tables, a crystal plate of food held clumsily in both his hands. Señor Rodríguez danced her through the rest of the crowd, through the doorway, and out into the hot Texas night.

They danced across the courtyard toward the fountain, its water splashing high and then burbling down. Oh, dear God, she prayed, let Señor Rodríguez know where to find Oñate! She couldn't live very many more days like this.

They waltzed around another dancing couple,

coming so close to the wall that the roses climbing up its face brushed Jennie's skin and her hair, then they whirled in a long, graceful spiral back out into the center of the patio.

The song ended.

Her host dropped his arms from around her.

Panic made her blood roar like thunder in Jennie's ears. This might be her very last chance.

"Do you know a trader name Ysidore Oñate?" she blurted, leaning toward her host so he could hear her hoarse whisper. "A trader who does much business with the Comanche?"

Señor Rodríguez bowed and took both her hands, squeezing them as he leaned close to give her that volatile look again.

"Please stroll around the wall and enjoy our flowers while I bring you a plate of refreshments, my dear," he said. She fixed her gaze on her host's departing back. In front of him, she caught a glimpse of Trammel in the broad, open doorway, and prayed that he wouldn't come out.

That squeeze of her hands, that look into her eyes, had been Rodríguez's message to her, not the words he had said. But what had it meant? Was he going to get Oñate, to produce him magically, somehow, out of the many people who crowded his house? Could it be?

Hope, a wild, leaping deer of a hope, crashed into her heart, made her breath come hard. She looked around for a shadowed spot, for someplace to talk with Oñate, should he come.

She turned her back on the curious onlookers and strolled quickly away from the fountain. The glowing lanterns were everywhere, but the thick adobe wall threw a few shadows, especially where the climbing roses grew thickest. She tried to pick out the darkest spot, while she stayed in view so

that her host could find her. She tried not to hope
too hard that Señor Rodríguez could help her.

But he *had* to help her! If not, what would she
do?

A tall man stepped out of the shadow she was
walking toward. The light from the lanterns
washed over him.

Jennie stopped so fast that the heavy skirts of
her costume swayed around her legs, pulling her
forward anyway. Pulling her toward him.

He was dressed as a Comanche, this guest; his
costume looked remarkably like an authentic one
of The People. Breechclout, moccasins, bare,
painted chest, an eagle feather tied in his hair.
Stripes of red and yellow paint formed the mask
for his face.

It stilled the blood in her veins.

He came toward her.

No, it was the way he moved, like a panther
on the prowl, that was squeezing the life from her
heart.

Then it leapt and hit against her ribs like a blow
from a giant's fist.

Windrider!

He moved toward her.

Jennie began trembling, shivering all over like
a tree covered with leaves being shaken by the
wind. Her mouth opened to cry out his name.

Then she instinctively bit her lips to keep from
drawing attention to him, and simply ran. Windrider met her, coming more than halfway in the
space of one breath, caught her hand, and turned,
running faster and faster, pulling her through a
gate in the wall that she hadn't noticed before.

"Stables this way," he murmured. "Kwahira
is there."

"Hurry," she gasped. "Oh, Windrider, hurry!"

If only she had time to shed the hindering skirts she wore, if only she could rip them off and wrap them around Windrider to hide him! If anyone saw that his was not a costume, he would be shot at that instant!

All sorts of crazy wishes crashed through her mind as she dashed through the night with him, running blindly into the breeze that blurred her eyes, clinging to his hand with both of hers, catching only glimpses of more climbing roses, yellow ones this time, and purple bougainvilleas, of winding paths paved with flagstones, of many, many carriages crowded to the edges of the long driveways. The lanterns, the hundreds of bright lanterns, were everywhere!

If only she had the breath to blow them all out!

They were even hanging in double rows along the front of the stables.

Windrider kept to the edge of the light there, running off the path, and Jennie caught a glimpse of Kwahira tied at the far side of the long, low building. If only she had a huge blanket to cover his white hide! He gleamed like a moon with four legs in the darkness!

Then they had reached him. She stood in one spot, panting for bits of life-giving air, too taken by the need to devour the sight of Windrider to remember, even, how to breathe. She fought her mind to make it believe her senses—tried to make it believe he was real.

His eyes gleamed dark and wild in the night, flashing at her as he reached to untie the stallion. Then he reached for her, too, making a low noise, a sound of surrender, deep in his throat. He crushed her to him with one arm hard around her waist, tangled in the rein, the other thrusting into her hair, its thumb caressing the comb she wore there, running up and down the carving on its edge, pressing it against her head as if he would brand her with it.

His lips took hers swiftly, swooping down like a hawk from the sky, and closed hers into such warm sweetness, she thought she could die. She tasted them hungrily, reaching with her tongue for more, always more, but he ripped them away.

"I could not live," he rasped hungrily. "I could not live without you, Fire Flower."

He kissed her again for the space of one heartbeat, a fast, bruising kiss that left her no breath and no mind, then he turned toward the horse.

"Don't move!"

The brusque command froze them where they were, Windrider with one hand on Jennie's shoulder and one on the horse, Jennie with hers still reaching for him. Like two creatures of prey, they turned together to look for the hunter at their backs.

Nate stood in the light of the nearest lantern swinging from the overhang of the stable. He held a long pistol in both hands, pointing it straight at Windrider and her. He had them in his sights at point-blank range.

"Hey, boy!" he shouted, barely turning to send the words over his shoulder toward the stable. "Go to the house and get Señor Nordstrom."

No one answered.

Then came the sound of heavy footsteps running.

Trammel bolted into the light, sweating and short of breath.

"Don't shoot the girl!" he ordered, and some insane corner of Jennie's mind took note that, even in this moment of crisis and conflict, he still wouldn't call her by her name.

"Why not?" Nate taunted. "She's leavin' you, Nordstrom, she's runnin' off with this here red Injun of her own free will. Any blind man could see that."

"Why *not*?" Trammel snarled. "Because she's the main attraction at the store, you idiot! Don't you know nothin'? Business is up seventy-five percent since them Rangers brought her back to me!"

He paused to take several deep breaths, his big stomach rippling as he tried to recover from the effort of running so fast.

"Besides, I ain't lettin' this filthy barbarian steal her from me again, whether she's live *or* dead."

"You're the barbarian, Trammel Nordstrom," Jennie said, the ice in her voice making it ring clear in the hot, heavy air. "Caring more about your business than the happiness of another human being, one you call your wife, declares that fact, plain as day!"

"Don't gimme none o' your sermons, missy," he said. "Save your breath."

"Save yours," she said, still in that same frigid tone. "Windrider is my true husband. You might as well let me go."

"Like hell I will!"

Windrider moved then, swift and sure as his medicine spirit. He scooped Jennie to his side with his left arm, threw the reins over Kwahira's neck with his right. He was lifting her to the stallion's back when the gun clicked, a sharp sound loud as a shout against the noise of Trammel's raspy breathing.

Jennie tensed for a bullet to rip through her, yet somehow she still flew through the air and onto their mount, floating on Windrider's incredible strength. He landed just behind her, his long legs hot and strong behind hers, his muscles rippling against her flesh, even through the wadded layers of the cloth of her dress.

His *puha* surged into her. The world belonged to the two of them once more. They could do anything.

His arms enclosed her, he pulled on the reins, Kwahira's head swung around.

"Wait!" Trammel yelled. "Wait, I say!"

He took a step toward them. "Give the girl to me, Indian! I'll trade you for her—Nate here, he's the man who killed your mother!"

Windrider whirled Kwahira, hooves pounding in the soft dirt, back to where he had been. Jennie felt his whole body tensing, muscles rippling instinctively to carry him off Kwahira and onto Nate.

The man was jerking and tugging on the gun's workings with both hands, his horrified eyes fixed on Trammel, his face full of astonishment. Then his gaze darted to Windrider, to see what he would do.

"Take *him*, Comanche!" Trammel hollered, pointing at Nate with a trembling forefinger. "Him and his drifter partner done the killings and the rapes of yore women; the girl done said so. You give her to me and take him. Stake him out in an anthill and take his scalp! He killed your own mother!"

Every muscle in Windrider's body screamed for him to leap down onto Nate and kill him with his bare hands, but his mind shrieked caution for the sake of the Fire Flower. That house had been full of people. White-eyes, armed with guns that would work. He had his love in his arms. He had no time for vengeance.

He drove Kwahira forward.

Nate whirled, pointed the gun and, holding it with both his shaking hands, pulled the trigger. This time it worked perfectly. The back-stabbing storekeeper was dead before he fell.

"A shot!"

"What happened?"

"*Madre de Dios!*"

The yells and shouts flew through the night from the house toward the stables fast, but not faster than Kwahira's feet flew away from them. They sounded loud, but not louder than the other pistol shots.

At their backs, Jennie could hear Nate shoot again and again as Windrider sent the stallion surging out of the stable yard, around it, and into the street. Then the noise of people running, yelling and calling, screaming for help, for a doctor, for Nate to stay where he was, filled her ears. Then they began to fade.

She wrapped her arms around Windrider's long, strong ones and wished she sat behind him instead of in front, behind him so her body could shield his from the bullets of the ones who would ride in pursuit.

How could they hope to get away?

Neither one of them knew which of the dark streets to take to find the edge of town and then the open plains, neither one of them carried a weapon, except for the knife strapped at Windrider's waist.

She scooted her back into his chest, fitted her body into the heavenly curve of his, and took note with every nerve and muscle in her, memorized with her very bones the way that he felt. If a bul-

let came through him, it would take her to the
Spirit Land, too. With him.

Tears sprang to her eyes.

It would take an act of God to get them out of
San Antonio alive.

Chapter 20

Windrider kept Kwahira at the gallop as they
turned a corner into a narrow alley that
ran between the walls of two huge adobe houses.
Jennie fought the panic tightening in her throat.

They could be trapped in here so easily! What
if their pursuers blocked the other end?

As soon as she had the thought, a horse and rider
materialized to fill the moonlit opening ahead. She
grabbed the iron muscles of Windrider's long
thighs, whispering, "Turn! Turn around, someone's there!"

He didn't even slow the stallion, and she
twisted to look up at him, desperate for Comanche words, unable to find a single one in the
screaming turmoil of her brain. She whirled back
to look ahead again just as they burst out of the
far end of the alleyway.

The apparition was there, right beside them,
turned to go with them, already moving in the
same gait as Kwahira. The rider raised one hand
and made a gesture that they were to follow, then
pulled ahead.

Windrider knew him, Jennie realized, and went
weak with relief. The two horses galloped around
one more corner, turned in to a wider street that

caught more of the moonlight, and came down into a slow trot.

"Galloping horses through town at night is a sign of alarm. We mustn't bring the good citizens of San Antonio de Béxar jumping out of their beds to chase after us," the other rider called softly, speaking English with a pronounced Spanish accent. "*Buenas tardes*, Señora Fire Flower!"

His lilting tone reminded Jennie of the music at the Rodríguezes' ball.

"Oñate," Windrider said.

"*Buenas tardes*," Jennie replied, her voice rattling thin as paper. She felt fragile as glass, yet tough as bois d'arc wood at the same time. "Thank you, Señor Oñate, for finding Windrider for me."

"Ah, but it is *he* who sent me to find *you!*" he said, chuckling. "I had that message long before I received the one from you!"

Jennie twisted in Windrider's arms to see his face. He smiled at her in the moonlight, and for one precious moment she knew they were safe.

"I thought Breaks Something would have told you such lies about me that you never would have come after me," she said, and leaned into his leg as they made another quick turn into an even darker street.

"She did," he said quietly. "But Ten Bears spoke unselfishly and wisely. He showed me the truth."

"Ten Bears!"

The surprise of that news took her speech away.

"Yes. Then the girl who lied was killed when the Rangers attacked."

Jennie's breath caught in her throat. Her voice cracked with grief. "So they did attack? I tried so hard to convince them that the band was all far away, but they had already seen us hunting buffalo.''

"A dozen or more of The People died," he said, and tightened his arms around her.

"Hukiyani?" she said, and then bit her lip.

"She is safe. And her husband and my nephew and my brother, his wives, and my father.''

"Thank God!"

She gave a great sigh of relief and grasped the hard-ribboned muscles of his forearms, wrapping them even more closely around her. She leaned her head into the hollow of his neck, letting her body move with his as they rode.

"I would never have left you of my own free will," she said. "Never."

"I know that now."

He tucked his chin against her head and held her even closer.

The hooves of the two horses, falling and lifting and falling again into the deeper sand of this street, provided the only sound except for the creak of Oñate's saddle. The horses trotted faster; Jennie rocked in Windrider's arms in rhythm with their hooves. She hardly noticed the quiet exchange of Spanish words between the two men.

He was here! He was real! They were together and would never be parted again!

Windrider was not killed by the Rangers, and she was in his arms at last. She leaned back against him, closing her eyes to let that reality soak in.

They turned once more, and then she realized that they were stopping. She jerked herself up to look around.

The moonlight picked out iron grillwork, a mass of flowers along a wall, an arched window. With a light in it.

"We're still in town!" she whispered. "We should be way outside it before we stop!"

Windrider didn't answer.

When she turned to look at him, from the corner of her eye she saw Oñate cross his reins on his horn and dismount.

"First I must give you the choice," Windrider said, and he let her go, moved his hands completely away from her, let them rest lightly on his legs. "I should have done so long ago."

"What choice?"

"To go or to stay."

"Of course I will go. I love you! I am your wife!"

"Onate tells me your mother is still alive."

The quiet words hit her like thrown rocks.

"Mama!" she gasped.

A great wave of guilt swept through her.

"In the wonder of being with you again, I forgot all about my *mother*!"

Her words, and the way she spoke them, made his heart sink like a stone in his chest. It made him want to bite off his tongue.

Why hadn't he simply ridden all night with her on the horse in front of him? So that by the time she thought of her mother or anything else, they would have gone so far out onto the plains that they couldn't come back?

Because, the voice of his honor shouted in the back of his mind. Because he had put off giving her her choice for far too long. He had to give it to her. Not only because of his honor as a warrior, but because of the desires of his heart.

He closed his mouth against more words crowding there, more words that would help to persuade her.

He wanted her to come with him of a will that

came out of the core of herself. A woman who wanted him, who loved him above all else. He must have that, and no less.

"Is Mama expecting us?" the Fire Flower asked, turning around, taking the beauty of her pale face, the brightness of her eyes, away from his sight. It was as if the Great Spirit had snuffed out the moon.

"She is," he said.

Oñate stepped out of the shadows of the house with a slight woman clinging to his arm. The Fire Flower threw her leg over Kwahira's withers and slid to the ground. She ran to throw her arms around her mother.

Windrider's heart caught, then fluttered like a wild eagle trapped in his chest. Would she come back to him? Would he ever hold her again?

The women embraced; they talked for a moment. Then the Fire Flower, with one arm still around the older woman, brought her closer to him. He dismounted, too.

"Mama, this is Windrider," she said. "Windrider, this is my mother."

He looked down into a drawn, faded face. A face that once had been beautiful.

A face so like that of his Fire Flower. Again he fought the instinct that told him to try to sway her to go, the urge to invite her mother to come with them, too.

The Fire Flower turned and took her mother's face in both her hands.

"I must tell you good bye, Mama," she said. "I'm going with Windrider's people far, far away."

"What . . . what about Mr. Nordstrom?"

"He's dead. Nate killed him."

She took a step toward Windrider and reached for his hand. "We must go."

So. She had decided. His heart leapt and danced.

"You are welcome to come to live with The People, Mother-of-My-Wife," he said, formally. "My band has much hospitality."

"Oh, Mama!" the Fire Flower cried, and threw both arms around her again. "Do! Please do come with us!"

For the space of one breath he thought that she might agree.

Then she shook her head. "No," she said, softly. "I am too old to learn to live outside like that, on the land. And that would be only another kind of charity. Here I make my own way."

The Fire Flower's face crumpled; he could see its sad lines in the moonlight. His heart stopped beating again.

But she didn't turn loose of his hand.

Which was it to be? The suspense tore at him with the teeth of a bear.

"Perhaps I might bring you sometimes to visit your daughter and your son-in-law, Windrider," Oñate suggested, in his courtly way. "I would be glad to have such charming company on a long ride."

"I would like that," the Fire Flower's mother agreed.

Windrider bit his tongue, but he could contain himself no longer. He spoke, the words rasping around the lump that had formed in his throat.

"So," he said. "Will you leave your mother and go with me?"

Kohtoo Topusana looked up at him, and her eyes were shining.

"Yes."

"You must know that we will be moving far, far away into the land of the Quohodi," he said, his conscience forcing him to be brutally honest. "We will be so far from this San Antonio, we cannot come back."

"I want to go with you."

"I want you to be free. You have told me how much you need your freedom."

"Then I must go with you," the Fire Flower said, and let go of her mother's hand to put both of hers around his. "You live so deep in my heart that I'm truly free only when I ride with you."

Epilogue

J ennie crossed her legs and sat back against the trunk of a cottonwood tree, enjoying the cool of its thick shade almost as much as the sight in front of her: her mother and her father-in-law, Half Horse, working together to swing her baby's cradleboard out of the shadows so they could see him better.

"Not too far," Kathleen O'Bannion cautioned, reaching up to steady the low-hanging limb to which she had tied the cradleboard. "If the sun hits him in the face, he'll wake up."

Jennie translated.

"He is *Nermernuh*, this small one," Half Horse grunted, sending Kathleen an irritated look from the side of his squinting black eyes. "He can sleep in sun."

Jennie told her mother what he said.

"Tish, tosh!" the other woman exclaimed. "If that isn't just like a man! Why, if you can't even tell that this baby looks Irish, then you certainly don't know how to take care of him. Don't you wake him up, now!"

Jennie stifled a giggle and glanced to Windrider for help. He and Oñate had stopped their lazy, rambling talk to watch, too.

Windrider winked at Jennie and took up her job as interpreter. "You are a wise man," he mistranslated tactfully. "Your people are brave and strong. They all can sleep in sun."

Half Horse turned toward Kathleen and inclined his head graciously to accept the compliment.

"Hmpf," she said, satisfied that he had taken the reprimand so well. "Now we need to talk about his name."

"He'll find his own name when he seeks his medicine vision, Mother," Jennie explained, hoping to head off yet another argument between the two proud grandparents. "Until then, we'll call him his pet name, *Kiyu*. It means Horseback, and we call him that because already he prefers to be on my back when I'm riding to when I'm walking or sitting still."

"And just how do you know that, missy?" her mother demanded, without taking her eyes from her grandson's beautiful face. "Since this lad is not talking?"

"I can tell," Jennie answered, confidently. "A mother knows such things."

Windrider translated for Half Horse, and all of them laughed.

"Even a mother of only six months?" Windrider teased.

"For his pet name, I'd think you'd have called him after me," Oñate drawled, smiling as he glanced from Jennie to Windrider. "A year and a half ago at this time I was the one who brought you two back together. If I hadn't, there would be no baby."

"Don't worry, Oñate," Jennie said, flashing a mischievous look at her husband, who had not taken his eyes off her. "I'll name this next one for you."

She touched her abdomen and leaned back, laughing, to watch her surprise sink in on the circle of faces she loved.

Her mother actually left her grandson in Half Horse's care to come to her. Her thin face was flushed with happiness.

"Really? Oh, Jennie, darling, really? Another baby so soon? I may just have to stay with you until then!"

Windrider translated for Half Horse, and all of them burst into laughter at the look on his face.

Then Windrider spoke, his eyes locked on Jennie's.

"*Two* babies," he said, pride vibrating in his deep voice as he pretended to frown. "I shall have to carry one of them on my back."

The heat of the gentle look he gave her then melted the cool shade away and warmed her like the sun.

Avon Romantic Treasures

*Unforgettable, enthralling love stories,
sparkling with passion and adventure
from Romance's bestselling authors*

AWAKEN MY FIRE *by Jennifer Horsman*
76701-5/$4.50 US/$5.50 Can

ONLY BY YOUR TOUCH *by Stella Cameron*
76606-X/$4.50 US/$5.50 Can

FIRE AT MIDNIGHT *by Barbara Dawson Smith*
76275-7/$4.50 US/$5.50 Can

ONLY WITH YOUR LOVE *by Lisa Kleypas*
76151-3/$4.50 US/$5.50 Can

MY WILD ROSE *by Deborah Camp*
76738-4/$4.50 US/$5.50 Can

MIDNIGHT AND MAGNOLIAS *by Rebecca Paisley*
76566-7/$4.50 US/$5.50 Can

THE MASTER'S BRIDE *by Suzannah Davis*
76821-6/$4.50 US/$5.50 Can

A ROSE AT MIDNIGHT *by Anne Stuart*
76740-6/$4.50 US/$5.50 Can

Buy these books at your local bookstore or use this coupon for ordering:

Mail to: Avon Books, Dept BP, Box 767, Rte 2, Dresden, TN 38225   C
Please send me the book(s) I have checked above.
❑ My check or money order— no cash or CODs please— for $_____is enclosed
(please add $1.50 to cover postage and handling for each book ordered— Canadian residents
add 7% GST).
❑ Charge my VISA/MC Acct#_____Exp Date_____
Minimum credit card order is two books or $6.00 (please add postage and handling charge of
$1.50 per book — Canadian residents add 7% GST). For faster service, call
1-800-762-0779. Residents of Tennessee, please call 1-800-633-1607. Prices and numbers
are subject to change without notice. Please allow six to eight weeks for delivery.

Name_____
Address_____
City_____State/Zip_____
Telephone No._____

                                                                        RT 0193

Avon Romances—
the best in exceptional authors and unforgettable novels!

THE LION'S DAUGHTER Loretta Chase
76647-7/$4.50 US/$5.50 Can

CAPTAIN OF MY HEART Danelle Harmon
76676-0/$4.50 US/$5.50 Can

BELOVED INTRUDER Joan Van Nuys
76476-8/$4.50 US/$5.50 Can

SURRENDER TO THE FURY Cara Miles
76452-0/$4.50 US/$5.50 Can

SCARLET KISSES Patricia Camden
76825-9/$4.50 US/$5.50 Can

WILDSTAR Nicole Jordan
76622-1/$4.50 US/$5.50 Can

HEART OF THE WILD Donna Stephens
77014-8/$4.50 US/$5.50 Can

TRAITOR'S KISS Joy Tucker
76446-6/$4.50 US/$5.50 Can

SILVER AND SAPPHIRES Shelly Thacker
77034-2/$4.50 US/$5.50 Can

SCOUNDREL'S DESIRE Joann DeLazzari
76421-0/$4.50 US/$5.50 Can

Buy these books at your local bookstore or use this coupon for ordering:

Mail to: Avon Books, Dept BP, Box 767, Rte 2, Dresden, TN 38225   C
Please send me the book(s) I have checked above.
❏ My check or money order— no cash or CODs please— for $_____is enclosed
(please add $1.50 to cover postage and handling for each book ordered— Canadian residents
add 7% GST).
❏ Charge my VISA/MC Acct#_____Exp Date_____
Minimum credit card order is two books or $6.00 (please add postage and handling charge of
$1.50 per book — Canadian residents add 7% GST). For faster service, call
1-800-762-0779. Residents of Tennessee, please call 1-800-633-1607. Prices and numbers
are subject to change without notice. Please allow six to eight weeks for delivery.

Name_____
Address_____
City_____State/Zip_____
Telephone No._____   ROM 0193